Normal Sheeple

Normal Sheeple

ROSS O'CARROLL KELLY

(as told to Paul Howard)

Illustrated by Alan Clarke

PENGUIN BOOKS

PENGUIN BOOKS

UK | USA | Canada | Ireland | Australia
India | New Zealand | South Africa

Penguin Books is part of the Penguin Random House group of companies
whose addresses can be found at global.penguinrandomhouse.com.

First published by Sandycove 2021
Published in Penguin Books 2022
001

Typeset by Jouve (UK), Milton Keynes
Printed and bound in Great Britain by Clays Ltd, Elcograf S.p.A.

The authorized representative in the EEA is Penguin Random House Ireland,
Morrison Chambers, 32 Nassau Street, Dublin D02 YH68

A CIP catalogue record for this book is available from the British Library

ISBN: 978-1-844-88550-3

www.greenpenguin.co.uk

Penguin Random House is committed to a
sustainable future for our business, our readers
and our planet. This book is made from Forest
Stewardship Council® certified paper.

To Rachel Pierce, my editor

Contents

Prologue

'We have taken back our country!' the old man goes, running his fingers through his hair slash wig.

There's, like, a huge roar of approval in the room, followed by a round of applause from all his dickhead mates.

He's there, 'We have taken back our country – and we now have a once-in-a-lifetime opportunity to reimagine Ireland and redefine its relationship with the rest of the world! We are no longer Éamon de Valera's nation of toothless, fat-ankled girls and big-boned, idiot boys, dancing a set in the village square after Sunday Mass! We are an intelligent, vital, hard-working people! And, after botching the first hundred years of our independence, we are ready at last to take our place among the nations of the world!'

This is us in, like, Dáil *Éireann* by the way? The old man is giving a little pep talk before handing out the ministerial seals of office. Sorcha is, like, holding her breath, the way she does when she's nervous.

'However,' he goes, 'Ireland will never be truly free until we break our ties with Brussels! This country has less representation in the European Parliament than it had in the British Parliament before Independence! We have no say over our own economic affairs, over how many fish we take from our own waters, over the fate of the oil and gas that sit beneath our seabed!

'One of the promises on which I was elected to office was to deliver – quote, unquote – Irexit! Therefore, my immediate priorities, as Taoiseach, will be to form new relationships, both economic and social, with countries outside of the European Union and to hold a referendum this autumn to repeal the Third Amendment to the Constitution, thus severing, once and for all, the ropes that shackle us to the innovation-crushing, creativity-stultifying European superstaat!'

I turn to Sorcha and I go, 'Bit of a bummer for you, isn't it? I thought you were a fan of the whole Europe thing.'

'Don't listen to him,' her old man goes. 'The most important day of your life and he's trying to drag you down to *his* level.'

'All I'm saying is that she was a major fan of Europe. She had one of those albums where you collect all the Euro coins from the different countries. I think you filled it in the end, didn't you, Sorcha?'

'Just because An Taoiseach and I have some differences of opinion,' she tries to go, 'doesn't mean that I can't serve as a member of his Government. Anyway, I'm still hoping to change his mind about Europe.'

'Or,' Sorcha's old dear goes, 'he might change yours, Dorling.'

Her old man's like, 'That's right. The important thing is that you're taking your first steps in the political career you've dreamt of since you were a child.'

'And so,' *my* old man goes, 'without further ado, it's time to hand out the – inverted commas – goodies!'

Everyone laughs.

'Hennessy Coghlan-O'Hara!' he goes. 'Attorney General and Captain of the Oireachtas Golf Society!'

Hennessy walks up to receive his little box while everyone claps and cheers.

'Gordon Greenhalgh!' the old man goes. 'Minister for Housing, Planning and Local Government!'

Behind me, a voice goes, 'Stordee, Rosser?'

I turn around and it ends up being Ronan.

I'm like, 'Hey, Ro, how the hell are you?'

'Ine gayum ball, Rosser,' he goes. 'Gayum ball.'

'How's the job going?'

'It's oately me foorst day.'

'An apprentice to Hennessy. Still, hopefully it won't be for too long. As soon as the old man gets those chorges against you dropped, you can go to the States and take up that internship offer in New York.'

'That's *if* he gets the cheerges thropped.'

'Er, he's the most powerful man in the country, Ro. Not to mention the most corrupt. Of course he'll get them dropped.'

Behind us, another voice is like, 'You'd be b . . . b . . . b . . . b . . . b . . . b . . . bethor off staying hee-or, Ro.'

It's Kennet, his father-in-law and the old man's driver.

He's like, 'You'll l . . . l . . . l . . . l . . . l . . . l . . . learden a lot mower from Heddessy than you would woorking for some crowd in Amedica for f . . . f . . . f . . . f . . . free. You've got responsibidities, doatunt forget. A wife and ch . . . ch . . . choyult. And I know Shadden would luvven anutter little babby.'

I turn around and I give him the most unbelievable filthy.

'Hee-or, Rosser,' he goes, the stuttering focker, 'me and you are godda be s . . . s . . . s . . . s . . . s . . . seeing a lot mower of each utter over the next few y . . . y . . . y . . . yee-ors.'

'The fock are you talking about?' I go.

'Cheerdles is arthur aston me to be S . . . S . . . S . . . S . . . Sudeka's full-time thriver.'

All I can do is go, 'For fock's sake!' and I realize that I literally can't spend another second in the focker's company, so I tip over to the old dear instead.

'Oh, hello, Ross,' she goes. 'Isn't your father doing wonderfully well? He's always *commanded* a room!'

I'm there, 'Where are the babies?' at the same time looking around me.

She's like, 'What babies?'

I swear to fock.

I'm there, 'Er, the six babies that you and *him* brought into the world using Eastern European women as surrogates. Ring any bells?'

'Oh, they're at home,' she goes. 'It wouldn't be fair to bring children to an event like this.'

It's a definite dig at me. Yeah, no, I forgot to mention that Brian, Johnny and Leo are jumping up and down on the old man's desk, trying to break it, shouting, 'Fock you, you focking focks! Fock you, you focking focks!'

The old man is having to pretty much shout to be heard over them.

'Declan Dennehy, my long-time friend from our Leggs of Lower Leeson Street days!' he goes. 'Minister for Finance!'

I'm there, 'Would you not think of spending time with them, no?'

She goes, 'We found this wonderful nanny, Ross, called Astrid. She's a German person.'

'What, and she's going to essentially raise them?'

'I'll do my bit. It's just that six babies are a lot of work – apparently. Plus we've got this move happening.'

'What move?'

'We're leaving Foxrock, Ross.'

'What, you're still planning to move into, like, the Áras?'

'As your father said to that Michael Higgins person, the leader of the country should have the best house. And that's all there is to it.'

The old man goes, 'Lastly – and that's not to suggest that I don't take the whole – inverted commas – global warming thing seriously – Sorcha Lalor! Minister for Climate Action!'

She walks up and collects her seal – a big Head Girl smile on her face.

'Can I say a few words?' she goes, and the old man reacts like she's whipped out one of her Milk Duds and is about to breastfeed a child in front of him.

He's like, 'Well, em, speeches weren't, em, port of the format for the day, Sorcha! But there will be plenty of other opportunities to speak, I promise!'

Honor sidles up to me.

'Oh my God!' she goes. 'Focking embarrassed for her!'

I'm there, 'Yeah, no, he pretty much slapped her down alright.'

'Granddad doesn't even believe in recycling! Why does he need a Minister for Climate Action?'

'Yeah, no, it's a bit of a mystery alright.'

'Now,' the old man goes, clapping his hands together, 'we have a very exciting summer ahead of us! And to use a phrase I recently learned . . .'

He picks his Russian mate, Fyodor, out of the crowd.

'Let me see if I can pronounce this correctly!' he goes. '*ValKOV beYATsa v LYES ni haDIT!* Which, roughly translated, means – if you're scared of wolves, stay the fock out of the woods!'

A Pain in the Áras

So we're standing outside this, like, pay-as-you-go gym on North Frederick Street and we're all looking up in the air, wondering which one is Sorcha's new office, as in which one is the Deportment of, like, Climate Action?

'It's on the – one, two, three, four – *fifth* floor,' Sorcha goes, squinting her eyes. 'So that must be it at the very top of the building.'

Her old dear is like, 'Oh!' failing miserably to hide her disappointment – like the time I turned up at her twenty-fifth wedding anniversary dinner in Dobbins Bistro wearing flip-flops and novelty board shorts with the words 'Choking Hazard' written across the crotch.

Yeah, no, you can tell that she's thinking the same thing as the rest of us – my old man is taking the serious P, I, double duckies here.

'Don't, em, take this as a criticism . . .' *her* old man goes.

And Sorcha's there, 'What?' because she genuinely *cares* what that tool thinks?

He's like, 'Is it not a bit –'

'Northside,' I go, because – yeah, no – I had to drive up O'Connell Street, then around Pornell Square to get here, with Honor curled up in the foetal position in the footwell, breathing in and out of a Hunky Dorys bag to try to stop her from hyperventilating.

Sorcha's old man closes his eyes and says fock-all for a few seconds, like he's waiting for a bad smell to clear.

'What I was *going* to say,' he goes, 'before I was rudely interrupted, is that it's a little bit, well, removed from the hort of Government.'

Sorcha's there, 'As in?'

'Again, not a criticism, but most of the important Government deportments are situated on the *other* side of the city. Finance is on Merrion Street. Health is on Baggot Street. Justice and Foreign Affairs are on Stephen's Green. I'm just concerned that you're a bit – like I said – remote from the centre of political action.'

Yeah, he means a bit Northside.

'It just goes to show what Granddad thinks of, like, environmental issues,' Honor goes. 'As in, he doesn't *give* a fock?'

I laugh, but I end up being the only one – the others just blank her.

'Dad,' Sorcha goes, 'when Barack Obama finished college and interned as a researcher for a global business consulting firm, he worked out of, like, a *stationery* closet? My point being that it doesn't matter where you work – it's the actual work you *do* that matters?'

He goes, 'Fair point, Minister!' like the complete and utter bellend that he is.

We all follow Sorcha up the steps to the front door – her old man, her old dear, then Johnny, Leo, and Brian, who's graduated from a wheelchair to crutches, then Honor, then me.

I'm carrying a lorge cordboard box containing all of Sorcha's shit – a paraffin-free candle; her biodegradable yoga mat; her signed copy of David Attenborough's autobiography; the framed thank-you letter she got from Greenpeace International when she sent them her Communion money; *An Inconvenient Truth* on Blu-ray; a globe that Fionn bought her which shows what the planet would look like if the polar ice cap completely melted; then a framed photograph of Sorcha with Swampy, taken in the Glen of the Downs in the late 1990s, when she camped out with the tree people to protest against the widening of the N11 but asked me to come and get her at two o'clock in the morning when she discovered she'd forgotten her night-time dental gord and the dampness in the tent was causing her hair to frizz.

Honor turns around to me and goes, 'Why is everyone ignoring me?'

'I think they're just a bit, I don't know, underwhelmed at seeing the place,' I go. '*I* laughed at what you said, in fairness to me.'

The noise inside the building is, like, deafening. Avicii's 'Wake Me Up' is blaring from the ground-floor gym and shaking the building right down to its foundations. Sorcha stops this girl – in her mid-twenties, I'm guessing, with tight yoga pants and an orse like two

6

balloons on a string – and asks her where the elevator is, shouting to make herself heard over the music.

The girl's like, 'THE WHAT?' at – yeah, no – the top of her voice.

'EL . . . E . . . VA . . . TOR!' Sorcha goes.

'I DON'T THINK THERE *IS* ONE?' the girl goes. 'I'M PRETTY SURE YOU HAVE TO USE THE STAIRS!'

So that's basically what we end up doing – we walk up eight focking flights of the things. I hand Sorcha her box of tricks and I carry Brian, whose leg in still in a plaster cast, all the way up. At the same time, Sorcha's old man keeps telling her that he's proud of her.

'I always knew you'd make your mork on the world eventually,' he goes. 'And I always knew it would involve public service.'

I'm there, 'Some people might say that she made her mork when she had a family. I would orgue her *children* are her biggest achievements?'

Then, behind me, Leo goes, 'Fock this focking focker fock,' sort of undermining my point.

'I'll tell you who's absolutely thrilled for you,' Sorcha's old man goes. 'Do you remember Ruaidhri Merriman? Environmental Protection Agency versus Wellbeck and Kaltz Chemicals 1997? He sought me out yesterday to offer me his congratulations. Which I thought was very nice of him, especially given his history of successfully defending some of the country's biggest polluters.'

'Oh my God!' Sorcha goes. 'That's *so* decent!'

'It's been like that all week. Well-wishers coming out of everywhere, wanting to shake my hand, and pat me on the back, and point out that, well, she didn't exactly lick it up off the ground, Edmund, did she?'

We eventually reach the top of the stairs and there's, like, a door to our left. There's a piece of foolscap paper Sellotaped to it, with the words 'Deportment of Climate Action' written on it in, like, green highlighter pen.

'Oh! My God!' Honor goes. 'This gets funnier and funnier!'

Sorcha's old dear is there, '*We'll* get you a sign made. It could be a present from your father and me . . . Minister!'

Seriously, there's a pair of them in it. Two dicks.

I put Brian down on the ground. Sorcha hands me back her

collection of junk, then sticks her key in the door, unlocks it and pushes it open. And into the room we go.

The office is, like, totally empty. There's not even furniture in there, except for a wooden school desk, facing the wall, with a plastic orange chair behind it and an old-school, wheel-dial telephone resting on top.

Sorcha lets out a long sigh.

'Oh, well,' she goes, her voice echoing off the bare walls, 'An Taoiseach did say it needed work.'

Honor's like, *'An Taoiseach?'* at the same time laughing. 'Focking spare me, would you?' but again she gets nothing back.

It's hord not to feel for the girl.

Even five floors up, we can still hear the music coming from the gym. It's something by David Guetta. Sorcha decides to try to make the best of a shit hand – the attitude that has kept our marriage together for, I don't know, I must check how long.

'Ross,' she goes, 'can you put my globe on the desk, please?'

I'm there, 'Will do. What about the picture of you and Swampy – is that going on it as well?'

'Just put everything on it for now.'

So I tip the box upside-down and it all spills out. Also in there, I notice, is the Mount Anville Past Pupils Union (in conjunction with Coopers & Lybrand) Green Business Award that she won for converting her boutique in the Powerscourt Townhouse Centre to solar energy, even though the cost was one of the reasons the shop went tits-up.

Leo storts chasing Johnny around the room, spitting on his back. It's just kids having fun, although Sorcha's old dear looks at them like she would a tradesman who's walked his muddy boots all over her cream corpet.

'You focking prick!' Johnny shouts.

Sorcha picks up the phone and holds it to her ear for a few seconds.

She's like, 'The line's dead.'

'Yeah, like your political career,' Honor goes.

It's an absolute zinger. But Sorcha just flashes her a grin – the kind you give the person sitting next to you on a flight when you've just snagged the last chicken chasseur and they've been told the vegan couscous or fock-all.

'Honor, I know you're looking for a reaction,' she goes, 'but you're not getting one from me.'

Honor's there, 'I can't believe you're still pissed off with me for calling you out on your bullshit in front of the United Nations General Assembly. You need to get over yourself.'

Sorcha's face suddenly hordens. I haven't seen her look so disgusted since she found out that Dakota, her teenage American pen-pal, was actually a twenty-stone Death Row inmate, wanking his final days away in a twelve-by-eight cell in Texas over the photographs that she regularly sent him.

'Believe it or not,' she goes, 'I *am* actually over it? I'm over *it*. And I'm over *you*.'

Honor's like, 'Excuse me?'

'I'm saying I don't care what you say any more. I don't care what you think any more. And I don't care what you do any more.'

'What, so if I got a tattoo on my lower back, or if I became friends with someone from Sion Hill –'

'I wouldn't give a damn, Honor. You see, I have a career now – the career I put on hold so that I could dedicate all of my time and energy to being a mother to you. And what did you do in return? You threw it back in my face.'

'What, just because I made a focking show of you in front of Mary Robinson and Michelle Obama?'

'No, I'm talking about time and time again, Honor. Your father can finish the job of raising you now. He'll enjoy that. He can see no wrong in you.'

'I actually can't,' I go. 'You crack me up, Honor, even when you're being a bitch.'

Sorcha's old man is just, like, staring at the girl, with a big, shit-eating grin on his face.

'Look at that!' he goes. 'That's softened her cough, hasn't it?'

Sorcha's old dear is like, 'Nothing to say for herself. Well, that's a first, isn't it, Edmund?'

Honor – I swear to fock – is on the point of basically tears.

e washed my hands of you, Honor.'

obviously doesn't mean that literally.'

bes, 'Oh, I do, Ross. I actually, actually do.'

of breeze blocks, in fairness to it.

JP has bought one of the new penthouses in Lansdowne Place, with a view of the – believe it or not – *Aviva*? And let's just say that the words 'fair focks' haven't been far from my lips all afternoon.

I'm there, 'This is obviously the money from the Vampire Bed finally coming through. Have I said fair focks, by the way?'

'Yes,' he goes, 'you've said fair focks.'

'Then I'm going to say it again. And go on saying it. Because you deserve this, Dude.'

People laughed at him when he said there'd *be* no housing crisis if everyone could just be persuaded to sleep standing up. And who's laughing now?

I'm there, 'Is that a focking tennis court down there?'

'It is, yeah,' he goes, at the same time handing me a stick of Heinemite from his – I shit you not – smort fridge.

I'm like, 'Clay?'

And he's there, 'Yeah, no, there's a grass court as well, though.'

I go, 'Un-focking-believable!' and then I turn around to Christian. 'Are you going to get one of these?'

The dude just shrugs.

I'm like, 'Dude, you're a millionaire – focking multi! – and you're renting in Stepaside along with the rest of Dublin's divorcee dads!'

Word for word, he goes, 'I want to make sure Lauren and the boys are looked after before I stort spending money on myself.'

I'm there, 'Lauren? After the way she treated you? You're a more forgiving man than I am, Christian.'

Fionn goes, 'Personally, I think that's pretty laudable, Christian.'

I'm there, 'Others might use the word mug.'

'I want to pay off the mortgage on the house in Booterstown,' Christian goes, 'then set up a fund for Ross's and Oliver's education.'

I actually laugh.

I'm there, 'You're a living saint. And, in the meantime, if you meet a bird, you're going to bring her back to that focking grief-hole you're renting in Stepaside? Make sure to take her shoelaces off her at the door.'

'I've no interest in meeting a *bird*,' he tries to go. 'I just want to be a good father to my kids.'

'Again, I think that's to be admired,' Fionn goes – a virgin until he was twenty-four, let's not forget.

I'm there, 'What about you, J-Town? Are you seeing anyone at the moment?'

JP's like, 'Er, not really, no.'

'Not really?' I go. 'So whose vaginal dryness cream is that in your bathroom cabinet?'

He rolls his eyes and goes, 'Fock's sake, Ross! That's a gross invasion of my privacy!'

Yeah, no, I always take a keen interest in what other people have in their bathrooms. You can pick up all sorts of useful information by having a mooch.

I'm there, 'So who is she?'

'She's just someone who's stayed over once or twice,' he tries to go. 'It's early days. I don't want to say anything yet to jinx it.'

'It's not Vanessa Orlean, is it?'

'Who?'

'Vanessa Orlean? She did German and Neuroscience in UCD. She pulled me off around the back of the Wicked Wolf the night Ireland lost to Scotland in the Foot and Mouth Six Nations.'

The focking looks I end up getting.

'No,' JP goes, 'it's not Vanessa Orlean.'

I'm there, 'Glad to hear it. Would have been awks.'

All of a sudden, the doorbell rings and JP makes his way over to the intercom. It ends up being Oisinn and Magnus, so he buzzes them in.

Five minutes later, they walk through the door of the aportment with their mouths wide open.

'Shit! The! Bed!' Oisinn goes. 'Dude, this *place*! You can see the actual Aviva from here!'

I'm there, 'He's got a fridge that literally tells you when your milk is about to go off,' and I'm saying it in, like, an *admiring* way? 'It sends you a focking text! Tells you that you're nearly out of Philadelphia as well and you might want to think about buying sausages for the weekend.'

'I shee there ish a clay tennish court downshtairs,' Magnus goes.

'There's a grass one as well, Magnus. And a Residents' Club – tell them what's in there, Dude.'

JP goes, 'Cinema, library, reading room,' trying to come over all modest, 'then a gym with weights, sauna and steamroom. Then you can get, like, a massage, spa treatments, everything.'

'Who's laughing now?' I go. 'That's my question. Who the fock is laughing at the idea of people sleeping standing up?'

Oisinn asks Fionn how he's doing. Yeah, no, he finished his chemo a few weeks ago, but his hair hasn't properly grown *back* yet?

'Still very tired,' Fionn goes. 'And still vomiting, believe it or not.'

Oisinn's there, 'When will you find out, well, you know?'

'The end of May.'

'And, like, what do you think? As in –'

'As in, do I think the cancer's gone?'

'I'm sorry, that's a stupid question.'

'It's actually not. I ask myself the same thing all the time. Some days I think, yeah, it's gone – every bit of it. Other days, it's like I can feel it inside my body. The truth is, there's no way of knowing. I just have to wait.'

JP hands Oisinn a Heineken and Magnus a bottle of – yeah, no – Coors Light. I know the world has changed and we're all supposed to be embracing each other's lifestyle choices, but I can't even look at him when he puts the bottle to his lips.

'By the way, Ross,' JP goes, 'how's Sorcha getting on? I saw her on the news getting her ministerial seal.'

I'm like, 'Yeah, no, she moved into her new office this morning – on North Frederick Street.'

'North Frederick Street?'

'Literally that.'

'Is that not a bit –'

'A bit Northside?'

'I was going to say far from the centre of things – but, yeah, when you put it like that.'

'She's putting a brave face on it. But I think my old man has stitched her up in a major way.'

'I still can't believe Chorles O'Carroll-Kelly is the leader of the country,' Oisinn goes. 'No offence, Ross.'

I'm there, 'Hey, none taken. I wouldn't trust the focker as far as I could throw you.'

'I mean, I used to love his letters to the *Irish Times* as much as the next man. But I can't believe the man who wrote them is now the most powerful man in Ireland.'

'He's going to lead us all over the edge of a focking cliff,' I go. 'Even though I'm bound to be biased.'

I suddenly notice that Magnus is grinning from ear to ear.

He turns around to Oisinn and he goes, 'Sho, can I tell the guysh my newsh?'

Oisinn laughs. He's there, 'Yeah, no, go ahead, Magnus.'

'I'm going to give a TED Talk,' Magnus goes, 'in the Mill Theatre in Dundrum.'

And I'm like, 'Whoa, fair focks, Dude! What the fock is a TED Talk?'

'A TED Talk ish where shpeakersh preshent ideash in front of a live audiensh – and alsho a potential audiensh of millionsh online.'

'I watched some great TED Talks,' Fionn goes, 'during the weeks when I was having my treatment. What are you doing yours on?'

'Well, ash you guysh know, when I went to work for Fashebook, I short of losht my mind a little bit.'

I'm there, 'A little bit? Dude, it was like you joined a cult! We had to break into the building and extract you!'

'Yesh, and I am shtill very grateful to you. And that'sh what my TED Talk ish going to be about. People who work in the clubby, collegiate atmoshphere of theesh multinational tech companiesh and who loosh their own identitiesh. If you look online, it ish a big, big problem.'

I'm like, 'Well, we'll all be there to support you, won't we, goys?'

And Fionn and Christian and JP are all like, 'Wouldn't miss it for the world.'

Oisinn turns around to JP and goes, 'Dude, can I use your Josh Ritter?'

JP's like, 'Yeah, no, it's the last door on the left.'

And I'm there, 'Just to warn you, there's a tube of vaginal dryness cream in there, although he's not saying who it belongs to, because it's early days.'

'Okay, I need a drink,' JP goes.

And Christian's like, 'This is the first time I've said this since I got sober – but so do I.'

'It's the end of an era,' the old dear goes.

She smiles then. And, oh my God, the focking state of her. She looks like – okay, just give me a second here – like an effigy of Donald Trump that's been stuffed with burned monkey meat, tied to the bumper of a flatbed Ford and dragged slowly through a coyote sanctuary.

'It's the end of one era,' the old man goes, 'but the beginning of a new one – eh, Kicker?'

I'm like, 'Whatever,' because it's weird – even *random*? – to think that they're moving out of Foxrock. We're just, like, walking around the house, saying our – I suppose – *goodbyes*?

We step into *my* old room.

The old man's there, 'If these walls could talk, eh, Kicker?' in his big, all-caps voice. 'What a story they would tell!'

'Yes,' the old dear goes, 'I lost count of the number of girls I had to chase out of here over the years.'

I'm there, 'Yeah, would you mind *not* talking filth in front of my daughter?'

Honor barely raises a smile. She definitely hasn't been herself since Sorcha said – yeah, no – what she said to her the other day.

'Oh, he'd sneak them in here,' the old dear goes. 'He thought I couldn't hear him on the stairs. They'd usually be called something like Bláithín, or Anna, or Rebecca, or Sadhbh. Complete fools for him – every single one of them!'

I'm there, 'Okay, wrap it up now, you focking, I don't know, drunken devil frog.'

'I used to say to them, "Those lines he's using on you, I heard him say exactly the same things – word for word – to the girl I chased out of here last night! And the night before that! That's right, young lady – sorry to disappoint you, but you're not the only one!"'

'That's funny,' Honor goes, not even smiling.

I'm there, 'I used to put temazepam in your Manhattans in the hope that you'd sleep through. But you built up quite a tolerance to it, didn't you, Mother dearest?'

'The only one who kept coming back,' the old dear goes, 'time after time, was Sorcha!'

'Focking sad bitch,' Honor goes.

'There was one week, I must have caught her in here three times. I said to Chorles, "I think this is the girl Ross is going to marry." Isn't that right, Chorles?'

'Oh, the girl was incorrigible!' the old man goes. 'The very same quality that's going to make her a wonderful Minister for Climate Action! If anyone is capable of convincing me that global warming isn't a hoax created by vested interests determined to prevent emerging economies like ours from becoming competitive, then it's your good lady wife, Kicker!'

Honor's like, 'We saw where you put her – hilarious, Granddad!'

Johnny, I notice, has unbuttoned the front of his chinos and is pissing against the wall, shouting, 'Focking piss on you!' and no one is saying shit to him.

Brian is watching him with a big grin on his face. Then Leo walks up behind him and kicks away one of his crutches. Brian goes down like a felled tree. Johnny and Leo laugh. But then Brian swings a crutch at Leo, catching him full in the face with the fat end of the thing, knocking him onto the flat of his back and sending his glasses flying across the room in two pieces.

'Come on,' I go, 'let's leave them to it.'

We step out onto the landing, then we tip down the stairs.

Honor goes, 'Will you miss it, Granddad?'

He's like, 'What, this house? I suppose I will! Like Fionnuala said, there are a lot of happy memories within these walls, Honor! But we'll make some new memories where we're going!'

I'm there, 'I still can't believe you're throwing Michael D. Higgins out on his ear.'

'The Taoiseach of the country should live in the country's finest house! I remember the late, great Chorles J. Haughey telling me that one night in Le Coq Hardi, when he stopped by our table to joke about Garret FitzGerald's money troubles while trying to look down your mother's top! Oh, wonderful times!'

I'm there, 'Where's he going to go, though? As in, like, Michael D.?'

'Who the hell cares?' he goes. 'Somewhere more modest – a place that befits a man who believes that the workers should control the means of production!'

All of a sudden, there's the sound of crying coming from the living room. The old dear tuts – seriously – and goes, 'Oh, for heaven's sake, what is it now?'

She's un-focking-believable.

I'm there, 'Er, one of your *babies* is crying?'

'Yes, I know that,' she goes. 'They keep doing it, don't they, Chorles?'

The old man's there, 'Yes, perhaps Kicker here could shed some light on the whys and wherefores of it, having been through it with Honor here and those three chaps upstairs!'

I'm like, 'The whys and focking wherefores of it? Are you actually serious?'

'Well, as your mother said, they cry all the time, Ross.'

'Yeah, that's what babies do!'

'But sometimes for hours on end,' *she* goes. 'One will stort, then set all the others off and that's it for half the bloody day!'

Suddenly – right on cue – a second one storts crying, then a third, then a fourth.

'You see?' she goes. 'And once it storts, there's nothing you can do except pour yourself a very lorge glass of wine, then go and sit in the gorden until it's over.'

The old man's there, 'Do you think there might be something wrong with them, Ross?'

I'm like, 'Jesus Christ, you talk about your kids like you've bought a trouser press with a busted element,' and at the same time I push the door and step into the living room.

They're lined up, all six of them, in their – I want to say – *cribs*?

'Well, it couldn't be hunger,' the old dear goes, 'because they've already been fed. Astrid, this wonderful German nanny I was telling you about, she saw to that when she was here earlier.'

I'm there, 'Er, maybe it's *love* they want?'

The old dear goes, '*Love?*' like I've just said a can of petrol and a box of focking matches. 'Surely they're too young to understand abstract concepts like love.'

All I can do is just roll my eyes and walk over to the first – again, I'm saying it – *crib*, where Hugo is roaring his hort out. I reach in with my two hands and I pick him up.

I hold him close to my chest and, in a gentle voice, I go, 'It's okay . . . shhh, shhh, shhh . . . your big brother's here now,' and I kiss him on the top of the head. 'Everything's okay . . . shhh, shhh, shhh . . .'

Honor reaches into the next crib and she pulls out Mellicent. 'Hey,' she goes, in the softest voice, at the same time gently bouncing her up and down in her orms. 'What's got you all upset? Hmmm? What's got you all upset?'

I look at the old dear and I nod in the direction of the others.

I'm like, 'Er, do you want to give us a focking dig-out here?'

So she picks up Cassiopeia and she basically copies what I'm doing.

I'm there, 'No, hold her in your left orm, not your right.'

'But my right orm is my strongest orm,' she goes – her focking pouring orm, in other words.

I'm like, 'Doesn't matter. You hold a baby in your left orm so its ear is next to your hort. That's if you have one, of course – which I seriously focking doubt.'

Hugo stops crying in my orms.

The old man goes, 'Good Lord! Will you look at that! Ross's one is smiling, look!'

The old dear – I shit you not – goes, 'Which one have you got, Ross?'

I'm like, 'Hugo! For fock's sake, he's dressed in blue and he's the only boy.'

'And which one have I got?'

'That's Cassiopeia. Honor has Mellicent. And that one over there, who Dad is just about to pick up – pick her up, Dad – is Diana.'

The old man does what he's told. He goes, 'Ear *next* to the hort, you say, Kicker?'

And I'm like, 'Yeah, but try not to hold her like she's an ormful of documents you're about to feed into a focking shredder.'

The old dear – again, this is word for word – goes, 'I wonder, Chorles, should we put little morks on their hands with coloured pens, just so we can tell them aport?'

I'm there, 'You wouldn't need to do that if you took an actual interest in them instead of leaving it all to Astrid. Talk to your daughter, will you?'

'Which one have I got again?'

'Cassiopeia! Jesus Christ, woman!'

She goes, 'Okay, stop crying now, Cassiopeia. That's enough of it now. We've all heard enough from you.'

By some miracle, this manages to somehow act as a comfort to the baby, who stops crying. Mellicent and Diana eventually stop too and suddenly the room is quiet.

The old dear looks at me like she's just invented the daiquiri.

'Ross!' she goes. 'Look what we've managed to do!'

I'm there, 'Like I said, it just takes a bit of love and affection.'

'I'm going to colour-code them.'

'Do *not* colour-code them.'

The old man goes, 'We're going to have a crèche for them in the Áras, Ross! Fully staffed, of course! You should bring your little chaps along! It'd be nice for them all to spend time together!'

At that exact moment, there's a loud crashing sound upstairs. Something has been thrown through the window of my old bedroom and I can only hope it's not one of my children.

I'm like, 'Yeah, no, it'd be nice if they were someone else's problem for a few mornings a week.'

The old man's there, 'Shall we take our leave of the place?'

'Yes,' the old dear goes, 'I can't wait to get into the new place and stort redecorating.'

18

I'm there, 'So what are you going to do with it? *This* house, I mean. Are you going to sell it?'

The old dear goes, 'Of course not. We'll need somewhere to live if Chorles loses the next General Election.'

'That's not going to happen,' the old man goes, running his hand through his hair slash wig. 'And, even if it does, it'll take a bloody well military coup to remove Chorles O'Carroll-Kelly from office!'

I search his face for signs that he's joking. But the worrying thing is that he's *not*?

Sorcha is wearing her famous Stella McCortney trouser suit – the one that says she is not a woman to be focked with. I once saw her reduce a clamper to tears while wearing it, after she porked her Nissan Leaf in a bus lane to run into Donnybrook Fair for a tub of sweet pea saffron hummus and possibly pitta pockets.

I can't even make eye contact with her when she has it on.

We're sitting in the back of her State cor, with the famous K . . . K . . . K . . . K . . . Kennet at the wheel, and we're on the way to the Áras via the Deportment of – yeah, no – Climate Action.

I'm looking at the boys. I stuck Leo's glasses back together by wrapping a plaster around the nose piece and now he's happily effing and blinding under his breath like the other two. I've actually got butterflies in my stomach at the thought of spending the day away from them.

Sorcha has her laptop balanced on her knees and she's writing presumably emails.

Bryan Dobson is on the radio saying that the Taoiseach, Charles O'Carroll-Kelly, has confirmed that he and his wife, Fionnuala, have decided to make Áras an Uachtaráin their official residence for the lifetime of this Government. He says they're going live now to Mícheál Lehane in their Leinster House studio and he goes, 'Mícheál, is it putting it too strongly to describe this as a Constitutional crisis?'

Sorcha looks up for the first time since we left Honalee. Seriously, she didn't even say goodbye when we dropped Honor off at Mount Anville.

She goes, 'Oh my God, I can't believe they're trying to make an actual story out of this thing.'

I'm there, 'It seems pretty major. They're saying that nobody knows where Michael D. Higgins even *is*?'

'What are they implying? That your dad has, like, bumped him off?'

'I wouldn't put it past him, would you?'

'Yes, I would, Ross. Honestly, there are far more important issues in the world than who lives in the biggest house.'

You'd never know she went to Mount Anville. Sister Philippine would turn in her grave if she was alive today.

'Focking focking focking fock,' Brian goes – my son, not Dobson, I probably should point out.

His leg is obviously driving him mad with the itch because he's stuck a wire coat hanger that Honor gave him underneath his cast and he's giving himself a serious scratching with it.

He's like, 'Focking focking fock.'

'Where are we?' Sorcha goes.

And I'm there, 'Lower Leeson Street.'

Then she looks down and storts going at the keyboard again.

I'm like, 'Who are you writing to?'

She stops and looks up again.

She's there, 'I'm not writing *to* anyone. I'm making notes for my Maiden Speech.'

I go, 'It's just you're typing like you're angry about something.'

'Of course I'm angry about something. The destruction of the Earth and the almost certain extinction of the human race.'

'Oh, that.'

'I'm going to use my first speech in the Dáil to call for a worldwide ban on the extraction of fossil fuels from the Earth.'

'Er, cool. So – yeah, no – Honor got off to school okay. I don't know if you've noticed she's no longer in the cor?'

'Ross, I've no interest in discussing that girl.'

'Yeah, that girl happens to be your daughter, Sorcha. And, even though I'm focking terrified of you in that suit, I'm just going to come out and say it – I think you're being *possibly* horsh?'

'Horsh?'

'What you said to her the other day about you basically washing your hands of her? I think she's genuinely learned her lesson, Sorcha. I honestly can't see her humiliating you on the international stage again.'

Sorcha suddenly goes, 'Shush, Ross. I'm trying to hear what they're saying on the radio. Kennet, can you turn up the volume, please?'

Kennet's like, 'N . . . N . . . N . . . No woodies, M . . . M . . . M . . . M . . . M . . . Ministodder.'

'That's right,' this Mícheál Lehane dude goes, 'in a separate development, the Taoiseach *has* confirmed that a Russian company called MasloGaz has been granted a licence to drill for oil in the sea off Malin Head in County Donegal. Now, this will be seen by many as very controversial – you'll remember that Charles O'Carroll-Kelly's confirmation as Taoiseach was delayed by almost a year due to allegations of election meddling by Russian interests. So it'll be interesting to hear the Taoiseach answer questions about this in the Dáil in the coming days.'

'Oh my God!' Sorcha goes.

I'm like, 'What? I'm not sure I fully understand what's going on.'

'What's going on is that here *I* am, about to make a statement calling for us to set a target date by which to end our reliance on fossil fuels. And there's your dad, handing out licences to extract more oil, gas and who knows what else from the ground. Oh my God, this was done without any discussion at Cabinet, by the way.'

I'm there, 'Yeah, no, I'm still not sure I fully get what's going on. Never mind.'

'Kennet,' Sorcha suddenly goes, 'stop the cor!'

He's like, 'You're the b . . . b . . . b . . . b . . . boss, Ministodder.'

We're on, like, Westmoreland Street.

I'm there, 'Sorcha, I'm not sure it's safe for a girl like you to be walking around here – especially dressed like that.'

'I'm not walking anywhere,' she goes – then I notice her putting bicycle clips around the ankles of her suit trousers.

I'm like, 'What the fock?'

'I've decided that I'm going to cycle the last two kilometres to the office every day,' she goes.

I'm like, 'Cycle it?'

'That's right, Ross. As the Minister for Climate Action, I owe it to the public to be *seen* to set a good example?'

'But what exactly are you going to cycle *on*?'

She gets out of the cor.

'The fock is *she* going?' Leo goes.

I'm there, 'I've no idea.'

Kennet gets out of the cor as well and walks around to the boot. He whips out one of those, like, folding bikes, while Sorcha puts on one of those sausage hats that men who discover cycling in the midst of a midlife crisis always wear. She fastens the strap underneath her chin, while Kennet snaps the bike into shape.

He's like, 'Th . . . th . . . th . . . there you are now, Ministodder.'

Sorcha's like, 'I'll see you tonight, Ross!' as she throws her leg over the thing. 'Have a good day in crèche, goys!'

We watch her wobble up the road in the direction of O'Connell Bridge.

'Focking state of her,' Brian goes.

And, of course, I'm thinking the exact same thing.

'I hate her,' Honor goes.

I'm there, 'Hate's a strong word, Honor.'

'Oh my God, do you know what I'd love? If you, like, died in your sleep and Mum ended up all sad and lonely.'

I laugh.

I'm there, 'You used to say that when you were, like, five. God, you were such a cute kid.'

'I actually *mean* it?' she goes. 'She's a stupid focking bitch.'

This conversation is drawing quite a few looks, it has to be said.

Yeah, no, we're sitting in the waiting room of The Beacon, where Brian is about to have the cast removed from his leg.

'Why don't you mind your own focking business?' Honor says to this nosy wagon sitting opposite, who's, like, glued to our conversation.

I'm like, 'Well said, Honor. Very well said indeed,' and the woman goes back to staring at her phone.

And that's when Honor – totally out of the blue – goes, 'I was telling Erika on FaceTime last night that I don't want to be called by that name any more.'

I'm like, 'Honor? Why not?'

'I just hate it.'

'I didn't know you hated it.'

'Well, now you focking do.'

'Hey, that's no biggie. So what do want to be called?'

'I want to be called by my middle name.'

'What, Angelou?'

'No, my *other* middle name?'

'Okay, refresh my memory?'

'Suu Kyi.'

I actually laugh.

I'm there, 'Suu Kyi! What the fock was your mother thinking?'

'I actually like it,' Honor goes. 'I much prefer it to Honor.'

'Hey, if you want to be called Suu Kyi, that's cool by me.'

All of a sudden, the doctor appears and goes, 'Brian O'Carroll-Kelly?'

The dude is from, like, Pakistan and I'm not saying that to be *deliberately* racist?

Honor, sorry, Suu Kyi, helps Brian to his feet and I hand him his crutches.

'Focking crèche,' he goes.

And I'm like, 'You're not going to focking crèche today. You're getting your cast removed.'

He picks his way into the examining room, then sixty seconds later he's lying on a bed and the doctor is cutting off the cast with this, like, electric saw thing. The plaster cast hits the floor with a hollow slap. Poor Brian's leg looks all white and withered – like my old dear's neck. The doctor puts the saw down and storts pressing down lightly on the bone.

I'm there, 'So how's it looking, Doc?'

'I was very happy with the X-rays,' he goes. 'Yes, the bone has healed very nicely.'

'And what about, you know, the obvious?'

'The obvious?'

'Er, *rugby*? Will he still be able to play the game?'

'Yes, of course.'

'Oh, thank God! Thank! God! Because there was talk before that he might end up with a gimp leg. In other words, one shorter than the *other*?'

'Well, yes, there may always be a slight difference between them.'

'Excuse me?'

'You see, while this leg was broken, this one was still growing as normal. So there is a chance he will have –'

'A gimp leg.'

'– a slight limp.'

'Tomato, tomayto. Jesus Christ, when I asked you if he could still play rugby, I meant at the elite level.'

Brian reaches for the saw and the doctor quickly whips it away, going, 'Sorry, little man, this is not a toy.'

Brian's like, 'Me want it!'

And I'm there, 'You better give it to him, Doc. He'll have a shit-fit otherwise.'

'But he could cut his fingers off.'

'From the way you're talking, he's not going to need them – certainly not for rugby purposes.'

'Mr O'Carroll-Kelly, you are taking this news very badly. I am saying he *may* have a limp. And, if he does, it will only be slight.'

I'm there, 'Come on, Brian,' trying to hide my annoyance with him, 'let's get you home. Honor, give your brother a hand there, will you?'

'Suu Kyi,' she goes.

I'm there, 'Sorry – Suu Kyi.'

She helps him to stand up. But then Brian goes to take a step and – I swear to fock – he goes down like a Templeogue College scrum. I'm looking at him lying on the deck and I'm like, 'What the fock? He can't even walk – never mind do all the things that a centre is required to do in the modern game!'

The doctor picks him up and sits him on the edge of the bed.

'The muscles in this leg will be very weak,' he tries to go, 'so he must continue to use the crutches until he builds up strength again.'

I'm there, 'A focking disgrace. The whole thing.'

The dude hands me a piece of paper with, like, pictures on it. He goes, 'Here are some exercises that Brian must do every day to build up strength in the leg again.'

I snatch it from him, give it the once-over, then hand it to Suu Kyi.

I'm like, 'Come on, Suu Kyi, let's get the fock out of here before there's any more bad news.'

Five minutes later, we're back in the cor.

'I'm focking fuming,' I go. 'Focking. Fuming.'

Suu Kyi's like, 'Dad, it's fine. I'll do the exercises with him every morning and every night.'

'Rugby, though.'

She puts her hand on my orm and goes, 'I know, Dad.'

I'm there, 'I can't say it enough times. Rugby.'

Suu Kyi reaches into her pocket then and whips something out. She goes, 'Here you are, Brian, I have a present for you.'

And – yeah, no – it ends up being the electric saw, which, it turns out, she swiped while the doctor was picking my idiot son up off the deck.

She turns around in her seat and hands it to him and he's like, 'Fock!'

I'm there, 'Is it not dangerous? I'm suddenly thinking about what that so-called doctor said.'

'No, it's not plugged in.'

'God, you're an amazing sister. See, this is the kind of shit you never get credit for – and that kills me.'

'Maybe I'll take the blade out later.'

'Again – amazing.'

I stort the cor and we get out into the industrial estate.

I'm there, 'When I saw his leg, though, I nearly got sick.'

'It looks like Fionnuala's neck,' she goes.

'That's exactly what I thought!'

'We should get some Vitamin E cream for it.'

'Are you talking about your granny's neck?'

'No, Brian's leg,' she goes. 'And maybe some Bio-Oil.'

I'm there, 'Yeah, no, let's hit the old phormacy, then.'

So, like, ten minutes later we're in Lloyds in Stillorgan Shopping

Centre and we're getting the various lotions and potions that, again, Suu Kyi mentioned, while Brian – hilariously – is crawling around on his hands and knees, looking for a socket to plug his new toy into.

And that's when I end up copping her. She's standing just in front of us in the queue for the till, pretending she doesn't know we're there.

I'm like, 'Lauren?' and she ends up turning around.

'Oh,' she goes. 'It's you.'

She literally says that.

I'm there, 'How the hell are you?' because, hey, I'm very relatable.

'I'm fine,' she tries to go.

I'm there, 'I met Christian last week. We had a few beers in JP's new pad, even though he obviously wasn't drinking himself, being a supposed alcoholic. He's not seeing anyone – just in case you're wondering.'

She goes, 'I wasn't wondering.'

'Are you seeing anyone yourself – just as a matter of interest?'

'That isn't any of your business.'

'Hey, I'm just being polite here.'

The woman at the till goes, 'Next!' and Lauren walks up to her to pay for whatever's in her hand. So suddenly I'm talking to the back of her focking head.

I'm there, 'We're just getting a few bits for Brian. I don't know if you noticed, Lauren, but he just got the cast removed from his leg.'

She says fock-all. I'm guessing it's down to guilt.

I'm there, 'Not that I want you to feel bad about it.'

I do want her to feel bad about it.

She actually turns around and goes, 'Why would *I* feel bad?'

I'm there, 'Er, because your son pushed him down a focking escalator.'

'Because *your* son slammed a piano closed on his fingers.'

'You're not comparing like with like.'

'Excuse me?'

'Brian might never play rugby again.'

She just sighs and rolls her eyes, picks up her – yeah, no – purchases and storms out of the shop without even saying goodbye, you're looking well, or blah, blah, blah.

'Oh my God – hilarious!' Suu Kyi goes.

I'm like, 'What?'

'Did you see what she was buying?'

'Again – what?'

And a shiver goes through my body when Suu Kyi goes, 'Vaginal dryness cream.'

The old dear is a good nine fingers of Tanqueray down the road to her usual porty piece of pissing herself in her chair.

'The decorators are arriving tomorrow!' she goes. 'I'm going to have absolutely everything ripped out. And these ghastly paintings will be the first things to go.'

Sorcha's like, 'But, Fionnuala, those are portraits of, like, all the past Presidents of Ireland,' and she looks around the table, hoping to make eye contact with someone who *gives* a shit?

The old dear's there, 'I don't care who they *were*, Sorcha. I didn't know any of them – why would I want pictures of them in my home?'

Sorcha's like, 'I think the idea is that they're supposed to be port of, like, the historic character of the *house*?'

'One of them gives me the absolute creeps. Which one is it, Chorles?'

The old man laughs.

'Ah,' he goes, 'the infamous Cearbhall Ó Dálaigh!'

'His eyes follow you across the room,' the old dear goes. 'I think we'll burn the lot of them, Chorles.'

Sorcha's there, 'Well, if you're definitely definite about getting rid of them, I'd love the Mary Robinson one – for my office.'

'Is that her there?' the old dear goes, pointing with her butter knife.

'Yes, she went to Mount Anville as well,' Sorcha goes.

'I'll have it wrapped and sent to you. Then we'll build a fire and get rid of the rest, Chorles.'

Yeah, no, the old pair invited us around to the Áras for, like, an intimate family dinner – we're talking me and Sorcha, we're talking Ronan and Shadden, and we're talking Hennessy and a prostitute named Davina, who comes from Russia and looks like Emmy Rossum.

Ronan goes, 'By the way, thanks again, Grandda – Rihatta-Barrogan is made up, so she is.'

The old man's there, 'Think nothing of it!'

I'm like, 'What the fock is this?'

Shadden goes, 'Your da's arthur buying Ri a pony.'

She hands me her phone across the table and – yeah, no – it's a photograph of the kid sitting on top of a piebald.

'She's arthur naming him Moxy,' Ronan goes.

Sorcha's like, 'Moxy! And can she ride?'

'Ah, she's a naturdoddle – idn't she, Shadden?'

Everyone on that side of the city can ride a horse. It comes as naturally to them as yachting does to us. Or committing perjury in front of a tribunal of inquiry.

I know the old man's game, by the way. He's trying to buy my son's loyalty.

'Do you know what *would* make a great gift,' I go, '*instead* of a pony? If you got the unlawful possession of a firearm chorges against my son dropped, like you focking promised you would when you became Taoiseach.'

The old man's there, 'All in good time, Kicker! We have to proceed with caution! Politicians cannot be seen to interfere in the administration of justice! Ask my Attorney General there!'

Hennessy just gives me a big, stupid grin. Yeah, no, Davina has her hand between his legs and she's playing with his testicles like they're stress balls.

We haven't even had our mains yet.

The old man's there, 'We're all very grateful to you, Hennessy, for using your world-famous contacts to keep the entire business out of the newspapers.'

'For what it's worth,' Hennessy goes, 'I don't think the DPP will send the case forward for trial.'

I'm like, 'Meaning?'

'Meaning,' Ronan goes, 'thee'll probably throp the cheerges in a few munts. Thee habn't addy ebidence, Rosser – except the woord of whoever reng the Geerds and touted on me, the doorty rat-bastard.'

'So what about the internship you were offered in the States?'

'Unfortunately,' Hennessy goes, 'Ronan's passport will have to remain surrendered until this business is sorted out.'

I'm like, 'Yeah – which suits you, of course. Means he has to take your apprenticeship offer.'

The old man's there, 'Young Ronan here will learn more about the workings of the law under the wing of the great Hennessy Coghlan-O'Hara than he would in some New York firm specializing in – what was it again, Ronan?'

'Humodden reets.'

'Human rights! I mean, the bloody nerve of these people! Plus, he's going to be working at the very hort of Government! No, I think you'll look back on this one day, Ronan, as the moment when two roads diverged in a wood – etcetera, etcetera!'

'In addyhow,' Ro goes, changing the subject, 'Ri's godda be competing in a jiddum kada this weekeddent. She'd lubben yous to be there.'

I'm there, 'She's competing in a what?'

'A jiddum kada.'

'Say it again?'

'A jiddum kada.'

'Okay, this one's a real head-scratcher.'

'A fooken jiddum kada, Rosser.'

'Maybe break it up for us,' Sorcha goes.

He's there, 'A jiddum –'

I'm like, 'Keep going.'

'Kada.'

'It's still not landing with me.'

'Jiddum.'

'Jiddum.'

'Kada.'

'Kada.'

'Jiddum kada.'

'Oh my God, I think he's trying to say gymkhana?' Sorcha goes. 'Is that what you're trying to say, Ronan?'

'It's what I *am* saying. It's an equesthrian evedent – for childorden.'

I'm there, 'Jesus Christ, that did *not* sound like gymkhana.'

'In addyhow,' he goes, 'yisser all invrit, so yous are.'

I'm like, 'When even is it?'

'Saturday arthur noon – in the keer peerk of The Broken Arms. She'd lubben yous *alt* to be theer.'

'Then we *shall* be there!' the old man goes. 'To witness my great-granddaughter take her first steps into the world of competitive sport!'

Three waiters – I shit you not – walk into the room and gather up our soup bowls.

'By the way,' I go, 'I've a bit of news myself. Honor's not called Honor any more.'

Sorcha is about to take a sip of wine. She stops, the glass frozen in the air, six inches from her lips.

'*Excuse* me?' she goes.

I'm there, 'Yeah, no, she says she wants to be known by her middle name from now on.'

'Angelou?'

'No, the other one.'

'Suu Kyi?'

'Nail on head.'

'She's doing that to embarrass me.'

'What do you mean?'

'I named her after Aung San Suu Kyi, Ross – who happened to be a hero of mine at the time.'

'Er, right.'

'Do you have any idea who Aung San Suu Kyi even is?'

'No, is he a poet?'

'*She*, Ross, was a winner of the Nobel Peace Prize and a prisoner of conscience in, like, Myanmor? She spent, like, fifteen years of her life under house arrest.'

'What's embarrassing about that? I suppose her clothes would have been pretty out of date after – what did you say it was, fifteen years?'

'Since Aung San Suu Kyi rose to power,' it's the old man who goes, 'she's been accused of various human rights abuses – isn't that right, Sorcha?'

Sorcha's like, 'Technically, all she's really been accused of is standing idly by while her military committed genocide. But her name is, like, oh my God, mud among the people who once admired her.'

'And you think that's why Honor wants to use her name?' I go.

'She's doing it to try to get a reaction from me. But she's not going to get one. You can tell her, Ross, that she can call herself Vladimir Putin for all I care.'

I notice the old man and Hennessy exchange a look across the table. I have no idea what it's about and no desire to know.

'So,' *he* goes, before clearing his throat, 'how have you enjoyed your first week in Government, Sorcha?'

She's like, 'It was mostly fine, Taoiseach – although it'd be nice if I had a working telephone in my deportment.'

'What, they still haven't put that line in?'

'No – and the mobile signal is awful. I have to walk down, like, eight flights of stairs and go out onto the street if I want to make a call.'

'I will sort it out next week. I want to assure you, Sorcha, that the work of the Deportment of Climate Action is very, very important to this Government!'

The door opens and the waiters walk in again with, like, our mains – we're talking roast lamb with rosemary and gorlic potatoes. It smells incredible and I horse straight in.

Sorcha goes, 'Chorles, seeing as we're on the subject of work, can I raise an issue with you?'

The old man's there, 'Of course!'

'I didn't know you were going to make a statement issuing licences for drilling. It sort of, like, caught me on the hop, because my Maiden Speech was going to be about how we need to, like, *stop* taking fossil fuels from the ground if we're going to survive as, like, a species?'

'Well, as you know, Sorcha, I remain unconvinced on the whole question of whether or not the planet is heating up – and whether we even *need* a bloody polar ice cap!'

'Well, I was just wondering why this decision wasn't discussed at Cabinet.'

'It *was* discussed – at an emergency Cabinet meeting. Isn't that right, AG?'

Hennessy just nods, still grinning like a moron while Davina tugs at his balls with one hand and eats with the other.

The old man goes, 'I can get you the minutes if you want.'

Sorcha looks confused. I'm thinking, welcome to my old man's world.

She goes, 'It's just that, well, why wasn't I *told* about the meeting? This is the first I'm even hearing about it.'

'Well, perhaps someone tried to contact you – but your phone isn't connected, remember?'

'Chorles – Taoiseach – that really isn't good enough. If I'd been at that Cabinet meeting, I would have spoken out against it and hopefully changed your mind.'

'Well, I will make sure that phone line is put in first thing on Monday morning.'

'Thank you. And – also? – some *staff* would be nice?'

'Staff?'

'Taoiseach, I can't run an entire Government deportment on my own.'

'I wouldn't be so sure, Sorcha. You're very capable.'

'But for it to actually *feel* like a deportment that's taken, like, seriously, I need to have actual people around me – for instance, *advisers*?'

I need to shit.

The old dear goes, 'Yes, thank you for that information, Ross,' because I must have accidentally said it out loud.

I stand up.

I'm there, 'Where's the jacks?'

'They're everywhere,' *she* goes. 'There's a lovely one at the top of the stairs. And make sure you flush afterwards – show some consideration for the next user.'

I walk out of the dining room and I tip up the stairs.

My phone beeps and I whip it out of my pocket. It's a message from JP on the Castlerock College Team of '99 WhatsApp group. I don't even bother reading it. I'm not in the mood for his shit right now. I'm thinking, Christian is not only his friend, he's also his business portner – and there's JP having sex with his still technically wife, albeit not great sex if the vaginal dryness cream is anything to go by.

I'm about to push the door into the bathroom when I suddenly hear someone behind me go, 'Psssttt!!! Psssttt!!!'

I turn around, except there ends up being nobody there. I'm thinking, okay, is this place focking haunted or some shit?

Then I hear a voice go, 'Up here!'

I look up and – oh my focking God – it's Michael D. Higgins – *actual* Michael D. Higgins – and he's literally in the attic.

I'm there, 'Jesus Christ, are you, like, living up there?'

He goes, 'It's only temporary, until we find something else.' The poor focker – you'd have to say. 'What are you having for dinner? It smells delicious.'

I'm there, 'Yeah, no, it's roast lamb.'

'Mrs Higgins and I are very hungry up here,' he goes. 'Do you think you might bring us something?'

So – yeah, no – I swing into Mount Anville to collect Honor slash Suu Kyi from school and I end up bumping into Roz Matthews, the *famous* Roz, who I shared a couple of scenes with while I was on a break from Sorcha. And don't be fooled by the La Rochelle midterm tan and the mint-green cable-knit sweater tied around her shoulders – the woman is an absolute potty-mouth when she's on the job, mixing gratuitous focking and blinding with angry threats about all the things you're going to be too sore to do tomorrow, although I won't go into the ins and outs of it.

'Piss straight' was mentioned once or twice.

Luckily, there's no awkwardness between us when we meet now. Embarrassment isn't really a thing in Goatstown.

She's like, 'You're early,' which is true, because school doesn't end for another, like, twenty minutes.

I'm there, 'Yeah, no, I was supposed to meet a friend of mine,' which is also true. I swung in to JP's aportment with the intention of asking him what the fock he and Lauren are thinking. 'Except he wasn't home. So I had a bit of time to kill. What about you?'

'I came early,' she goes, 'because I wanted to sneak a look at how rehearsals are going.'

I'm there, 'Rehearsals? As in?'

'Sincerity is writing and directing the school show this year. They're putting on *Samantha Power: The Musical* next month.'

'Samantha Power? The, er –'

'The US Ambassador to the United Nations – who went to Mount Anville, albeit the Junior School and only for a short while. We're still claiming her, though!'

Modesty wouldn't be big around here either.

'So I'm presuming Sincerity's in it,' I go, because her daughter is one of those girls who always *has* to be the centre of attention?

She's like, 'Yeah, as well as writing and directing, she's also playing the port of Samantha. Oh my God, listen to me – I've turned into one of those awful stage moms! I'm so embarrassed!'

Er, no, she isn't. I have this sudden memory of Roz sitting astride me with the heels of her hands pressed into my eye sockets, telling me that I was going to be in the morket for a 'focking mobility scooter' by the time she was finished with me.

I'm there, 'There's no embarrassment between us, Roz. None whatsoever,' and into the school we walk.

We can hear the music from outside the concert hall. Roz pushes the door and we slip in unseen and sit in the back row.

Sincerity is standing on the stage, wearing a red wig and holding a suitcase. She's surrounded by six or seven girls dressed up as nuns and they're singing:

> *Samantha Power,*
> *This is the hour,*
> *For you to leave! Goodbye, sweet girl!*
> *Samantha Power,*
> *Beautiful flower,*
> *You'll make your mork upon the world!*

I spot my daughter at the very back of the choir. She's not even singing with the rest of them. She's on her phone, texting or, *more* likely, shopping.

Roz – as if reading my mind – goes, 'How's Honor doing these days?'

And I'm like, 'Yeah, no, she's in cracking form,' being obviously a fan. 'Although she's not *called* Honor any more? She's called Suu Kyi.'

'Oh, yes, Sincerity told me.'

'After some woman who everyone seemed to love until she failed to stop a genocide. Sorcha thinks she's possibly doing it for attention.'

'Ross, can I tell you something – in confidence?'

'You can say anything to me, Roz – I thought you knew that.'

'Sincerity said that Honor is being, well, ostracized by the other girls.'

'Jesus, I would have thought it was the other way around. She hates everyone in this school – your daughter included. No offence. She just thinks she's a sap.'

'Sincerity said that ever since, well, what happened at the United Nations –'

'When she said the death of human civilization was something to be welcomed? You can say it, Roz.'

'Well, yes, ever since *that*, everyone has been ignoring her. Like, when she sits down in the cafeteria, all the other girls who are sitting at the table get up and walk away.'

'Girls can be bitches. That's not sexist. I'm just laying out facts.'

'It's the Sixth Years who are behind it, apparently. They're telling all the other girls to stay away from her – well, you know what girls can be like. They think she's damaged the school's reputation abroad.'

I look down at Suu Kyi and my hort literally breaks for the girl. There's something about the thought of her being bullied that brings me to the point of actual tears.

My phone all of a sudden beeps. It's a text message from her. It's like: Why the fock are you talking to that stupid bitch's mother?

Well, whatever's going on, it's nice to see that it doesn't seem to be affecting her. I give her a smile and a wave and she gives me the finger back.

> *Samantha Power,*
> *This is the hour,*
> *Remember us in all that you do!*

Samantha Power,
Beautiful flower,
Mount Anville will always love you!

I'm there, 'That's a banging tune, Roz, in fairness to Sincerity.'

Roz goes, 'She worked so hord on it! I'm so proud of her!'

Samantha Power,
Beautiful flower,
Mount Anville will always love you!

When they finish rehearsing, Suu Kyi and Sincerity make their way over to where we're sitting. Sincerity throws her orms around Roz like they've been ported for ten years rather than the length of a school day, while Suu Kyi looks me up and down and goes, 'Why the fock are you even here? You should be outside in the cor.'

I'm there, 'I just stuck my head around the door to see how the rehearsals were going.'

In fairness to Sincerity, she makes the effort with her. She's like, 'Suu Kyi, do you want to come to my house to study together over the weekend?' which is really decent of her, even *if* she's a knob?

'With you?' Honor goes. 'I don't focking think so,' and then off she literally focks.

I apologize to Sincerity and Roz – well, I give them one of my famous 'what can you do?' eye-rolls – then I follow Suu Kyi outside to the cor.

We get in and I'm like, 'So how was school today?'

She just goes, 'School was school. I focking hate it and everyone in it.'

'Suu Kyi, you're not being –'

'Being what?'

'Well, people aren't giving you a hord time, are they? Just because you stood up in front of the United Nations and called out a few people who needed calling out?'

She doesn't say shit for ages. Then, eventually, she goes, 'What did *she* say when you told her that I'd changed my name?'

I'm there, 'Who, your old dear? Yeah, no, she said she was cool with it.'

'*Cool* with it?'

'Well, what she *actually* said was that she didn't care.'

'What, if I take the name of someone who people are now calling a war criminal?'

She just, like, stares straight ahead. I don't think I've seen her look this crushed since I took the matches off her while she was trying to set fire to the moving crib in Archbold's Castle five or six Christmases ago.

'Hey,' I go, 'I've an idea. Why don't we go to Dundrum Town Centre and see how long it takes us to burn through a grand? Would you like that, Suu Kyi?'

And she's just there, 'I don't want to be called Suu Kyi any more. My name is Honor.'

The cor pork of The Broken Orms pub in Finglas is absolutely rammers. It's fair to say that the whole community has turned out in its finest for the seventh annual St Margaret's Pony Club Gymkhana and Rodeo Competition, Incorporating Steer Wrestling, Calf Roping and Bronc Riding.

Even Tina – as in, like, Ronan's old dear – is wearing actual clothes, rather than her usual pyjamas and fake Uggs. I say it to her as well.

I'm there, 'I nearly didn't recognize you without your PJs on. Nice to see you making the effort. For once in your life.'

She goes, 'Will you ebber fook off, Rosser?' and I honestly don't know how I ever went there. 'What are you doing about yisser sudden?'

I'm like, 'My what?'

'Ronan.'

'Oh, my son! Yeah, no, what about him?'

'Is he going to jayult?'

'No, he's not going to *jayult*. Hennessy's going to hopefully get the chorges dropped.'

'I doatunt like him woorking for that doort-boord. He's the fedda sent me a lethor threatening me when I fell pregnant with Ro.'

I'm there, 'I'm not exactly pleased about it either, Tina. Leave it to me. I'll sort it, okay?' and I walk off.

Rihanna-Brogan is sitting on her pony – the famous Moxy – and she's looking nervous. Her old dear isn't exactly helping matters. She's looking around at the other competitors in the Go for Broke Bookmakers Dot Com Cup and she's going, 'There's no bleaten way that girdle theer is thirteen or under!' and 'That's not a pony oaber theer – that's a bleaten horse, so it is!'

I try to give my granddaughter the benefit of my experience in the area of competitive sport. I'm like, 'Don't worry about anyone else, Rihanna-Brogan – just focus on what *you're* going to do?'

Ronan goes, 'Listen to what Rosser is tedding you, love. And joost remember, at the end of the day, it's oately a birra fudden.'

Jesus Christ, I never said that. But I don't get the chance to correct the record because Shadden gets in there first.

'It is in its boddicks a birra fudden,' she goes. 'There's a thousand eurdos for the widder.'

Ro's there, 'There's mower to life than muddy, Shadden.'

'Says the fedda who wanthed to go to Amedica to woork for people for nuttin.'

He goes, 'Alls I was wanton to do was help people – the fook is wrong with that?' and I'm picking up on the vibe that Ronan might still be open to the idea of going to the States if the illegal possession of a fireorm and obstructing the course of justice chorges were somehow dropped.

She goes, 'Yeah, *you* woody about helping the rest of the wurdled, Ro. Hab you nebber hoord of the phrase, chadity begiddens at howum?'

It's horrible to listen to – and I'm not just talking about her pronunciation. The only consolation for me is that I told him it was a mistake to marry her.

Rihanna-Brogan goes, 'I want to walk the cowurse wit Moxy.'

Ronan's like, '*I'll* take you, love.'

She goes, 'No, I want me ma to do it,' and it's pretty obvious whose side she's on here.

Hey, she got a pony out of the deal.

So Shadden grabs the animal by the – I suppose – *reins* and walks him, with Rihanna-Brogan – six years old, bear in mind – up on his back, past the series of traffic cones and oil drums that she's going to have to weave through or jump over.

Ro's there, 'Alls Shadden bleaten cares about is muddy, Rosser.'

I'm there, 'It gives me no pleasure whatsoever to say I focking told you so. So how's the so-called job going?'

He goes, 'Er, moostard, Rosser. Moostard,' except I know he doesn't mean a word of it.

I'm there, 'So what does it actually involve, this so-called apprenticeship? And don't bullshit me, Ro. I did work experience for Hennessy when I was in school, remember. I was the only kid in Transition Year who had to write up his report at gunpoint.'

'You know yisser self,' he goes, 'little birra this, little birra that.'

I'm there, 'Ro, I'm so sorry.'

'Ah, it's not too bad, Rosser. He's paying me good muddy – and he's putting me through Blackhoddle Place. Ine steering in September, so I am.'

'I know, but you wouldn't be in this position if Leo hadn't fired that gun in Foxrock Church that day. You did what you did to cover for him.'

'I was cubbering for Shadden's da, Rosser. It was his gudden.'

'What I still can't understand is how Leo managed to get his hands on it in the first place?'

That's when I hear my old man's big, loudhailer voice go, 'There she is! My great-granddaughter – the future Aga Khan winner!'

I turn around. He's standing about twenty feet away, surrounded by – yeah, no – six or seven Special Branch officers without a neck between them.

I'm like, 'What the fock are you doing here, you big foghorn fock?'

'I'm here for the same reason as you, Kicker!' he tries to go. 'To see young Rihanna-Brogan ride her mount to victory in her very first gymkhana!'

Hennessy is standing beside him, smoking a cigor long enough to inseminate a whale. Then beside him is Kennet, with the famous Dordeen in tow.

He goes, 'How's she c . . . c . . . c . . . c . . . cutting, Ro? I habn't m . . . m . . . m . . . missed athin, hab I?'

'No,' Ro goes, 'it's joost about to steert, Kennet. Rihatta-Barrogan's not odden till last.'

The first rider out ends up being eight-year-old Shania Madden from Con Colbert Terrace in Coolock on her albino pony, Henrik Lorsson. She's got a big fan club with her, judging from the noise of the crowd. She storts pretty well – makes it over the first two jumps cleanly, then does the figure-eight and the key. But halfway through her round, she suddenly falls aport. Yeah, no, she storts hitting fences and knocking over traffic cones, racking up more penalty points in sixty seconds than Hennessy has collected in a lifetime of driving.

'Moy Jaysus,' Kennet goes, '*she* was apposed to be w . . . w . . . w . . . w . . . wooden of the f . . . f . . . f . . . f . . . f . . . favourduts.'

The second rider up is nine-year-old Idrina Moiles from Desmond Connell Gardens in Edenmore on her jet-black Connemara pony, Bieber. I don't really watch her round, though, because – being honest? – I find anything to do with ponies or horses really boring, so instead I just stare Kennet and Hennessy out of it, while a horrible thought storts to take shape in my head.

The whole thing was a fit-up!

It's so focking obvious to me now. The old man and Hennessy want Ronan to take over their business – whatever business it is they're in these days.

Evil, basically.

The old man knows I wouldn't be capable of doing it, what with me having nothing but focking bingo balls in my head. But, with Hennessy's training, Ronan definitely could. Which was why he had to stop him from going to New York.

The crowd gasps. I look up to see that Bieber has thrown little Idrina Moiles clean off his back. Luckily, she's not injured, but Bieber has decided to have a lie down in the middle of the cor pork and the organizers end up having to disqualify him and drag him off the course by throwing a rope around his neck and hitching the other end of it to the tow bor of a Ford Transit Connect.

How did Kennet's gun end up in Leo's hands? Kennet must have given it to him. Knowing that Leo would fire it. Knowing that me and Sorcha already had Tusla sniffing around us and that Ronan, being Ronan, would do whatever he had to do to stop his little brother from being taken into care, even if that meant taking off with the gun and stashing it. And who told the Feds that it was Ro who hid the gun?

Focking Kennet, of course. Or Hennessy. Or maybe the old man.

And, just when I stort to wonder am I being possibly paranoid, there's suddenly a humungous crash. Amanda Neeson of Medjugorje Villas in Artane has ploughed through the first fence on her Shetland pony, Argos. I hear Kennet have a little chuckle to himself. Argos wobbles but clears the second fence before stopping halfway through the figure-eight to drop a load in the middle of the cor pork, the shit pouring out of him like Guinness from a dirty tap.

And that's when I cop it – and half the crowd cops it as well, certainly judging from the angry noises I'm suddenly hearing. The horses have been poisoned. My eyes automatically turn to Kennet. He's down on one knee.

For me, there is no sight in the world more unsettling than a working-class Dublin man pretending to tie his shoelaces – especially when he's wearing slip-ons.

I watch in just, like, shock as Hennessy produces what I can see, from even ten yords away, is a syringe filled with something. He slips it to Kennet. And pretty quickly it's clear that it's different to the something that the *other* ponies had?

Rihanna-Brogan's name is called over the tannoy. Kennet, still down on one knee, looks over both shoulders, then jams the syringe into Moxy's orse. The pony takes off like a bullet, clearing the first fence, then the second, while poor Rihanna-Brogan clings desperately onto his neck and all the crowd can do is just go 'oooh' and 'aaah'.

'She's an absolute natural!' the old man goes. 'The O'Carroll-Kelly genes are strong in her!'

And, in that instant, I suddenly realize what I have to do. As his old man, I owe it to Ronan to get him away from these people once and for all.

2.

Truth to Power

Sincerity Matthews fell through a trapdoor and bruised her coccyx. Honor breaks this news to us while she's helping Brian to do his morning exercises and I'm hoping and praying that my face doesn't give away what I'm thinking.

She stares at me and goes, 'What?'

And I'm like, 'Nothing. I wasn't thinking anything. You know my head, Honor – empty, thank God.'

'Dad, I saw the look on your face. Brian, try to lift your leg higher – that's it. You think I pushed her, don't you?'

'Hey,' I go, 'all I'm saying is that Fionn had the exact same look on *his* face?' trying to hopefully deflect.

Fionn is sitting at the kitchen table, trying to feed Hillary, except the kid keeps shouting, 'Unkon Yoss! Unkon Yoss!' which is his way of saying Uncle Ross.

Fionn goes, 'It's a family matter, Ross. It has nothing to do with me,' and I'm thinking, yeah, no, thanks for the back-up, Dude.

Honor's there, 'So do *you* think I pushed her?' except she's not looking at me – she's, like, staring at Sorcha, who has her head down, reading a magazine while eating her muesli.

I'm like, 'Yeah, what do *you* think, Sorcha? The spotlight's very much on you now.'

But Sorcha just goes, 'I'm reading here, Ross,' like she doesn't *give* a fock. Which is probably *actually* the case?

Fionn's there, 'Is that the piece in *The New Yorker*?'

'Yeah,' she goes, 'it's about the Doomsday Thermometer. The United Nations Intergovernmental Panel on Climate Change is now saying that an increase of even one point five degrees Celsius in the global temperature would mean the loss of the world's coral reefs,

44

the displacement of millions of people by rising sea levels and a drastic decline in global crop yields.'

'I have to say,' Fionn goes, 'I always thought the limit of two degrees Celsius that they set in Paris had more to do with politics than geophysics. I'd love to read the piece when you're finished with it, Sorcha.'

Honor tells Brian to lie down on his side, which he straight away does – yeah, no, he absolutely adores the girl. She puts this, like, giant rubber band around his two knees, then she tells him to lift his top knee while keeping his two ankles together.

I remember Luke Fitzgerald doing the exact same exercises when he was coming back from his knee injury back in the day. Three nights a week, me and JP would drive up to West Wood in Leopardstown with a Nando's and watch him do his rehab from the mezzanine while we horsed into a couple of ten-wing roulettes with Peri-Peri chips. We were both massive, massive fans of Pivot – still are – and he apparently name-checked us when he talked about his comeback on Blackrock College Transition Year radio, although he also mentioned that he now associates the smell of borbecue flame chicken with that unhappy period of his life and has gone through periods of vegetarianism.

'Fock!' Brian goes, because it's obviously hurting him. 'Focking fock!'

Honor's like, 'I know it's sore, Brian, but this will strengthen your hip. We don't want you ending up with a limp, do we?'

I'm there, 'It's too late for that – that's according to the doctor. His legs are already banjoed.'

Leo goes, 'Silas – say, "Go fock yourself!"'

And from the speaker next to the Nespresso, a sexy robot voice goes, 'Go fock yourself!' and Leo, Brian and Johnny all laugh.

I'm there, 'I'm already regretting buying that thing.'

'Silas,' Brian goes, 'say, "Fock you, you focking motherfocker!"'

But Honor's there, 'Forget about Silas for the moment, Brian. If we do these exercises every morning and every evening, we can prove the doctors wrong. I know we can. That's it – lift your leg.'

Sorcha's there, 'When I look at that globe that you bought me,'

Fionn, and I see the Maldives not even *there* any more, that's when I remember the enormity of this responsibility I've been given. Mom and Dad took us there for the Easter holidays when I was, like, twelve and it's like, Oh! My God!'

This time, Fionn just nods along with me – there's not a lot else to say.

'Anyway,' Honor goes, 'it means Sincerity isn't going to be able to play Samantha Power. So they're having, like, auditions for the port next week. I was thinking of going for it.'

She says this while stealing a look at Sorcha, obviously trying to gauge her reaction. But, without even looking up from her magazine, Sorcha goes, 'Ross, will you get the boys ready for crèche and Suu Kyi ready for school?'

Honor's like, 'I'm not *called* Suu Kyi any more? I've gone back to being Honor,' except Sorcha continues to just, like, blank her.

I'm there, 'Honor, come on, let's get going,' so we bring the boys upstairs to get them dressed.

'Oh my God,' Honor goes, 'she's being *such* a bitch.'

I'm there, 'I don't want to take sides, but she definitely seems to be, alright.'

Fifteen minutes later, Kennet arrives in the limo and the whole happy family piles into the back of it. Then we hit the road.

Kennet looks at me over his shoulder and he's there, 'S . . . S . . . S . . . S . . . Suddem resudult, w . . . w . . . wadn't it, Rosser?'

'The fock are you talking about?' I go.

'Ine th . . . th . . . th . . . thalken about little Rihatta-Barrogan widding the j . . . j . . . j . . . j . . . jiddum kada on Saturday.'

There's so much I feel like saying to the focker. I want to tell him that I know he drugged all the ponies, just like I know he gave his gun to Leo in Our Lady of Perpetual Whatever She Was Going Through Church in Foxrock that day. Except I don't say shit.

I just go, 'Does this thing go up?' meaning the glass screen that separates the front of the cor from the back.

He goes, 'The b . . . b . . . b . . . button's on the soyid of the d . . . d . . . d . . . d . . .' and I press the button and – hilariously – shut him out before he manages to say the word 'dowur'.

I'm there, 'I rue the focking day that my son got mixed up with that focking family of scumbags.'

Honor's like, 'Dad, are you absolutely sure he can't still hear you?'

I look at the back of his head. Yeah, no, he's just staring at the road ahead.

I'm there, 'Yeah, no, I don't care if he *can* still hear me? The stuttering scumfock.'

'Stuttering scumfock,' Leo goes.

Then Brian laughs and repeats what he said.

He's like, 'Stuttering scumfock.'

It's at that exact point that Honor storts singing. Yeah, no, out of literally nowhere, she's suddenly giving it:

> He's from Hawaii,
> And from Kenya,
> He's also Irish,
> Like me and Enya,
> He called to ask,
> 'Samantha, can ya –
> Help me bring hope to the world?'

I'm like, 'That's lovely, Honor. Is that from, er . . .'

'*Samantha Power: The Musical*,' she goes. 'It's the bit where Barack Obama asks her to be his Senior Foreign Policy Adviser during the 2008 Presidential campaign.'

Sorcha looks up from her laptop and goes, 'Sorry, is this conversation for *my* benefit or something?'

'Would you not be worried,' Honor goes, 'if I went for the port and got it?'

But Sorcha's there, 'I told you, I have absolutely zero interest in anything you do any more. Have a good day, Suu Kyi.'

Yeah, no, we've arrived at the gates of Mount Anville.

Honor just stares at her old dear like the woman is made of corbs and she's been told she has to eat her before bedtime. She gets out of the cor and slams the door shut again, then morches into the school in an absolute rage.

I'm like, 'Do you have to keep calling her Suu Kyi?'

'I don't know,' Sorcha goes, 'there's something about the name that pretty much encapsulates the way I feel about her right now. And she definitely pushed Sincerity through that trapdoor.'

'I don't know how you can even think that.'

'We're all thinking it, Ross – including you.'

'Why would she do it?'

'Because she wants to play Samantha Power – so she can use it to embarrass me all over again in front of yet another audience.'

'I'm actually wondering should we possibly give her the benefit of the doubt this time?'

'How many more chances do you intend giving that girl, Ross?'

'I was thinking a good few.'

She's like, 'You're a fool for her,' and then she goes back to her laptop.

Leo – for absolutely no reason – slaps Johnny around the side of the head and Johnny storts screaming blue murder.

I'm like, 'For fock's sake, Leo, you'll dislodge his grommets again.'

'Focking prick!' Johnny goes, grabbing two fistfuls of Leo's hair and shaking his head until his glasses fall off his face.

I manage to – yeah, no – separate them.

'Oh my God!' Sorcha goes. 'I don't believe it!'

She looks up from her laptop.

She's like, 'It's An Taoiseach –'

I'm there, 'Yeah, can you just call him Chorles? It's way too random otherwise.'

'According to the *Irish Times*, he's agreed to sell off hundreds of square kilometres of Ireland's forest-land to a Russian logging company. Avondale Forest Pork in Wicklow. Coole Pork Nature Reserve in Galway. Knockbarron Wood in Offaly. Killorney National Forest in Kerry. All these areas are going to be completely cleared of trees. We're talking – oh my God – literally millions of them are going to be cut down and shipped out of Ireland to be presumably burned.'

I'm there, 'Hey, I warned you about my old man, Sorcha. But you didn't want to listen.'

'I didn't think he'd do something like this.'

'Sorcha, he's done way worse than this.'

'What are you talking about?'

'I'm pretty sure he set up Ronan. Him and Hennessy and focking K . . . K . . . K . . . K . . . Kennet there.'

'There's no way he'd do something like that, Ross. Have you asked him about it?'

'No, but I'm going to go and see the tool this morning.'

I'm like, 'What do you mean, who am I?'

I can't figure out whether the dude at the gate on Merrion Street is serious or if he's just being a dick.

'I'm Ross O'Carroll-Kelly,' I go.

He acts like the name means fock-all to him – thus answering my question.

'Rugby,' I go. 'My old man is Chorles O'Carroll-Kelly. Er, this is where he *works*?'

He's there, 'But you can't just walk in here off the street.'

'What, even though he's the leader of the country?'

'Especially because he's the leader of the country. Do you have a pass?'

I'm like, 'Do you know what? Forget it,' and I whip out my phone. 'The power has obviously gone to your focking head.'

I ring Ronan's number.

He answers by going, 'Rosser, Ine up to me boddicks hee-or.'

I'm there, 'I'm outside on Merrion Street and I can't get in.'

I swear to fock, he goes, 'Have you not got a pass?'

I'm there, 'I'm not even going to dignify that with a response. Come down here and sign me in, will you?'

I hang up on him, then I turn around to the dude on the gate and I go, 'Can I get your name, please?'

He's like, 'My name is on my badge,' because he couldn't be bothered to just tell me.

I'm there, 'Robert Tyner? Is that actual?'

'What do you mean is it actual?'

But then I spot Ronan walking across the cobbled courtyord with a laminate swinging from his fingers. He ends up handing it to me through the gate, then he goes, 'He's moostard, Robbie. That's me auld fedda.'

This Robbie Tyner dude is like, 'You're joking me! Him?'

And Ronan laughs – focking laughs! – and goes, 'I know. Heerd to belieb, idn't it?'

I flash the pass at the dude and he opens the gate and I go, 'Yeah, good luck getting a new job after I get you focking sacked in about five minutes,' as I walk past him and give him *the* filthy of a lifetime.

I walk with Ronan across the courtyord and he goes, 'What are you doing hee-or in addyhow?'

I'm like, 'I'm here to see my old man. I want a word with him.'

'He's up to he's boddicks this morden, Rosser. Did you see it was in the paper about him sedding off a load of Arelunt's foddests to the Rushiddens?'

'I saw that, yeah.'

'And then the papers is all aston where's Michael D. Higgins and he's missus?'

'What do you mean? They're living in the attic.'

'Thee habn't been seen in public for two weeks, but. There's rumours that Cheerlie's arthur –'

'No, I was talking to them the other night. I brought them up a bit of dinner. He had the lamb and she had soup.'

It's only then that I notice the absolute state of Ro. The white shirt he's wearing is, like, covered in stains and he smells like – and this isn't me being a dick – a hot day in Ballyogan.

I'm like, 'Ro, have you been sleeping rough or something?' because my first thought automatically is that Shadden must have caught him up to his old tricks again.

He goes, 'I told you, Rosser, I've been woorking.'

I'm there, 'What are you working on? A focking trawler?'

He looks around to make sure no one's behind him.

'Mon,' he goes, 'I'll show you.'

I walk with him along a corridor, then up a flight of stairs, then along another corridor, until we reach a door. He presses a four-digit code into a keypad and it opens. Beyond that, there's another door and he presses a second four-digit code to open that one.

We walk into this, like, small room and I can't even begin to describe the hum in there. I look around me. There are bags of, like, literally rubbish piled up everywhere. We're talking black refuse sacks with tea bags and Chinese food cortons and stale bread spilling out of them.

'Okay,' I go, 'what the actual fock? Whose rubbish is this?'

He's there, 'That's Frances Fitzgedoddled's. That's Micheál Meertidden's. That's Meerdy Lou McDonoddled's.'

'You are taking the literally piss. What the fock are you doing with Mary Lou McDonald's rubbish?'

'Ine seerching it.'

'Searching it for what?'

'Addything of inthordest.'

'Excuse me?'

'An hour befower the binmen cub arowunt, Heddessy has some wooden collect the rubbish from outside the gaffs of evoddy member of the Opposishidden to brig it hee-or.'

'Ro, do you know how dodgy this is? Jesus, whose is that one with all the copies of my old dear's books spilling out of it?'

'That's Meerdy Mitchiddle-O'Coddor,' he goes. 'She must have had a cleer-out of her office.'

I laugh.

He goes, 'They're peersonoddy signed to her as weddle. *To Meerdy, moy deerdest friend, Fidooda.*'

I'm there, 'I can't wait to tell her.'

'You caddent ted her, Rosser. No one's apposed to know addything about what goes on in this roowum.'

'Fine, my lips are sealed. Where the fock is my old man's office?'

'Rosser,' he goes, 'I doatunt want me grandda to think Ine ungratefuddle.'

'Ro, you're getting sucked into something here. Something very, very bad. And I need to get you out of it. Plus –'

'What?'

'That day in the church. Ro, I'm convinced you were set up.'

'By who?'

'The old man. Or Hennessy. Or Kennet. Maybe even all three of them.'

'Thee woultn't do that, Rosser.'

'They're capable of anything, Ro. Where's his office?'

'It's up anutter lebel – end of the coddidor, turden left, then reet and you caddent miss it.'

I follow his instructions – well, insofar as I understand them – and I eventually find my way to the old man's office after asking one or two other people who speak English for further directions.

Yeah, no, Hennessy is sitting at a desk outside the door, obviously deciding who goes in and who doesn't. I just walk straight past him.

He's like, 'Where the fuck do you think you're going?'

I'm there, 'I'm going to talk to my old man,' and I push the door into the office.

The dude is sitting behind *the* most humungous desk I've ever seen.

He's like, 'Ross, I didn't expect to see you this morning!'

I'm there, 'You set my son up.'

'I *beg* your pordon!'

'You wanted him working for Hennessy, which meant you had to stop him going to the States. So you got K . . . K . . . K . . . Kennet to give Leo his gun in Foxrock Church that day, knowing full well that Leo would fire it.'

'You think I would do something like that? Any one of us could have been killed! Me? Your mother? One of the babies?'

'Not if the bullets were blanks.'

'What you're saying isn't rational, Kicker!'

'And you knew, given the kind of kid that Ronan is, that he'd take chorge of the situation and try to get rid of the gun. Here's an interesting question, though – who *called* the actual Feds?'

'I've no idea where this is leading, Ross! Objection! Relevance? Strike from the record with order for costs – eh, Hennessy?'

'Like Ronan said, someone focking touted. As in, someone who was at the christening told the Gords that Ronan took the gun away and disposed of it.'

Hennessy goes, 'We won't know that until the Book of Evidence is presented.'

'I already know,' I go. 'It was either you or focking K . . . K . . . K . . . K . . . K . . . K . . . Kennet.'

He's there, 'That is a very serious allegation you are making.'

'You're being paranoid!' the old man tries to go. 'Look, I know you're upset that Ronan couldn't take up that wonderful offer to work for a firm for absolutely nothing in New York! But trust me when I say that he'll look back on the whole sorry business one day and agree that it was a blessing in disguise! This is where young Ronan belongs, Ross, working with your godfather and me in the best interests of our country!'

I'm there, 'Do you know what Hennessy has my son doing this morning?'

'I'd prefer not to know, Ross! I promised your godfather that I would keep the office of Attorney General free from political interference! The separation of powers – quote-unquote! If I don't know what the hell is going on, I can't be accused of perjuring myself at a future tribunal! That was another one of Haughey's! Dear, oh dear, he really was a tonic!'

The old man stands up from his desk. He walks over to a photograph on the wall of him having a couples massage with Donald Trump – yeah, no, someone focked up the booking in the spa in Doonbeg and they decided to just go along with it. Got on like a house on fire as well. He checks his reflection in the glass, then storts puffing up his wig with the tips of his fingers.

Hennessy goes, 'Now, if you don't mind . . .' and he flicks his head in the direction of the door, telling me to basically hit the bricks.

The old man goes, 'Yes, we've a busy day ahead. The press has found out about this deal I've done with Fyodor – it's only a few trees, for heaven's sake. And there's all these bloody Michael D. conspiracy theories on Twitter. You know, there are people out there who think I've bumped the chap off, Ross!'

I'm there, 'You better get those chorges against my son dropped,' and I turn around and storm out of the room.

Outside in the corridor, I end up literally running into Fyodor.

I'm there, 'Alright, Dude?' but he just, like, stares at me and doesn't say shit. I can't help but wonder has he found out that I rode his wife in a Mitsubishi i-MiEV in the Glen of the Downs. 'How's

Sergei?' because – yeah, no – his son played for me when I coached Pres Bray. 'Have you heard from him?'

'I think you have sex with my wife,' he goes.

I'm there, 'Er, which one is your wife again?' playing for time.

'Raisa,' he goes. 'When she meets you, she tells me she likes you. You are handsome, she says. You have big shoulders and nice smile.'

'Hey, I can take a compliment as well as the next man.'

'Then, last week, she says you are bastard and she thinks you are probably kind of man who likes other men –'

'I'm not sure if you're allowed to *say* shit like that any more?'

'– because you cannot satisfy woman with your tiny penis that keeps falling down like a cheap tent in the wind.'

'Can I just ask, are those *actual* quotes or are you, like, paraphrasing?'

'And I think to myself, what has made Raisa hate this man so much? Only one thing, I think. He has disappointed her when he has the sex with her.'

'The sex?'

'Yes, she can have a very – how to say? – cruel mouth if you fail to satisfy her in a sexual way.'

'Dude, I'm going to put my hand on my hort here and assure you that I did not have the sex, as you call it, with your wife.'

'Yes, she says this also.'

'Then I hope it's put your mind at ease.'

'Perhaps a little. But if you are lying to me, Ross, I will find out. And then I will fucking kill you with my hands.'

Today is a big day – you'd even be tempted to use the word humungous – for JP and Christian. Yeah, no, the Ant Farm at Cherrywood – 'a truly revolutionary residential development', according to the brochure, 'that reconceptualizes what we consider living space' – is about to be officially opened by Gordon Greenhalgh, the Minister for Housing, Planning and Local Government.

I'm genuinely stoked for the goys, since the Ant Farm at Cherrywood is the perfect showcase for their Vampire Bed, combining it with another exciting Irish innovation, the Homedrobe, to demonstrate how – again, this is all me quoting from the brochure – 'humans can be accommodated in a way that's simple, pragmatic and space-efficient'.

'What do you think?' Fionn goes, whispering the words out of the side of his mouth. He's holding little Hillary, who's going, 'Unkon Yoss! Unkon Yoss!" because – like I said – he's a fan.

And I'm there, 'Yeah, no, fair focks to them. Fair very much focks to them, in fact.'

'Are you joking?' Fionn goes. 'Ross, it's like something out of a science fiction movie.'

'You obviously mean that in a *bad* way?'

'I'm thinking about that one that's set on a spaceship – we watched it – and all the crew are in an induced coma in these, like, pods.'

'Is that the one where Chris Pratt wakes Jennifer Lawrence up because he wants to ride her?'

'That's possibly an oversimplification, but yeah.'

I open one of the famous Homedrobes, invented by Éadbhard – spelt the Irish way – Ó Cuinneagáin, who played blindside flanker for Wesley back in the day. It's pretty poky, it has to be said. It's about the size of, like, a standard hot press, but it's just about big enough to accommodate one vertical bed, then there's a pocket where you can fit, like, your wallet and your cor keys, and also a shelf with a wireless phone-chorging station on it.

Hand on hort, a hundred Ks seems pretty pricey for what you're actually getting, but then you also have access to a communal living room and kitchen, as well as a communal shower and – yeah, no – a communal shitter.

I'm there, 'Dude, this is apparently how the next generation *want* to live?'

He's like, 'Is it, though? Or are we telling them it's how they want to live?'

'Hey, I'm only going by what my old man said during the election when he was talking about the housing crisis.'

'All I know is I wouldn't want this for Hillary. You put all those years and all that money into educating a child – Montessori, junior school, secondary school, college, postgrad – and they end up living in a cubby-hole.'

'There's apparently a communal roof gorden as well – we're talking architect-designed.'

A girl's voice suddenly goes, 'Smile, goys!'

We both turn around and it ends up being Lychee, the Minister's twenty-two-year-old – I can't help but notice – foxy daughter. Yeah, no, she's pointing her phone at us.

She's like, 'I'm doing my dad's social media. I want to get a picture of you in front of the Homedrobe.'

Fionn's there, 'Look, I'm not sure if I want my image used to endorse –'

But before he can finish his sentence, Lychee has taken about thirty focking shots of us.

'Oh my God,' she goes, checking her phone, 'that one's, like, perfect for Instagram – *such* a cute baby! – and that's an amazing one for Twitter. Can I get something for, like, TikTok?'

Me and Fionn are both like, 'TikTok?' the two of us suddenly feeling our age.

She's like, 'Yeah, a short video where you, like, *do* something.'

I'm there, 'In terms of?'

'It's up to you. But something that, like, millions of people will want to share. Oh my God, can your *baby* actually do anything?'

Fionn suddenly loses it with her. He's there, 'I could strap him into one of the vertical beds if you like and get him to say, "The future is communal living!"'

'Oh my God,' she goes, 'could he do that?'

Me and Fionn end up just staring at each other. But luckily we don't have to explain it to her because – this is young people for you – she suddenly spots something more interesting happening somewhere else.

'I think my dad is about to make his speech,' she goes, whipping out a second phone. 'I'm supposed to be live-streaming it on Facebook,' and off she focks, the gorgeous idiot.

Me and Fionn follow the crowd up to the communal roof gorden, where the speeches are supposedly happening. I spot Christian and

JP standing next to Gordon Greenhalgh, and also Éadbhard – spelt the Irish way – Ó Cuinneagáin, looking all delighted with themselves. JP smiles at me, but I look away, because I'm still struggling with the idea of him and Lauren doing it behind Christian's back.

'The Ant Farm at Cherrywood,' the Minister goes, 'is the first and last word in intelligent, twenty-first-century accommodation solutions. As you probably know, our need, as a society, to embrace new types of tenure is very much port of New Republic's vision for the future of our country's housing market. And I, for one, am proud that the Vampire Bed and the Homedrobe are two Irish innovations which, when synergized like this, can help us totally reimagine what we, as a species, consider a habitable space.'

Gordon, by the way, lives on Serpentine Avenue in a house that used to be the Chinese embassy. The old man told me once that you could wander around it for days without ever seeing your wife and children.

'As a Government,' he goes, 'we believe that it's time we moved away from this, frankly, twentieth-century, post-colonial idea that we should all aspire to *own* a house. I'm happy to say that young people are keen to embrace a brand-new paradigm for living, one that doesn't involve the heavy monthly burden of mortgage debt, meaning they have more money in their pockets to buy the things they really want, such as Apple products and takeaway coffees. The new generation don't look on where they live as a home in the traditional sense; they see it as somewhere to sleep, cook and go to the toilet in between having all these wonderful experiences that, well, old farts like me only get to enjoy by taking a peek at our children's Instagram accounts!'

Everyone laughs. I don't know why. It just feels right and we all go with it.

'As the Minister for Housing, Planning and Local Government,' the dude goes, 'it is my great pleasure – even privilege – to officially launch The Ant Farm at Cherrywood and kick-start what I know will be a revolution in how our children live their lives tomorrow.'

Everyone claps, while I head for the free bor and ask for a Heineken, only to be told that they're only serving – fock's sake – wine.

JP sidles over to me.

'How our children live their lives tomorrow?' he goes, looking over his shoulder to make sure no one's listening. 'Not Lychee. She'll be inheriting that palace on Serpentine Avenue.'

I'm there, 'The dude did you a favour by showing up today and endorsing your bed. It's a pretty shitty thing to stort dissing him behind his back.'

He stares at me, wondering am I ripping the piss, then he sees that I'm not.

He's like, 'Ross, what's wrong? You haven't been returning any of my calls. You haven't reacted to any of the videos or pictures I've posted on WhatsApp and you're usually the first in there with an emoji or two.'

Yeah, no, one of the videos was of a seagull walking out of Insomnia on Camden Street with a packet of Keogh's salt-and-vinegar crisps and it killed me not to be able to acknowledge it with a Beaming Face with Smiley Eyes, or a Laughing Face with Tears of Joy, or even just a Winking Face with Tongue.

I'm there, 'Maybe I should have held off with the emojis a bit more often. But then that's just my big hort.'

'Dude,' he goes, 'what are you talking about?'

'I know who she is, JP. The bird you've been seeing.'

Oh, that rattles his molars, because he suddenly looks away.

I'm there, 'She was buying vaginal dryness cream in Lloyds in Stillorgan and I put two and two together.'

'Ross, look –' he tries to go.

I'm there, 'She's a married woman, JP.'

'I know she's a married woman.'

'And you know who she's still technically married to?'

'Yes, of course I do.'

'And you don't see anything wrong with that?'

He tries to get smort with me then.

He's there, 'Who the fock are you to judge anyone, Ross?'

'Oh,' I go, 'you're going to stort throwing my past in my face now? This is a hell of a lot different to me riding Christian's mother.'

'And Fionn's sister?'

'Again – different.'

'Look, she's separated, Ross.'

'Yeah, only just.'

'Her marriage is over.'

'And what about *his* feelings? I presume she hasn't told him yet?'

'No, she hasn't. We're taking things slowly.'

'If she's ended up with thrush, you are *not* taking things slowly.'

'Ross –'

'She's got a tube of it in your bathroom and she was buying more. Don't shit a shitter, J-Town.'

'Look, I would appreciate your discretion on this.'

'I'm sure you focking would.'

'We don't know where it's going yet. Yeah, no, there are obstacles. She hasn't met Isa yet and then there's obviously *her* kids to think about.'

I'm there, 'You need to tell him, Dude.'

'Well, *she* doesn't think that would be such a good idea,' he tries to go.

I'm there, 'Oh, I bet she doesn't. But he needs to know.'

'Ross,' he goes, 'I don't understand why you're being so moralistic about this.'

I'm there, 'Then you don't know me, JP. Either you tell him or I'll focking do it for you.'

'I've resigned,' Sorcha goes, 'as Minister for Climate Action.'

This is in response to me asking her why she's in such shit form tonight.

I'm there, 'Resigned? The reason being?'

'The reason *being* that your father seems determined to sell off all of Ireland's trees to a logging company – which, I found out, just so happens to be owned by that Russian friend of his who *always* seems to be hanging around?'

'Are you talking about Fyodor?'

'Yes, him.'

'But I thought you knew all of this.'

'Excuse me?'

'Erika told us two years ago what my old man was planning to do. He was going to sell off all of Ireland's natural resources to the Russians in return for them rigging the election.'

'Well, pordon me for being naive, Ross, but I genuinely believed I could change his mind.'

Suddenly, from the living room, we can both hear the sound of Honor singing, while accompanying herself on the piano. She's going:

> *Once in lifetime*
> *There comes along*
> *A woman who cares*
> *But is also strong.*
> *Hillary Clinton*
> *Was heaven-sent.*
> *And I meant what I said*
> *As a com . . . pli . . .meeennnttt . . .*

I'm there, 'Her audition is tomorrow.'

Sorcha's like, 'I already told you, Ross, I don't care.'

'Oh my God, *listen* to her!'

'What am I listening to? The sound of a girl looking for an opportunity to embarrass her mother in front of the world again?'

'We don't know if that's definitely the case this time.'

'We do know. She's well aware that Samantha Power is one of my – oh my God – heroes and one of my dream dinner porty guests, along with Al Gore, Stella McCortney, Greta Thunberg and Marissa Corter, the woman who set up Cocoa Brown. And obviously Nelson Mandela if we're allowed to invite people from, like, the spirit world.'

'Well,' I go, '*I'm* going to give her some positive feedback even if you're not,' and I walk out of the kitchen and head for the living room.

Through the door, I can hear her going:

> *I didn't say she was a bitch!*
> *I didn't say she was a bitch!*
> *I didn't say she was a bitch!*
> *And, anyway, it was supposed to be off the record!*

I knock, then in I go.

I'm there, 'Hey, Honor! How the hell are you?'

She stops singing and playing.

She's like, 'What?' already on the big-time defensive.

I'm there, 'Your voice! Jesus!' and I sit down on the piano stool beside her.

She goes, '*She* doesn't want me to audition, does she?'

I'm there, 'I wouldn't go that far, Honor. She doesn't give a fock one way or the other.'

'So, like, if I get the port of Samantha Power, she's not going to come to see it?'

'She thinks you're only doing it – okay, don't go ballistic! – just to embarrass her in front of everyone again.'

'But I'm not. I actually *want* the port?'

'It's just, you know, given your history, Honor, it'd be understandable if she thought this was another one of your famous set-ups.'

'Do *you* think it is?'

'I've no idea. The point is, I'm prepared to take a chance that this time it'll be hopefully different.'

'Thanks, Dad.'

'You just concentrate on nailing that audition. I'll talk your old dear into changing her mind – work my famous chorm.'

I kiss her on the top of the head, then I stand up. My work here is done.

As I reach the door, Honor goes, 'Dad, I didn't push Sincerity through the trapdoor.'

And I'm like, 'I know you didn't,' even though I suspect she *probably* did?

I tip back out into the hallway and I suddenly hear *his* voice coming from the kitchen – as in, like, my old man's. He's obviously read Sorcha's resignation letter because he's going, 'I'm sorry, Minister, I simply refuse to accept it!'

So – yeah, no – I tip back down to the kitchen.

'Well, you're going to *have* to accept it, Chorles,' Sorcha goes. 'I'm resigning on a point of principle.'

He's like, 'Principle? What principle?'

'The principle that my job – *as* Minister for Climate Action? – is to act as a custodian to Ireland's environment and you're, like, thwarting that by selling off hundreds of thousands of acres of forest-land.'

'They're only trees, Sorcha! Ireland is covered in the bloody things! Eleven per cent of the island, would you believe!'

'So?'

'It just seems like rather a lot, that's all! Overkill!'

'Well, it's not, Chorles. It's actually not *enough*? We should be planting more trees, not chopping down the ones we have, then exporting them off to God knows where.'

The old man suddenly cops me standing there. 'Kicker!' he goes. 'I'm just trying to talk some sense into your good lady wife here!'

I'm like, 'Yeah, no, leave me the fock out of it.'

Sorcha goes, 'The worst thing of all, Chorles, is that this decision to just destroy all these areas of scenic beauty was taken at yet another Cabinet meeting from which I was excluded.'

'It was an emergency Cabinet meeting – Fyodor needed a quick answer – so we just gathered together whoever happened to be around Leinster House at the time!'

'This is what I mean, Chorles. I agreed to be port of your Government because I thought I could make an *actual* difference, which I realize now I can't. The phone in my office *still* hasn't been connected?'

'I will see to it first thing tomorrow morning!'

'I'm sorry, Chorles, it's too late.'

I'm like, 'This is focking hilarious, by the way. Let me grab a cold one from the fridge and sit down for it.'

He goes, 'You can't do this, Sorcha!'

She's like, 'Do what?'

'Pirouetting on the plinth! Threatening to walk away every time you suffer a reverse! It's not how politics works! You're port of a Government!'

'I'm not any more.'

'And when you're port of a Government, Sorcha, there is a thing called Cabinet responsibility! Quote-unquote! It means that we stand by every decision we make as a Government whether, as individuals, we agree with them or not!'

'I'm sorry, Chorles, but I don't *feel* port of a Government – and I haven't for the two weeks that I've been a Minister.'

'What do you want, Sorcha?'

'I want to feel like I'm – oh my God – helping to formulate policy. I don't have electricity in my office either, by the way.'

'There you are – you're already running the greenest Government department in the history of the State!'

She doesn't laugh.

'Okay, name something!' he goes. 'Anything! A major policy initiative in respect of the environment and I will support it! No matter what it is!'

'Are you *actually* serious?'

'I'm one hundred per cent serious!'

'Well, I'd have to think about it? You're kind of putting me on the *spot* here?'

'Take as long as you need! But in the weeks ahead, I want you to bring forward some kind of legislation to tackle this famous climate change of yours!'

'I didn't think you believed climate change was even a thing?'

'Well, let's just say that my mind is a lot more open than it was before!'

'I want to hire a Special Adviser, Chorles. At the moment, I'm working on my own.'

'Hire away – as many as you need!'

'And I want a phone line that actually works.'

'Consider it done! So is that it, then? You'll withdraw your resignation?'

Sorcha just sighs.

She's like, 'No more deforestation, Taoiseach.'

'All I can promise you,' he goes, 'is that the issue will not be discussed at Cabinet again without you being present to throw in your tuppence' worth!'

'Then I accept. Do I have to remind you, Chorles, that we have made commitments to the European Union to reduce greenhouse gases?'

'Do I have to remind you, Sorcha, that I was elected with a mandate to take this country out of the self-same European Union?'

'As it happens,' she goes, 'I'm still hoping to change your mind on that subject.'

The old man sort of, like, stares into the mid-distance and grins, like he's in Daniel's in Glasthule and he's just spotted the lobster he wants.

'You and I are going to do wonderful things for this country!' he goes. 'I can taste it!'

I ring Roz Matthews – yeah, no, her number's still in my phone – and I ask her if I can talk to her about something. She says she's having coffee with the girls – meaning, presumably, some of the other *moms*? – and she'll just step outside.

Twenty seconds later, she's like, 'Is everything okay?'

And I'm there, 'Yeah, no, I was just wondering, how's Sincerity's coccyx? Hopefully that doesn't sound too weird.'

She laughs.

'It's very badly bruised,' she goes. 'She can't even sit down, the poor girl.'

I'm like, 'Yeah, no, shit one. Roz, can I ask you a random question?'

'Of course.'

'How did she fall through the trapdoor? As in, did someone maybe give her a shove? As in – let's be honest – did my daughter give her a shove?'

She just laughs.

'God, no,' she goes. 'Sincerity was giving the cast some notes on the scene where Samantha Power is appointed by Barack Obama to the National Security Council and she didn't notice that it was open.'

'Honor didn't leave it open, did she?'

'No, Sincerity did. I don't think Honor was even at rehearsals that day.'

'Okay, that's a definite weight off my mind.'

'Oh my God, did you really think that Honor pushed her?'

'Of course not. Yeah, no, maybe a little bit.'

'No, I promise you it *was* a total accident, Ross.'

'It's just that Honor is going for the port of Samantha Power now and obviously I wondered was there any connection between the two things.'

'Look, just between ourselves, Ross, Sincerity really wants Honor for the lead.'

'Does she?'

'She's by far the strongest singer. Plus, she thinks the world of Honor and she hates that the Sixth Year girls are being – God forgive me – *such* bitches to her.'

'That's, er, lovely to hear.'

'Isn't the audition happening today?'

'Yeah, no, I'm driving to the school for it now.'

'Well, wish her luck from me. Hey, by the way, I noticed that Sorcha left the Merrion Tree Bistro Chat Group.'

'The what?'

'Oh, some of the moms from Sincerity and Honor's year – we have our own WhatsApp group, just to talk about school stuff. I suppose she's probably so busy now that she's a Government Minister!'

'I wouldn't be so sure of that. She's not even on the electricity yet.'

'Oh my God, Ross, *you* should join!'

'Me?'

'It's a really good way to stay connected to what's going on. I'll add you to the group, okay?'

I tell her – yeah, no – that'd be great, then I say I have to go, because I've just pulled into the school cor pork. My phone beeps as I get out of the cor. Then I head for the concert hall.

Except this time I don't actually go *in*? I just, like, stand at the door, with the thing a little bit ajor, so that Honor can't actually see me, even though I can see her.

She's standing to the side of the stage with, like, five or six other girls, who are all presumably going for the same port. Mrs Husqavarna, the music teacher, is sitting at the piano and I spot Sincerity, who's standing in front of the stage, because she obviously can't sit down, and I actually feel sorry for the girl, having once picked up the exact same injury falling off a high stool in Café en Seine when I leaned backwards to get a better view of a girl I thought was Lindsay Armaou from B*Witched but turned out *not* to be?

The first girl steps up to audition, but I end up missing it because that's when my phone beeps. It ends up being a WhatsApp message from Alva Crowe – as in, like, Ginny Crowe's old dear? – who wants to know if anyone knows the best place to buy a gumshield. A second or two later, my phone pings again. Amanda Mangan – as in, Tess Mangan's old dear – goes, 'Elverys', and then, a few seconds later, Rachel Lynch – as in, Eponine Lynch's old dear – goes, 'Elverys', and then a few seconds after that, Grainne Lessing – as in, Hester Lessing's old dear – goes, 'Would anyone be interested in sponsoring my cleaner, who's doing a ten-day virtual walk of either the Pennines or the Apennines in aid of fibrodysplasia?'

I switch my phone to Silent then because I hear Sincerity go, 'Okay, Honor O'Carroll-Kelly is next!' and – again – I peek around the door and I watch her step up to the mic. Mrs Husqavarna storts tinkling the old ivories and I watch Honor take a deep breath. And that's when it happens:

> *Mount Anville*
> *Instilled in me,*
> *The courage, the brains and the nous,*
> *Now look at me,*
> *Making histooorrryyy!!!*
> *Red hair,*
> *Black man,*
> *White House!*

Everyone in the concert hall is instantly blown away. You can actually see it. Honor is, like, jaw-droppingly good – and I'm not just saying that because she's my daughter and I'm terrified of her. Everyone is just looking at each other and laughing, as if to say, Oh my God, am I *actually* hearing this?

It's a pretty sassy number, by the way, and Honor is really giving it loads, it has to be said, swinging her hips and doing the whole Catherine Zeta-Jones in *Chicago* thing? I can see Sincerity looking at Mrs Husqavarna with her mouth wide open, obviously thinking, Holy fock! We have *so* just found our Samantha Power.

> *Power's my name,*
> *And power's my game,*
> *Now hand me my suit*
> *And my blooouuussse!*
> *Oh, Washington,*
> *You turn me oooooooonnn!*
> *Red hair!*
> *Black man!*
> *White House!*
>
> *I'm doing my thing*
> *In the famous West Wiiinnnggg!!!*
> *Red hair!*
> *Black man!*
> *White House!*
>
> *Red hair!*
> *Black man!*
> *Whiiiiiite Hooouuussseee!!!*

It's like, 'Whoa!'

When she finishes the final note, everyone storts clapping, including the other girls who are here to audition. At the same time, you can see it in their faces – they know they're never going to match that. It kind of reminds me of being in Krystle back in the day and Rob Kearney catching the eye of a girl you were in the process of chatting up – you knew instantly that you might as well fock off home now.

I end up joining in the applause. I can't help it – it's, like, an *automatic* thing? And that's when Honor spots me standing in the doorway. She stares at me for a few seconds. I'm wiping away literally tears.

Then she suddenly jumps down from the stage and runs towards me. She throws her orms around me and I hold her close.

I go, 'You nailed it, Honor! You totally smashed it out of the ballpork!'

She's there, 'Thank you for believing in me, Dad.'

Yeah, no, it's a moment. It's a definite, definite moment.

Honor says that Samantha Power is coming.

Sorcha looks up – she can't actually *help* herself? It's, like, a reflex thing. Then she remembers that she *supposably* doesn't *give* a fock what our daughter gets up to these days, so she goes back to her laptop, probably kicking herself for seeming interested.

I'm like, 'Samantha Power? As in, like, *actual* Samantha Power?'

'As in, like, *actual* Samantha Power,' Honor goes. 'I was telling Erika about it last night on FaceTime. Sincerity sent an email to her office and said, if you happen to be in Dublin in May and blah, blah, blah. And Samantha Power wrote back and said she wouldn't miss it for, like, the *world*?'

I'm like, 'I'm going to jump in here and say fair focks. Did you hear that, Sorcha – the woman who's on your fantasy dinner porty list is going to be at the musical?'

Except she just looks straight through me and goes, 'Kennet, we have to make an extra stop this morning. We're picking someone up at the bottom of Foster's Avenue, opposite the Radisson St Helen's.'

Kennet's like, 'N . . . N . . . N . . . Norra b . . . b . . . b . . . b . . . b . . . b . . . botter, M . . . M.. M . . . M . . . M . . . Ministodder.'

We pull into the grounds of the school. Honor kisses her three brothers, then hugs me, then mutters 'Sad bitch' in Sorcha's general direction before getting out of the cor. I notice Sincerity waiting for her on the other side of the cor pork. They wave at each other like normal friends do and it makes me genuinely happy to see it.

Kennet pulls out again onto Mount Anville Road.

'So did she *get* the port?' Sorcha suddenly goes.

And I'm there, 'She doesn't know yet. Mrs Husqavarna has told Sincerity they should see everyone in the interests of fairness. But she absolutely nailed the audition. It seems to be pretty much in the bag.'

'I know you want me to feel something, Ross, but I don't.'

'So you're saying you wouldn't go to see it – even if she does get the lead?'

'That's exactly what I'm saying.'

'And even though Samantha literally Power is coming over from the States specifically for it?'

'Kennet, pull in here,' she goes. 'That's her there, with the dreadlocks.'

He's like, 'F . . . f . . . f . . . f . . . f . . . feerd enough.'

I'm there, 'Who are you talking about, Sorcha? Who's *she*?'

'Yeah,' Brian goes, 'who the fock is *she*?'

Leo's there, 'The focking fock!'

And Johnny's like, 'Focking focker!'

'Her name is Simone, except it's pronounced Sea-mon,' she goes. 'She's my new Special Adviser.'

I'm there, 'How do *you* know someone with dreadlocks?' and I genuinely mean it. This is a girl who refuses to go to Electric Picnic because she has nightmares about head lice.

'She has a degree in Marine Biology,' Sorcha goes, 'and she's just finished a Masters in Environmental and Natural *Resources* Law? She's, like, *the* greenest person I've ever met – which is saying something, given that I've been a member of Greenpeace since I was, like, six.'

I'm like, 'That doesn't answer my question.'

Kennet pulls in and the girl walks towards the cor.

'She sent me an email,' Sorcha goes, 'telling me what she thought my key policy priorities should be in my first hundred days in Government.'

'What,' I go, 'and instead of telling her to go fock herself, you offered her an actual job?'

The girl opens the back door and in she gets. She's in her, like, mid-twenties, I'm guessing, with these famous dreads of hers and she's wearing a red raincoat, even though there's not a cloud in the sky, along with – I shit you not – shorts and black Vans with a white stripe down the side.

She goes, 'Hi, Minister!' and she doesn't even look at me and the boys.

Sorcha's like, 'Ross, this is Sea-mon – and Sea-mon, this my husband, Ross, and my boys, Brian, Johnny and Leo.'

'Dirty focking hair!' Leo goes, pointing at her, and we all pretend we didn't hear it.

I'm there, 'Hey, See-mon, how the hell are you?' being my usual chorming self.

But she goes, 'It's Sea-mon!'

I'm like, 'Excuse me?'

'It's pronounced Sea-mon!'

'See-mon.'

'No, Sea-mon!'

'See-mon.'

'Sea-mon!'

'The weird thing is, See-mon, I feel like I'm actually *saying* that?'

'Just listen to the way I'm saying it. Sea-mon!'

'See-mon.'

'Sea-mon!'

'See-mon.'

'Okay, I give up,' she goes. 'Seriously, how difficult could it be to say? How are you, Minister?'

Sorcha's like, 'I'm fine, Sea-mon,' and she says it the exact same way *I* focking said it? 'Although I was up half the night trying to decide what my major policy initiative is going to be.'

'It needs to be something radical,' Simone goes, 'but, at the same time, something that makes a statement, that climate change is not something on which you're prepared to compromise.'

My phone beeps. Amanda Mangan – as in, Tess Mangan's old dear – wants to know what's fibrodysplasia?

Sorcha goes, 'What about making Climate Change Denial an actual crime, like Holocaust Denial is in some countries, and make it punishable by – I don't know – up to ten years in prison?'

Simone is like, 'I don't think so, Minister.'

'Do you think twenty years?'

'No, I'm saying the idea, while obviously well-intentioned, is not going to do anything to reduce Ireland's corbon footprint.'

'Okay, then I was thinking maybe I'd make putting non-recyclable materials into the green bin an actual crime, and make it punishable by – I don't know – up to two years in prison?'

'Again, Minister, I'm not sure that jailing people is going to bring down our greenhouse gas emissions to any significant degree.'

My phone beeps. Cho Hye-Ji – as in, Jang Hye-Ji's old dear – says, 'Elverys.'

'Kennet, stop the cor,' Sorcha goes, because – yeah, no – we've suddenly reached Westmoreland Street. 'We can talk about this more while we cycle the rest of the way to the office.'

Simone's like, 'Cycle?'

'Yeah, I hope you don't mind, Sea-mon, I brought a fold-up bicycle for you as well.'

Simone's eyes light up like a focking jukebox. 'Okay,' she goes. 'I think I'm going to love working with you!'

Jesus Christ, they're some pair. They get out of the cor.

I'm like, 'Nice to meet you, See-mon.'

And she just goes, 'Again, it's actually Sea-mon.'

Kennet opens the back door of the limo and the boys spill out of it like a knocked-over bottle of mayhem.

They go chorging across the gravel towards the actual Áras – well, Leo and Johnny do, while Brian limps after them with his still gammy leg.

The old dear steps out of the front door with a Bellini in her hand, squinting her eyes to try to focus on me in a way that suggests it might not be her first drink of the morning.

I'm like, 'Kennet, get in the focking cor and step on it, will you?'

Except it ends up being too late. She's walking towards me like something from Michael Jackson's *Thriller* video and I end up having no choice but to open the window a few millimetres to talk to her.

'Why do you always do that?' she goes.

And I'm like, 'Always do what?'

'You drop those boys off here and then you rush off. Why don't you ever come in?'

'I don't know.'

Yeah, no, she *does* this? She guilt-trips you. You could call it her superpower.

I'm there, 'I actually have to go. A friend of mine is doing, like, a TED Talk in Dundrum this afternoon.'

She's like, 'This afternoon? But it's only nine o'clock in the morning! At least come in and see the nursery!'

So – yeah, no – I end up being shamed into getting out of the cor and I stort walking towards the house like I'm caught in some kind of tractor beam.

'What's that ghastly man's name?' she says to me – thinking she's whispering, except she's not. 'That driver person?'

I laugh. She can be alright sometimes.

I'm there, 'That's Kennet. He's Ronan's father-in-law.'

She turns around to him and she goes, 'There's a portrait of Mary Robinson in the pantry, with her face to the wall. Could you bring it to Sorcha's office?'

He's like, 'N . . . N . . . N . . . N . . . Norra bodder, Mrs O'C . . . C . . . C . . . C . . . C . . . C . . . C . . . C . . . Cattle-Keddy.'

The old dear goes, 'What did he say, Ross?'

I'm there, 'In a roundabout way, he said yes.'

'And then come back here, will you,' she goes, 'and collect Ross?'

'F . . . F . . . F . . . Feerd enough.'

Anyway, into the gaff we go. It's definitely changed from the last time I was here in that – yeah, no – everything has been ripped out and there's, like, workmen everywhere, slapping paint on the walls and laying corpet and throwing up wallpaper.

I'm there, 'You weren't joking when you said you were gutting the place, were you?'

She goes, 'Will you have a Bellini?'

'Yeah, but only so you don't end up feeling like the total focking dipso that you are.'

'I'll have one of the kitchen staff bring it. Would you like a lorge one?'

'Obviously, yeah – again, thinking about your feelings.'

My phone beeps. Grainne Lessing – as in, Hester Lessing's old dear – says that, according to Wikipedia, fibrodysplasia is a disorder in which skeletal muscle and connective tissue, such as tendons and ligaments, are gradually replaced by bone.

The old dear leads me downstairs, then along a passageway, at the end of which is a door that's firmly closed.

She grabs the handle.

'Are you ready?' she goes, preparing me for the big reveal.

I'm like, 'Yeah, no, whatever.'

She's there, 'Three, two, one . . .' and I have this sudden flashback to when I was seven years old and she made me remove her bandages after a Hungarian surgeon hacked an inch of cortilage off her nose to try to make her look less like a giant, pissed crow.

She pushes the door and my mouth just falls open. I'm not even sure I have the words to describe the sight that's revealed to me.

The room is like – I shit you not – the Disney Store. There's, like, giant toys everywhere – we're talking the Seven Dwarfs, we're talking Buzz Lightyear and the gang, we're talking Winnie the Pooh and *his* whole crew? Then there's, like, giant zoo animals – we're talking elephants, we're talking bears, we're talking hippos, we're talking giraffes – big enough for *me* to sit on their actual backs.

But that's not the thing that *most* throws me? It's, like, the peace and – I'm tempted to use the word – *tranquillity*? Yeah, no, there's soft music playing and the lights are soft as well and so are the furnishings and the colours on the walls.

I spot my brother and sisters. They're all lying on their backs on a giant playmat in the middle of the floor and they're, like, happily goo-goo-goo-ing and gah-gah-gah-ing while staring at moving shapes on the ceiling above them.

Then – and this is the real shocker – I spot my three boys. They're sitting at this, like, low table, playing with cors – but playing nicely, not killing each other like they usually do.

I'm like, 'What the fock? Are you drugging my children?'

Then I hear laughter behind me. I turn around and standing there is this woman in her maybe mid-forties, we're talking six feet tall with glasses and short, grey hair.

'Ross,' the old dear goes, 'I want you to meet Astrid.'

In other words, the German nanny.

She's like, 'Hello – is nice to meet you! Let me tell this to you – you have the most beautiful boys!'

'Jesus,' I go, 'they haven't been at the Bellinis as well, have they?'

The woman laughs, in fairness to her. A lot of people get a kick out of me.

She goes, 'I will tell you that, yes, sometimes they can show challenging behaviours. But always I like to say that there is no such thing as bad children, Ross – there are just bad environments.'

Leo – I shit you not – walks over to her, looks up and goes, 'Nanny Astrid, me want raisin!'

And Astrid – she seems like *such* a cool person, by the way – goes, 'What is magic word?'

Leo's there, '*Bitte!*' and he opens his mouth like a bird.

She drops a raisin into it and he's like, '*Danke!*' and it's hord to believe this is the same kid who tried to stab me between the shoulder blades with a Sabatier paring knife while I was bending down to tie his shoelaces this morning.

My phone beeps. Amanda Mangan – as in, Tess Mangan's old dear – says that sounds awful and asks how much everyone else is giving.

I switch my phone to Silent.

The old dear goes, 'Come and see your brother and sisters, Ross,' and I follow her over to the mat. I get down on my hands and knees and I tickle little Mellicent's face.

I notice a red dot on the back of her hand. I'm there, 'You went ahead and colour-coded them, didn't you?'

The old dear has this, like, swatch in the hand that *isn't* holding a Bellini?

'It just makes it simpler for me,' she goes. 'Red is Mellicent.'

I'm there, 'Yeah, I know it's Mellicent. I'm the one who can actually tell them aport, remember?'

She's like, 'Oh, yes, Astrid, he has some kind of trick! It's like something a magician would do!'

I pick Mellicent up off the floor and – I swear to God – she properly, full-on smiles at me. She's gorgeous.

'I've been doing that thing you showed me,' the old dear goes. 'I

74

hold their heads here, next to my hort – and it works, Ross, it really works!'

I'm just, like, staring at her – as in, my old dear.

I'm there, 'So how many hours a day do you actually spend in here?'

She goes, 'I'm in here *all* day – except when Astrid and I put them down for their nap. That's when I go and consult with the decorators and find out if they've done something that warrants me sacking them. Then I'm back in here until they go to sleep for the night.'

'So you've storted to get into it – as in, the whole, like, motherhood thing?'

'Having children was the best thing I've ever done, Ross. And maybe the only good thing.'

I'm left literally speechless, so much so that I end up forgetting to tell her that Mary Mitchell O'Connor focked out all of her books.

My drink arrives. The woman who brings it tells me that my driver is outside. But I just go, 'Tell him to come back later, will you? Tell him to come back in, like, two or three hours.'

'I wash very losht,' Magnus goes. 'Ash a pershon, I no longer knew who I wash any more.'

The Mill Theatre in Dundrum is absolutely rammers for his TED Talk and he has the entire audience eating out of the palm of his hand.

'It got sho that I literally could not have a convershashion that did not involve Fashebook. No matter who wash talking, I had to find shome way to bring the convershashion back to Fashebook again. "Your father hash a heart attack, you shay? Well, in Fashebook we have a weekly cardiac shcreening ash part of the company'sh Healthy Body, Productive Worker plan."'

Everyone cracks up, in fairness to them.

'Yesh,' he goes, 'I hear you laughing becaush it ish true, yesh?'

There must be a fair few former, or even current, staff here because he ends up getting a round of applause. Behind me, I hear Christian tell Oisinn, 'He's absolutely nailing it,' which he is, in fairness to him.

My phone beeps. Marissa Arnold – as in, Jessica Arnold's old dear – asks Alva Crowe if she managed to get a gumshield in the end.

'The problem for me,' Magnus goes, 'ish that I became a shlave to what I call the hamshter cage. You are all familiar with thish conshept, yesh? A cage in which everything ish laid on for the hamshter – he hash hish wheel for exshershishe and he hash hish little food bowl which ish filled every day. Well, in Fashebook – shee, there I go again! – we had a gym for exershishe and food that wash both plentiful and shubshidished. Sho why would you ever want to leave? The truth ish, my friendsh, I didn't.'

JP turns around to me and goes, 'A black polo-neck really suits some people, doesn't it?'

I'm like, 'Yeah, no, he looks well alright,' but I'm still pissed off with JP, so I make sure to go, 'Have you told him yet?' keeping my voice low so that Christian doesn't hear.

'*She's* going to tell him,' he goes.

'Her?'

'Yeah.'

'Do you not think it'd sound better coming from you?'

'Me?'

'Yeah, you.'

'She said she'd prefer to do it.'

'When?'

'Ross, I still don't see how this is any of your concern.'

'Oh, do you not? Well, maybe *I'll* tell him. Maybe I'll tell him right now.'

He's there, 'She's going to do it next weekend, okay?'

'Well, make sure she does,' I go. 'I hate knowing this when he's in the total dork.'

My phone pings. Susan Ó Roileacháin – as in, Lilian Ó Roileacháin's old dear – says there's a speed van on the Stillorgan dual-carriageway just beyond the Galloping Green travelling south and be careful because she thinks she got caught and she's already on, like, nine penalty points.

'My marriage wash in tattersh,' Magnus goes. 'Absholute tattersh. I shtarted shleeping in Fashebook in one of the shnooze

podsh they provide for shtaff working late. My hushband, Oisinn –
the mosht patient man in the world – he shaysh to me, "Magnush,
you are never home any more." And I shay to him, "Why do I need
to come home? Everything I need ish in Fashebook."'

There are quite a few – let's just say – nods of recognition.

He goes, 'Hish friendsh – thish amazing bunch of rugby guysh –
deshided there wash no other way to bring me to my shenshesh other
than to break into the building and forshefully extract me from
there. But even ash they were dragging me out onto Grand Canal
Shquare, I wash kicking and shcreaming and telling them that I had
an important preshentashion to make to the EMEA Regional Training Team and that I wash shupposhed to be partnering Karim from
Content Moderashion (Happy Shlappingsh, White Nationalishm
and Ishlamic Shtate Execushionsh) in the Fashebook Interdepart-
mental Piggy-Back Championshipsh.

'I wash very lucky that I had theesh guysh. If they had not shtaged
an intervention, I would probably shtill be there today, working
every shingle hour I wash not ashleep, never sheeing shunlight,
never having a convershashion about anything that didn't involve
Fashebook. Sho I shay to all of you who are in the shame shituation –
or perhapsh it ish your hushbandsh, wivesh, brothersh, shishtersh,
friendsh, even parentsh who have dishappeared into one of theesh
multinational tech companiesh – there ish hope. There ish life outshide Google. There ish life outshide Twitter. There ish life outshide
Zendeshk. There ish life outshide LinkedIn. There ish life outshide
Shalesforsh. There ish life outshide Indeed. And – yesh, my friendsh –
I am living proof that there ish even life outshide Fashebook. Thank
you for lishening.'

There's, like, a loud cheer from the crowd, then an actual standing ovation. I'm so proud of the dude, and so are the other goys. We
want to tell him, except we can't get anywhere near him afterwards.
The dude is, like, surrounded by people, showing him photographs
of their husbands, their children, their best friends, going, 'He didn't
even phone the children on Christmas Day!' and 'She only joined
for the Dental Plan – now it's like talking to a zombie!'

Suddenly, the dude is, like, sympathizing with total strangers, hugging them, offering them words of consolation and hope. Then he whips out his phone and – yeah, no – he storts taking numbers, going, 'I know shome people who are alsho working for Workday. I will make shome inquiriesh for you!' and 'Where doesh she work? Intel? And when wash the lasht time you shaw her alive?'

There's a woman bawling her eyes out, going, 'My husband talks to me like he's my team leader! He said to me, "If you have capacity and availability after lunch, could we maybe circle back and discuss what we're going to have for dinner?"' and Magnus puts his orms around her and pulls her close.

'I will help you,' he goes. 'I will help you all.' And I'm thinking, there will be definitely be a high-five in this from me the second this crowd clears.

That's when my phone all of a sudden pings again. Alva Crowe – as in, like, Ginny Crowe's old dear – says: Hey, did anyone hear about Honor O'Carroll-Kelly? She thought she was going to get the lead in *Samantha Power: The Musical*, but they gave it to Imogen Cranny instead, and Honor ran out of the school crying. Good enough for her, after what she did, disgracing the name of Mount Anville in front of the United Nations General Assembly, the f**king evil bitch.

I turn around to Oisinn and I'm there, 'I have to go. Will you tell Magnus fair focks from me?'

I run through Dundrum Town Centre, all the way back to the cor pork. Five minutes later I'm doing, like, eighty on Taney Road, with the cor pointed in the direction of Mount Anville.

My phone pings again. Roz Matthews tells Alva Crowe that Ross O'Carroll-Kelly – as in, like, Honor's dad – is actually a member of the group. Then, a minute later, Alva Crowe says that she's mortified but obviously she meant no offence by it.

I swing into the grounds of the school and I spot Honor pretty much straight away. She's sitting on the steps leading down to the hockey pitches. I pull up on the side of the road with a screech of tyres and I hop out.

She doesn't even look around at me. She's sort of, like, hugging her knees and – yeah, no – she's been crying. Her breathing's still a bit all *over* the shop?

'Imogen Cranny is a focking knob,' she goes.

And I'm there, 'She definitely sounds it,' instantly taking my daughter's side.

'She can't sing for focking shit either,' she goes. 'The only reason they gave her the port was because they said they couldn't trust me.'

I'm there, 'How could anyone *not* trust you, Honor?'

At the same time, I look up and I notice that someone has made absolute shit of the main hockey pitch – there's, like, lumps kicked out of it everywhere. Then I see the mud on Honor's black loafers, but I don't ask her if she did it.

In many ways, I don't *want* to know?

'They thought it was another one of my tricks,' she goes. 'That I was going to bring shame on the school in front of *actual* Samantha Power.'

I'm like, 'Fock them, Honor – and fock their bullshit musical.'

She rests her little head on my shoulder and doesn't say anything for ages. Then she goes, 'The thing is, Dad, I wasn't doing it to embarrass Mom this time. I wanted to make her proud of me.'

I'm there, 'Oh, Honor!' because she can be so sweet sometimes.

'I shouldn't have called her a sap and a phoney in front of the United Nations General Assembly. But I was pissed off with the stupid focking bitch.'

'And not without reason, some would say. She sent you away to Australia because she thought you tried to poison Hillary.'

'I just thought, if I got the port, and then she came along, I might be really good, and everyone would be saying it to her that she had an amazing daughter, and then she wouldn't hate me any more, and she wouldn't think I was a horrible person.'

She just bursts into tears. I put my orm around her shoulder and I tell her she's not a horrible person – although the Senior Hockey Coach might have a different take when she sees her pitch turned over like a ploughed field.

She goes, 'It's not just *her*. I thought if I was good in it, then the girls in school would change their minds about me as well.'

I'm there, 'When have you ever cared what other people thought of you?'

'Everyone hates me, Dad.'

'Sincerity doesn't hate you – even though she's a focking sap.'

'The Sixth Years are, like, total bitches to me. They tell all the other girls not to talk to me because I damaged Mount Anville's reputation abroad.'

I'm there, 'What reputation abroad?' because I'm sick to the back teeth of hearing about it. 'Seriously, who've they actually got? Mary Robinson, Alison Doody and now your old dear. It's not exactly a long roll of honour, given the breeding of the kids who go here and the focking fees they chorge.'

'They've also got Samantha Power,' she goes.

'Yeah, she left when she was, like, eight,' I go. 'No disrespect to Samantha, but that's seriously scraping the barrel.'

'She didn't even go to, like, *actual* Mount Anville? She only went to, like, the junior school.'

'Taking. The. Piss. I've honestly never understood why they're so up themselves in this focking school. Even Coláiste Íosagáin produced Bláthnaid Ní Chofaigh and that woman your old dear loves who set up Cocoa Brown.'

That seems to definitely cheer her up because she suddenly sits up straight and wipes away her tears with the palm of her hand. Then she goes, 'I'm so lucky to have you as a dad.'

And I'm there, 'Hey, I'm the lucky one, Honor.'

'I just wish –'

'What? What do you wish?'

'I wish Mom didn't hate me.'

'Your mom doesn't hate you, Honor.'

'She does.'

'Why do you think that?'

'Because I heard her tell her mom. On the phone. It was the day after we came home from New York.'

'People say all sorts of shit when they're angry, Honor. How many times have you heard me say that I hate Owen Farrell? And yet if I was picking my fantasy Lions team tomorrow, he'd be the first name on the team sheet.'

'She didn't actually tell her mom she hated me.'

'There you are, then.'

'She said something worse.'

'What could be worse?'

'She said that when she was pregnant with me, she nearly, like, miscarried at four months. And she said sometimes she thinks she would have been happier if she did.'

'There's no way she said that.'

'Dad, she definitely did.'

'Yeah, no, you must have, like, *misheard* her?'

And yet, at the same time, I know she probably didn't. I just think to myself, holy fock, who says something like that? And what has happened to the woman I married?

3.

A Baahd Night Out

Sorcha's old dear is wearing – I swear to fock – a fascinator. It looks like someone has strapped a half-plucked roadkill pigeon to her head and I'm tempted to tap her on the shoulder and tell her that.

'She looks like someone's ugly spinster aunt,' Honor goes, 'waiting for the bouquet to be thrown at a shit wedding in Celbridge.'

I just crack my hole laughing. And, of course, Sorcha's old man doesn't like it one little bit. He turns fully around in his seat and goes, 'What the hell are you two sniggering about?'

Yeah, no, we're sitting in the public gallery in, like, Leinster House, waiting for Sorcha to make her famous Maiden Speech, during which she's going to announce her major policy initiative, whatever it is that her and Simone have cooked up.

'We're laughing at the focking state of your wife,' Honor goes. 'I said she looks like someone's ugly spinster aunt waiting for the bouquet to be thrown at a shit wedding in Celbridge.'

There's no fear in the girl. I like to think she got that from me.

Sorcha's old man goes, 'For once in your life, could you please show a little decorum?' which is a weak comeback and I think he knows it as he turns to face the front again.

Leo Varadkar is on his feet. He's telling my old man that his treatment of President Michael D. Higgins and his wife, Mrs Higgins, has been nothing short of shameful. The old man shouts, 'They've got food, a bed and a roof over their heads! And they're free to leave at any time!'

Sorcha is sitting in the middle of this guffawing sea of jowly, red-faced, middle-aged men, staring straight ahead, looking – yeah, no – definitely tense. Her old man gives her a little wave, except she doesn't see him and Honor sniggers and, in his ear, goes, 'Focking dying for you!'

Her spinster aunt comment has definitely hit a nerve with Sorcha's old dear because she half turns around and goes, 'I don't know why they bothered coming at all.'

And Honor – quick as a flash – goes, 'Go get your flip-flops, Auntie Phyllis – the *Grease Megamix* will be on in a minute.'

Again, I crack my hole laughing. I'm like, 'Pure brilliance, Honor. Pure, pure brilliance.'

'At least *some* members of that household know how to behave themselves,' the woman then goes – because she's always been a last-word freak. She looks to her left, where Brian, Johnny and Leo are sitting quietly and calmly, waiting for their old dear to say her piece.

'*Ja*,' the famous Astrid, sitting behind them, goes, 'they are good boys. *Stimmt das?*'

'*Wir sind gute Jungen!*' the three of them – together – go.

I wish they behaved like that for me. I still say she's drugging them.

Sorcha's old dear is delighted. She's like, 'You have them speaking German!'

'*Ja*, just a few words and phrases,' Astrid goes. 'They are very quick to learn.'

Sorcha's old man is there, 'You see? I've been saying it for *how* long now? All those boys ever needed was a firm hand!'

I'm about to say something when Honor nudges me and shows me the click-lighter up her sleeve.

Sorcha's old dear goes, 'We should talk to Sorcha about sending them to St Kilian's next year. It's a wonderful school. I loved it there.'

And suddenly I shush her because the dude in the chair – I think he's called, like, the *Ceann Comhairle* or some shit? – is announcing that the Minister for Climate Action, Senator Sorcha Lalor, is going to make a statement to the House.

At that exact moment, someone slips into the seat to my right. It's, like, Simone, or See-mon, or however the fock you're supposed to say it. She's wearing – I'm not making this up – combat shorts with Birkenstocks, a yellow rain mac and then obviously the dreads. She looks like a focking hitch-hiker in a Danish porn video.

She doesn't say shit to anyone. She just gives a thumbs-up as Sorcha climbs to her feet and Sorcha smiles at her, then takes a deep breath and storts reading her speech.

'Ceann Comhairle, Taoiseach, members of the House,' she goes, 'it is my great privilege today to be standing here before you, making what is my Maiden Speech to Dáil Éireann. I don't use the word privilege lightly, since I'm well aware that I have no mandate from the electorate to serve as a member of this House. However, as one of the Taoiseach's appointees to the Seanad, I have been invited to serve at Cabinet as the head of what I myself personally think is *the* most important government deportment of all. I am, of course, referring to the Deportment of Climate Action.'

I notice quite a few TDs get up and leave. It's a pretty boring subject, to be fair to them. Sorcha responds to this, like, basically snub by raising her voice, like she's shouting to be heard in Finnegan's at ten o'clock on Christmas Eve.

She's like, 'The success and exponential growth of human society over the past ten thousand years has placed considerable pressure on our precious natural resources. Our reliance on fossil fuels to meet the increasing energy demands of a rapidly increasing global population, as well as our reliance on intensive forming to feed ourselves, has brought the planet that we call Earth to a critical juncture.'

I notice that Honor is holding the flame of the click-lighter to one of the feathers on Sorcha's old dear's fascinator. All I can do is just laugh and shake my head.

She'd really put you in great form.

'In laying out my legislative goals today,' Sorcha goes, 'I want to remind you all of the words of the amazing, amazing Greta Thunberg, who said, "I don't want you to be hopeful. I want you to panic. I want you to feel the fear I feel every day. I want you to act. I want you to act like you would in a crisis. I want you to act like your house is on fire – because it is."'

I'm watching the feathers on Sorcha's old dear's fascinator shrivel up under the heat of Honor's flame and I sort of, like, chuckle to myself.

How could anyone hate that girl?

'Animal forming,' Sorcha goes, 'is the single biggest contributing factor to the warming of our planet. In Ireland, methane from cows, sheep and other ruminant animals accounts for fifty-eight per cent of all agricultural emissions.'

'Oh my God, your head is on fire!' some random dude behind me shouts.

Oh, fock, he's right. There's, like, a piece of netting on Sorcha's old dear's fascinator that's obviously highly flammable because – like the dude said – there are literally flames coming off her head.

Sorcha's old man takes his coat off with the intention of throwing it over her to quell the blaze, but Honor is already on the case. She's ripped a fire extinguisher from the wall. She points the hose at Sorcha's old dear's head and she lets her have it – a good thirty-second blast of foam – and she's, like, laughing while she does it.

It *is* very funny, in fairness to it.

Sorcha becomes aware of this, like, kerfuffle in the public gallery and she stops reading her speech. The – like I said – Ceann Comhairle dude goes, 'Can we have complete silence while the Minister is speaking, please – otherwise, I shall be forced to clear the gallery.'

Sorcha's old man helps his wife up off the floor and wipes some of the foam from her head. He shouts, 'Carry on, Dorling!' which Sorcha then does.

She goes, 'Ireland has already committed itself to reducing agricultural emissions to between seventeen-point-five and nineteen million tonnes by 2030. It is clear to me that this commitment can only be met by pursuing a course of action which, on the face of it, seems drastic – but which, I believe, is also necessary. That is why, as part of my legislative agenda for 2018/2019, I will be introducing a Bill before this House that will ban the forming, breeding and sale . . . of all sheep and cows in Ireland.'

There's, like, literally gasps in the chamber. Then the, I don't know, clamour storts to build from the Opposition benches. They're, like, muttering among themselves and this suddenly builds up into full-on shouting-of-the-odds and giving-out-of-yords.

Even Sorcha's old man stops picking the pieces of blackened, foam-soaked fascinator from Sorcha's old dear's head and goes, 'Did she just say she's going to ban sheep and cows?'

I'm looking at my old man and – yeah, no – he's obviously cool with it because he's just, like, roaring at the Healy-Raes to allow the Minister to finish, then he calls them Gombeens and tells them to piss off back to Kerry.

'What class of a *liúdramán* is this girl at all?' the one *without* the beard goes? 'You can't ban sheep and cows! You're a disgrace!'

The Ceann Comhairle ends up having to ring the bell for a good, like, two minutes before order returns to the chamber. He goes, 'Can we please hear what the Minister has to say?'

Sorcha seems definitely *shaken* by the reaction? She looks up at Simone, who indicates to her that she should stand up straight, which is what Sorcha then does.

'Thank you, Ceann Comhairle,' she goes. 'Like I said, I will be bringing legislation before this House, when the Dáil returns after the summer recess, that will have the effect of banning the keeping of cows, sheep and other ruminant animals for forming purposes.'

The entire chamber is suddenly in uproar again.

Sorcha has to shout, 'I have spoken to the Taoiseach about this and he has agreed to make it a priority of this Government to gradually phase out the existence of these animals from our country by the year 2022.'

And suddenly the screams of, 'This will devastate rural Ireland!' and 'Where the feck is she even from with that fecking accent?' are pretty much deafening.

Under her breath, I hear Simone go, 'Well done, Sorcha. Well done.'

Brian is lying on his back on the cold kitchen floor and Honor is standing over him. She's going, 'Lift this leg up, Brian – that's it, about twelve inches off the floor – and try to hold it like that for ten, nine, eight, seven, six . . .'

I'm there, 'I don't know why you're even bothering, Honor.'

'Five, four, three, two . . .'

'I said I don't know why you're even bothering.'

'The doctor said if he does his exercises, there's a chance he *won't* end up with a limp?'

'His leg's focked, Honor. Move on. I know I have.'

I'm sitting at the table with Leo and Johnny, who are horsing into their breakfast.

'*Ich will mehr focking Pfannkuchen!*' Johnny suddenly screams at the top of his lungs.

I'm like, 'What the fock does that mean?'

Honor laughs.

'It's German,' she goes, because she does grinds after school two days a week with Mrs Hölzenbein. 'He said he wants more focking pancakes. I'll make more pancakes in a minute, Johnny. *Ich werde in einen moment mehr Pfannkuchen machen.*'

'*Ich will mehr focking Pfannkuchen!*' Leo shouts.

She goes, 'I'll make some more for you as well, Leo.'

Johnny takes a mouthful of orange juice then and spits it right in Leo's face, all over his ridiculous glasses.

I'm there, 'I wish they behaved here the way they behave for Astrid. I'd genuinely love to know what her secret is.'

Leo bursts into tears.

I'm like, 'Leo, don't let him get away with that. Deck the focker.'

He picks up his plate and – I swear to fock – smashes it over Johnny's head, like in a comedy movie.

I'm there, 'Again, watch his grommets, though,' but at the same time I'm laughing as I pick him up and move him to the other end of the table.

'*Fünf, vier, drei, zwei, eins,*' Honor goes. 'That's very good, Brian! *Das ist sehr gut! Du hast dich angestengt.*'

Brian's like, '*Danke.*'

'*Jetzt,*' Honor goes, pouring more batter into the pan, '*machen wir noch mehr Pfannkuchen!*'

I'm like, 'So how *are* you, Honor?' because I'm still a bit thrown by our conversation the other day and what she *thought* she heard Sorcha say? 'I hope I managed to put your mind at ease about, well, you know.'

But Honor thinks I'm talking about *Samantha Power: The Musical*.

She just shrugs and goes, 'I didn't want to be in the stupid focking thing anyway.'

I'm there, 'Er, cool. That's the spirit. It'll be a long time before anyone plays hockey on that pitch as well.'

'And like *you* said, Dad, these people would want to get over themselves. Samantha Power left the school when she was, like, eight.'

'I'm going to be honest with you, Honor, I'd never even heard of the woman until you mentioned her. That'll show you how important she must be in the grand scheme of things.'

'They have – literally? – no embarrassment.'

'I'll tell you who *I* blame? That Sincerity Matthews. I mean, she *wrote* the focking thing.'

'It's not her fault, Dad. She actually *wanted* me for the lead? She even threatened to quit as the Director when Sister Consuelo told her not to cast me.'

'If she had any balls, she would have walked.'

'I told her not to.'

'I stand by my statement.'

'It's only a stupid musical – and Mom said she wasn't going to go anyway, the fat bitch.'

Your hort would actually melt for the girl.

'Hey, it's Saturday morning,' I go. 'Why don't we hit Dundrum Town Centre? You can go mad with my credit cord!'

She's like, 'Really?' shovelling a pancake onto a plate and putting it in front of Leo. '*Kinder, Mochter ihr nach Dundrum gehen?*'

The boys are like, '*Ja! Ja!*'

I'm there, 'I'll just tell your old dear we're going.'

I get up from the table, then I tip up the hallway to the study, where Sorcha and the famous Simone have been hord at it since, like, eight o'clock this morning, even though it's, like, the *weekend*?

I push the door.

Simone is going, 'No one has ever suggested anything this radical to try to reverse climate change. But you're going to make a lot of enemies. Most of our TDs are from rural backgrounds and represent the interests of farmers. It's important to keep stressing, Minister, that you don't hate sheep *or* cows.'

'Oh my God,' Sorcha goes, 'I actually love them! I've got an original Deborah Donnelly upstairs on the landing – it was a thirtieth birthday present from my mom! It's also my computer screensaver!'

I'm like, 'Hey, See-mon! How the hell are you?'

'It's Sea-mon!' she goes.

I'm like, 'Yeah, no, I'm not going through that again. So what are you goys up to?'

Sorcha goes, 'We're planning my media strategy, Ross. I have to persuade people that ridding Ireland of sheep and cows is actually a *progressive* step?'

Simone – I swear to fock – goes, 'Yeah, we're kind of busy of here, so if you wouldn't mind . . .' and she nods at the door.

The focking state of her, by the way. She's wearing, this time, a yellow raincoat with a white Aran sweater underneath, grey combat shorts and then a pair of those focking origami shoes with the Orgentina flag on the back.

I'm there, 'Yeah, no, I'm just going take the kids to Dundrum for the day. Honor could do with cheering up.'

Sorcha's just like, 'Why?'

'I don't know if you heard,' I go, 'but she didn't get the port of Samantha Power in the school musical in the end.'

'I know she didn't.'

'Oh, did I already tell you?'

And that's when she says it.

She goes, 'I was the reason she didn't get it, Ross. I rang Sister Consuelo and I told her that, as her mother, I didn't want Honor cast in the school musical.'

I'm there, 'You did what?' hearing the shock in my own voice.

'Sister Consuelo wanted to give her another chance. Can you believe that? After what she did in New York and yet – typical Mount Anville – she was still prepared to offer her the benefit of the doubt. I said she didn't deserve another chance.'

I'm there, 'I thought you said you didn't give a fock what Honor does any more?'

'I don't,' she goes. 'But I told Sister Consuelo that Honor was probably planning to use it as an opportunity to further humiliate me – even damage me politically – and to bring the good name of Mount Anville into further disrepute, including internationally. And I wasn't prepared to take that chance, not with *actual* Samantha Power coming. So I told her, "Do not put that girl on the stage!" '

That girl?

There's something about the way she says it – cold and hord – that reminds me of the way my old dear used to talk about me.

I'm there, 'Sorcha, can I ask you something – in, like, private?'

She goes, 'Anything you have to say to me, Ross, you can say it in front of Sea-mon.'

'Honor says she heard you talking on the phone to your old dear. It was just after we came home from New York.'

'And?'

'She said you told your old dear that you nearly lost Honor when you were, like, four months pregnant. And that sometimes –'

'Sometimes I think I'd have been happier if I had?'

'Words to that effect,' I go. 'Yeah, no, I was hoping you were going to tell me that you didn't say it.'

And she's there, 'I did say it, Ross. And I meant every word.'

'Hugo's got your nose,' the old dear goes. And, of course, I'm just about to smile when she turns around and goes, 'How old does a child have to be before they'll do corrective surgery?'

I'm there, 'Er, I'd imagine you'd have to wait a few years. I suppose that'd be considered cosmetic, wouldn't it?'

'Would it?' she goes. 'Even for one that size and shape?'

'Do you genuinely think it's that bad?'

'There's a chance he'll grow into it, I suppose. Mind you, your father said the same thing about yours!'

'Yeah, I do have focking feelings, you know?'

She whips out her swatch of colours.

'Purple,' she goes. 'That means this one I'm holding is . . . Louisa May.'

I'm there, 'Can you genuinely not tell them aport? It's not like they're even identical.'

'I'm getting there, Ross. I'm nearly sixty, remember.'

'Yeah, your sixtieth is long focking gone – like all the maids you had deported over the years for using the front door instead of the side entrance.'

She smiles at me – a mouth on her like a dropped kebab.

She goes, 'This is nice, Ross, isn't it?'

I'm there, 'Is it?'

'Yes, us spending time together like this. You and I. Your children and my children.'

I look over at Leo. He's holding Diana in his outstretched orms and for a second it looks like he's about to Garryowen her across the room.

I'm like, 'Watch he doesn't kick her, will you?'

But Astrid goes, 'He will not kick her, will you? Leo is good boy!'

'I am good boy,' Leo tells me.

'*Ich bin ein guter Junge*,' she goes. 'Can you that say that, Leo?'

He's like, '*Ich bin ein guter Junge*.'

He kisses the baby on the cheek, then he suddenly pulls a face like he smells something bad.

'Broken!' he goes, handing her to me. 'Is broken! *Kaput!*'

I laugh.

The old dear's like, 'What does he mean by broken?'

And I'm there, 'He means she's either pissed or shat herself.'

The old dear looks over the top of her glasses at Astrid and goes, 'Astrid, this one needs its nappy changing. Green – let me see which one that is.'

I'm there, 'It's Diana. And, Astrid, you stay where you are. My old dear is going to change her.'

'Me?' she goes, like it's the most random thing she's ever heard. 'But I've never changed a nappy in my life.'

I'm like, 'What do you mean? You must have changed *my* nappies when I was a baby?'

'No, we had an Eastern Health Board nurse who used to visit the house once a day.'

'Once a day?'

'Yes, I think your father used to pay her to keep an eye on things.'

'So what happened if I pissed or shat myself when she wasn't there? Oh my God, you left me in my own muck, didn't you, until *she* arrived the following day?'

'It was the 1980s, Ross. People didn't change their babies' nappies every single time they had a little accident.'

'Yeah, I'm pretty sure they focking did.'

'Well, I wouldn't have had the first idea what to do.'

'Right, you're going to learn now.'

I carry Diana over to the changing table and I lie her down flat on it. I'm like, 'Okay, off you go.'

I swear to fock, she goes, 'Well, what should I do?'

I'm there, 'I've seen you mix a Mortini with one hand while tweezing your beard hair with the other. If you can manage that, you can manage this. Okay, first, take the old nappy off.'

Which is what she does. She actually gags at the whiff. It's all new to her, I suppose.

'When you pooed your nappy as a baby,' she goes, 'I would just put you upstairs where I couldn't smell you.'

I'm there, 'Yeah, no, maybe you shouldn't tell me any more stories about my childhood.'

'So what now?'

'Now, take one of those wipes there – that's it – and you wipe her, you know, various bits.'

'And you do this *every* single time?'

'Yes, *every* single time.'

'It was just a question, Ross. How's Honor, by the way?'

'Yeah, no, she's fine.'

'I rang her the other day. She said she wasn't going to be in the school musical after all.'

'Yeah, no, it turns out she didn't get the port.'

'Didn't get the port? Why on Earth not?'

'Because the entire school has it in for her – just because she called her old dear a phoney bitch and supposedly disgraced the name of Mount Anville in front of the United Nations.'

'Would you like Hennessy to send the school one of his letters?'

'Yeah, no, that was my first thought as well.'

'He could drag them into the High Court and force them to cast her.'

'Great minds – blah, blah, blah. But then I thought, if they don't want her, then fock them. It's their loss.'

'You're a wonderful father to that girl, Ross.'

'Do you genuinely think that?'

'Oh, I say it to Chorles all the time. You didn't exactly have the best parental role models and yet when I see how you are around your own children, not to mention ours – well, it's a miracle, Ross.'

'I'm amazing with kids. I'm happy to admit that. It just comes naturally to me. Now, put the new nappy on her. No, the other way around. That's it.'

All of a sudden there's a loud crash upstairs. The old dear looks up and roars, 'Will you please keep the focking noise down?' because she's definitely had one or two this morning. 'Honestly, it's like having two ghosts pottering around the place!'

I'm there, 'Are Michael D. and the missus *still* living in the attic?'

'Chorles said they could stay until they found somewhere else to live. All hort – that's your father. I'd have put them out on Conyngham Road.'

She finishes putting the nappy on Diana in a way that I would have to describe as *textbook*?

I'm like, 'That's it! Done!'

'Did I do it right?' she goes.

'Yes, you did it right! Fair focks!'

Suddenly, I hear her go, 'Delma!' and I look up to see – yeah, no, like she said – her best mate standing in the doorway of the nursery.

I'm going to be honest and say there's been a definite awkwardness between us ever since I rode the woman bandy-kneed on the rainwater butt in the back gorden in Foxrock. For reasons best known to herself, Delma decided that she couldn't live with the guilt of what she'd done and she ended up telling my old dear about the whole episode – we're talking blow for *literally* blow?

And now my old dear *has* that over me. And, of course, I just know she's going to use it to embarrass me at every opportunity.

She goes, 'Delma, it's lovely to see you! I forgot to tell you, Ross, that Delma was going to be popping in! Oh my God, look at you in that black wool dress! Doesn't she look wonderful in that black wool dress, Ross?'

See, this is what I'm talking about.

I'm there, 'Yeah, no, I'm *agreeing* with you?'

She goes, 'And look at your legs, Delma! You have the figure of a woman forty years younger! Ross, look at Delma's legs in her black tights.'

'Yeah, no, they're fine,' I go. 'I've seen better and I've seen worse.'

And then I suddenly realize – oh, Jesus Christ – I've got a focking slide trombone in my chinos. I sort of turn sideways and I go, 'I, er, better head off.'

The old dear goes, 'Nonsense! It's only ten o'clock.'

I'm there, 'I'm just worried about Kennet still sitting outside in the cor,' which I'm not, by the way. I couldn't give a fock about him.

The old dear goes, 'That's what he's paid to do. To wait for people and then to drive them around. I'll order some tea from the kitchen. Or Bloody Marys. Let's have Bloody Marys.'

Delma, by the way, is every bit as mortified as I am – which she should be, given that she was the one who couldn't hold her piss.

'I, em, brought this,' she goes and she hands the old dear a copy of an interiors magazine.

The old dear's like, 'Delma, what have you done with your hair? Have you had it cut?'

She has had it cut – in a sort of, like, *bob*?

'Oh, em, yes,' she goes. 'I thought I'd try something different.'

The old dear's there, 'It's taken years off you! If that husband of yours could see you now, he'd soon realize his mistake! Don't you think she looks ravishing, Ross?'

I'm there, 'I, er, definitely have to go,' because I'm horder than Wayne Shelford here. I stort making my way to the door.

'Aren't you going to say goodbye to Delma?' the old dear goes and I'm thinking, What a focking idiot I was to think that we were actually bonding, that we could ever have a normal mother–son relationship.

Me and Delma just look at each other.

I say an awkward, 'Yeah, no, bye, Delma.'

And Delma's like, 'Bye, Ross.'

'What is wrong with you two?' the old dear goes. 'Give your Auntie Delma a kiss, Ross!'

So – yeah, no – we end up having to do the whole air-kissing thing, except I go left and Delma goes right and – I swear to fock – we end up kissing each other on the actual mouth.

The old dear claps her two hands together and goes, 'You two have always got on *so* well, haven't you?'

I pretty much leg it out of that room. And outside I end up nearly crashing into Michael D. Higgins, who's on his way back to the attic in his dressing-gown with a tray of tea and toast. He must cop the anger in my face because he goes, 'Your father said it was okay for us to use the kitchen – just until we find somewhere else to live.'

From the attic, I hear the wife go, 'Don't forget the marmalade, *a stór*!'

I'm there, 'Don't worry, Dude, it's not *you* I'm pissed *off* with?'

I grab a piece of toast from his plate.

'It's *her*,' I go, taking a bite of it. 'That tattered sack of gin, walrus spunk and trafficked organs who calls herself my mother.'

Other people's toast always tastes nicer than your own.

I'm there, 'I thought we were making an actual connection – as, like, parents? But she's just like him. As in, the old man. They're both evil.'

Michael D. smiles at me.

'As I said when I became the very first recipient of the Seán McBride International Peace Prize,' he goes, 'the conservative can exist in comfort only by averting his gaze. To choose to know is to risk being presented with a dilemma. That dilemma, put simply, is that once one knows, one can from that moment live only in the bad faith of guilty silence – or act.'

He's right. I mean, I didn't understand most of it, but I think I got the general gist.

I'm like, 'Thanks, Michael D.'

He goes, 'It's, em, President Higgins,' but I totally blank him, because I'm suddenly a man on a mission.

I go back to the nursery and I push the door. The old dear is look-ing at her swatches, trying to find out which baby she's given Delma to hold.

'Hey,' I go, to catch the woman's attention.

The old dear looks at me and she's like, 'Oh, look who's here, Delma – it's Ross!'

And I go, 'Mary Mitchell O'Connor focked all your books in the bin.'

The old man is having his portrait painted. I shit you not. He's pos-ing behind his desk with a big, fat Cohiba burning between his fingers and a pleased-with-himself face that's just crying out to be slapped.

A few feet in front of him, there's a dude with a goatee, in a smock, standing behind an easel, squinting his eyes, probably wondering how he's going to fit the old man's fat head onto the canvas.

'Kicker!' he goes. 'You're back again!' and I can tell that he doesn't mean it in, like, a *good* way? 'Can't keep you away from the place, it seems! Drawn to the beating hort of Government like a moth to the proverbial what's-it! Full point, new por!'

I'm like, 'Yeah, don't focking flatter yourself. I actually called in to see did Ro fancy going for lunch slash early afternoon pints – except he's not *around*?'

'He's at the tailor's,' Hennessy goes.

Yeah, no, Hennessy is standing behind the painter dude, following each and every brush stroke like he's watching a man defuse a bomb.

'How am I looking?' the old man goes.

Hennessy's like, 'Positively Churchillian!'

'The tailor's?' I go. 'What focking tailor's?'

The old man's there, 'He's gone to see Solly Sitwell in Portobello! He's been making Hennessy's suits for – what is it now, old scout? – must be nigh on forty years?'

'It's pushing on fifty,' Hennessy goes.

'Dear, oh dear – where *do* the years go? Anyway, since he's now mentoring young Ronan, your godfather thought that the chap should have his very own bespoke wardrobe! So he sent him along to Solly to have him fitted for his very first handmade suit! He's collecting it right now!'

Hennessy suddenly points at the canvas.

'Hey,' he goes, 'how many fucking chins are you giving him?'

The ortist dude is like, 'I'm just painting what I see!'

'Well,' Hennessy goes, 'you can drop one of them right now. Matter of fact, drop two.'

I'm there, 'What's all this in aid of anyway?'

'Every Taoiseach who has ever served this country has his portrait hanging in the hallowed hallways of Leinster House!' the old man goes. 'By the way, how's that wonderful wife of yours?'

I'm there, 'Why are you asking me? You see more of her than I do these days.'

'I hope she's bearing up alright under the weight of the backlash from – inverted commas – rural Ireland! I see our friend Miriam Lord called her . . . what was it, Hennessy?'

'Ireland's very own Eireann Flockovich.'

'Eireann Flockovich! Have you ever heard the likes of it, Kicker?'

'She also called her Diana, Princess of Kales.'

'I'll have to send the woman a cord, Hennessy! I'm happy to say that the editorial in the *Times* was largely supportive of what she's proposing to do! Radical, but necessary! Although I suspect our cow- and sheep-loving friends in Europe won't see it that way!'

All of a sudden, the door opens behind me. I turn around and it ends up being Ronan – except I very nearly don't *recognize* him? He's dressed – I swear to fock – in the same black-and-white-pinstriped suit that Hennessy has worn for as long as I've known him – the same suit he's wearing now. And not only that, he's also wearing the same black Fedora.

The old man's face lights up when he sees him.

He's like, 'Ronan! Look at the cut of you! You look like a young Hennessy Coghlan-O'Hara!'

And Ronan goes, 'Thanks,' like that's an actual compliment. 'Soddy threw in the hat as a gift.'

'That's Solly for you,' Hennessy goes. 'He's never forgotten how many times I've stopped him going to prison.'

Ronan's there, 'He toawult me. He's some bleaten boyo, idn't he, Heddessy?'

And I'm suddenly staring at my son and then at Hennessy, then back at my son, then back at Hennessy again, and I'm thinking, You have to do something, Rossmeister – before it's too late.

Ronan goes, 'Are we going for luddench, Rosser?'

And the old man's there, 'Take him across the road to Guilbaud's, Ross! Let him show off that new suit! They serve their beef with roast *foie gras* and Madeira and truffle *jus*! Have it with something from the Burgundy region and put it on my tab!'

I'm like, 'Just, er, give me a minute, Ro, will you?' and I step out of the office and into the corridor.

I whip out my phone and I call up the number. I still have it stored from when we were in New York slash the States. It rings three times, then it's answered by – and this is probably sexist – but a *woman*?

She goes, 'Good morning! Shlomo, Bitton and Block – Civil Rights Attorneys! How may I direct your call?'

I'm there, 'Can I speak to Hazel Rochford, please?'

'Who shall I say is calling?'

'It's Ross O'Carroll-Kelly.'

'And will she know what it's in connection with?'

'It's in connection with my son, Ronan.'

There's, like, a click on the line, then it beeps for maybe, like, ten seconds, then all of a sudden I hear her voice.

She's like, 'Ross, how lovely to hear from you!' because we definitely hit it off the day she gave us all the tour of the office. I'm tempted to say there was chemistry.

I'm like, 'Hazel, how the hell are you?' because she looks like Marisa Miller.

'I'm wonderful!' she goes. 'How's Ronan?' and I actually love the way she says his name. He definitely made an impression too.

I'm like, 'Yeah, no, he's cool. Look, I know you were disappointed that he turned down the internship in the end.'

'Of course!' she goes. 'We were looking forward to having him work here!'

'Look, just between ourselves, there were reasons – and they probably weren't the actual reasons he told you.'

'He said that a family friend had offered him an apprenticeship.'

'Yeah, no, that bit's true. But, well, the main reason he can't go to the States is because he had to, like, surrender his passport.'

'Okaaay. Can I ask why?'

'Because he's been chorged with the illegal possession of a fire-orm and obstructing the course of justice.'

There's, like, silence on the other end of the phone. She's sup-posedly a human rights lawyer. I thought she would have heard most shit at this stage.

I'm there, 'He's innocent, Hazel.'

And she doesn't even hesitate. She just goes, 'I believe you.'

'Seriously?'

'Hey, I met him, remember?'

'Yeah, no, I do. Strictly between us, he's got himself mixed up with some bad people, Hazel. And when I say bad people, I mean my old man and his crooked-as-fock solicitor. I'm pretty sure they set him up because they didn't want him to go to the States. They want him here, helping them do their dirty work.'

'We deal with cases all the time where people are accused of crimes they didn't commit. We know the territory. But we can't rep-resent your son, Ross. Ireland is not within our jurisdiction.'

'I'm not asking you to represent him. I'm just asking –'

'– if the offer of the internship still stands?'

I'm like, 'Yeah, no, *does* it?'

She just goes, 'Absolutely.'

That's all I need to hear. Now, I just have to make the case against my son go away. And, already, a plan is storting to come together in the back of my, I suppose, *brain*?

It's, like, Sunday afternoon, the sun is blazing down, and me and the goys are enjoying a – believe it or not – play date with our kids in – yeah, no – Herbert Pork.

It was actually, like, *Fionn's* idea?

We're talking me with Brian, Johnny and Leo; we're talking JP with Isa; we're talking Christian with Ross Junior and Oliver; and we're talking Fionn with little Hillary.

It's a good opportunity for us all to meet up, although there's a definite where-did-all-the-years-go vibe to it.

'Hillary is getting big,' Oisinn goes – yeah, no, him and Magnus are *also* there? Magnus has brought along a soccer ball, but I say nothing, much as it kills me to see him kicking it to Oliver. In terms of his development as a rugby player, he could be setting him back years, but it's Christian's place to say something – he's the one who's going to have to clean up the mess – and he decides to just leave it.

Oisinn takes Hillary out of Fionn's hands and goes, 'Give me a little hold there. Oh, you're a beautiful boy, aren't you? Yes, you are! Yes, you are!'

Hillary goes, 'Unkon Ocheen,' which is what he calls the Big O.

Fionn is quiet today. He's been the same at home. He's obviously thinking about Friday, the day he gets his results.

'It's going to be good news,' I go.

He's there, 'I hope so.'

'Dude, I'm not one for, like, praying to, like, Holy God and shit, but I've been basically talking to Father Fehily every night in my mind, telling him to have a word with the right people up there.'

Fionn smiles and goes, 'Thanks, Ross.'

'And if anyone knows how to find the right people, it's him. He got me into UCD on a Sports Scholarship, bear in mind, despite N.G.s in literally everything in the Leaving Cert.'

'We'll all be there,' Oisinn tells him. 'Three o'clock, St Vincent's, right?'

'Private,' I quickly add. 'Don't forget the Private.'

My phone pings. Joanne McAuley – as in, like, Ruth McAuley's old dear – says she's thinking of doing the whole Invisalign thing. Roz Matthews – as in, Sincerity's Matthews old dear – says she so should. Rebecca Leahy – as in, Diva Leahy's old dear – says she won't regret it. Rachel Lynch – as in, Eponine Lynch's old dear – says, 'OMG! Want!'

Oisinn starts throwing little Hillary up in the air, going, 'Whoooooo-sha! Whooooooosha! Whooooooosha!' and Hillary squeals with delight.

I'm there, 'By the way, Magnus, I'm sorry I had to shoot off at the end of your TED Talk. I have a high-five here with your name on it.'

I hold my hand up and he comes to collect.

'Yesh, it went down fantashtically well,' he goes, then he goes back kicking the ball backwards and forwards with Oliver. 'Lot of people talked to me afterwardsh to shay they alsho have friendsh and family membersh who are in the shame boat. Alsho, on shoshial media. Sho now I am thinking perhapsh I will shet up a counselling shervish to help people readjusht to life after they leave one of theesh big multinational companiesh.'

I'm like, 'Fair focks, Magnus. Even though I'm tempted to give out to you for bringing a soccer ball here today, knowing full well there was going to be children in the pork, but I'll just be grateful that my kids aren't showing an interest in it.'

'Where *are* your kids?' JP goes.

Actually, that's a good point. I haven't a focking clue.

'They're over there, Roth,' Ross Junior goes, at the same time pointing to an area of trees. 'Leo climbed up a three and he ith sthtuck!'

The little focking tell-tale. I don't even stir.

Christian goes, 'Do you want to go and maybe help him down, Ross?'

I'm there, 'Are you talking to me or your son?'

'Er, you.'

'Fock him. He'll find his way down when he's hungry.'

'Roth,' Ross Junior goes, 'my mom wenth out for thinner latht night and she looked *tho*, tho hoth. She wath wearing thkinny jeanth and knee-high booth and she altho thmelled amathing!'

Jesus Christ, he's eleven years old now. I'm about to say something. As his godfather, I'm supposed to be in chorge of his – yeah, no – spiritual and moral upbringing. And if that doesn't give me the right to tell him to stop perving over his own mother, I don't know what does. But then I'm thinking, whoa back, did he say that Lauren went out for dinner last night? Then I'm suddenly looking at JP, tickling little Isa, who's rolling around the ground in hysterics, and I'm thinking, has she even told Christian yet what's going on?

Christian goes, 'I'm going to go and help Leo out of that tree.'

And I'm like, 'Yeah, no, please yourself, Dude.'

Then the second he's gone, I tip over to JP and I'm all, 'Well?'

He goes, 'What?'

That's what he has the actual balls to say.

I'm there, 'Has she told him yet?'

He goes, 'I still don't see how it's any of your business, Ross. But for what it's worth, yes, she told him.'

'Really? When?'

'During the week.'

'And how did he take it?'

'He's, like, totally cool with it.'

'That's weird. Seriously?'

'As a matter of fact, he told her that he was very pleased for her.'

'What is he, a mug?'

'Their marriage is over, Ross. They've both moved on. Hopefully, you can as well now.'

'Well,' I go, 'at least I don't have to carry around the burden of your dirty little secret any more.'

He just shakes his head like he doesn't know what I'm talking about.

Anyway, about thirty seconds later, I notice Christian emerge from the trees, carrying little Leo, who's crying his eyes out.

Christian's like, 'It's okay, Leo. Your Uncle Christian has got you.'

Johnny goes sprinting past me, shouting, 'Fock you, you focking motherfockers!' with Brian limping after him. Leo instantly cheers up and goes, 'Me focking chase! Me focking chase!' Christian puts him down on the ground and Leo goes haring after his brothers.

'He managed to climb about twenty feet up the tree,' Christian goes, 'then he must have lost his nerve.'

'The last thing any father wants to hear,' I go. 'What would he be like squaring up against a really tough tackler.'

'Ross, don't be so hord on him.'

'There's not one of them who's turned out any good, Christian. Between Leo's skronky eye and lack of bottle, Johnny's inner ear issues and Brian's focked leg, there isn't a rugby international of the future among them.'

'Maybe they'll play some other sport.'

'They can find somewhere else to live if they do that. And I genuinely mean that.'

He smiles.

I'm there, 'Hey, I'm glad Lauren finally told you what was going on. It was actually killing me carrying that secret around. I hate seeing you being taken for a fool.'

'Taken for a fool?' he goes, screwing up his face. 'What are you talking about?'

'Hang on, he said you already knew.'

'Knew what?'

'For fock's sake,' I go, looking over at JP. 'He said Lauren told you.'

Christian's there, 'Ross, you better tell me what the fock you're talking about – and tell me right now.'

'Okay,' I go, 'but don't overreact, okay? It's probably not as bad as it sounds – but, well, JP has been riding your wife behind your back.'

His jaw literally drops – yeah, it's pretty obvious that Lauren *didn't* actually tell him and also that he is most definitely *not* cool with it?

He's like, 'JP? And Lauren?'

I'm there, 'The only reason I found out about it is because I saw *her* in Stillorgan Shopping Centre buying a tube of – I'm trying to think of a nice way of saying it – cream for her growler. She had a tube of the same shit in JP's gaff. She seems to have tubes of it all over town. I'm just sorry you had to find out from me.'

He's suddenly just, like, staring at JP. 'Supposed to be my focking friend,' he goes.

I'm there, 'And business portner. You were the one who put the money up to help him get the Vampire Bed off the ground – literally. That's why I thought he should have at least consulted you before he storted – again, I'm trying to be as delicate as I can with my words here, given that your children are here – knobbing your wife.'

He goes, 'You total focking –' but he doesn't say another word after that.

He makes a run at JP, who obviously thinks the dude is messing around because he sort of, like, smiles, even as Christian is getting closer and closer to him, with his fist cocked and ready to fire.

Then, all of a sudden . . .

Bang!

Christian hits him square on the cheek and JP goes down like a focked deckchair.

Fionn, Oisinn and Magnus are like, 'Whoa!' and Ross Junior screams like he's on a focking funfair ride. I just hope the kid never gets to experience some of the shit that goes on in the average ruck – which I seriously doubt he will, by the way.

Christian reaches down and grabs JP by the scruff of his shirt and he's about to hit him again when Oisinn arrives on the scene and drags him off.

'You wanker!' Christian goes. 'You total focking wanker!'

JP is like, 'What the fock was that for?' playing the total innocent, as Fionn helps him up from the ground.

And I'm there, 'Sorry, Dude, it turns out she didn't tell him after all.'

JP's like, 'Seriously, what the fock did I do?' and you can tell by his voice that he's still a bit groggy.

Christian goes, 'Ross told me. You've been having sex with my wife.'

Poor Oliver and Ross Junior, by the way, having to stand there and listen to their old dear being discussed like this.

JP goes, 'No, I haven't,' at the same time holding his cheekbone. 'Ross, what the fock are you talking about?'

I'm there, 'Er, I thought it was Lauren you were riding. She was buying – again, sorry, Oliver and Ross Junior – but ointment for *thrush*?'

'I'm not *having* sex with Lauren!' he goes – and he actually shouts it. 'I'm having sex with Delma!'

'Oh my God,' Honor goes, 'is she having, like, a nervous breakdown or something?'

I'm there, 'You'd have to wonder what the fock is going on in her head alright.'

Yeah, no, Sorcha is on *Claire Byrne Live*, having a debate with some dude from the Irish Formers' Association.

'I want to stress,' she goes, 'that I don't hate cows. I have an original Deborah Donnelly at home – I was one of the first in Ireland to buy one – and I actually had black-and-white cow-print seat covers in my very first cor, which was a Toyota RAV4.'

Honor's like, 'Oh my God, she's focking babbling. I'm actually *embarrassed* for the woman?'

Claire Byrne's there, 'Can you maybe address the specific issue that has been put to you, Minister, which is that this proposal is going to destroy one of Ireland's most profitable industries?'

Claire looks fantastic, by the way. I remember asking her for her number at a porty in the Red Cow Inn to celebrate the launch of TV3's 2003 autumn schedule. Colette Fitzpatrick had taken me as her plus-one. Anyway, I ended up sneezing and there was a zip wire of snot between my nose and Claire's right hand, which happened to be holding a pint of West Coast Cooler. I did the gentlemanly thing, of course, and let her wipe it on my shirt, but the girl was not amused. And, while I stuck around for another hour, I have to be honest and say the conversation never really recovered. Like the contents of my left nostril, you could say, I totally focking blew it.

The dude from the Irish Formers' Association goes, 'Can I just interject here with some figures, Claire? Ireland is the fifth largest beef exporter in the world and the largest beef exporter in Europe. Last year, we sold more than half a million tonnes of beef overseas, worth almost two billion euros, as well as sixty-two thousand tonnes of sheep meat, worth almost three hundred million euros. These exports are vital to the Irish economy.'

Sorcha goes, 'Can I answer that, Claire, and say that, as the Minister for Climate Action, I am responsible for reducing Ireland's greenhouse gas emissions. I'm not saying what I'm proposing isn't radical –'

'It's ridiculous,' the dude goes.

Sorcha's like, 'I didn't interrupt you and I'd thank you to pay me the same respect. I'm not saying it's not radical. It's never been tried anywhere in the world before, but I genuinely, genuinely believe that it will help Ireland achieve a net-zero corbon emission rate in the medium term.'

'Minister, what consolation is that to farmers,' Claire Byrne goes, 'who are maybe worried about their futures tonight? You've told them that keeping cows and sheep will be illegal from 2022. What are they supposed to do?'

Sorcha's there, 'I'm happy to answer that question.'

'Well, then, please do,' Claire Byrne goes, 'because I've asked it three times already,' and I'm suddenly wondering does Claire know that she's married to the man who snotted all over her.

'The whole point,' Sorcha goes, 'of the four-year phasing-out period, Claire, is to give formers the opportunity to transition into other types of forming that don't produce these hormful methane levels that are destroying this planet that we call –'

'What *types* of farming, Minister?'

'What, you're asking me to name different types? Well, for instance, *wind* forming?'

The dude from the Irish Formers' Association actually laughs at that one.

'This girl,' he goes, 'is living in Cloud Cuckooland. Let me ask you, have you ever been on a farm, Minister?'

'Of course I've been on a form,' Sorcha goes. 'And please don't patronize me.'

He's like, 'Where? Which farm was it?'

'Airfield Estate in Dundrum,' she goes. 'Although it's actually more of a formers' morket, but they do have a petting zoo. So, yes, if that's what you're getting at, I've *seen* actual cows and sheep.'

'Oh my God,' I go, 'I can't watch any more of this,' and I reach for the remote.

Honor's there, 'Don't you focking dare change the channel.'

'It's a total cor crash, Honor.'

'I want to watch it. It's hilarious.'

'Honor, I know you two aren't seeing eye to eye at the moment – and yeah, no, a lot of that is definitely *her* fault? – but she's still your mother.'

'Dad, I know what happened.'

'Happened? What are you talking about?'

'I know she rang Sister Consuelo and told her that she didn't want me to be in the musical.'

'That's totally untrue. I don't know where you're getting your information.'

'Sincerity told me.'

'Okay, right – yeah, no, it *is* true.'

'And I totally understand you keeping it from me – she's your wife.'

'Well, it's also because –'

'What?'

'I want it to end, Honor. This tit-for-tat thing that you two have had going on for the last few years. You do something on her and then she does something to you.'

'It sounds like you're taking her side.'

'I'm not. I'm taking yours, Honor. I'm just saying, the reason I didn't mention it was because I didn't want this thing escalating again.'

On the TV, Sorcha is still getting called out in a major way.

'According to this phased plan, which you've published,' Claire Byrne goes, 'the export of cows and sheep will be stopped from the end of 2019.'

Sorcha's there, 'That's to discourage formers from continuing to breed the animals.'

'So what's going to happen, Minister, to all of these cows and sheep that we're left with after that date?'

'I don't know. I suppose they'll all have to be eaten.'

The dude from the Irish Formers' Association goes, 'Eaten? There are seven million cows in Ireland and three point eight million sheep. We'd want to be very hungry.'

I stand up. I'm there, 'Seriously, I can't watch!' and that's when my *phone* all of a sudden rings? I check the screen and it's – believe it or not – Delma.

Holy shit, I think.

I'm there, 'Honor, I'm just going to step outside for a second,' which is what I end up doing.

I'm like, 'Delma? To what do I owe the *pleasure*?' and the way I say 'pleasure' makes it sound possibly pervier than I possibly *meant* it to sound?

'So you know about me and JP?' she goes.

I'm there, 'Yeah, no, he told me. I got the totally wrong end of the stick, you possibly heard.'

'Fionnuala doesn't know anything about it. And I'd prefer to keep it like that – just until JP and I have figured out how we feel about each other.'

'It's all so random. I'm talking about the two of you. Although he did always have the big-time hots for you. Do you remember your Hermès scorf that . . . actually, it doesn't matter.'

'The other thing I wanted to say was that he doesn't know anything about, well, you know.'

About me curling her toes that day around the side of the old pair's gaff.

'And if it's alright with you,' she goes, 'I would prefer if he didn't find out.'

I'm there, 'Hey, Delma, discretion is my middle name. Of all the words used to describe me, gentleman is the one that tends to come up time and time and time again.'

There's, like, silence on the other end of the line – like she doesn't quite *believe* me?

She's there, 'I need to talk to you about something else, Ross.'

I'm like, 'Is this about what happened that day in the Áras? Embarrassing, wasn't it? I'm sorry about the old Super Soaker sticking out of my chinos. Don't go getting a big head now. The thing has a mind of its own. It wouldn't know the difference between an attractive woman and a Subaru Signet.'

'Fionnuala seems to have no memory, Ross, of what I told her – about us?'

'What are you talking about? She was loving seeing me squirm. Kept banging on about how any man in his right mind would love to – in fairness – ride you.'

108

'That's what I'm trying to explain, Ross. It didn't have anything to do with making you and me feel uncomfortable. I genuinely think she has no memory of me telling her.'

Ronan asks me if Sorcha's okay.

I'm like, 'Yeah, no, why do you ask?'

'Why do I ask?' he goes. 'There's moorder going on, Rosser, over her wanting to badden sheep and cows.'

I'm there, 'Yeah, no, it's definitely random. I blame See-mon – she's this, like, Special *Adviser* she's hired?'

'She's arthur making herself a lot of edemies, Rosser. Heddessy's phowun is arthur been rigging all morden – the beef baddens, the whole bleaten lot of them.'

'She says my old man's backing her, though.'

'He is, yeah. I heard him saying he's godda give Shanahan's the use of the Gubbermint jet to fly in their beef from Scotland once a week. In addyhow, you were looking for me, were you?'

Yeah, no, I just remembered he's returning my call from yesterday.

'Dude,' I go, 'would you still be interested in going to the States?'

He's like, 'What?'

'The States, Ro. To take that internship you were offered.'

'Ine arthur been cheerged with a seerdious croyum, Rosser.'

'If I could somehow get the case against you dropped – would you go?'

'I altreddy toordened it down. I toawult them I was godda be woorking for Heddessy.'

'I spoke to that Hazel Rochford. I think I was right about her having a thing for me, by the way. I'm pretty sure I made her day by ringing.'

'You what?'

'Yeah, no, I rang her. And I explained the situation to her. The point is she believes you, Ro. She believes you're innocent.'

'I'm not iddocent, but. I took the gudden and I fooked it in the pond in Cabiddenteedy Peerk.'

'You know what I mean. You were set up.'

'We doatunt know that I was serrup, Rosser. Cheerlie and Heddessy is arthur being veddy good to me.'

'Ro, if I could somehow make this case against you go away, would you go to the States?'

There's, like, silence on the other end of the phone.

Then he goes, 'I'd lubben to, yeah.'

I'm like, 'That's good – because I've come up with, like, a plan.'

'What's your pladden?'

'I'm going to talk to the dude who arrested you. What was his name?'

'Who, Garda Sergeant John Haskins? Prick of the highest order? You're wasting yisser toyum, Rosser – he woatunt throp the cheerges.'

'He will when I tell him what I'm planning to tell him.'

'And what *are* you pladding to ted him?'

'I'm going to take the blame myself.'

'You're what?'

'I'm going to tell him that it was actually me who got rid of the gun – to cover up for Leo.'

'He woatunt belieb you.'

'Yes, he will. I'll even tell him where he can find it. In the lake in UCD.'

'I caddent let you do it, Rosser.'

'It's the only way to get you your passport back.'

'Rosser, you wouldn't last pissing time in jayult.'

'They don't send people like me to jail, Ro.'

'How can you be so shewer?'

'Because (a) I've got five kids, (b) I come from what they call a good background, meaning I went to a rugby school, and (c) my old man happens to be the leader of the country. There's also (d) I haven't been in trouble with the Feds since the time Leinster lost a Celtic League match to Connacht at the Sportsground in 2008 and I stuck my orse out of the window of the Galway-to-Dublin train to moon a bunch of old-age pensioners who were standing on the opposite platform on their way to Knock.'

'Rosser, I doatunt waddant you to do it.'

'I'm doing it, Ro.'

'Rosser, I mean it. I doatunt waddant Hodor and the boys being wirrour their fadder for two or tree yee-or.'

'I genuinely can't see a judge sending me down.'

'Rosser,' he goes, suddenly raising his voice, 'probise me you woa-tunt do athin, do you hear me?'

I don't say anything.

'Anyway,' I just go, 'I have to head here. I'm in St Vincent's, obvi-ously Private, Hospital. Fionn's about to find out if his – yeah, no – *cancer's* gone?'

'Ah, Jaysus, wish him all the best from me, will you, Rosser? And text me when you hear the resudult, will you?'

'I will.'

I hang up on him and I tip back into the waiting room.

All the goys are sitting around – we're talking Christian, we're talking JP, we're talking Oisinn and we're talking Magnus.

I'm there, 'Is he still inside?' meaning inside with the consultant.

All the goys just nod.

'The fock is keeping him?' I go. 'Jesus, he's been in there, like, half an hour.'

'We know,' Oisinn goes, handing little Hillary to me.

I'm there, 'Is that a good sign? A bad sign? What?'

'Unkon Yoss!' Hillary goes. 'Unkon Yoss!'

I'm picking up on some definite tension between JP and Chris-tian. Mind you, Christian did pretty much fracture his cheekbone. JP's eye is black and swollen like a pool ball.

I'm there, 'That's a hell of a shiner you've got there, J-Town. Don't take it out on Christian, though. If anyone's to blame, it's portly me.'

'It's focking totally you,' Christian tries to go. 'You told me he was sleeping with my wife.'

'Hey, it was a genuine mistake.'

'You know,' JP goes, 'I was wondering why you were so worked up about the thing, insisting that I tell her husband. I kept thinking, why the fock does Ross care so much about Breffni's feelings?'

I'm like, 'You see, Christian? I had your best interests at hort, even though I got the shit-end of the stick. So when did it stort, Dude? As in, you and Delma? It's still random, by the way.'

'We met at your old pair's christening,' he goes. 'I got chatting to her and we ended up going for a round of golf the next day, then a drink, and blah, blah, blah.'

I'm there, 'I know you always had a thing for her. Do you remember when we were kids and you stole her Hermès scorf from the coat stand in our gaff because it smelled of her *Obsession* by Calvin Klein? I remember you bringing it to Irish college that summer and you stuffing it in your mouth and wanking yourself to sleep at night. I'm actually delighted for you, despite the – whatever it is – twenty-year age difference. How old are her kids now?'

'Belle is the same age as me,' he goes, 'and Bingley is thirty-five.'

'Belle and Bingley. The focking names on them.'

'And they're cool with it, are they?' Oisinn goes.

JP's like, 'Yeah, matter of fact, we all went out for dinner last night to Hortley's in Dún Laoghaire. Belle teaches Chemistry and Physics in the Institute and Bingley is a hedge fund manager.'

'Bingley,' I go. 'I'm still laughing here.'

All of a sudden, the door opens and we all automatically jump to our feet. Fionn steps out of the office looking, I don't know, pale and shaken. I'm still holding little Hillary and the kid's going, 'Dada! Dada!' and reaching out for him. Fionn takes him out of my orms, but he still doesn't say shit.

I'm like, 'Dude, what the fock?'

He just shakes his head.

Christian's there, 'Fionn, you're freaking the shit out of us here. What did he say?'

And in a tiny little voice, Fionn goes, 'It's gone.'

JP's like, 'What?'

And then, finally, Fionn laughs and – a little bit louder – goes, 'It's gone! My cancer is gone!'

All hell breaks loose then – and fock what the other people in the waiting room think. We're, like, dancing around and hugging each other and I'm not going to lie and say that one or two Castlerock chants aren't heard.

'He focking beat it!' Oisinn goes. 'He focking beat it!' and he's got, like, tears streaming down his face.

But then, what am I saying? Yeah, no, we *all* do?

*

The concert hall in Mount Anville is absolutely rammers and there's a real buzz in the air as we await the arrival of Samantha *actual* Power. Sorcha keeps looking over her shoulder, determined to be the first up out of her seat when the woman walks through the door.

I spot Joanne McAuley – as in, Ruth McAuley's old dear – and I'm wondering did she end up doing the whole Invisalign thing in the end.

Mallorie Kennedy – as in, like, Courage Kennedy's old dear – tips over to where we're sitting and goes, 'I thought you were wonderful on the television the other night, Sorcha.'

Yeah, no, that seems to be the *general* consensus here tonight? It's Dublin 14, bear in mind. I doubt if many of these people would know what end of a cow to milk if they were dying of focking thirst.

Sorcha's there, 'Thank you. Even though the priority for me isn't to win TV debates, Mallorie – it's a net-zero corbon emission rate in the medium term.'

Jesus, I'm thinking, have a focking night off, Sorcha.

'I thought Claire Byrne was a focking disgrace,' the woman goes, 'and I'm saying that as a vegan.'

Sorcha's like, 'That's unfair. Claire Byrne is a tough but totally importial interviewer.'

'She grew up on a form, though. I thought she should have declared that at the stort of the interview – again, as a vegan.'

'I wasn't aware that Claire grew up on a form.'

'Surrounded by cattle is the story I've heard. Cattle and sheep.'

'She actually hides it very well.'

'Well, *I've* made a complaint to the BAI. Do you mind if I sit here?'

'Er, sorry, Mallorie, these seats are, like, *reserved*?'

'Reserved?'

'Yeah, no, it actually says 'Reserved' on them. For Samantha Power and her –'

Sorcha suddenly twitches like a deer that's heard a twig snap in the distance. 'She's here,' she suddenly goes, then she turns and she's off down the aisle with me following her, practically running to match the length of her stride.

I watch her pretty much shove Carmencita Blake – as in, like, Sally Blake's old dear – out of the way, then she does the same to Cho Hye-ji – as in, like, Jang Hye-ji's old dear.

She pushes the double doors at the back of the hall, then steps out into the cor pork just as Samantha Power's cor is pulling up. Sister Consuelo is standing there with a crowd of about fifty others, we're talking teachers, we're talking members of the Board of Management and we're talking members of the Mount Anville Parents Council, including Alva Crowe, as in, like, Ginny Crowe's old dear.

Sorcha – I swear to God – pushes her way through them like Brodie focking Retallick, so that when Samantha Power gets out of the cor, she finds herself standing pretty much nose-to-nose with her.

'Sorcha Lalor,' she goes, air-kissing her on both cheeks. 'Minister for Climate Action and member of Seanad Éireann. And, like you, Samantha, I'm a former alumna here.'

'Well,' Samantha Power – in fairness to her – goes, 'I only went to the Montessori Junior School until I was –'

'Nonsense!' Sorcha goes. 'We're still claiming you!' and then she puts her hand on Samantha's back and storts – I swear to fock – steering her through the crowd and into the concert hall.

'Make way!' she's going. 'VIP coming through! Let us get to our seats! Thank you! Move, please!'

Poor Sister Consuelo is left standing there with her mouth open, looking like something that's been washed up on Booterstown Strand.

I follow the crowd inside. Everyone is on their feet and clapping as Sorcha steers Samantha Power to the front row. Of course, Sorcha thinks the applause is for her and she storts giving the crowd little waves of acknowledgement.

It's un-focking-believable.

I make my way up to the front, by which time Sorcha is already sitting down next to Samantha and boring the ear off her about her political problems.

'Another thing that you and I have in common,' she's going, 'is that we've both seen up close the obstacles that women face every day in the patriarchal world of politics. Am I right, Samantha?'

Samantha Power's there, 'Er, did I read in the *New York Times* that you were planning to banish sheep and cows from Ireland?'

'That's a *slight* oversimplification,' Sorcha goes, 'but, if you're asking if I'm taking measures to help Ireland become the first country in the world to achieve a net-zero corbon emission rate in the medium term, then the answer is yes.'

There's no introduction for *me*, by the way? And my seat, as it happens, has been taken by the famous Simone, so I end up having to sit, like, three or four seats down, beside one of Samantha Power's crew.

Anyway, the show eventually storts and – yeah, no – it's rattling along nicely. Imogen Cranny is actually pretty good as Samantha Power, insofar as I'm a critic of musical theatre.

Honor is a member of, like, the chorus and I give her a big thumbs-up at the end of the opening number, 'We Will Teach This Ginger Child'.

Then I sit forward in my seat and I notice that *actual* Samantha Power is watching with a look of open-mouthed either shock or wonder on her face – it's difficult to tell from this angle.

Anyway, about ten minutes in, they get to the scene where little Samantha is leaving Mount Anville to move to the actual States. Imogen is standing in the middle of the stage, surrounded by nuns, and everyone's singing:

> *Samantha Power,*
> *This is the hour,*
> *For you to leave! Goodbye, sweet girl!*
> *Samantha Power,*
> *Beautiful flower,*
> *You'll make your mork upon the world!*

The girls in the chorus stort humming the tune then, while one of the nuns goes, 'Samantha Power, you are going to grow up to do – oh my God – amazing, amazing things in the world! You will receive a Bachelor of Orts degree from Yale, as well as a Doctor of Jurisprudence degree from Horvord Law School!'

Then the next nun is like, 'You will cover the Yugoslav Wars as a foreign correspondent and win a Pulitzer Prize in 2003 for your book *A Problem from Hell: America and the Age of Genocide*!'

The next nun is there, 'You will become the Founding Executive Director of the Carr Center for Human Rights Policy at Horvord's Kennedy School, where you will later serve as first Anna Lindh Professor of Practice of Global Leadership and Public Policy!'

Fock me, it sounds like Sincerity just cut-and-pasted this shit from Wikipedia.

'You will become a friend,' the next nun goes, 'as well as a confidante and Senior Adviser to the amazing, amazing Barack Obama! You will serve as Special Assistant to the President and as Senior Director for Multilateral Affairs and Human Rights on the National Security Council! You will later chair the newly formed Atrocities Prevention Board!'

The next nun is there, 'You will be appointed as the US Ambassador to the United Nations, in which role you will focus on such issues as women's and LGBT rights, religious freedom and human trafficking! You will also play a key role in persuading President Obama to intervene militarily in Libya!'

'In 2016,' the last nun goes, 'the American business magazine *Forbes* will list you as the forty-first most powerful woman in the world!'

Then the chorus storts up again:

> *Samantha Power,*
> *This is the hour,*
> *Remember us in all you do!*
> *Samantha Power,*
> *Beautiful flower,*
> *Mount Anville will always love you!*

And that's when it happens. The first thing I hear is, like, a bleat coming from the back of the concert hall – as in, like, '*Baa-aaah!*'

Then I hear another one, then another, then a series of

high-pitched screams coming from behind me. I turn around and I have to tell you, I am not prepared for the sight that greets me.

Er, *no one* is?

The double doors have been thrown open and hundreds of sheep are flooding through them into the concert hall, going – like I said – '*Baa-aaah!*'

People are screaming and jumping up onto their chairs. As I climb up onto mine, I hear a kid behind me go, 'Monsters, Mommy! Monsters!' because – yeah, no – they wouldn't be exposed to form animals on a regular basis around here.

'I think they're sheep,' his old dear tells him.

The things keep flooding into the concert hall, up and down the aisles, until they're covering literally every inch of floor space. I see Orlaith Stapleton – as in, Liesel Stapleton's old dear – and Helen Hall – as in, Thia Hall's old dear – and they have their backs to the wall, clutching each other, their eyes glazed over, like they can't take in what they're seeing and they're trying to just wish it away.

Then I hear *actual* Samantha Power – up on her chair – go, 'What the hell is going on?' and, bear in mind, this is a woman who's seen some seriously focked-up shit in her time, judging from the CV that we just heard being read out.

Sorcha, standing beside her, goes, 'Oh my God, Samantha, I am *so*, so embarrassed!'

The animals stort making their way up the steps and onto the stage, sending the cast of *Samantha Power: The Musical* fleeing in terror. I notice Sister Consuelo, standing there, surrounded by sheep, with her eyes closed, singing 'Nearer, My God, To Thee', as panic rips through the crowd.

Suddenly, a group of formers step into the concert hall and they unfurl a banner that says, 'SAVE OUR COWS! SAVE OUR SHEEP!' and they stort chanting, 'LALOR OUT! LALOR OUT! LALOR OUT!'

Actual Samantha Power turns around to Sorcha and goes, 'Is this because of you?'

Sorcha's there, 'I am *so* sorry, Samantha! This wasn't on my

official ministerial schedule – someone must have tipped them off that I was going to be here.'

My head automatically turns and my eyes quickly find Honor. She's standing in the wings, with her orm around Sincerity Matthews, who's in tears, her entire production ruined.

And what I can't take my eyes off is the humungous smile on Honor's face.

4.

The Book Thief

So it's, like, lunchtime the following day and I'm sitting in Kielys. I notice that I've got, like, a tonne of WhatsApp messages and of course I make the mistake of actually reading them.

Cho Hye-ji – as in, like, Jang Hye-ji's old dear – asks did anyone get bitten by a sheep last night? Mallorie Kennedy – as in, Courage Kennedy's old dear – says that she didn't personally but she still found the whole thing deeply distressing and she's saying that as a vegan. Helen Hall – as in, like, Thia Hall's old dear – says a ram tried to dry-hump her leg and she'll never be able to look at her Gianvito Rossi suede boots in the same way again. Alva Crowe – as in, Ginny Crowe's old dear – says that if it's not Honor O'Carroll-Kelly bringing shame on the school, then it's her mother. Mallorie Kennedy reminds her that Sorcha's husband is a member of the Merrion Tree Bistro group. Alva Crowe says oh my God, she's mortified – she thought she was messaging the Orchestra Moms group!

I close WhatsApp, then I open Safori and Google the number for Donnybrook Gorda Station. Yeah, no, despite what Ronan said, I've decided that I *am* going to take the rap for him so that he can move to New York. I'm going to tell them that it was me who took the gun from the church and I'm going to tell them exactly where they can find it.

The phone is answered on the third ring.

'Good afternoon,' a woman's voice goes, 'Donnybrook Garda Station.'

And I'm like, 'Yeah, no, hi, Donnybrook Gorda Station!' because I just can't help being a chorming bastard. 'This is Ross O'Carroll-Kelly. Can I speak to John Haskins, please?'

'John Haskins?' the woman goes. 'There's no John Haskins here.'

I'm there, 'As in, like, Gorda *Sorgeant* John Haskins? He arrested my son – Ronan Masterson – a few weeks ago. I'm ringing to tell you that he's innocent. I'm actually the guilty porty. I'm across the road in Kielys. I'm about to come in.'

It's all very Jason Bourne.

But then she says it again – the exact same thing. She's like, 'I don't know who you're talking about. There's no Garda Sergeant John Haskins here,' and she literally hangs up on me.

I'm thinking, okay, that is seriously, seriously strange.

So I ring Ronan and I'm there, 'Ro, where are you?'

He goes, 'Ine in Rathgeer, Rosser.'

'Are you trying to say Rathgor?'

'Yeah, Ine at the Rushidden embassy. It's on Orweddle Roawut. Cheerlie is about to gib a press conferdence.'

'Why's he giving a press conference in the Russian embassy?'

'I doatunt know. It's all veddy hush-hush, so it is.'

'I need to talk to you about something. I'll be there in, like, fifteen minutes.'

I end up being there in ten.

I pork the cor on Orwell Road. An absolute giant of a dude, who's as wide as a focking portaloo, is manning the gate.

I point to myself and I go, 'Journalist.'

And he's like, 'You have press card?'

I end up whipping out my membership cord for the Sporting Emporium Casino on Anne's Lane, which has been in my wallet since the weekend of Jamie Heaslip's stag, along with an unopened, strawberry and cream frappuccino-flavoured condom. The dude stares hord at it for a good thirty seconds, like he'd know a fake press cord if he saw one, then he lets me in.

I find the room where the press conference is about to stort. It's totally rammers. The old man is sitting at a table at the top of the room along with Hennessy, who's doing the introductions, then three or four Russian-looking dudes, one of whom is the famous Fyodor.

The old man's there, 'Thank you, Hennessy! As my Attorney General and long-time political jousting portner has just explained, the reason we're staging this press conference here, in the wonderful Russian consulate, is to deliver some very exciting news for Ireland! Exclamation mork, exclamation mork, exclamation mork!'

'Several weeks ago, I extended an invitation to the President of Russia, Mr Vladimir Putin, to visit our country! And I'm happy to report to you this afternoon that he has accepted that invitation and plans to visit Ireland in the coming weeks – itinerary to follow!'

I'm looking around the room for Ronan. There's, like, no sign of him, but I spot Raisa, Fyodor's wife – again, the woman I rode in the back of a Mitsubishi iMiEV, and I'm not saying it in a braggy way. I'm only mentioning it because it's relevant to the story.

She's staring hord at me, not even blinking, while at the same time chewing her bottom lip, similar to the way Lucy Kennedy used to look at me across the floor of The Queens back in the day.

'Ireland and Russia are two countries with a great many things in common,' the old man goes, 'and I look forward to strengthening our relationship further during the course of President Putin's visit! Now, as Hennessy said at the beginning, you will be offered the opportunity to ask questions, so I'm going to throw it open to the floor!'

'Can I ask you, Taoiseach,' some random journalist dude goes, 'for your reaction to Jean-Claude Juncker's comment that the Government's proposed ban on sheep and cow farming is incompatible with membership of the European Union?'

The old man's there, 'I've just delivered some wonderfully exciting news about the first visit to our country by a Russian head of State since Boris Yeltsin very nearly got off the plane in Shannon – and you want to talk about sheep and cows?'

'With respect, Taoiseach,' the same journalist dude goes, 'this ban threatens to destroy the livelihoods of tens of thousands of farmers and decimate rural Ireland. I think the views of the President of the European Commission are very relevant.'

The old man just, like, smiles. He's there, 'Well, as you know, I was elected on a promise to take Ireland *out* of Europe! I've promised the people a referendum in the autumn! Perhaps, by the time this bill comes before the house, the views of the no doubt highly estimable Jean-Claude Juncker will no longer be relevant!'

'Have you spoken to the Minister about the concerns expressed in Brussels?'

'I speak to the Minister all the time! She's a member of my Cabinet and also my daughter-in-law!'

'But *she's* still in favour of Ireland's continued membership of the European Union, isn't she?'

'The Minister believes she can change their minds! As you said, she has a lot more faith in the – quote-unquote – European project than I do!'

'Taoiseach, would you care to comment on reports on social media that farmers drove a herd of sheep into the concert hall in your granddaughter's school last night as a protest against the Minister's plan?'

'My views on formers will be well known to anyone familiar with the letters page of the *Irish Times*! They're port of the old Ireland! The Ireland of Costello and de Valera! The Ireland of country-and-western music and sexually frustrated priests trying to beat the left-handedness out of children!'

'Taoiseach, was the Minister present at the time?'

'Yes, she was.'

'Was she hurt?'

'Hurt? They were sheep!'

Yeah, try telling that to Helen Hall's good suede boots.

I suddenly feel a hand on my shoulder. I turn around and it ends up being Ronan. In a sort of, like, hushed voice, he goes, 'Alreet, Rosser? What's the stordee?'

I'm there, 'Ro, you're not going to believe what happened.'

He's like, 'What?'

'I rang Donnybrook Gorda Station – with the intention of, like, turning myself *in*?'

'I bleaten toawult you to leab it, Rosser.'

'Well, as it turned out, I'm glad I didn't listen to you.'

'Why? What happent?'

'He doesn't exist, Ro.'

'Soddy?'

'I'm talking about John Haskins. The Gord who supposedly

chorged you. I rang Donnybrook Gorda Station and the woman who answered the phone had never heard of him.'

'That's cos he's not based ourra Doddybruke, Rosser. He's in the Peerk.'

'What?'

'Doddybruke is where they breng me for to be interviewed. He woorks ourra the Phoedix Peerk.'

I look over at Raisa, who's staring at me now while licking her teeth. I know a lot of people prefer complicated relationships to simple ones, but there's clearly some weird, I don't know, *want* in me, which makes any woman whose husband has threatened to kill me about a hundred times more attractive in my eyes.

'Taoiseach, where is President Higgins?' someone then asks. 'He hasn't been seen in public for weeks. Leo Varadkar has challenged you this morning to provide proof of life.'

'Proof of life!' the old man goes, then he sort of, like, chuckles to himself. 'All I can do is confirm for you that President Higgins is alive and well! As a matter of fact, I bumped into him in the kitchen last night when he was getting his cocoa! We are sharing the living space in the Áras and it is working out very amicably! Now, does anyone have any questions about the visit to Ireland of a great friend of our country, Mr Vladimir Putin?'

My *phone* all of a sudden rings? It's, like, a withheld number. The only reason I end up answering it is because I notice that Raisa has her own phone to her ear, so I just presume it's her. I step away from Ronan and outside into the hallway.

I'm there, 'I've been thinking about those gorgeous lips of yours for the last twenty minutes.'

Except it ends up *not* being Raisa? Yeah, no, it's a man's voice.

He goes, 'Ross, this is Garda Sergeant John Haskins.'

And I'm like, 'Oh – you *do* exist,' and I can hear the disappointment in my voice when I say it.

'You were looking for me?'

'Yeah, no, I wanted to . . . hang on, how did you know?'

'The girl you were talking to is new in Donnybrook. One of the lads overheard her and told her I was based in the Park. She remembered your name – she thought you sounded a bit full of yourself, by the way – and all numbers come up on the computer when you ring the station.'

'Fair enough.'

'What can I do for you?'

'I'm glad you asked me that question. I want to make a confession.'

He sort of, like, laughs to himself. It's noisy in the background. Yeah, no, it sounds like he's in a pub.

He's there, 'A confession, is it?' sounding Scooby Dubious.

I'm like, 'Yeah, no, you've chorged my son –'

'Ronan.'

'That's right – with unlawful possession of a gun. Well, it was actually *me* who disposed of it?'

'Is that right?'

'I swear on my old man's life.'

'You wouldn't be trying to take the blame for him, would you?'

'Dude, I'm telling you the honest to God truth.'

'Your son is going to jail, Ross. That's as sure as I'm having three types of potato with my carvery lunch today.'

In the background, I hear him go, 'Three types of potato – and all the veg, yeah.'

I'm there, 'Dude, it was me who got rid of the gun. And to prove it, I'm going to tell you where you can find it.'

'We've already found it,' the dude goes – and for a few seconds I think he's possibly *bluffing*? 'Yesterday. In the lake in UCD.'

I'm like, 'That's what I was going to tell you. I was the one who focked it in there.'

'Your son threw it in the lake,' he goes. 'And I have a witness who saw him do it.'

I walk into the Áras with the boys and Leo lets a scream out of him like he's just seen my old dear without her foundation and her false teeth. Yeah, no, Michael D. Higgins is standing, like, twenty feet in front of us with two plates of beans on toast.

He goes, '*The* focking *President's Glasses!*' because – yeah, no – Sorcha bought them the book for Christmas, then he makes a run at him and Michael D. pulls a face like he's about to be tackled by Eben Etzebeth. But Leo just grabs a hold of his leg and goes, 'Michael D. Higgins! Michael D. Higgins! Michael D. Higgins!'

The other two make a chorge for him as well. Johnny grabs the other leg and I go, 'Goys, don't lift him! He's got two breakfasts in his hands!'

Michael D. chuckles to himself, in all fairness.

I'm there, 'Sorry, Dude, they're major fans.'

'That's quite alright,' he goes. 'It's nice to know someone is.'

Leo's there, '*Guten Morgen*, Michael D. Higgins!'

'*Guten Morgen* indeed!' the dude goes. '*Wie geht's?*'

'*Gut, danke.*'

Michael D. smiles at me.

'They speak German?' he goes.

I'm there, 'Yeah, no, Astrid, their nanny, is teaching them. They're possibly going to be storting in St Kilian's German School in September. Well, me and Sorcha have got, like, an *interview* this week?'

Michael D. just, like, stares into the distance.

'Education,' he goes, 'is the most vital gift we can bestow on the next generation,' and he seems to have genuine tears in his eyes. 'I don't know if you remember my speech to the Yeats International Summer School in 2001?'

I'm there, 'Er, give me the *gist* of it again?'

'I said there was too great an emphasis placed on preparing young people to be useful within the knowledge economy and what was being lost was the capacity of young people to critically evaluate, question and challenge.'

'Yeah, no, it's storting to ring a bell alright.'

'I said that there is a very real danger that we will come to forget the powerful and vital force of creative thinking as the fundamental basis of a truly functioning society, while we pursue, in a very narrow sense, the skills and outcomes that will prepare young people for the world of paid work.'

'I said don't lift him, goys!'

'It's okay.'

'People are worried about you out there.'

'Are they?'

'No one's seen you for weeks. Yeah, no, they're worried the old man might have, well –'

Michael D. laughs, in fairness to him.

'Sabina and I have started looking for alternative accommodation,' he goes. 'But there aren't a lot of suitable properties out there.'

I'm there, 'Have you checked out the Ant Form at Cherrywood?'

'The Ant Farm?'

'Yeah, no, it's this, like, communal living gaff and it's out – let's call a spade a spade here – Loughlinstown direction. Two mates of mine supplied their beds. I'll make a few inquiries for you, if you want.'

'That's very kind of you, Ross.'

'Hey – ain't no thing but a Chandler Bing, as we used to say back in the day. Here, your beans are going cold there.'

I manage to remove the two boys from Michael D.'s legs, then we head for the crèche, the boys shouting, '*Auf Wiedersehen*, Michael D. Higgins!' over their shoulders.

The crèche is the usual scene of serenity – we're talking soft lights and classical music. The boys run squealing across the floor to Nanny Astrid for hugs. The old dear is sitting on the playmat with the babies and she's making nonsense talk to them.

She's going, 'Who the lovely babies? You the lovely babies! Yes, you are! Yes, you are! You the lovely babies!'

Actually, maybe she's just had a skinful.

She storts tickling one of them on the tummy, then, with her other hand, she whips the swatch out of her pocket.

'It's Louisa May,' I go.

She looks up and sees me for the first time.

She's there, 'Yes, I thought it was Louisa May! You know, I'm almost at the point now where I don't need to check!'

'What, six months in? I'm tempted to say yay!'

'How *are* you, Ross?'

'Yeah, no, I'm coola boola.'

'Will you have a Grapefruit Mojito?'

'Er, are your breasts likely to burst if you go up in a plane?'

'You can just say yes or no, Ross.'

'Yes. Focking definitely.'

'You're obsessed with my breasts. Your father warned me that's what would happen if I bottle-fed you.'

'A lovely way for a mother to speak to her son.'

'He said you'd be tits mad. And that's how you've turned out. Tits mad.'

She stands up, walks over to the wall and presses a bell.

She's like, 'How was the musical? I haven't spoken to Honor this week.'

'Yeah, no,' I go, 'good moments and bad would my review. I'll, er, let her fill you in on how it ended. Wouldn't deny her that particular pleasure.'

'Where is that bloody borman?' she goes.

I actually laugh. At least she's giving him his proper job description.

I pick Hugo up off the floor and he smiles at me. Yeah, no, he's definitely storting to recognize me.

'So, er, that was random seeing Delma in here the last time,' I go.

I've been thinking a lot about what the woman said to me – the old dear having literally no memory of her telling her what happened between us.

She's like, 'Yes, you've always got on wonderfully well with Delma, haven't you?'

I'm there, 'Yeah, no, just as friends, though.'

'Well, of course just as friends! What an odd thing to say!'

'It's always been, like, purely plutonic.'

Hugo laughs. It's almost like he knows that his big brother is a legend.

The old dear goes, 'Can I let you into a little secret, Ross?'

I'm there, 'Yeah, no, what?'

'I think Delma is having a secret romance!'

'Why do you say that?'

'Oh, I can just tell these things! There's an aura about her at the moment, don't you think?'

'I haven't noticed any aura. Like I said, I've never looked at her in that way.'

'The new hairstyle! The clothes! The way she can't stop smiling!'

'Like I said, if that's your thing – blah, blah, blah.'

She goes, 'You still haven't got your Grapefruit Mojito, look!' and she presses the bell again.

I'm there, 'So, er, how long have you known Delma again?' just trying to subtly test her memory.

She goes, 'Delma and I have been friends since the very first Move Funderland to the Northside protest, which means that it was January 1987. She storted the picket, of course. That ridiculous funfair of theirs was pulling in poor people from all over Dublin – as it still is today! Well, Delma said as much on the news. I said to your father, "At last! Someone in this country who *is* prepared to speak their mind! This is a woman I simply have to become friends with!" We were living in Glenageary at the time.'

We were living in Sallynoggin at the time, but I decide to let it go.

'I got into the cor – this was in the days when it was perfectly acceptable to drink and drive – and I headed straight for the RDS,' she goes. 'I introduced myself to Delma and I told her that, while I didn't live in Ballsbridge myself, I cared about the area very, very deeply and I didn't want to see it destroyed by the borbarian masses. I told her I could introduce her to people. Influential people, including Peter Sutherland, the former Attorney General, with whom I'd had a fling back in the day. He took me to the Gonzaga debs, you know? Don't mention that to your father, by the way – he gets very jealous, even though poor Peter's gone now. It was in November 1963, just before John F. Kennedy was assassinated.'

Okay, there's clearly fock-all wrong with her memory.

'Anyway,' she goes, 'Delma and I manned the picket until the funfair finally packed up and focked off somewhere else. But we remained in touch. Because we discovered that we had so much more in common than our desire to be advocates on behalf of people with money. Golf, for instance. She took me to Foxrock Golf Club – my very first time playing the course. The twelfth of Morch 1987. She shot 99 and I shot 137.'

'Yeah,' I suddenly go, 'you can stop telling me your life story now,' and I can hear the definite relief in my voice. 'You're focking boring me and Hugo rigid here. Isn't that right, Hugo?'

The old dear goes, 'I'm going to go to the kitchen and see about this drink of yours!'

As she's leaving, I'm like, 'Hey, I'm sorry for saying that Mary Mitchell O'Connor focked all your books in the bin. Even though she did – because she's clearly got taste.'

And the old dear just fixes me with a look and goes, 'Who on Earth is Mary Mitchell O'Connor?'

Sorcha says she will not be intimidated – by formers or by anyone else.

I'm there, 'Fair focks, Sorcha. I said it the other night and I'll go on saying it.'

'A columnist in the *Gordian* said this morning that what I was proposing was the most radical – if somewhat misguided – effort to reverse the effects of global warming in history and Greta Thunberg Liked the orticle on Twitter.'

'Did she Retweet it?'

'No, she just Liked it. But Sea-mon has sent her a message saying that if she Liked it, she might consider *sharing* it?'

'She's definitely earning her money, that girl.'

'One thing she's really big on is just, like, shutting out the negative voices. Like, can you believe that Thia Hall's mother sent me a solicitor's letter, demanding €900 for a pair of Gianvito Rossi boots and €50,000 for emotional distress.'

'The focking nerve of the woman. Although a ram tried to ride her leg.'

'Sea-mon took the letter, tore it in two and dropped it in the recycling bin. She's *so* amazing, Ross!'

'I'll take your word for it.'

'The only thing that bothers me is the question of, like, who tipped off the formers?'

'As in?'

'As in, who told them that I was going to be there?'

'No focking way. I know what's being alleged here, Sorcha, and I don't like it one little bit.'

'It had to have been Honor, Ross.'

'I genuinely, genuinely don't think it *was* this time?'

'Have you asked her?'

'I don't need to ask her. I'm backing her one hundred per cent and I hope that's the end of the matter.'

I kill the engine. Yeah, no, we've pulled into the cor pork of St Kilian's on Roebuck Road. I open the back door and the boys come tumbling out of the cor, then I turn to Sorcha and go, 'So how do you want to play this?'

She's like, 'In terms of?'

'In terms of, do you want me to do the talking?'

'You?' she goes with a level of disdain in her voice that I personally think is unnecessary. 'You just keep your mouth shut and leave it to me, okay?'

I'm telling you, those formers don't know who they're focking with.

Into the school we go. Sorcha tells the woman in the office that we're here to see Herr Schwarzenbeck, then we're shown into this office where there's this – not being sizeist – but big fat dude with a blond, pudding-bowl haircut and thick black glasses sitting behind a desk.

He stands up and he holds out his hand.

He's like, 'Minister Lalor, it is a pleasure to welcome you to our school!' and Sorcha shakes it and I'm thinking, yeah, no, that's not a bad stort, until Brian goes, 'Look at this fat focker!' and I realize we may well have an actual job on our hands here.

'A fat focking prick,' Leo goes.

And Sorcha's there, 'I'm so sorry about that. They're not usually *like* this?' lying to the dude's face.

She's only been a Minister a few weeks as well.

'That's quite alright,' he goes. 'I have heard much worse things said in this room!' and we all laugh.

Yeah, no, a lot of rich kids go here.

'This is Brian, Johnny and Leo,' Sorcha goes, making the introductions. 'And, well, I've heard so many good things about this school, Mr Schwarzenbeck, mostly from my mom, who went here from, like, junior school, right the way through to her Leaving Cert year.'

'Of course, I know Mrs Lalor very well,' the dude goes. 'She was on the school fundraising committee for many years.'

Sorcha goes, 'She would love to *still* be? But she's just got – oh my God – *so* many other commitments at the moment.'

'She raised lots of money for this school and we are very grateful to her. So, what, you would like for your boys to come to this school in September?'

'Oh my God, definitely,' Sorcha goes – a little bit *too* keen, if you ask me?

I decide to dampen down the dude's enthusiasm, let him know that we're not without options, even though we are without options. There's hordly a decent fee-paying school south of the Liffey that doesn't know all about our children's reputation.

I'm there, 'What would St Kilian's have to offer that the likes of Blackrock and Michael's wouldn't have?'

'Fock this shit!' Leo goes. 'You focking pricking fock-stick!'

The dude goes, 'Well, we don't compare ourselves to other schools,' as if Leo never even spoke. 'Instead, we ask one simple question – does this child have an interest in, or an aptitude for, languages?'

'Well, in the case of Brian, Johnny and Leo,' Sorcha goes, 'the answer is, oh my God, *definitely* yes? At the moment, they're in a crèche with this amazing, amazing German lady named Astrid and she's the one who's been teaching them German phrases.'

'*Guten Tag, Jungen,*' the dude goes. '*Wie geht es Ihnen?*'

Leo's like, '*Super!*'

'*Super? Wie war das Wochenende?*'

Brian's like, '*Wir haben* focking *Rugby gespielt.*'

And Johnny's there, '*Und ins Kino* focking *gegangen.*'

'*Ah!*' Herr Schwarzenbeck goes. '*Welchen Film habt ihr gesehen?*'

'*Death Wish,*' Leo goes.

'*Death Wish?*' Herr Schwartenbeck goes, looking at me.

I'm there, 'Er, yeah, they grew out of kids' movies a long time ago.'

The dude looks at Sorcha then.

'Their pronunciation is flawless,' he goes. 'They speak like little Germans – except for the occasional F-word!'

'I'm embarrassed to say,' Sorcha goes, 'that they have better

German than they have English – and that's after only a few weeks of Astrid looking after them.'

'Well, in this school, they will learn everything through German. There is no better way to learn a language, we believe, than to totally immerse yourself in it.'

'I probably should also mention that I very nearly did an Erasmus year in Heidelberg,' Sorcha goes.

He's like, 'That's not necessary for me to know. I would be happy to enrol these boys for September.'

'Oh my God,' Sorcha goes, 'you won't regret this.'

He will regret it. Very focking quickly as well.

I'm there, 'Before we accept, can I just ask about rugby?'

'Ignore my husband,' Sorcha goes, suddenly standing up. 'Thank you so, so much. My mom is going to be – oh my God – so, so proud that they're going to be following in, like, *her* academic footsteps?'

'Please give your mother my best wishes,' the dude goes.

Then, before I know it, we're walking out of there and back to the cor.

'Oh my God,' Sorcha goes, out of the corner of her mouth, 'I can't focking believe you, Ross.'

I'm there, 'What do you mean?'

'*What would St Kilian's have to offer that the likes of Blackrock and Michael's wouldn't have?*'

'Hey, it always pays to let the other porty know they're not the only show in town.'

'They *are* the only show in town, Ross. Michael's gave us a flat no. Willow Pork just hang up on me every time I ring.'

'Did you see the look on his face when I asked about rugby? I'm pretty sure they don't have a team, by the way.'

'Rugby is the least of my focking concerns,' she goes.

When we're all back in the cor, Sorcha, in a frosty voice – and totally out of left field – goes, 'And by the way, Honor is going to Irish college this summer.'

I'm there, 'Excuse me?'

'You heard me, Ross. She's not spending the summer watching TV and trolling celebrities on social media. She's going to the Gaeltacht.'

'So, what, this is, like, *your* revenge, is it?'

'It has nothing to do with revenge. You heard what Herr Schwarzenbeck said about the value of immersing yourself totally in a language.'

Johnny's there, '*Ich* focking *will nach Dundrum gehen!*'

Sorcha goes, 'You wouldn't believe how many young people have fluent Irish these days, Ross. Sea-mon was telling me that it's actually considered random if you *don't* speak it fluently?'

I'm there, 'But hang on a second, it's already the first week in June. Surely all the best courses are already booked up?'

'I couldn't get her into the one in Lurgan, where practically the whole of South County Dublin goes. And I couldn't get her into Spleodar in Galway, which is where – oh my God – *all* the politicians and RTÉ people send their kids.'

'So where's she actually going?'

'She's going to a place called Muiríoch.'

'Jesus, where even *is* that?'

'It's on the Dingle Peninsula.'

'The Dingle Peninsula? In focking, I don't know –'

'Kerry, Ross.'

'Kerry. It was on the tip of my tongue to say it. She won't like that. She's paranoid about picking up an accent. Jesus, she mutes the TV every time Dáithí Ó Sé comes on.'

'*Ich* focking *hasse* Dáithí Ó focking Sé!' Leo goes.

Sorcha's like, 'Ross, Honor is going to Irish college whether she likes it or not.'

I'm there, 'All I can say is good luck breaking the news to her.'

And Sorcha just goes, 'I'm not telling her, Ross. *You* are?'

I'm like, 'Me?'

But there the conversation suddenly ends – because Sorcha is just, like, staring at her phone.

'It's a message from Sea-mon,' she goes. 'Oh my God!' and then, a few seconds later, she says it again. 'Oh! My! God!'

I'm like, 'What?'

'You're not going to believe what Phil Hogan said about me in an interview with Bloomberg.'

I'm there, 'Who's Phil Hogan?' because the name definitely rings a bell. 'Refresh my memory again?'

'He's the EU Commissioner for Agriculture.'

'That's it!' I go, the penny suddenly dropping. 'Yeah, no, he's a mate of my old man's. I played a three-ball with them in Druids Glen a few years ago and the dude cleaned us out.'

'Well,' she goes, still staring at her phone, 'he's done the same thing to me this morning – as in, like, politically? Have a listen to this, Ross. He said I was wilfully ignorant of the ways of rural Ireland and that I lacked empathy or understanding for anyone who didn't enjoy my privileged South Dublin upbringing.'

I don't say anything.

She's there, 'Are you listening to me?'

'Yeah, no,' I go, 'I was waiting to hear more.'

'More?'

'Well, I was going to let you tell me *all* the shit he said, then give you a big, big reaction at the end.'

'He said I was naive in the extreme to think that Ireland could remain port of the European Union while carrying out what was effectively a purge of a whole class of people and their way of life. He compared me to Stalin, Ross.'

'Well, he didn't seem like that when I met him. He seemed sound.'

'Oh my God!' she just goes. 'Oh! My! God!'

JP is surprised to find me standing at his door – although shocked is possibly *more* the word?

He's like, 'How the fock did you get into the building?' and this is one of my best friends in the world, bear in mind.

I'm there, 'I slipped in behind some randomer as the door was closing.'

'Well, what do you want?' he goes and I'm getting the vibe that he's not exactly happy to see me.

'I was talking to Michael D. Higgins. Him and the missus are obviously looking for somewhere to live. I was trying to remember the name of the dude who owns the Ant Form at Cherrywood.'

'Could you not have, like, texted me that?'

'Well, I also wondered did you fancy a few of these?' and I hold up two six-packs of the good stuff. 'Are you going to invite me in or what?'

'Dude, it's not really a good time.'

And that's when I hear *her* voice coming from inside.

She's like, 'Who is it, Jay Dorling?'

And I actually *laugh*?

I'm like, 'Jay Dorling?' at the same time nudging my way past him. 'No wonder you're being weird. You're on a date,' because I can suddenly smell *her Obsession* by Calvin Klein and *his* shrimp fettuccine Alfredo pasta bake.

'Fock's sake,' JP goes, chasing me down the hallway. 'We're in the middle of dinner, Ross.'

The room is in almost total dorkness. Delma is sitting at the table. In the flickering candlelight, she looks – yeah, no – definitely younger than her sixty-five years.

When she sees me, she goes, 'What are *you* doing here?'

Seriously, a goy could develop a complex.

I'm there, 'Hey, I just popped in to be social. Didn't realize I was interrupting a romantic dinner for two,' and I turn to JP then. 'You did your shrimp fettuccine thing, did you?'

He rolls his eyes and goes, 'Fock's sake, Ross.'

I'm like, 'This is my first time seeing you two together as an actual couple. It's still so random.'

'Can you please leave?' she goes – like it's *her* gaff?

I'm there, 'Okay, I can take a hint. By the way, Delma, you were spot-on about my old dear.'

'What are you talking about?'

'Er, about her *forgetting* things? She didn't know who Mary Mitchell O'Connor was the other day. Mary Mitchell O'Connor! The woman who told her that she wasn't too old to wear leather trousers. The woman she placed ahead of me in her list of emergency contacts when she had her frequent faller alorm fitted.'

'Yes, it's worrying,' Delma goes.

'The weirdest thing is that she can remember shit from, like, *ages* ago? As in, she can remember the exact date that you two first met and she can remember what score you both shot the first time you ever played golf.'

'So it's just her short-term memory?' JP goes. 'Is she on any medication at the moment?'

I actually crack my hole laughing.

'Dude,' I go, 'she's like Ozzy focking Osbourne!'

He's there, 'Well, has she storted taking any new medications recently?'

'I know she's on fecal incontinence tablets,' I go. 'I found them when I was going through her handbag, looking for the alcohol breathalyser kit that I bought her for her seventieth birthday.'

I stort racking my brains, trying to remember what they were called.

I'm there, 'Was it ShiteRight? No, I think I made that up at the time. Hang on,' and I whip out my phone. 'I'll Google fecal incontinence and see what comes up.'

JP goes, 'Ross, we're about to have Chocolate Mess for dessert.'

I'm like, 'No, thanks, I ate earlier.'

I end up finding it straight away. It's called ZenBowel.

I'm like, 'Here we go. They have, like, a website,' and I stort reading it out loud. '*Fecal incontinence is the inability to control bowel movements, causing stool to leak unexpectedly from the rectum. The problem can range in seriousness from occasional leakage of matter while passing gas to a complete loss of bowel control.*'

'Oh, for God's sake!' Delma goes, pushing her dessert away.

I'm there, '*Chronic, recurring fecal incontinence, especially in elderly women, is most commonly caused by the weakening of the muscles in the area of the bowels as a result of ageing or giving birth.* Jesus, I might have known it was my fault. *People with this condition may be unable to stop the urge to defecate, which comes on so suddenly that they don't make it to the toilet in time.*'

JP goes, 'Ross, can you not read this at home later on?'

'Okay, I can see the way you're both looking at me, so I'll skip forward to the side-effects. Here we are. *Do not drive or operate heavy machinery while taking ZenBowel. Side-effects may include skin rash, dry mouth, drowsiness, nausea, insomnia, thrush* – hey, you're not alone,

Delma! – *dizziness, abnormal hort rhythms, hallucinations and* – happy days! – *short-term memory loss!* Mystery solved, Delma!'

She suddenly stands up.

'I need to use the bathroom,' she goes. 'JP, please make sure he's gone when I come back.'

Then off she jolly well focks.

I'm there, 'You've obviously told her you like *Obsession* by Calvin Klein,' I go. 'I presume that's why she's wearing it?'

But he storts shoving me towards the door, going, 'Seriously, Ross, you need to get the fock out of here – as in, like, *now*?'

'Just wait a second,' because I suddenly find myself overcome with feelings of happiness for him. I can be like that sometimes. 'Just let me say something.'

He's like, 'What?'

And I'm there, 'I'm happy for you, Dude.'

'Really?'

'Genuinely. I have to admit, when you first told me about you and Delma, I thought it was just you trying to get that weird perversion you had for her as a teenager out of your system once and for all. Now, I can see that it's obviously more than that.'

'I'm in love, Ross.'

'Big word.'

'I know.'

'Big, big word.'

'I was thinking of telling her – tonight.'

'Go for it would be my advice.'

He's like, 'Thanks, Ross. You're a good mate.'

I'm about to say goodbye to him when he suddenly goes, 'Hey, wait!' and he slips into his bedroom, then steps back out thirty seconds later holding a black bin liner that's, like, *filled* with something?

He's like, 'Will you throw this down the rubbish chute – it's opposite the lift.'

I'm there, 'What is it?' at the same time taking it from him.

'It's my collection of women's underwear,' he goes, sounding almost embarrassed. 'Knickers and bras from, you know, girls I've known over the years.'

I'm there, 'What, you're throwing out your screwvenirs?'

'Yes, I am.'

'Why, Dude?' at the same time looking into the bag. I notice that they've all got little labels stapled to them with names and dates on them.

'I can't keep them here, Ross. What if Delma finds them?'

'Just hide them really, really well.'

'I don't want them any more.'

'That's how you feel now. I'm just worried that you might one day regret it. Like Sorcha did when she ended up rebuying her entire DVD collection on Blu-ray.'

Inside the aportment, I hear Delma go, 'Has he gone yet?'

He's there, 'Ross, promise me you'll put them down the chute?'

And I'm like, 'Dude, don't sweat it. A promise is a promise.'

'Yeah, but you didn't make one.'

'Come on, what are we, thirteen? I'll give you a bell tomorrow, Dude.'

Then I make my way down to the cor park and I throw JP's collection of women's smalls into the boot of my cor.

My phone pings. Alva Crowe – as in, like, Ginny Crowe's old dear – says she's thinking of taking up boxercise and does anyone know if it's good for, like, cordio?

I didn't know that JP was with Jane Balfe – as in, like, *with* with? *Or* that she was into black lacy thongs, which is a genuine shock given that she's a Minister of the Eucharist in Booterstown Church and a chaperone on the annual parish pilgrimage to Fatima.

Yeah, no, this bag of women's underwear is proving to be full of surprises.

Just as another example, I would have thought Criosa Luhan – this apparently sex maniac who JP was with, on and off, for about two years – would have been the one wearing the bootlace to cover her vajayjay. Instead, hers are these, like, giant white bloomers that look like my old man's Y-fronts – and I say that as someone who walked in on him and the old dear while they were hord at it in the kitchen the night Leinster beat Munster in the famous

O'Driscoll–O'Gara intercept match and *she* was helicoptering the things above her head.

I'm thinking, either Criosa didn't know she was going to be having sex when she got dressed that morning, or JP has stapled her name to the wrong Diana Vickers.

There is so much history in this bag that it seems definitely wrong to just, like, throw it away. I genuinely think that JP would one day regret it, especially if this thing with Delma ends up being just another one of his weird phases.

Speaking of which, *her* Hermès scorf is in here as well – the one that famously went missing from the old dear's coat stand all those years ago.

There's a knock on the bedroom door and I hear Honor go, 'Dad?'

I'm like, 'Just a second, Honor,' and I shove everything back into the bin liner and I fock it into the bottom of my wardrobe.

Then I open the bedroom door.

I'm there, 'What's up? I was just, em, reading.'

She doesn't pull me up on it.

She's just like, 'I've got something to show you.'

'Show me?' I go. 'In terms of?'

She's there, 'Brian, will you come out here?'

The door of the boys' bedroom flies open and – yeah, no – *he* steps out wearing the full Leinster kit that I bought him for Christmas last year and which I've literally never seen him wear.

'So it still fits,' I go, 'despite the amount of shite he eats.'

Honor's there, 'Show your daddy what you can do, Brian,' and suddenly he storts running figure-eights, up and down the landing, shouting, '*Fick dich*, Munster! *Fick dich*, you focking Munster focks!'

I'm there, 'You didn't give him Red Bull again, did you?'

But Honor goes, 'Dad, look at his legs!'

I'm like, 'What about them?'

'His limp!' she goes. 'It's gone!'

She's right! Holy fock, she's actually right! He's running like a normal kid!

Until, that is, Leo steps out onto the landing and trips him up – I like that competitive streak in him – and Brian falls flat on his face.

'Honor,' I go, throwing my orms around her, 'you're un-focking-believable!'

She's like, 'Do you think?'

'You believed in him, Honor. I'm remembering all those mornings when you helped him with his physio, even though I said you were wasting your time and that Brian was basically dead to me – certainly in terms of rugby. But you never, ever gave up on him.'

'Er, he's my *brother*, Dad?'

'I know, Honor – but even so.'

I watch him pick himself up off the corpet – no tears, no complaints to the ref – then walk over to Leo and deck him with a short punch to the left temple. Suddenly, the two of them are rolling around the landing, punching the head off each other like they're on the last Nitelink to Saggart.

Honor goes, 'Will we break it up?'

And I'm like, 'Only if Leo storts to get the upper hand. I have a duty to protect the future Leinster number ten, bear in mind!'

She smiles. It's a great line, in fairness to me.

I'm like, 'Thanks again, Honor.'

'You're welcome,' she goes.

She's such a great kid – so great that I feel bad about what I have to tell her.

'Honor,' I go, 'how would you like to go away this summer?'

She's there, 'Oh my God, are we going to Quinta do Lago?'

'Er, not *quite* Quinta do Lago?'

'Where are we going then?'

'*We're* not going anywhere. Your old dear is going to be busy this summer with the whole banning sheep and cows thing. But *you're* going to get to go away – isn't that exciting?'

'Where the fock am I supposedly going?'

'Very good question. And, bear in mind, this isn't *my* idea – it's all coming from her – but *she* thinks it'd be a good idea if we sent you to the Gaeltacht for three weeks.'

'The Gaeltacht?'

'Again, I'm dead against it. I put up one hell of a fight. You should have heard some of the things I said to her. Unbelievable.'

'Which Gaeltacht?'

'Try not to lose your shit, Honor.'

'Lurgan?'

'Unfortunately, it was late in the day.'

'Spleodar?'

'No, not Spleodar either. You're going to Kerry.'

'Kerry?'

'I'm afraid so.'

'She's doing this to get me back, isn't she? Just because I rang the Irish Formers' Association and told them that she was going to be at *Samantha Power: The Musical*.'

'What, you actually *did* that?'

'Yeah, I did. So focking what?'

'Yeah, no, nothing.'

'You said you thought it was funny.'

'It was funny. From stort to finish.'

'Do you know what? Fock *her* shit. I'll go.'

'What? Seriously?'

'She thinks I won't survive down there. I'll prove the stupid bitch wrong.'

'I love your attitude, Honor.'

Suddenly, I hear raised voices downstairs. Sorcha and Fionn are having, like, a blazing row – which is pretty unusual. As a matter of fact, I don't think I've ever heard them exchange two cross words before.

I'm there, 'What the fock is that about? Do I even *want* to know?'

Honor's there, 'She's pissed off because the EU called her out on her bullshit and now she's being a total bitch to everyone.'

'Yeah, no, she can be a bit of a drama queen alright. I better go down and see what the deal is. Maybe pull the boys aport there, Honor. Leo seems to be getting the better of him.'

So she does that while I tip downstairs.

And – yeah, no – Sorcha and Fionn *are*, like, roaring at each other. They're, like, so worked up about, I don't know, whatever it is they're arguing about that they don't even notice that I've walked into the kitchen. They're both, like, red in the face, hot spittle coming out of the sides of their mouths.

Fionn is holding little Hillary, who's crying his little hort out – but, again, they don't even seem to cop it.

I'm like, 'What the fock, goys?' taking the little lad out of Fionn's orms. 'They can hear you up in the Druid's focking Chair.'

They stop shouting and they just, like, stare at each other across the free-standing island, trying to get their breath back.

I'm there, 'I'll repeat my question – what the fock?'

Fionn goes, 'Why don't you ask *her*?'

But Sorcha's like, 'I'm not the one with the problem, Fionn. You are.'

'Whoa, whoa, whoa,' I go. 'Let's all just take a chill pill here. Is this about Phil Hogan?'

Sorcha looks at me like she's already considering how to dispose of my remains.

'No,' she goes, 'it has nothing to do with Phil Hogan. Fionn wants to take my baby away.'

He turns to me then?

He's like, 'I want to go travelling – that's all. I've had this, like, brush with death and I've realized that there are so many places in the world that I want to see. Machu Picchu. Uluru. The ancient city of Petra. And I want to do it before it's too late.'

'Well, focking do it,' Sorcha goes. 'But you are not bringing my son with you.'

'It's only for a year, Sorcha.'

'He won't even recognize me when he comes home.'

That's when Fionn says it.

'Well,' he goes, 'I'm surprised he recognizes you now.'

There's, like, silence in the kitchen.

'*Excuse* me?' she goes.

He's there, 'I'm just saying that you're not exactly in his life these days. You're never here.'

She goes, 'I'm trying to do something positive – to save the planet that we call Earth, which will benefit Hillary in the long term.'

'And I'm sure he'll be very grateful – if you succeed.'

Holy fock, the face on her. It's like the time she had her credit cord declined at Pippa O'Connor's pop-up shop in Dundrum Town Centre. Fionn needs to tread very, very carefully here.

She goes, 'You are not taking my son around the world for a year and that's the end of the matter.'

And he's like, 'So you'd prefer to put him in a crèche where he doesn't know anyone rather than leave him with me? We've formed a bond, Sorcha.'

'I can't believe what you just said, Fionn.'

'What did I say?'

'That I was a bad mother.'

'I didn't say you were a bad mother.'

'You implied it.'

At that exact moment, I hear a series of loud thuds as something – or someone – comes tumbling down the stairs. Sorcha doesn't move a muscle, just keeps staring Fionn down. I stick my head out the door into the hallway.

'Panic over,' I go. 'It's only Leo.'

Fionn takes Hillary out of my hands.

He's there, 'I'm going on a round-the-world trip, Sorcha. And I'm taking my son with me,' and with that he storms out of the room.

Sorcha shouts after him.

She goes, 'As I said in a voice message to Phil Hogan, you'd better not underestimate me, because I will fock your shit up!'

Ronan says he's boddixed.

I tell him not to think that way. Yeah, no, I'm channelling Johnny Sexton at half-time against Northampton in the 2011 Heineken Cup final.

I'm there, 'It's not over until it's over,' and I'm actually giving myself goosebumps here.

He goes, 'It's oaber now, Rosser. Thee hab the gudden.'

I'm there, 'So they have the gun – what does that actually prove?'

'And thee hab a witness who saw me thrun it in the lake.'

'I still say it's possible to turn it around. An early try in the second half could change everything.'

'What?'

'Sorry, I storted thinking about rugby there. Ro, could you possibly slow down?'

Yeah, no, we're walking down Kildare Street and I'm having to pretty much run to keep up with him.

'I caddent slow down,' he goes, 'I hab shit to do.'

I'm like, 'Where are you even going?' as he turns left onto, like, *Nassau* Street?

'That Putin fedda's arriving tomoddow,' he goes. 'Cheerlie's asked me to pick up a predent for him – joost to say welcuddem to Arelunt.'

'*That's* what he has you doing now? His focking shopping?'

'If I get sent dowun, Rosser, that's all I'll ebber be good fowur.'

'What are you talking about?'

'If Ine convicted of a seerdious offence, I woatunt be able to get a Certificate to Practise Law – ebber!'

'Fock.'

'This John Haskins sham is deteermined to send me dowun, Rosser.'

'Can't Hennessy arrange to have him –'

'What? Kilt?'

'I was going to say transferred. He used to use his influence to do that all the time. Any Gord who tried to do him for, I don't know, drinking after hours, or driving while suspended, suddenly found themselves moved to some shit-hole of a town in the middle of nowhere. He has friends – and he has a lot of dirt on them.'

'He dudn't think there's athin he can do now that thee hab the gudden and the witness.'

I'm there, 'Well, I still haven't given up hope,' and I'm thinking maybe I'll get Johnny Sexton to send him a text, or possibly even ring him, to remind him what can happen when you *don't* quit?

Er, his drop goal against France, anyone? Eighty-third minute? Thirty-nine phases? Give me a focking break! Jesus, I can feel my eyes tearing up as I head for the door of the Kilkenny Shop – a definite first for me.

And that's when I realize that Ronan isn't with me any more. Yeah, no, he's carried on walking.

I'm like, 'Ro, it's *here*?'

He's there, 'Ine not going to the Kilkeddy Shop, you flute.'

'Where are you getting this present, then? Please don't say Caddles Irish Gifts.'

'Mon,' he goes, suddenly crossing to the other side of Nassau Street. 'Foddow me.'

I'm there, 'Dude, you're going to be getting a call from Johnny Sexton later on. I'm going to text him and ask him to talk some focking sense into you.'

'Rosser,' he goes, 'will you joost fooken leab it? New York wadn't to be – alreet? Ine godda get sent dowun. Ine arthur accepting it. Might be oatenly a yee-or. Heddessy has said he'll pay me wages for howebber long Ine insoyut – make shewer that Shadden and Ri doatunt waddant for athin. Then when I gerrout, he's probised there'll be woork for me.'

'What kind of work are we talking?'

'Well, I woatunt be a solicitodder, but it'll be quasi-legal woork.'

'What, like shopping?'

He takes a right turn into, like, Trinity College.

I'm there, 'Where the fock are you going?' and at the same time I notice – I swear to fock – six or seven uniformed Gordaí standing at the entrance.

Ronan walks up to them and goes, 'Howiya, feddas? Yeah, Ine from the Office of the Attordeney Generdoddle. Foddy me.'

Then into the actual college we go.

Sixty seconds later, we're crossing this, like, cobbled courtyord, Ronan striding ahead with a real sense of – you'd have to say – *purpose*? Then up a set of stairs we go to this, like, humungous library. I can imagine how it'd be seriously impressive if books were your thing.

People turn around and stare as we walk in. Yeah, no, we're some sight, it has to be said. We're talking Ronan in his black, pin-striped suit, all these Gords in – like I said – full uniform, then me in my usual Leinster jersey and chinos.

I'm thinking, what the fock are we even doing here? And, of course, I'm about to find out.

This, I don't know, librarian woman, wearing a grey cordigan, and tiny round glasses on the end of her nose, walks up to our porty and she's like, 'Can I help you?'

And Ronan looks the woman square in the eye and goes, 'I've come for the Book of Keddles.'

'For the what?' the woman goes.

'The Book of Keddles.'

'I'm sorry, I'm struggling with your, em –'

I'm there, 'I think he's trying to say he's come for the Book of Kells,' but, to be honest, I'm sort of, like, struggling with it myself. This is what the old man is giving to this famous Putin dude?

'What do you mean you've come for it?' the woman goes.

Ronan doesn't answer her – not with words anyway. He just reaches into his trouser pocket and whips out a folded-up letter, which he opens out and hands to her.

The woman gives it the old left to right, then she goes, 'I'm sorry, the Office of the Attorney General doesn't have the jurisdiction to just demand the Book of Kells.'

You'd have to feel sorry for her. Hand on hort, I couldn't tell the Book of Kells from a focking Neven Maguire cookbook, but I've heard Fionn bang on about it loads and I know it's supposably – in inverted commas – important.

'I'm sorry,' the woman goes, handing Ronan back the letter, 'I have no idea what this is about. You'll have to speak to the Provost.'

Ronan doesn't say shit. He just reaches inside his jacket and he whips out – I swear to fock – a hammer. There's, like, gasps in the room. The librarian woman turns white, presumably thinking he's going to give her the business end of the thing. Except he *doesn't*? Yeah, no, he walks up to this, like, glass-topped table, lifts the hammer high above his head, then brings it down hord on the table.

There's the sound of, like, glass shattering, then an alorm goes off. Ronan reaches in and pulls out a book. The thing is open and he just, like, tips it upside-down to get rid of all the broken glass from it, then he slams it shut and sticks it under his orm.

The librarian woman rushes towards him, going, 'That's Ireland's greatest cultural treasure,' which sounds like a bit of an exaggeration to me. It's still just a book. 'You can't just come in here and take it!'

One of the Gords steps in front of her and goes, 'If you lay one finger on that man, Madam, I'll be forced to arrest you.'

The woman just, like, bursts into tears. I'm guessing it must be worth a few shekels.

Two security dudes come racing into the room then, in response to the alorm. They see Ronan coming towards them with the thing under his orm.

One of them goes, 'What in the name of –'.

But one of the Gords just roars, 'Stand aside!' which is what they end up doing – no choice in the matter. Then thirty seconds later, I'm watching my son walk back across the cobbled courtyord with the Book of Kells jammed into his ormpit and his mission – you'd have to say – very much accomplished.

It's, like, nine o'clock at night and the kids are all in bed, but Sorcha is still working. Yeah, no, she's sitting at the island in the kitchen, tapping away on the keys of her laptop, occasionally chuckling to herself or saying shit like, 'Oh, good line, Sorcha! He can't deny the science!'

I'm there, 'What are you doing?'

She goes, 'Sea-mon thinks I should put out a strong statement, expressing my deep disappointment with Phil Hogan's position.'

'Right.'

'So I'm saying that, while I'm a lifelong supporter of the European Union and the work it does, I don't believe they're doing enough to try to combat global warming. I'm also making the point that these – oh my God – beef barons have held Ireland to ransom for way too long and it's about time someone took them on.'

'Fair focks,' I go. 'Fair, fair focks.'

She goes back to her keyboard.

'So,' I go, 'that, er, got pretty heated between you and Fionn the other night, didn't it?'

She's there, 'I was stating my position, Ross – as I'm doing now.'

'I'm wondering should you maybe let him go away, though?'

'Excuse me?'

'The dude nearly died, Sorcha. It stands to reason that he'd have a whole new – I want to say – *prospectus* on life?'

'No one's stopping him from going away.'

'You know what I mean – *with* Hillary.'

'He's not taking my son away from me.'

'Like he said, Sorcha, they have an actual bond.'

'Then he needs to decide if going away for a year is the right thing for him to do.'

All of a sudden, speak of the devil, Fionn steps into the kitchen. At first I'm wondering did he hear what was just said, but then he mustn't have because he just, like, stares at me and goes, 'Your old man has stolen one of the four volumes of the Book of Kells.'

I'm like, 'Word certainly travels fast.'

'It was the lead story on the nine o'clock news. He marched into Trinity College and just took it.'

'*He* didn't take it. Even though I'd usually be the last person to defend him. It was actually Ronan who took it, acting on Hennessy's instructions. I was actually there.'

'And, what, you just stood back and let it happen?'

'I was never a fan of books, Fionn. You know that. How many times did I set fire to your schoolbag when we were in Castlerock?'

'It's not *just* a book, Ross. It's Ireland's greatest historical treasure.'

'That's pretty much what the librarian said.'

'What's he planning to do with it?'

'He's, em, giving it to that Something Something Putin dude.'

'He's *what*?'

'Yeah, no, as a gift to say welcome to Ireland. I'd have got him a Newbridge Silver cheese plane. Or a set of Jonathan Knuttel place-mats. But the old man is obviously going all out to impress.'

Fionn turns to Sorcha then and he's like, 'And you're okay with this, are you?' and there's a real, like, nasty *edge* to his voice?

She just goes, 'I don't have to agree with absolutely everything the Taoiseach does. And I can't be pirouetting on the plinth every time something happens that I don't like. I'm in politics to make an actual difference – and if that means having to occasionally bite my tongue, then so be it.'

'Even if it means standing idly by while a priceless, thousand-year-old manuscript is stolen?'

'See? Not nice, is it, Fionn? When there's something that's – oh my God – so precious to you and someone threatens to take it out of the country.'

'Yeah, at least I'd be bringing Hillary back, Sorcha.'

I honestly can't listen to the two of them going at it again, so I tell them that I'm heading out to maybe grab a late one in Finnegan's.

I get into the cor and that's when I notice that I have a missed call from, believe it or not, Raisa. I think about maybe *not* returning it, what with her husband threatening to kill me with his bare hands if he catches me sniffing around her. But then I'm also thinking about – being *honest*? – how hot she looked at the press conference at the Russian embassy and how *into* me she seemed to be?

So, naturally, I end up ringing her back. On top of everything else, it's good manners – something I've always been big on.

She answers by going, 'Hello, Ross.'

I'm like, 'Raisa, how the hell are you?' just making conversation with the girl. 'I'm sorry I didn't get to chat to you at the press conference that day. You were looking well. Extremely well.'

I have a real way with words.

She comes straight out with it. She's like, 'We have business that is not finished.'

She's clearly talking about our little game of push and shove in the Glen of the Downs.

I'm there, '*I* seem to remember finishing – very quickly as well. And I'm saying that as a compliment to you.'

'You do not give me pleasure,' she goes. 'And now you must.'

I'm there, 'I've heard a lot of women say that they don't necessarily have to experience orgasm to enjoy sex,' just trying to get her to hopefully lower her sights. 'I may have even read it in one of my wife's magazines, even though I think they were talking specifically about seniors' sex. I'll see can I dig it out for you either way.'

She's like, 'You come to house now.'

Yeah, no, her and Fyodor are renting this massive, four-storey gaff in Monkstown.

I'm there, 'What about your husband?'

'He is at airport with your father,' she goes, 'for arrival of President Putin. He will not be home for many hours.'

I'm there, 'We're not going to need many hours, Raisa,' trying to sell it to her as a positive. 'I think it's only fair to warn you.'

I pork the cor in Monkstown Village – a discreet distance from the house – then I tip around to Longford Terrace, a pretty much dinosaur bone in my chinos at the thought of what I'm going to do to the woman.

Raisa opens the door wearing a white, fluffy bathrobe and a look of, like, vague disgust on her face.

'Upstairs, in bedroom,' she goes, flicking her thumb over her shoulder, like I'm here to bleed the radiators, or fix the focking Sky box.

I'm there, 'Fair enough,' and I start trooping up the stairs, with her following behind me, no doubt checking out my orse, her breathing slow and laboured, like Tony Soprano when he's trying not to lose his shit.

Into the bedroom we go. No words end up being exchanged between us. She shoves me backwards onto the bed and storts tearing at my chino buttons like she's opening her Christmas presents.

I'm not exactly hiding behind the door, by the way. Yeah, no, I'm a full and active porticipant in the proceedings. I give the belt of her bathrobe a tug and the thing falls open, revealing the full sweetshop window.

'You've an unbelievable body,' I tell her, because I can give a compliment as well as I can take one. At the same time, I'm squeezing her goodies, which she seems to love. 'I don't think I properly appreciated it the last time because we did the deed in a Mitsubishi iMiEV, which isn't much roomier than a Peugeot 106. I'd nearly compare it to the Honda Fit.'

She covers my mouth with her hand – it's a little bit *Fifty Shades of Grey*, in fairness to it – and goes, 'Do not talk. You have voice like a girl's voice.'

She pulls the clothes off me like she's stripping a hospital bed.

I'm like, 'There's a Johnny in my wallet there, Raisa. I don't know if you're a strawberries and cream frappuccino kind of woman, are you?'

And she's there, 'No, I have this,' and she picks a condom up from her bedside table. 'It is for woman's pleasure.'

'Hey,' I go, 'anything that speeds up the process for you.'

I open the foil, take the thing out and then pull it on. It's, like, white, blue and red stripes.

'The colours of Russian flag,' she goes. 'Fyodor love Mother Russia.'

They're Fyodor's? Using another man's Johnnies to ride his wife is another item about to be checked off the bucket list.

She sits – I want to say – *astride* me, pulls out my nine-iron and holds it in what anyone who knows anything about golf would have to describe as a textbook Vardon grip. She's standing over me – working it, working it, working it – and I'm going at her lady bubbles like a kid with a Fisher-Price Jungle Gym.

And it's there that I'm going to have to go dork on the rest of the details. I've always been a firm believer that the things that happen in the bedroom should remain in the bedroom, another reason why women tend to see me first and foremost as a gentleman.

All I will say, by way of helping the story along, is that Raisa ends up riding me like a SoulCycle bike, muttering compliments, put-downs and threats, sometimes in the same breath, and squeezing my windpipe like I owe her money, while I cup my two hands around Fred and Ginger and squeeze them one at a time, until the whole workout comes to a screaming end (my screams) after approximately ten minutes, and that's me rounding up.

I sort of, like, push her off me and she goes, 'No! You cannot be finished! You are not a man who likes women! You are man who likes other man!'

I'm there, 'See, I'm not sure you're allowed to use that as a term of abuse any more, Raisa.'

'You are gay man.'

'I've got a very good friend who's gay. Two, if you count his husband.'

I stand up from the bed and I catch sight of myself in the full-length mirror. I've gone all soft and deflated, like a New Year's Eve 2017 helium balloon. I snap the Johnny off, wrap it in tissue and slip it into the pocket of my chinos just as I'm getting ready to step into them.

And that's when Raisa suddenly turns violent. She storts throwing shoes at me, picking them up off the floor and focking them at me. I bend down and I stort gathering up my t-shirt, my jocks and my Dubes, as the Saint Laurents and the Aquazurras bounce off my head and my back like designer leather hailstones.

I clutch my clothes to my chest and I peg it – still *naked*, bear in mind? – out onto the landing, running in a zigzag pattern to try to avoid being hit.

I reach the bottom of the stairs and that's when I hear voices outside in the front gordon.

'Shit,' Raisa, standing at the top of the stairs, goes. 'Is Fyodor.'

I'm like, 'Okay, don't panic,' because it's not the first time I've had to run stork-naked from another man's house. It's not even the twenty-first. 'Is there a back door? Or even a lorge window with not more than a ten- to twelve-feet drop?'

A lifetime of this kind of thing has left me with the ankles of a man twice my age.

She's there, 'There is back door, but is locked, and is no time to find key.'

She pulls on her bathrobe and she chorges down the stairs, then she shoves me into this, like, living room.

'Hide,' she goes.

I'm like, 'Where am I supposedly hiding?'

'Behind here,' she goes, pulling this, like, sofa out from the wall. At the same time, I hear the front door open and the hallway outside suddenly fills up with voices. I dive head-first behind the sofa and Raisa pushes it back into position, jamming me – again, bucknaked – up against the wall.

She goes out into the hallway and I hear her go, 'I am so sorry! I am just out of bath!' and then a second or two later I hear her gasp and go, 'I am honoured that you visit our home, President Putin. And also you, em . . . I am so sorry to say that I cannot remember what is the title for you.'

'Taoiseach!' I hear the old man go. 'But you can call me Chorles!'

Oh, fock a focking duck!

'And this is my Attorney General,' he goes. 'Mr Hennessy Coghlan-O'Hara!'

You have *got* to be focking shitting me.

'Raisa,' Fyodor goes, 'why don't you bring for us some vodka from the freezer. We have much to talk tonight.'

Oh, shit, he pushes the door and steps into the room. They all do – we're talking one, two, three, four of them. I can see their feet through the gap underneath the sofa.

'Come,' Fyodor goes, 'let us sit. For you, Mr President, the best seat in the house,' and a few seconds later the dude – yeah, no – plonks himself down on the sofa. It moves back a few inches, basically pinning me to the wall.

I'm suddenly shitting myself like a wildebeest at a watering hole.

'As I said to you at the airport,' the old man goes, 'I want Ireland and Russia to be firm friends, Mr President! I think we can do business together in a way that serves the interests of both our countries! Especially as we seek to form new allegiances once we exit the European Union!'

I hear Fyodor translate it into Russian, then this Putin dude says something back to him in presumably the same language.

'President Putin says that Ireland is a backwards nation,' Fyodor goes, 'full of idiot people with very poor-quality genes and women that look like pigs. He says for Russia there is nothing of interest in this country except for oil and gas and trees and also space to bury Russian waste.'

The old man laughs nervously. He's like, 'Well, I hope to change his mind over the course of his visit!'

My phone suddenly pings in my pocket and I quickly whip it out – my phone, I mean. Carolanne Bradley – as in, like, Juanita Bradley's old dear – says she did pork shoulder with port, juniper and orange in the slow cooker today.

'What was that?' this Putin dude goes.

The old man's like, 'What was what?'

I quickly switch my phone to Silent as a picture of Carolanne

Bradley's dinner comes through, along with the news that it's the first time she's used her slow cooker in years, but she's definitely going to use it a lot more now.

Putin says something in, like, Russian then, which Fyodor translates.

He goes, 'The President says he heard a ping.'

'A ping?' the old man goes. 'I didn't hear a ping! Did you hear a ping, Hennessy?'

'I didn't hear any ping,' Hennessy goes.

Carmencita Blake – as in, Sally Blake's old dear – says Wow! Then Joanne McAuley – as in, Ruth McAuley's old dear – says Yum! Mallorie Kennedy – as in, Courage Kennedy's old dear – says they don't eat meat in their house because they're obviously vegans, but she wonders would it work if she swapped out pork for root vegetables?

Fyodor goes, 'The President says he thought he heard a ping. He wants to be sure that you are not recording this conversation.'

The old man's there, 'I can assure you, Mr President, that nothing that's said within these four walls will travel beyond these four walls!'

Grainne Lessing – as in, Hester Lessing's old dear – says she would LOVE to become a vegan and the only things she would miss would be roast chicken, Hick's sausages and her mother's spaghetti Bolognese. Vanessa Mitchell – as in, Treasa Mitchell's old dear – says she's sorry she's late to this, but what's boxercise?

Raisa arrives in with the vodka. I can see her bare feet on the wooden floorboards.

'Thank you, my Darling,' Fyodor goes, then I hear the sound of him pouring it into glasses while Raisa focks off out of the room.

'Fyodor, can you tell the President that he does have a point!' the old man goes. 'Ireland was, for centuries, a backward, peasant country, but that's all changing now! We are advancing at a pace towards becoming a post-agricultural society! My Minister for Climate Action, who also happens to be my daughter-in-law, is about to introduce a bill that will have the effect of banning cows and sheep from Ireland!'

Putin says something and Fyodor goes, 'President Putin says she is like your St Patrick and the snakes, yes?'

The old man and Hennessy crack their holes laughing.

Amanda Mangan – as in, Tess Mangan's old dear – asks Mallorie Kennedy if she eats fish. Mallorie Kennedy says no, she never eats fish because she's a vegan. Amanda Mangan says that's a shame because she has an amazing recipe for a monkfish and cauliflower chowder that's both healthy and restaurant-worthy, which it should be because she got it from someone whose sister cuts Derry Clarke's hair.

The old man's like, 'What a wonderful sense of humour you have, Mr President! You'd humour a dying man! Anyway, this move – along with our mutual friend Fyodor's efforts to strip the country of its forests – moves us closer to my vision of Ireland's future outside of the European Union! I look forward to outlining it for you in full during the course of your visit!'

There's, like, silence for a good, like, ten seconds.

'Fyodor,' Hennessy goes, 'can you please translate what the Taoiseach just said?'

Except Fyodor doesn't. He just goes, 'What is this on floor?'

I look across the room and that's when I notice it. Oh, holy focking shitcakes! I must have dropped one of my socks. Yeah, no, I can see it on the floor across the other side of the room. He walks over to it and he picks it up off the ground.

He's there, 'It is sock. Blue sock.'

'A blue sock?' Hennessy goes. 'So fucking what?'

'I do not wear blue socks.'

'Well, maybe it's your wife's.'

'I do not recognize. What is this symbol?'

'It's a yellow horp!' the old man goes.

'But what does it mean?'

The old man's there, 'It's the insignia of Leinster rugby, don't you know!'

'Leinster rugby?' the dude goes.

'Yes, I recognize it because Ross has a pair of socks just like it! We bought him a pack of six for Christmas in the Leinster Rugby Store!'

Him and his big focking mouth.

'So now I wonder,' Fyodor goes, 'why is your son's sock in my living room?'

The old man's there, 'A mystery on a par with that of the famous Bermuda Triangle – exclamation mork, exclamation mork, exclamation mork!'

I swear to fock, I think I'm going to have an actual hort attack. Luckily, someone in the room has a bit of cop-on.

'It's *my* sock,' Hennessy suddenly goes. 'You, er, probably don't remember, Charlie, but you bought me a pack of six as well.'

The old man's there, 'Did I? I don't remember that, old scout!'

'Yeah, you did. Anyway, I got my laundry back this morning and it must have somehow gotten stuck in the pocket of these trousers.'

There's, like, silence from Fyodor and I know he doesn't believe him – except he doesn't want to call him a liar to his face.

'Mystery solved!' the old man goes. 'Now, let us toast the relationship between our two countries – and the end of the so-called European Union!'

'*Za ná-shoo dróo-zhboo!*' I hear this Putin dude go, then I hear the sound of glasses clinking. '*Pa-yé-kha-lee!*'

5.

A Shellfish Lover

It's, like, six o'clock in the morning when I finally get out of Fyodor's gaff. They end up talking all focking night. About bullshit mostly. Fyodor says he believes there is a lot of oil off the coast of Dalkey and probably off the coast of Kinsale too, while the old man says that Ireland could be a useful strategic ally to Russia, especially at the United Nations, whatever the fock that even means.

Putin challenges the others repeatedly to punch him in the stomach. And, over the course of the night, they bond while I lie on my side, wedged between the sofa and the wall, buck-naked and shivering with fear.

At some point, Putin says he wants to add a visit to Croke Pork to his itinerary. They've all had a lot of vodka at this stage. The old man tells him – 'word from the wise, old chap' – that it would be a complete and utter waste of his time. Putin says he heard it was a place of significant cultural and historic interest. The old man says someone has obviously got their stories twisted because the Aviva Stadium – formerly Lansdowne Road – is the real sporting hort of Ireland.

'I could ask young Ross to show you around!' the old man goes. 'He's my son! He could tell you a thing or two about the stadium's storied past – including his own role in it! St Patrick's Day, 1999 – eh, Hennessy?'

But Putin insists that it's Croke Pork that he wants to see and the old man says that, for the sake of relations between our two countries, he would ask his wonderful grandson, Ronan, to give him the tour.

Putin tells a few stories about his sexual conquests – he does very well for himself, even if only half of it is to be believed. Fyodor tells dirty jokes, few of which I actually get.

Finally, after what seems like an eternity, Putin focks off, followed by the old man and Hennessy, then Fyodor goes upstairs to bed. I crawl out from behind the sofa, throw on my clothes, then tiptoe to the front door.

I step out onto Longford Terrace, blinking in the bright dawn of a sunny June day – the eyes sunk in my head from literally, like, *no* sleep? I walk back to the cor, my hort rate finally coming down as relief washes over me.

My phone pings. Alva Crowe – as in, like, Ginny Crowe's old dear – says boxercise is a high-intensity interval training class based on boxing training. And, as I point the cor in the direction of Killiney, I stort to think about my next problem – what am I going to tell Sorcha? As in, where the fock have I been all night?

I could say I changed my mind about Finnegan's, I think, and I hit The Bridge instead. And there ended up being a lock-in – yeah, no – to celebrate Seán O'Brien's birthday. Except Sorcha knows that Seán O'Brien was born on Valentine's Day because I send him flowers every year without fail and it always ends up being a bone of contention when I forget to also send them to her.

I put my key in the door and I let myself in as quietly as I can. I head for the kitchen to grab a glass of water. And that's when Sorcha suddenly steps out of the study. She fixes me with a look and goes, 'Morning, Ross!'

Of course, I instantly go into babbling mode.

I'm there, 'It was, em, Dave Kearney's birthday drinks – the great, great, great, great Dave Kearney,' no idea what I'm even saying. 'One of the most underrated players ever to play the game in my humble view. When you think of some of the tries he scored for Leinster over the years, Sorcha. Against Castres? Against the Dragons? Come on, Sorcha! Give the goy his due!'

But that's when, totally out of left field, Sorcha goes, 'You're up early this morning. You do know that it's only half six?'

Now, I may not have played the game at the same level as Dave Kearney, but I'm smort enough to know when I've been thrown a dream pass.

I'm like, 'Yeah, I, er, must have set my alorm wrong.'

She goes, 'I didn't even hear you come in last night.'

'Yeah, no, it ended up being an early one in the end. Have you been in the study all night?'

'Yeah, I've been writing a speech. Fianna Fáil and Fine Gael have tabled a motion of no confidence in me.'

'Holy shit.'

'It's fine, Ross, they don't have the numbers for it to pass. But Seamon thinks I should use it as an opportunity to persuade people – including my counterports in all the other twenty-seven EU countries – that what I'm proposing here is, like, necessary if we're going to reverse the effects of global warming before it's too late.'

'That sounds pretty cool.'

'She also thinks I should make the point that banning cows and sheep shouldn't spell the end for rural communities – as long as the people who live in them actually embrace the change and stort thinking imaginatively. There are *other* types of forming? I've mentioned obviously wind. But then Claire and Garret have storted keeping chickens.'

'Nothing would surprise me about that pair – focking yokels.'

She goes silent for a bit then and, like, stares at a point just over my left shoulder. There's something else on her mind, and, for a second, I'm wondering can she see the toothmorks that Raisa made in my earlobe.

'I had another row with Fionn last night,' she goes. 'Worse than the last one.'

I'm like, 'Oh – er, bummer.'

'Do you think I'm being maybe *too* horsh, Ross?'

'Horsh? In terms of?'

'In terms of not letting him go away with Hillary?'

'Hey, he's your son as well, Sorcha.'

'He said tonight that I had a guilty conscience.'

'You can overcome that by pretending that you didn't do the thing that you actually *did* do? Does that make sense?'

'Well, I think he possibly had a point. I do feel bad – *as* a working mom – that I'm not getting to spend as much time around my boys as I want.'

'You've got a job to do, Sorcha. And it just so happens to be saving the planet.'

'That's what Sea-mon said. She said that if Hillary found himself growing up in a world where sea levels are rising at a rate of a quarter of an inch per year – and I had a chance to stop that but *didn't*? – I would never, ever forgive myself.'

'See-mon is one smort cookie. She could wash her focking hair once in a while, but she's talking definite sense in this case.'

'I'm just worried that Hillary will forget me, Ross.'

'Fionn won't let that happen.'

'You don't think?'

'Sorcha, me and Fionn have had our differences over the years. There's been a lot of bad blood, which goes back to me shitting in his shoes, shitting in the boot of his cor, shitting in his mother's MacBook. Then, of course, he got you pregnant. But when he got sick and very nearly died, it helped me realize something.'

'What?'

'I actually love the dude. And I don't just mean I love him for the rugby player he used to be, or for the assistant he was to me when I coached Pres Bray to the Leinster Schools Senior Cup this year. I mean I love him for the man he is and the man I would genuinely, genuinely love to be myself – obviously minus the glasses.'

'Oh my God, you're being very deep, Ross.'

It's obviously lack of sleep.

I'm there, 'Hey, it happens from time to time. And, when it does, I can't switch it off. Fionn is the very best of us, Sorcha. He won't let Hillary forget you. If I know Fionn, he'll be talking to him the entire time about his amazing mother back home who's doing important work trying to save the world.'

She smiles at me.

'Hey,' she goes, 'do you know what we should do now?'

I'm like, 'What? Seriously?'

'We've got, like, half an hour before the boys wake up. We haven't done it in ages.'

Speak for yourself, I nearly feel like saying.

'Oh my God,' she goes, 'do you remember how horny I used to get when I stayed up all night cramming for exams?'

I'm there, 'Why do you think I was always so keen for you to do courses? I used to leave those Smurfit Business School brochures all over the house.'

My phone all of a sudden rings.

'Who is it?' she goes.

I check the screen. I'm there, 'It's, er, Hennessy.'

She's like, 'Oh my God, why is he ringing so early? Do you want to maybe answer it?'

'Definitely, definitely not,' I go, then I grab Sorcha's hand and I lead her upstairs to the bedroom.

Astrid is a miracle worker. I say it to her as well.

I'm like, 'They're totally different children when they're here with you, Astrid. I'll get them home tonight and they'll be three little pricks again within about five minutes.'

'Is not a mystery,' the woman goes. I think I mentioned that she's not great in terms of looks. 'While they are here, they do not eat sugar. And when they use bad language, or they are violent to each other, I tell them to stop.'

'Well, I'm still using the phrase miracle-worker,' I go, 'because to me that's what you are.'

'The boys tell me they are going to German school in September.'

'Yeah, no, Sorcha managed to blag them into it. To be honest, we're lucky anyone's taking them. They'd be fairly widely known. Joe Duffy's done entire shows on them.'

'*Sehr gut*, Leo!' she suddenly goes.

Yeah, no, he's just finished a jigsaw of a dog. He's managed to put about ninety per cent of the pieces in the right places – the rest he's just sort of, like, forced in there with his fat thumbs.

He's like, '*Danke*, Nanny Astrid!'

I'm there, 'I'd say they'll be expelled pretty quickly, though, without their miracle nanny there. I'm using that word – you're just going to have to accept it.'

The old dear goes, 'You loved jigsaws when you were their age, Ross.'

I'm there, 'Did I?' because I'm beginning to really love these mornings, listening to stories about my childhood while hanging out with my brother and sisters, and – yeah, no – even her as well.

'Oh, yes,' she goes. 'As a matter of fact, I could leave you in the house on your own for five or six hours – go shopping, have lunch, maybe even visit the National Gallery with the girls – once you had a jigsaw in front of you.'

I'm there, 'Seriously, it's a genuine wonder that I wasn't taken into care.'

'When I'd arrive home, you wouldn't have completed very much of it. But you'd have this intense look on your face – this little frown of concentration on your forehead. And will I tell you something wonderful, Ross? Louisa May has exactly the same frown!'

I look at her. The old dear is holding her in her arms and – yeah, no – she's totally right. She looks like she's thinking really, really deeply about something, exactly the way I sometimes do?

'I have photographs of you as a baby,' the old dear goes, pointing at her Birkin bag on the changing table. 'Get them for me, will you please, Ross?'

I open her bag and I look inside.

She goes, 'It's a little album with a red cover,' and I find it pretty much straight away. I end up, like, flicking through it and – yeah, no – it's full of pictures of me as an actual baby.

I'm there, 'I didn't know you had this,' at the same time handing it to her.

'What?' she goes.

'Pictures of me in an album. In your actual handbag.'

'Just because I was a bad mother, Ross, doesn't mean I didn't love you – on *some* level.'

She finds the photo she was thinking about – me at, I don't know, maybe six months old.

'Here,' she goes, showing it to me, 'look at your little face and then look at Louisa May.'

I laugh. No choice in the matter. She *is* an absolute ringer for me?

'Why are you looking at me like that?' the old dear then goes.

I'm there, 'I don't know. I just love the way we are these days. As in, like, me and you – when we're, like, *around* each other?'

'Yes, it's nice, isn't it? By the way, I was right about Delma!'

'As in?'

'She is seeing someone. A younger man, Ross. Indecently young. Good for her, I say.'

'Did she tell you who it was?'

'Oh, she said his name. It didn't mean anything to me.'

'It's JP.'

'Yes, it might have been something like that.'

'No, I'm saying it *is* JP – as in, like, my *friend* JP?'

'I don't think I've met *him*, have I?'

'JP Conroy. His old man ran Hook, Lyon and Sinker. He was always in our gaff – especially if Delma was around. You caught him in the hallway once sniffing her good coat.'

'No, I can't place him.'

I stare at her face and I realize that she's being actually serious here. She has no memory of the dude at all.

I'm there, 'I'm just going to, er, pop down to the kitchen and grab another Bloody Mary. Do you want another one?'

'What a silly question!' she goes, meaning presumably yes.

She gets down on her hands and knees on the playmat then and storts making shite-talk to Cassiopeia and I use the distraction to go back over to her handbag. I poke around inside and I manage to find her fecal incontinence tablets, next to her Say Goodbye to Sweat Patches roll-on antiperspirant and a pamphlet on strengthening your pelvic floor.

I whip out the bottle and I go, 'Okay, two more Bloody Marys coming up. Extra voddy in yours,' and then I slip out of the crèche and down the corridor to the jacks.

I whip open the medicine cabinet and I notice a jor of just, like, regular paracetamol on the shelf. I open it and I spill some into my hand. Then I whip out the other tablet bottle, twist the cap and look inside. Yeah, no, they look pretty much the same – we're talking little white bullets. I lift the lid of the toilet and I empty the old dear's medication into it, then I flush it and I refill the bottle with the paracetamol.

And that's when I suddenly sense someone standing in the doorway, watching me. It ends up being Michael D. Higgins.

'I was hoping to use the bathroom,' he goes.

I'm like, 'Yeah, no, I'm sure that's allowed. I was just, er, swapping out my old dear's fecal incontinence meds for a – I *think* it's a word? – *pracebo*?'

He just, like, stares at me, obviously not knowing how to respond. I'd say people like us must come across as, like, total weirdos to him.

I'm there, 'So how's the house-hunting coming along?'

He goes, 'We went to see that Ant Farm place you recommended.'

'And?'

'Well, Ant Farm is an apposite description. I can't believe they expect human beings to live like that.'

'Are you talking about sleeping upright? Apparently you get used to it after a few weeks.'

'I'm talking about those little storage closets.'

'Yeah, no, the Homedrobes.'

'I don't know if you remember the speech I made at the switching-on of the Christmas lights in Eyre Square in 2006, but I said it wasn't enough for someone simply to have a home – it must be a home that affords them dignity.'

'I must have missed that one.'

'Ross, I know the Taoiseach is your father, but, for the first time in my life, I would say I'm deeply, deeply worried about the future of this country.'

'We are at a crossroads in history,' Sorcha goes. 'And what I would say to the leaders of the other twenty-seven EU countries is that our children, not to mention our children's children – *and* our children's children's children – will not thank us if we choose the wrong path.'

'Hear, hear!' the old man shouts, then all of his mates on the Government benches join in.

'MOOOOOO!!!!!!' the Fianna Fáil and Fine Gael heads shout. 'MOOOOOO!!!!!! MOOOOOO!!!!!! MOOOOOO!!!!!!'

I watch Sorcha's old man's entire body tighten, then out of the corner of his mouth he goes, 'How dare they subject my daughter to this kind of treatment – this baying mob!'

I think she's actually nailing it, although it's the Opposition's turn to speak next and they're apparently planning to be total dicks about the whole thing.

Which, by the way, they're *already* being?

'MOOOOOO!!!!!!' they keep going, with the occasional, 'BAA-AAAHHH!!!!!! BAA-AAAHHH!!!' until the Ceann Comhairle dude ends up having to ring his bell and go, 'I will have order or I will suspend the debate and clear this chamber. Deputy Cowen, get down off that chair!'

Sorcha's there, 'Thank you, Ceann Comhairle. Often in life, the easiest thing is to do nothing at all, while the hordest thing is to be brave. As Nelson Mandela – the late, great Madiba – once said, "Courage is not the absence of fear, but the triumph *over* it."'

'Hear, hear!' the old man shouts.

'MOOOOOO!!!!!!' the taunts stort up again. 'MOOOOOO!!!!!! MOOOOOO!!!!!!'

But Sorcha just shouts over it this time. She goes, 'Tackling the climate crisis is going to mean taking drastic steps. Yes, I would say to Phil Hogan, there will be pain in the short term for a great many people, especially in rural Ireland, but the payoff for future generations will be incalculable. In a hundred years' time, people will hopefully look back and say that the planet was saved *because* of the tough decisions taken by our generation – and by this Government. Thank you, Ceann Comhairle.'

There's, like, a roar from all the men – it's only men – on the Government benches and they all jump to their feet and give her a round of applause.

I turn around to Simone and I go, 'Nailed it.'

'It was a great speech,' the girl agrees.

The clamour then dies down and I shout, 'Fair focks, Sorcha!'

which she seems to appreciate, even though the Ceann Comhairle warns the people in the public gallery as to their future conduct.

'Now,' the same dude goes, 'I'm going to call on Deputy Barry Cowen, the Fianna Fáil spokesman for Agriculture.'

This dude climbs to his feet and goes, 'Ceann Comhairle, Minister Lalor mentioned in her speech certain alternatives to cattle and sheep farming in Ireland and one of those was wind. Well, if we were to harness the amount of wind in her statement, we'd never have to put up another turbine in this country again.'

The Opposition all laugh.

I'm there, 'It's a good gag, in fairness to it,' but Sorcha's old man turns around and just, like, glowers at me. It reminds me of the night of Sorcha's twenty-fifth, when he showed up in the Ice Bor wearing – quite literally – a bow-tie and I was paying people all night to go up to him and try to order a round of drinks from him.

'Hey, just because I'm married to the girl,' I go, 'it doesn't mean I can't appreciate a good one-liner.'

This, again, Cowen dude goes, 'What we are seeing, in the Minister's statement today, is nothing less than a full-frontal assault by this Government on rural Ireland and, in particular, on the farming community. Banning cows and sheep – does the Taoiseach not realize that we are the laughing stock of Europe?'

'We'll be the envy of Europe,' Sorcha shouts, 'and the rest of the world when we manage to reduce our emissions in accordance with the commitments we made when we signed up to the Paris Agreement!'

It's not a great comeback – and I'm saying that with the greatest will in the world – and the Ceann Comhairle dude ends up having to remind her that she has already had her opportunity to speak.

This Cowen dude is like, 'Minister, you will no doubt survive this Confidence Motion today with the help of your pals on that side of the House. But I'm going to make you a promise, Minister. Fianna Fáil will fight, with tooth and nail, any attempt by this Government to introduce a bill bringing this ridiculous idea into law, a move that would mean devastation for the Irish countryside, to say nothing of the beef industry that is the cornerstone of our indigenous economy.'

The old man jumps to his feet. 'The Deputy's roots are showing!' he shouts.

The Ceann Comhairle goes, 'Taoiseach, please take your seat!'

'He talks about the beef industry!' the old man goes. 'Yes, the very same beef industry to which Fiánna Fail has been beholden for years! Well, I'm happy to say that the notion that what was good for beef barons like Larry Goodman was good for Ireland has had its day, just like all of your other tired ideas! That's why the electorate rejected you and your Fine Gael cohorts there – by an overwhelming majority, need I remind you?'

'Sit down, Taoiseach!'

'Formers have held this country to ransom since Independence! I'll not take lectures on the economy from a man with the smell of shite off his boots!'

Suddenly, I feel a tap on my shoulder. I turn around and – oh, holy fock! – Hennessy is standing there.

I'm there, 'Er, hey, Dude – how the hell are you?' trying to keep it light and airy. 'Sorry I've been missing your calls.'

He's like, 'Come with me,' and I end up having no choice but to stand up and follow him out of the public gallery. Once we're outside in the corridor, he doesn't beat around the bush.

He's there, 'Did you fuck Fyodor's wife?'

I'm like, 'A gentleman never reveals these –'

I don't even manage to get the next word out. He reaches down and – I swear to fock – grabs a firm hold of my nuts and storts squeezing.

'Nnnggghhh!!!' I go.

He's like, 'Did you fuck her?'

I sort of, like, nod my head.

He goes, 'Your father and I are in a phase of negotiations with Fyodor and the Russian President that I would describe as –' and he suddenly gives my testicles a shorp twist like he's opening a jor of pickled beetroot.

'Nnnggghhh!!!' I go.

And he's like, '– delicate. I've just spent twenty-four hours trying to persuade Fyodor not to kill you. Do you know how close you came to ruining it all? Everything your father and I have worked for?'

I'm like, 'Nnnggghhh!!! I'm sorry! I didn't . . . Nnnggghhh!!! . . . realize I dropped the sock.'

'The sock?' he goes. 'How did you know he found the sock?'

'Because I was . . . Nnnnggghhh!!! . . . in the room. I'd just finished doing the deed when you goys walked in. I hid behind the . . . Nnnnggghhh!!! . . . sofa.'

'Wait a minute, you were in the room?'

'Yeah.'

'What, all night?'

'All night.'

'What did you hear?'

'Not much. I sort of, like, zoned in and out . . . Nnnggghhh!!! . . . I find it hord to follow conversations that aren't about either rugby or me.'

'I'm going to make you a promise now.'

'Nnnggghhh!!!'

'If Fyodor finds out about you and his wife, he won't have to kill you . . .'

'Nnnggghhh!!!'

'Because I'll fucking do it for him!'

'I thought we'd seen the last of this place!' the old man goes.

He's looking around him like we've just landed on some hostile, alien planet. It's Ballybough, so – yeah, no – I suppose we *have*?

'I'm having flashbacks to 2007!' he goes. 'All of us being bussed across town from Ballsbridge like bloody well animals! You know, until we emerged from the famous Port Tunnel, I don't think any of us had any idea that people still lived like this in the twenty-first century.'

The old dear's there, 'It's like *Strumpet City*, Chorles!'

'*Strumpet City!*' *he* goes. 'You took the words right out of my mouth, Dorling!'

Ronan seems to be enjoying himself, though. He's showing the famous, I don't know, Putin around and telling him a little bit about the supposed history of the place. They're surrounded by, like, Russian secret service agents wearing black leather jackets and permanently pissed-off faces. They look like the kind of dudes who would have turned you away from Club 92 back in the day because your shoes were too casual.

'You've heerd of Bloody Suddenday,' he goes, 'hab you?'

There's a dude doing the translating.

'Ah, U2!' Putin goes.

But Ronan's like, 'No, that was a diffordent Bloody Suddenday – happened in Deddy. There was anutter Bloody Suddenday happened hee-or at a match between Dublin and Tipperdeerdy. The Brits – the doorty, moorderding bastards – meerched in hee-or and opened foyer on the crowut, kidding fourteen iddocent people, including Mick Hogan, the Tipperdeerdy player. That stand oaber there is named in he's hodder.'

Putin hears all of this translated and he sort of, like, nods thoughtfully.

Then we all hear a sudden rip.

'Is your stomach a little unsettled, Dorling?' the old man goes out of the corner of his mouth.

The old dear's there, 'It's been upset all day, Chorles. Perhaps it was the thought of coming here.'

'Well, thank you again!' he goes. 'As I said to you this morning, this is above and beyond your duties as a First Lady!'

The press are all here as well, by the way, listening to Ronan doing the whole tour guide thing. Then, all of a sudden, I spot his mate Nudger walking across the pitch with a hurling stick in his hand. I'm not the only one who spots it either. The secret service agents suddenly draw their weapons and rush towards him and before Nudger has time to say, 'What's the stordee, feddas?' they have him pinned face-down to the pitch with six pistols pointing at the back of his head and a shiny George Webb pressing down on his neck.

Ronan goes, 'It's alreet, feddas, it's norra weapodden. It's called a hurdle. You use it for playing hurdling – which is one of eer nationod-dle gayums.'

The dudes help Nudger to his feet and they dust him down, all apologies. He's there, 'You're gayum ball, feddas,' as he hands the hurling stick over to Putin. 'Jaysus, they're strong lads, wha'?'

The photographers all crowd around as Ronan pulls a hurling ball out of the pocket of his pin-striped trousers and hands it to Putin. The dude stares at the two things like he has absolutely no idea what one has to do with the other.

'The stick – like I said to you – is called a hurdle,' Ronan goes, 'and the ball is called a shlithor. See the posts down theer? Well, you hab to hit the shlithor with the hurdle and try to get it eeder oaber the bar for a point or in the goawult for tree points.'

Putin nods like he understands. He's a better man than me. Ronan's explained it to me hundreds of times over the years and I still don't fully understand the point of the whole exercise. The dude could be just humouring him of course.

'So go odden,' Ronan goes, 'gib it a go.'

Everyone steps back to give the dude space. He sizes up the goal.

'Now,' Ronan goes, 'you've got to thrun the shlithor in the air, wait'll it comes dowun, then gib it a bleaten beddelt with the hur-dle. Do you get me?'

So – yeah, no – Putin does what he's told. Except when he throws the ball up in the air, there's another sudden rip from the general direction of my old dear's orse. Putin swings the stick too early and manages to totally miss the ball.

Everyone turns and just, like, stares in my old dear's general postcode.

'Road works,' the old man goes, trying to cover up for her.

Ronan's there, 'Gib it anutter go, Mister Presserdiddent. Doataunt swig it too eerdy. You've got to wait till it falls – do you get me?'

Putin nods. Then he tries it again. Same result. He ends up swing-ing at fresh air as the ball hits the ground with a clump. Putin hands the two things back to Ronan and says something to him in Russian.

'The President says that your bat and ball are broken,' the transla-tor goes.

The old man sidles up to me then.

He's like, 'It seems your mother has had something of an accident! It must be all the lead in the air out here! We're going to discreetly slip away! I'll see you tomorrow night, won't I?'

I'm there, 'What's tomorrow night?'

'The State banquet in President Putin's honour! Sorcha's going to be there – I just presumed she'd be taking you as her significant other!'

'Yeah, no, she did mention it now that I remember it.'

'I can't wait to see President Putin's face when he sees the gift I have for him!'

I notice the old dear walking towards Kennet's cor cowboy-style.

'Anyway,' the old man goes, 'like I said, your mother requires a change of clothes! I'm wondering should we maybe see about switching those tablets she's on!' and off he focks.

Ronan's still gabbing away. He'd have made a good teacher.

He's there, 'The utter spowurt what's played hee-or is Gaedic footbalt.'

'Gay dick,' Putin goes.

'No, Gaedic.'

'Gay dick.'

'Gaedic.'

'Gay dick.'

'Gaedic footbalt.'

'Gay dick footballed.'

The dude says something to the translator, who then goes, 'The President wants to know is this a game for homosexuals?'

God, they're focking gay-obsessed, the Russians.

'No, no,' Ronan goes, 'addyone can play. It dudn't mathor if you're gay or sthraight.'

'In Russia, it matters very much,' the translator goes. 'The President says perhaps the less he knows about this game, the better.'

Ronan takes Putin and his entourage off then to see the Croke Pork museum. That's when I catch Nudger's eye and gesture to him that I want a word. So – yeah, no – we step to one side.

He's like, 'What's the stordee, Rosser?'

And I'm there, 'I'm worried about Ronan.'

'Woodied?'

'Yeah, no, I'm talking about these, like, *chorges* that he's facing?'

'He toawult me thee fowunt the gudden.'

'Yeah, no – and also a witness who saw him fock it into the lake in UCD.'

'He's boddixed so, Rosser. At least Heddessy is godda keep him odden the payroll, eeben if he does toyum.'

'Hennessy set him up, Nudger.'

'What?'

'I'm convinced of it. To stop him going to the States. Him and that K . . . K . . . K . . . K . . . K . . . Kennet.'

Nudger is no fan of the stuttering fock.

'I wouldn't put it past that fedda,' he goes.

I'm there, 'It was *his* actual gun, Nudger.'

'Ro toawult me, yeah.'

'So what are we going to do about it?'

'What cadden we do?'

'Come on, Nudger, you're one of the dodgiest fockers I've ever met – no offence to you. Surely, you can think of some way of getting him out of this.'

'I'll ted you what,' he goes. 'I'll arrange a sit-down – me, you, Buckets of Blood and Gull. We'll put our bleaten heads togetter in The Broken Eerms. And, howebber long it takes, we'll cub up wirra way to gerrim ourra this Jaysusin mess.'

The old man is in his element. By that I mean he's already half-titted and this is before we've even had our storters. He stands up and raises his glass – his third toast in the last, like, fifteen minutes.

'To new friends!' he goes.

Everyone is just like, 'To new friends!' lifting their drinks in the air, then he sort of, like, flops back down onto his seat again.

Out of the corner of her mouth, Sorcha tells me she's – oh my God – *so* embarrassed.

I'm like, 'What are you embarrassed about?'

'I told you it was black tie,' she goes, because – yeah, no – out of the hundred or so people who are seated for dinner, I'm the only one wearing just a Leinster jersey and chinos.

I'm there, 'I thought you just said it was a formal dinner.'

'And what do you think a formal dinner means?' she goes.

'I don't know. One where you're on your best behaviour. Don't talk with your mouth full. Don't take food from anyone else's plate without asking them first. Blah, blah, blah.'

'You focking *know* what formal means, Ross. You got dressed up for Jamie Heaslip's big night.'

She's talking about the night me and Oisinn blagged our way into the Leinster Awards Ball in the Mansion House to see the big man collect the Player of the Year Award. I'm tempted to point out that she's not Jamie Heaslip, but I'm not sure it would do anything to advance my case.

She's not the only one at the table who's, like, fixated with what I'm wearing, by the way. Fyodor is just, like, staring at my jersey – or, more specifically, the yellow horp on my right pec. He's obviously finding it – what's the word? – *triggering*?

Raisa, sitting next to him, is acting like she's totally oblivious to it. And – yeah, no – I decide to just, like, brazen it out as well.

I'm there, 'It's great to get out of the house, isn't it, Raisa? You look fantastic, by the way. I love your dress, and I mean that genuinely.'

She just, like, glowers at me.

To my right, I've got Gordon Greenhalgh, the Minister for Housing, Planning and Local Government, who's brought his foxy but equally irritating daughter Lychee as his plus-one.

'Oh my God!' she goes. 'Ross, can you do that again?'

I'm like, 'Do what again?'

'When you told Raisa that she looked well, you sort of, like, made your pectoral muscles move?'

'That was, like, an unconscious thing. So focking what?'

She shows me her phone.

'I just wanted to film it,' she goes, 'and put it on, like, TikTok?'

Focking millennials.

She goes, 'Excuse me?' because it seems I said it out loud.

I'm there, 'We're not all, like, actors in the focking movie of your life, Lychee.'

All of a sudden, at the next table, the famous Putin dude stands up. He looks like he's had a skinful as well. As a matter of fact, my old man puts his hand underneath his elbow to steady him as he gets to his feet.

The old dear taps her fork off her glass. She's either asking for silence or letting the sommelier know that she needs a top-up. She ends up getting both.

'Good . . . evening!' Putin goes – yeah, no, he's mashed alright.

His interpreter stands up beside him and storts translating.

He's like, 'Good evening!'

Everyone laughs because it's the same thing his boss just said.

Putin launches into this, like, long and rambling speech then. When he eventually stops to take a breath, the interpreter goes, 'When I first come to Ireland, I did not expect to like very much. I think is backwards country with backwards people. Also, lots of rain and the women so ugly as to make you sick in your stomach.'

I watch the old man and Hennessy both nod, like the dude has said something of, I don't know, real significance.

Off he goes again. Sixty seconds of blah, blah, blah in Russian before the interpreter goes, 'But in the days that I have spent here, I have fallen a little bit in love with Ireland. Not just the country but also the people, who are very much like Russians in that they always wear shit clothes and they are miserable when they are not drinking the alcohol.'

Everyone laughs. I don't think he was joking, though.

'On my trip,' the dude continues, 'I met a very special man, who extended the hand of friendship to me and to all Russians. That man is Charles O'Carroll-Kelly. He is strong leader – much like me. Our countries have very much in common and I hope, through my growing friendship with this man, Russia and Ireland can forge a very special relationship.'

'I'll drink to that!' the old man shouts, attempting to get to his feet but failing.

It's Putin's turn again. He bangs on for another thirty seconds, then the interpreter goes, 'I would like to mark my visit with a special award for my new friend. That is why I am very proud to give to Charles today –'

Putin reaches into the pocket of his tux and whips out a little box.

And the interpreter dude goes, '– the Order of Friendship!'

There are, like, gasps all around the room. It's obviously a pretty big deal. The old man stands up and puts his hand over his hort. For a second, I'm wondering is his *ticker* going to give way again?

'What an honour!' he goes, as Putin opens the box and whips the thing out. It's, like, a medal on a long piece of red ribbon. 'A signal honour! Exclamation mork! Exclamation mork! Exclamation mork!'

The old man dips his head and Putin hangs the thing around his neck.

Lychee stands up and she's like, 'Oh my God, I missed it! Can you, like, do that again?' except everyone just ignores her and she sits back down again.

'I thought we were going to do presents *after* dinner!' the old man goes. 'But, seeing as you've given me this wonderful gift, I should like to reciprocate now by presenting you with a gift of my own!'

Ronan is sitting next to Shadden at the same table. The old man gives him a nod and Ro reaches underneath his chair before whipping out – yeah, no – the famous Book of Kells. He hands it to the old man.

'Can you please explain to President Putin that this is the Book of Kells!' the old man goes. 'It's more than one thousand years old! I don't know much more about it than that, just that it is one of our country's most priceless treasures and I would like you to have it as a token of our new-found friendship!'

He hands it across the table to him while the interpreter fills the dude in on the story. Putin just, like, stares at the thing. You can tell he's disappointed and you wouldn't focking blame him.

I remember Sorcha buying me a Harry Potter book for Christmas once after I made some comment about possibly wanting to improve my mind. Poor Putin is obviously going through pretty much the same thing as I went through then. I don't care how old the thing is, a book is the shittest present you can give to someone and I genuinely mean that.

Everyone waits for the dude to say something by way of thanks. After, like, ten seconds of silence, he mutters something under his breath and the interpreter goes, 'President Putin has asked me to say that the Order of Friendship is a very, very special honour and this book you have given him in return does not please him.'

He's totally within his rights to say it. I remember saying something similar to Sorcha and she practically focked the gift receipt at me. As it turned out, the shop would only give me a credit note, so I exchanged it for three black Shorpies, which me and JP used to write slanderous things about Blackrock College on every bus shelter between Temple Hill and the Horse Show House the night before the 2005 Leinster Schools Senior Cup final. I've heard a few people say that it was one of the reasons Blackrock lost.

There ends up being, like, silence in the room.

Sorcha goes, 'Oh my God, I can't believe he's not happy with the actual Book of Kells!'

'I can't believe I missed another moment,' Lychee goes.

And I'm there, 'Have your phone ready – from the look on his face, I think he's going to fock it across the table at him.'

'Like I said,' the old man goes, 'it's a very, very important book. I think it might even be the oldest book in the world.'

Putin mutters something else to the interpreter, who goes, 'President Putin has asked me to say that this afternoon he visited the wonderful passage grave at Newgrange. He would consider this to be a suitable gift from Ireland as a sign of our friendship.'

'You want me to give you Newgrange?' the old man goes.

Putin just nods.

'And what would you do?' the old man goes. 'Just dig it out and then ship it back to Mother Russia?'

The interpreter goes, 'President Putin says this will not be a difficulty. He can send men who will do this work.'

The old man looks across the table at Hennessy, who just shrugs his shoulders like he couldn't give a fock one way or the other.

'It's yours!' the old man goes. 'Take it whenever you wish!'

'A wonderful gesture!' Gordon Greenhalgh turns to me and goes. 'Your father is a terribly generous man!'

I'm there, 'I don't know about that. I saw Newgrange once on a school trip and I thought it was boring. I'm not even sure it's that much of an improvement on the book.'

Sorcha suddenly throws her two hands over her eyes. She's like, 'Oh my God, Shadden has just knocked a glass of wine all over the Book of Kells!'

She stands up then.

She's like, 'I have to go to the bathroom,' and off she goes.

I stort telling Raisa the famous Harry Potter story, but she has zero interest in it and I abandon it mid-sentence when our storters finally arrive.

We're having, like, Clew Bay oysters and I'm trying to remember if I like them or not. I pick up one of the shells and I tip its contents into my mouth and I suddenly remember that I don't like them. They remind me of nearly drowning.

I decide to spit the thing out. And, given that this is – Sorcha's words – a formal dinner, I decide it would be bad form to just gob it into my hand, which is why I reach into my pocket and I pull out a tissue.

And that's when it happens.

Something flies out of it across the table and lands smack bang in the middle of Fyodor's plate. He stares down at it for a good, like, ten seconds, like he's trying to figure out if it really is what it looks like, or whether his mind is playing tricks on him.

I know straight away what it is. And, judging from the way the colour is draining from her face, it's pretty obvious that Raisa knows what it is too.

It's the used Russian flag Johnny that I borrowed from Fyodor to have sex with his wife.

I go, 'Dude, you can buy those bad boys anywhere – Tesco, Boots . . .' and I realize that I'm suddenly babbling, something I tend to do when I'm in fear of my life. 'Lidl, Aldi, blah, blah, blah.'

He storts muttering something madly under his breath, then he picks up his oyster shucker, holds it in his clenched fist, and launches himself across the table at me, sending glasses flying everywhere.

I end up actually screaming as the dude grabs me by the front of

my Leinster jersey and he holds the oyster shucker in front of my face like he's getting ready to jam it into my eye.

'You fuck my fucking wife!' he goes. 'You fuck my fucking wife!' and, out of the corner of my eye, I can see that Lychee is filming the incident.

I'm going, 'McCabes Phormacy,' still naming places where you can supposedly buy the dude's signature zepps. 'I'd be shocked if the Allcare in the Merrion Centre doesn't do them.'

He's just about to bring the shorp end of the shucker down on my beautiful face when all of a sudden someone grabs his wrist. I'm relieved to see that it's Ronan. He manages to wrestle the weapon out of his hand, then five or six members of Putin's security detail arrive on the scene, pick poor Fyodor up and carry him outside. Raisa runs out after them.

There's, like, total and utter silence in the room again.

The old man goes, 'No more vodka for table two!' then everyone laughs and goes back to their storters and their conversations.

Literally twenty seconds later, Sorcha arrives back at the table, totally oblivious to what's gone down.

'Oh my God,' she goes, 'who knocked over all the glasses?'

And, cool as the bed of crushed ice on which Fyodor's used Johnny still sits, I turn around and go, 'Yeah, no, it was Fyodor. It turns out he's allergic to shellfish.'

'Oh my God,' Sorcha goes, 'one of my best friends in UCD had the exact same thing. She had to carry an epi pen with her everywhere she went. Hey, Ross, I've been thinking about what you said – about Fionn.'

I'm like, 'Yeah, no, what about him?'

'You were totally right. He would never let Hillary forget about me. So I'm going to tell him I don't mind him taking him around the world for a year.'

I'm there, 'Er, yeah, no, cool.'

'And I'm sorry I gave you such a hord time for not wearing a tux tonight,' she goes, leaning in and kissing me. 'You're an amazing husband, Ross.'

And, in that moment, I just happen to catch the eye of President

Putin at the next table. He has this, like, expression on his face – one that I recognize only too well from my days as the best schools rugby player in the country.

It's a look of total and utter awe.

The Broken Orms is quite literally heaving. People are standing on chairs and tables and the walls are dripping with sweat. And the roars would nearly deafen you.

Nudger's girlfriend, Blodwyn, is taking on the famous Rashers Falvey for the Finglas All-Comers Dorts Championship and the atmosphere is electric.

She has this, I don't know, interesting playing style, insofar as I'm a judge of working-class people and the things that amuse them. Yeah, no, she doesn't, like, compose herself between her throws the way that Rashers does. She stands behind the line of masking tape on the floor and stares at the board for ages – we're talking, like, totally zen – with the dorts in her left hand, then she suddenly explodes into life, passing each dort in turn from her left to her right, then focking them at the board, one after the other – bam, bam, bam – in an absolute flurry of movement.

But – yeah, no – it's obviously working for the girl because she's handing Rashers his orse here and she looks on course to win the De'Longhi La Specialista Bean to Cup Pump Espresso Coffee Machine – which I'm guessing is so focking hot, you'd need focking oven gloves to operate the thing.

'One hundred and fooortyyyyyy!!!!!!' roars the owner's son. I don't know his name, but they call him The Yank because he wore a baseball cap once about thirty focking years ago.

See, that's what they're like around here. As a matter of fact, some total randomer shouts at me, 'Where'd you peerk the boat?' which is obviously a reference to the red Helly Hansen crew jacket I'm wearing and obviously my Dubes.

I spot Nudger, sitting with Buckets of Blood and Gull at a low table, absolutely glued to the action.

I'm like, 'Hey, goys,' and the three of them turn and look at me. Nudger and Buckets go, 'Howiya, Rosser!' but Gull says nothing – because he never does – then they all go back to watching Rashers throw.

'One hundred and eightyyyyyy!!!!!!' the Yank goes and there ends up being a roar from – let's just call them – the *away* fans?

'Hee-or, Annalise Murphy,' another randomer shouts in my general direction, 'sit the fook dowun!' and everyone laughs.

Side note – I'm actually a little bit in love with Annalise Murphy. I remember one night she porked her Mercedes X-class pick-up right next to my Audi A8 in an otherwise empty Royal Irish Yacht Club cor pork and managed to bump my door when she was getting out. She must have caught me rolling my eyes – there was, like, two hundred empty spaces in there – because she was suddenly standing at my window, going, 'Have you got a problem?'

I was like, 'Er, no,' suddenly realizing who she was – not just someone I seriously fancied, but someone who'd done it at the highest level of her sport.

'Are you sure?' she went, raising her voice to make herself heard through the glass. 'Because you *seem* to have a problem?'

I was there, 'Yeah, no, I don't, Annalise – I definitely, definitely don't,' and I wanted so much to buy her a Teddy's and watch her eat it as we walked the pier together, but I lost my nerve and I just couldn't ask.

'I said sit the fook dowun,' the same randomer goes again. 'I caddent see what's going odden.'

So I end up sitting down, next to – I'm presuming – Nudger and Blodwyn's three kids, who are far too young to be in a pub at nine o'clock at night, by the way. One of them's an actual baby. But then my old dear left me on my own in a shitty nappy to go and have lunch with her mates in the National Gallery, which makes Nudger look like Father of the Year material.

I'm like, 'How's it going, goys?'

They're all there, 'Howiya, Rosser?' because they're all big, big fans of mine.

Buckets goes, 'Nudger was saying you think Kennet set Ronan up.'

I'm there, 'Yeah, no, I do. Him and Hennessy. To stop him going to the States. Goys, ever since Ro was a kid, you three have looked out for him and tried to keep him on the straight and narrow. I honestly don't want to think what might have happened if he didn't have you watching over him, making sure he didn't go down a bad road. But, goys, he's going down that road now. Hennessy and my old man have him doing all sorts of dodgy shit. He needs your help, goys – now more than ever.'

My little speech obviously works because Nudger, Buckets and Gull are all suddenly looking at each other with big, serious heads on them.

'John Haskins is a boddicks,' Buckets goes. 'Fitted a mate of moyun up – Psycho Byrne – and the fedda ended up doing a ten-sthretch.'

I'm like, 'Ten years?'

'That was arthur persuading him to plead giddilty,' he goes, 'on the probise of oately seerving two.'

I'm there, 'Could we maybe –'

'What?'

'I don't know, *threaten* him in some way?'

Three sets of eyes go wide.

'You want to threaten a member of An Geerda Síocháda?' Nudger goes.

Buckets is like, 'What are you godda threaten him wit, Rosser? A whack over the head wit one of those sailing shoes?'

I'm there, 'Maybe if we keyed his cor? Or wrote something in red paint on it, telling him to back off – this case is too hot, blah, blah, blah?'

The goys get a good kick out of that – even Gull laughs.

'Hee-or,' Buckets suddenly goes, 'do you know what was odden the teddy the utter night? *The Genderdoddle*!'

I'm like, 'The what?'

'The filum. About Meertin Cahill. *The Generdoddle*.'

I smile. I remember when Ronan was a child, I used to read the book to him before he went to sleep. He used to make me do the accents and everything.

'There's a bit in the fillum,' Buckets goes, 'where he breaks into the office of the Didector of Public Prosecutions and he steals a buddench of foyuls ourra the place.'

Nudger's face lights up. He's there, 'Are you saying what I think you're saying?'

''Thee hab the gudden,' he goes, 'and thee hab a witness to say thee saw Ronan fook it in the lake. But what if the gudden was to go missing? Vital ebidence mislaid – the case would have to be thrun out. Wouldn't eeben get to cowurt.'

I'm like, 'Are you talking about, like, stealing it?'

'All the ebidence in seerdious crimidal cases,' he goes, 'is stored in the Phoedix Peerk. Ine saying we do what The Generdoddle did.'

'Break in?'

'You bethor fooken belieb it.'

I look at Nudger. He's, like, deep in thought. This is a man, bear in mind, who's tunnelled his way into actual bank vaults. The *Sunday World* nicknamed him The Mole. I think it was actual Paul Williams who came up with it.

I'm there, 'Is it possible – to, like, break in?'

'It's possible to break in addywheer,' he goes. 'The question is, is it woort the risk. I've tree kids now, Rosser, and anutter on the way,' and I'm thinking, Yeah, no, I thought Blodwyn looked pregnant throwing the dorts up there. 'Me and Blod made an agreement that needer of us was going back insuyut.'

Buckets goes, 'But this is Ronan, Nudger. He's in thrubble. He gets a record, it'll desthroy he's bleaten life.'

Nudger just nods. 'Ine godda need a map,' he goes, 'showing the layout of the place.'

Buckets is there, 'Gull will get you a map.'

Gull just nods.

I'm there, 'This has turned very *Mission Impossible* all of a sudden, hasn't it?'

Nudger goes, 'It's no fooken joke, Rosser. We get caught doing this, we're looken at jayult toyum eerselves, do you wontherstand?'

'Yes,' I go, 'I understand.'

I can feel my hort suddenly beating fast.

He's like, 'This idn't like breaking into the bank, where the aleerm goes off and you've twenty midutes befower the Geerds arroyuv and the lead steers floying. In this case, the Geerds are altreddy theer.'

Buckets sort of, like, laughs to himself. 'If we madage to pud this off,' he goes, 'it'll go dowun as one of the greatest sthrokes in histoddy. Stealing edibence from reet unther the noses of the Geerds.'

'The oately question,' Nudger goes, 'is how do we do it? Do we go under the wall? Do we go troo the wall? Do we go troo the roof? That's what I hab to woork out.'

Nudger suddenly grips my leg hord. He's like, 'Double top to win it, Rosser!'

Blodwyn throws just one dort this time and it ends up being, like, bang on the money. The entire place goes ballistic. And, as he and five or six others lift the pregnant Blodwyn up onto their shoulders, Nudger turns around to me and goes, 'Doatunt woody, Rosser – I'll cub up with a pladden and I'll be in touch.'

I'm there, 'Dude, I owe you for this big-time. If there's any way I can ever repay you–'

'There is,' he goes.

I'm like, 'Fock, I didn't mean literally. It was a more a figure of –'

'You can buy the coffee machine off Blod,' he goes. 'Two hundoord snots.'

'Well, *someone* made an impression on Vladimir Putin!' the old man goes.

This is on, like, the phone.

I'm there, 'Really?'

'Oh, he couldn't stop talking about you,' he goes, 'all the way to the airport!'

I'm there, 'In terms of specifics, what was said?' because I'm a sucker for a compliment.

'He said, "Your boy has ice in his veins!" '

'Right,' I go, 'and he definitely meant that as a compliment, did he?'

'I said to him, "You should have seen him play rugby, Mister President! He was absolutely ruthless on the field!" '

'I was.'

'Although I don't know what the hell has got into Fyodor! He's very upset, Ross!'

'Yeah, I was the one he tried to stab in eye with an *oyster* shucker, bear in mind?'

'He seems to have gotten it into his head that something happened between you and the lovely Raisa!'

'Nothing happened.'

'That's what I said! Ross is a happily married man, I told him! Anyway, Hennessy is with him now! I told him to sell him the Cloosh Valley! Four thousand hectares of trees! I'm sure that will help appease the chap!'

'Whatever.'

'Yes, a successful week all round, I would have said! Ronan dropped the Book of Kells back to Trinity! They weren't a bit grateful to have it back either! All they could talk about was the bloody wine that was spilled on it!'

'I hate books. They cause nothing but trouble.'

'Speaking of Ronan, I wanted to have a word with you about something, Kicker! Well, as you know, it's his twenty-first birthday in September and your mother and I were trying to come up with a suitable present for him!'

'I usually buy him hash.'

'We were thinking of giving him the house in Foxrock!'

'Jesus.'

'What?'

'I don't know. Ronan and Shadden living in Foxrock. It's funny.'

'You wouldn't have any objection, Ross, would you – as our eldest son and heir?'

'No, like I said, it'll be worth it just to see how the neighbours react.'

'It's just that I'm anxious that Shadden and young Rihanna-Brogan should have a roof over their heads – in the event of Ronan, well –'

'He's not going to prison.'

'Look, Hennessy is still doing his best to get the chorges dropped, but the eyewitness and the discovery of the gun have changed everything!'

'He's not going to prison because I'm not going to let it happen! I've got a plan! End of conversation!'

'Right – well, anyway,' he goes, 'I'd better go and check on your mother! She had the doctor earlier!'

I'm like, 'The doctor? Is she okay?' and I can hear the concern in my voice.

'No, just a small issue of a personal nature,' he goes, 'that we probably don't need to go into! Bowel leakage and so forth! It turns out the idiots in the chemist who filled her prescription gave her paracetamol! Have you ever heard the likes of it, Ross!'

'No. It's, er, definitely random.'

'Anyway, I've told the doctor to put her on something different! The last tablets she was on made her terribly forgetful!'

'Maybe if she didn't *drink* with them?'

He laughs like this is the most ridiculous thing he's ever heard.

'Drink?' he goes. 'Your mother barely touches the stuff! Anyway, tell Honor I'll ring her tomorrow! I want to wish her all the best before she sets off for the famous Gaeltacht!'

He hangs up and I go back to trying to set up the De'Longhi La Specialista Bean to Cup Pump Espresso Coffee Machine. There's, like, no instruction manual with it. It didn't even come with a box. On the underside, written in Tipp-Ex, it says: Property of Richard Bruton TD – DO NOT REMOVE FROM CONSTITUENCY CLINIC!

I've been forting around with it for a full hour now and – unlike my old dear, I'm tempted to say – there hasn't been so much as a dribble of brown water out of it. So – yeah, no – I decide to ask Honor if she can maybe try to get it working. I tip up the stairs. When I reach the landing, I can hear Erika's voice coming from Honor's room and it's obvious they're, like, *Skyping* again?

I'm about to knock on the door, because I'm interested in seeing how Erika's looking – *if* that's not too weird a thing to say about your own half-sister – and also what she's wearing.

But, just as my knuckles are poised, I hear Honor go, 'My dad is my best friend in the world – I mean, how focking sad is that?'

Which – yeah, no – I have to admit, *stings* a bit?

Erika goes, 'Ross is not nearly as bad as people say,' at least defending me. 'Yes, he's in love with himself and totally deluded about a lot of things, including rugby. But he's a good father, Honor.'

'He's an amazing father,' Honor goes, and, for a second, I manage to blank out Erika's crack about my rugby, which I thought was definitely unnecessary. 'But I don't have any friends my *own* age?'

Erika's like, 'What about Sincerity?'

'She's only nice to me because she feels sorry for me. And anyway, she's a focking knob.'

'But maybe that's *why* you don't have any friends, Honor.'

'Excuse me?'

'Because you talk about people like that. She might not be cool, Honor, but there are more important things in the world.'

'Are you actually being serious right now?'

'I'm only saying this, Honor, because I can see so much of myself in you. Ask your dad what I was like when we were teenagers.'

Gorgeous, I think. She looked like Denise Richards except even hotter.

'I was a bitch,' Erika goes.

Yeah, no, that's *also* true?

Honor's like, 'I love that you're a bitch. It's one of the things we have in common.'

'But where has it gotten me?' Erika goes. 'I'm nearly forty –'

'You'd pass for thirty,' I whisper under my breath. 'Certainly in terms of body.'

'And look at me, Honor. I'm a single mom, still living with my mother. I have no one.'

Honor's like, 'You have Amelie.'

'She's my daughter, Honor. What I mean is, I have no friends. I have no man in my life. All I'm saying is, don't be too quick to push people away. Because, believe me, it will lead to a life of loneliness.'

'Okay.'

'When are you going to Irish college?'

'The day after tomorrow. Dad's driving me.'

'Is it Lurgan or Galway?'

'Neither.'

'Neither?'

'Yeah, no, my stupid bitch of a mother left it too late to book. So I've ended up going to some shithole in Kerry where, like, *no one* I know is going to be?'

'Well, that's good.'

'Er, *how*?'

'Because it means you're not arriving with any baggage. No one knows the first thing about you. So you can be whoever you want to be.'

'I suppose.'

'Just give people a try, Honor. They're not so bad.'

All of a sudden, I feel a hand on my shoulder and I end up nearly having a focking prolapse.

'Jesus Christ!' I go, spinning around.

It ends up being Fionn, who's standing there with little Hillary in his orms. He doesn't say shit. He just throws one orm around me and hugs me tight.

I'm there, 'Sorcha obviously mentioned that I had a word with her.'

But he just goes, 'I love you, Ross.'

My phone pings. It ends up being a photograph from Carmencita Blake – as in, like, Sally Blake's old dear – of a glass of red wine. Then a couple of seconds later she says the kids are off to Irish college tomorrow – plenty more of these over the next three weeks! Joanne McAuley – as in, Ruth McAuley's old dear – says OMG yes! Grainne Power – as in, Conwenna Power's old dear – asks her if she's driving to Lurgan and Joanne says yes, she couldn't expect her daughter to get on a train or a bus. Alva Crowe – as in, Ginny Crowe's old dear – says does anyone know which Irish college Honor O'Carroll-Kelly is going to and she just hopes it's not Spleodar. Grainne Power says this isn't the Orchestra Moms group and Alva Crowe goes, OMG mortified!

I look up and I see the three dudes walking towards me. I actually laugh.

'Where the fock did you get the uniforms?' I go.

Yeah, no, Nudger, Buckets and Gull are all dressed up as, like, Gords. They look like a really shit striptease act.

Buckets goes, 'Ways and means, Rosser,' at the same time tapping his nose. 'Ways and means.'

Nudger still hasn't told me shit about this plan of his. Which is understandable enough. He couldn't exactly explain it to me over the phone. He just told me to meet him and the goys at the Wellington Monument at, like, six o'clock and that was all he said.

I'm looking around, wondering where the shovels are.

'In terms of the actual digging,' I go, 'I probably should mention now that manual labour wouldn't be my *strongest* suit? I damaged my rotator cuff back in the day.'

Nudger's there, 'We're not digging our way in, Rosser.'

I'm like, 'So, er, how are we going to get in there?'

'We're godda walk in,' he goes, 'through the fruddent dowur.'

Buckets is like, 'That's why we're thressed as Geerds.'

'But hang on,' I go, 'we can't just morch in there. I mean, presumably, there's, like –'

'What?'

'I don't know – laser tripwires? Retina-scan door locks?'

The three of them act like this is the funniest thing they've ever heard.

'You're arthur watching too meddy Tom Carooz fillums,' Buckets goes. 'It's the fooken Geerds, Rosser!'

'Okay, cool,' I go. 'So we morch in the front – and do we know where we're going from there?'

Nudger is like, 'The basemiddent. The ebidence roowum is down theer, next to the ceddle block.'

I'm there, 'So, like, where's *my* uniform?'

'We habn't got wooden for you,' Nudger goes.

I'm there, 'Dude, don't you focking dare try to cut me out of the plan. Ronan is *my* son and I'm going in there with you.'

'Oh, you're cubbing in wirrus alreet,' he goes. 'It's just you're godda be the fedda we addested.'

I'm there, 'I'm what?'

'We're godda prethend we're arthur nicking you,' Nudger goes.

'We'll say you were doing a shit on the steps of the Weddington Modument.'

I'm like, 'Okay, why does it have to be a shit?'

'Accorton to Ronan,' Buckets goes, 'you're altways shitting on things. He said you did a shit in a wooban's laptop.'

I'm there, 'Yeah, it's called a Waffle Press and it was an actual thing at the time, like the Ice Bucket Challenge, except with a twist.'

'We'll say you were boozen wit your bleaten rubby wanker mates,' Nudger goes, 'and you did a shit on the steps for a dare, like.'

I'm there, 'Can we maybe say piss? Piss sounds a lot less bad than shit.'

Gull produces a set of handcuffs. Without saying anything, he spins me around, he pulls my orms behind my back and snaps the things on my wrists.

'Jesus,' I go, 'is this not a bit OTT?'

'We hab to make it look readistic,' Nudger goes. 'The whole thing is about confiddidents. We hab to look like we're in cheerge of the situation and no one will gib us a second look – do you get me?'

Then he gives me a hord shove in the back.

He's like, 'Mon, rich kid, let's go,' and he pushes me towards the main gate of the Gorda Headquarters.

It's as we're entering the actual building that the verbal abuse *really* storts?

Buckets storts going, 'You fooken rubby prick! Let's see will your rich auld fedda be able to get you out of this wooden.'

I'm there, 'Okay, can I just check that we're definitely still pretending here?'

'The fook in theer,' Nudger goes, shoving me into the reception area. 'Shitting on a public memorial. You're an absolute disgrace.'

I look over my shoulder at him. I'm there, 'I thought we agreed to say it was piss.'

Buckets is like, 'Rubby – a gayum for pricks if ebber there was one. Pricks of the highest fooken echelons.'

A fair few Gordaí hanging around look at us.

Nudger goes, 'You rich feddas disgust me – think you can cub oaber to eer side of the city and joost vandadize evoddy thing?'

They're putting on a real show. And, while I'm not exactly enjoying the abuse, everyone seems to be buying it. As a matter of fact, doors literally stort opening for us. Gords – as in, like, *real* Gords? – hold them for us to let us through.

'Did a shit on the Weddington Modument,' Buckets tells them.

'The dirty bastard,' comes the typical reply.

And Nudger's like, 'Fooken rubby – I'd badden it tomoddow.'

It ends up being a lot easier than I expected. Five minutes after walking through the front door, the goys are escorting me downstairs and now my hort is, like, seriously racing.

And that's when Gull all of a sudden pipes up. Bear in mind, it's literally years since I've heard the man say a single word. 'Ine godda put you in that ceddle,' he goes, 'and Ine godda split your skull like you're a fooken coconut.'

Nudger's like, 'Cool the jets, Gull. I think you're habbon one of yisser anxiety attacks.'

Yeah, no, the dude apparently did a peacekeeping tour in Angola when he was in the Ormy and, according to Ronan, has never been right since. He's got, like, post-traumatic stress and blah, blah, blah.

'Ine godda smash every bleaten toot in yisser fooken head,' he tells me then. 'You fooken yachting bastard.'

'Deep bretts,' Buckets goes. 'Mon, Gull, you're not in Angoda addy mower.'

Down a long corridor they push me, then Nudger's like, 'It's that dowur at the veddy end.'

Luckily, the thing ends up being unlocked. Buckets pushes it and in we go. The room is, like, the size of a rugby pitch and it's filled with, like, hundreds and hundreds of metal shelving units – we're talking floor to ceiling here – and on every shelf there's a line of, like, cordboard *document* boxes?

'Okay,' Buckets goes, taking the handcuffs off me, 'what's Ronan's case number?'

I'm like, 'Case number? I haven't a focking bog.'

'You doataunt need the case number,' Nudger goes – he's done his homework, in fairness to the dude. 'They're foyult by nayum and they're all in alphabeticoddle order.'

Gull storts going, 'It's a bleaten amboosh – Ine tedding you,' and I can hear that his breathing's all, I don't know, *ragged*? 'They're godda bleaten shoot us.'

Buckets goes, 'Gull, you're being padanoid. You're not in Africa addy mower.'

'If I doatunt make it out aloyuv,' the dude goes, bursting into tears, 'will you teddle Janet that I lub her and teddle Tony that he can hab me mothorbike.'

Buckets is there, 'You can teddle him yisser self, Gull. We're godda get ourra this aloyuv, my friend – that's a probiss.'

Nudger goes, 'Rosser, you go and look for the ebidence while we thry and get this fedda caddem.'

I'm like, 'No probs,' and I go looking for Ronan's box.

My hort is beating like a focking drum, by the way, and I notice that my hand is shaking as I trace my finger along the O's.

O'Callaghan. O'Canny. O'Carroll. O'Carroll-Kelly.

Paydirt!

Fock me, there's a lot of them. We're talking, like, one, two, three, four boxes for Fionnuala O'Carroll-Kelly – obviously from the time she murdered her second husband. And one, two, three, four, five, six, seven, eight, nine, ten for Chorles O'Carroll-Kelly.

We're some family, it has to be said.

But there's fock-all there for Ronan. Then I remember that his second name is Masterson. I'm about to go looking for the aisle with the M's, except curiosity suddenly gets the better of me and I decide to have a peek inside one or two of my old dear's boxes.

I can hear Nudger, in a soft voice, telling Gull, 'We're all godda gerrout of this, Gull. And you're godda be stanton on Hill 16, watching the Dubs wit your auld fedda this weekend – that's a probiss,' and then Buckets – in a sort of loud whisper – goes, 'Rosser, huddy up to fook!'

I lift one of the old dear's boxes down onto a table, then I lift the lid and look inside. And it's fair to say that I am not ready for what I end up seeing.

There's a humungous black rat sitting in the middle of the box, staring up at me. I swear to fock, I get such a fright that I actually scream. And it's, like, a proper *horror* movie scream?

It's like, 'Aaaaaarrrrrrggggggghhhhhh!!!!!!'

From the door, I hear Buckets go, 'The fook is happening, Rosser?'

And of course the rat ends up getting a fright and he springs at me, sinking his teeth into my thumb.

I'm suddenly screaming, 'He's got me! He's focking got me!' because the thing is literally attached to my left hand and I'm shaking it frantically, trying to throw the little focker off.

Nudger goes, 'What in the nayum of Jaysus is going on, Rosser?' because – yeah, no – I'm making quite a bit of noise and I can hear Gull growing more and more agitated.

He's going, 'It's an ambush, feddas! Someone's arthur gibbon away err posishidden!'

I'm still trying to shake the focking thing off my hand, going, 'FOCK! FOCK!!! FOOOCCCKKK!!!' but he sinks his teeth in even deeper.

'What is it, Rosser?' Buckets goes.

And I'm like, 'IT'S A RAT! IT'S A FOCKING RAT!'

I hear Gull go, 'I bleaten toawult yous! Some wooden's arthur squealing!' and then he's like, 'Let's get the Jaysusing fook out of hee-or!' and I hear the door open.

Nudger shouts, 'Abandon mission, Rosser! Abandon mission!'

But I'm there, 'If I could just get this focking –' and then suddenly, for reasons best known to himself, the rat decides to let go of my thumb, drops to the floor, then scurries underneath one of the metal shelving units, like the prick that he is.

'Rosser,' Buckets goes, 'mon, we're out of hee-or!'

I'm there, 'Just give me, like, a minute to find Ronan's box,' and I notice that the blood is, like, pouring from my thumb.

'There's no bleaten toyum,' Nudger goes. 'The fooken noise Gull is making out theer, this place is godda be full of Geerds in about thoorty seconds – real Geerds, Rosser! You'll do toyum for this, Rosser. You'll get eeben longer than Ronan's godda get.'

So I end up having no choice but to – like he said – abandon the mission. I make a run for the door. Ten seconds later, the four of us – first Gull, then Nudger, then Buckets, then me – are taking the steps up from the basement three at a time, then sprinting along a corridor, then a second corridor. Then we're running through the reception area, passing Gords drinking tea, who go, 'What in the name of God is going on?' then we're bursting out of the main doors, through the cor pork, then out into the actual Phoenix Pork.

All of the *actual* Gords are too in shock to even react until we're out the gate and gone, with Gull shouting, 'You'll nebber take me aloyuv, yous pack of African bastards!' over his shoulder, and me feeling sick in my stomach, portly due to the pain in my thumb, but mostly due to the knowledge that I have focked up my son's best chance at freedom.

6.

Dingle White Female

'I've decided to stop being a bitch,' Honor goes.

This is while we're passing the famous Obama Plaza.

I'm like, 'Really?' playing the innocent. 'That's, em, certainly a new deporture for you. I kind of *like* you being a bitch?'

'Well, I was talking to Erika,' she goes, 'and she thinks I should maybe try to be, like, *nicer* to people?'

'Random – especially coming from her. She was the biggest bitch in Ireland when we were growing up, and I'm saying that as a compliment.'

'She says I could have, like, loads of friends if I was, like, *kinder*? So I'm going to try it for the next three weeks.'

You're not going to last three weeks in Kerry, I nearly feel like telling her. I'd be stunned if she lasts a full day. Which is why I've decided to stay in Dingle tonight – just so I don't have to drive all the way back down tomorrow to collect her.

'By the way,' she goes, 'what happened to your thumb?' because she's obviously copped the plaster on it.

I'm there, 'Yeah, no, I got bitten by a rat.'

'A rat?'

'It's a long story. I had to go to the SwiftCare in Balally last night for a tetanus shot.'

'That's like, Oh! My God!'

'Yeah, no, it definitely was at the time. Hey, the smell of cow shit, Honor, huh? Of course, that'll be a thing of the past if your old dear has her way!'

She's like, 'I don't actually *mind* the smell?' and all *I* can do is laugh. I'm there, 'That's because we're still in technically Tipperary.

Wait until we hit *actual* Kerry. It'll singe your focking nose hairs – trust me.'

She goes, 'I know what you're thinking, Dad.'

And I'm like, 'Okay, what am I thinking?'

'That I'm not going to last a *day* down here? That I'm going to ring you tomorrow morning and tell you I want to go home?'

'Not true.'

'So why have you booked yourself into a guesthouse in Dingle?'

'Er, I *haven't*?'

'Dad, I heard you on the phone. *You've a lovely voice, Nuala! Yeah, no, I'm a sucker for a girl with a country accent!*'

'That voice you do when you're impersonating me is pretty cruel, Honor.'

'*I once dated a member of the Mayo women's football team and another bird who worked in FBD and was originally from Tubbercurry.*'

'Okay, what happened to you being kinder?'

'We're not actually *there* yet?'

'Fine, I booked myself into Grangetown Manor because I've heard good things. And – yeah, no – also in case you change your mind and you want to come home with me.'

'Dad, I'm not going to change my mind. I don't want to go back to that focking house.'

Yeah, no, that ends up *stinging* a bit? But I don't say anything and we listen to songs from Honor's iPhone until we're in pretty much Abbeyfeale, then I go, 'You are going to miss us, aren't you?'

And she's like, 'I'll miss the boys. I *already* miss them?'

'Seriously, you couldn't – focking idiot kids.'

'And I'll probably miss you. A little bit.'

'Well, I'm definitely going to miss you, Honor – and I don't mind saying it. As a matter of fact, I'm actually hoping that you hate it, then we can go home and tell your old dear that it just didn't work out. You know, we took you to Castletown-Bearhaven when you were, like, five years old and you complained that you could smell fish for about a year afterwards.'

'Dad –'

'We had to send you to a child psychologist.'

'Dad, I'm going to be fine!'

'I'm just saying, don't be afraid to use that excuse if you're looking for a way out.'

We eventually reach Dingle, which means we're, like, a twenty-minute drive from Muiríoch, our final destination. And I stort to feel – yeah, no – sad in my hort.

I'm there, 'Do you have everything? Hair straighteners? Fake tan?'

'Yes, I have everything,' she goes.

'Nothing we need to go back for, no?'

'No.'

'What about the De'Longhi La Specialista Bean to Cup Pump Espresso Coffee Machine? You're not going to be able to get coffee out here in the wilds. I'll turn the cor around.'

'Dad, just keep driving!'

We cross over the water and I take the right turn for the road to Muiríoch. I'm watching entire fields zip by, full of cows and sheep – all of them focked, even though they haven't got a clue – then suddenly a view to the sea opens up to the left below us and it's, like, so beautiful that it pretty much takes my breath away.

'Wow,' I go. 'Focking . . . wow.'

We eventually pass a church with obviously a Londis opposite it and Honor tells me to take the next right, which I do, then suddenly I'm driving up this, like, narrow boreen that looks like it was last surfaced back in the days when my old dear still had her original facial features. There's, like, big clumps of grass growing out from between the cracks – of the road, just to be clear, not my old dear's face.

'According to the satnav,' Honor goes, 'Bean Uí Chuill's house is up here on the left.'

I'm there, 'Bean Uí Chuill? It'll be interesting to see what kind of an operation this woman is running with a name like Bean Uí focking Chuill.'

'There it is! Stop!'

I pull up outside this, like, lorge but generic bungalow. Out front, I notice that a big crowd of girls is gathered – some Honor's age, some older, all chatting away, obviously getting to know each other.

Honor gets out of the cor first, then I do the same. I walk around to the boot and I take out her two pink Globe-Trotter suitcases.

I'm there, 'I'll carry them in for you.'

Except *she* goes, 'Dad, no – I've got this, okay?' obviously worried about her old man embarrassing her.

I'm like, 'You'll text me, won't you, if it turns out there's no Wi-Fi? Or if they ask you to milk a cow? Or make your own bed?'

'Dad,' she goes, finally losing her patience with me, 'stop making a show of me, okay?'

She grabs her two suitcases by the handles and I end up just standing there with a definite lump in my throat, watching – with my hort in my mouth – as my daughter does something that I never thought any child of mine would ever have to do: walk over a cattle grid in Pretty Ballerinas.

When she makes it safely to the other side, she looks over her shoulder at me, just to let me know that she's going to be okay from here, then she walks up the driveway and suddenly all the other girls – in bogger accents – are going, '*Dia dhuit*,' meaning, obviously, what's your name?

I get back into the cor, put it into Drive and slam my foot on the pedal – unfortunately without checking my blind spot first. I hear a sudden scream, then a bump, then another scream, then I look in my rearview mirror and I spot a woman on a bicycle, wobbling from side to side, like my old dear leaving the prosecco tent at Bloom, then her front tyre hits the wall and she's thrown orse over tit onto a grass verge.

I decide to – yeah, no – stop. It's the right thing to do – and anyway, there's a pretty good chance that she saw my reg before she was flipped over the handlebors.

I get out of the cor, going, 'Are you okay?' making sure to tread that fine line between sounding sympathetic and admitting liability. 'Did you have a dizzy spell or something?'

I think Hennessy, in his own way, has damaged us all.

She's there, 'You just pulled out.'

I'm there, 'That's not what happened.'

'You pulled out without looking.'

And I'm there, 'Well, maybe you should have anticipated what I was going to do,' because there's no focking way I'm taking penalty points for this.

She's like, 'You should have checked your blind spot.'

And I'm there, 'No high-viz safety vest, I see,' subtly making the point to her that, if she even thinks about claiming off my insurance, I'll drag her through every focking court in the land.

I put my hand out to help her up, because I'm still a gentleman, even if she's on the obvious make here. She grabs a hold of it. And that's when our eyes suddenly meet.

A lot of people talk about love at first sight. It's something I myself personally have never actually *felt* before? But there's no doubt that that's what this woman is experiencing as she clocks my face for the very first time.

'Are you alright?' I go, pulling her to her feet.

She's like, 'I don't know,' her mouth slung open. 'Yes. I think so.'

I'm there, 'So you're definitely not hurt?'

'No.'

'No?'

'I don't think I am.'

'Do you mind if I record this conversation?'

She's just, like, staring at me. She's not exactly bet-down, in fairness to the woman. She's, like, my age, I'm guessing – with long black hair. If I had to say she looks like anyone, it'd have to be Marisa Tomei, except she dresses like a librarian – one of the cross ones who are constantly shushing people – we're talking black cordigan, black trousers, men's shoes.

I'm there, 'I'm sorry about what happened to you,' and, at the same time, I'm looking at the side of my cor to make sure she hasn't damaged the paintwork. 'Even though that's not an admission of responsibility.'

She's there, 'Em. Yes. Right.'

She sounds like she's from Dublin.

I'm there, 'The name's Ross, by the way,' picking up her bike for her – a big, heavy, black thing that seems to be made of, like, cast iron.

She's like, 'Hi.'

And I'm there, 'Hi.'

'I, em –'

'What?'

'– have to go.'

'Right.'

'Sorry.'

'It's cool.'

'Okay.'

'Are you sure you're alright?'

'I'm grand.'

'It's just you seem –'

'What?'

'– I don't know. I want to say –'

'What?'

'– *flustered*?'

'It's nothing.'

'Are you sure?'

'It's nothing.'

'Right.'

'I'm grand.'

'Okay.'

'Grand so.'

'Right.'

She throws her leg over the crossbor and steadies herself.

Then she's like, 'I'm sorry.'

I'm there, 'Hey, no horm done.'

'Goodbye.'

'Yeah, no, bye.'

Then she wobbles off down the road and I'm wondering has she maybe got a concussion. It's only when she's gone that I notice that all of the girls from the famous Bean Uí Chuill's gaff have rushed down the driveway to find out what the commotion is all about. They're just, like, staring at me. And right in the middle of the crowd is Honor, with her face all red and her hand over her mouth, looking as embarrassed as I've seen her since the famous Bring Your Dad to School Day in Mount Anville Junior School, when I told Mrs

Delmege – her fourth-class teacher – to sit on my back while I performed push-ups in front of the class and it turned out I was only able to do one.

And, who knows, maybe even more embarrassed than that.

'Oh, 'tis in fine form you are this morning,' the famous Nuala goes – she's not great, as it turns out. ''Tis as if all the birds in the kingdom of Kerry are singing just to delight thine own heart!'

It turns out her voice was making promises that her face couldn't honour. I decide not to be a dick about it, though.

I'm there, 'That's a pretty a good way of putting it, in fairness to you,' because it's not *her* fault?

She's there, 'Is it plans for the day you have?' because they all talk like focking Yoda down here.

'Yeah, no,' I go, 'plans for the day I have alright! I'm bringing my daughter home from, like, *Irish* college?'

'Oh! And was it a good time she had?'

'I seriously doubt it. And that's no offence to you. She wouldn't be a major fan of – let's just say – the *country*? My wife took her to the Newbridge Silverware Visitor Centre once and Honor refused to get out of the cor.'

Nuala picks up my empty plate and goes, 'Is it more coffee you'll have?'

And I'm there, 'No,' at the same time standing up, ''tis heading off I'd better be. The girl will have an absolute shit-fit if I leave her waiting here five minutes longer than is necessary.'

Twenty minutes later, I'm in the cor and heading back to Muiríoch, with a bit of a head on me, in all fairness. Yeah, no, I spent the night drinking pints in the famous Dick Mack's and I got chatting to this American couple, who told me they wanted to learn a traditional Irish song, so I taught them 'She Was Only the Gravedigger's Daughter – But She'd Lie Under Any Old Sod' and they posted a video of themselves singing it on their Insta for all their friends back home to see, even though they'd no idea how actually filthy the lyrics were.

I was getting on great with one of the bormaids as well, doing that flirty thing I invented where I hold out a fifty-yoyo note to pay for my drink, then when the bormaid goes to take it, I quickly pull it away. The first three or four times I did it, I think she found it cute, but I have this vague memory of the manager eventually hurdling the bor and manhandling me out the door.

Still, I've had worse nights out.

I pull up outside the famous Bean Uí Chuill's gaff and there's no sign of Honor. I honestly expected to find her sitting on her suitcases in the gorden with a face on her like she's sucking a lime. I go to, like, text her, but I notice that I've got no signal, which possibly explains why I haven't heard a word from the girl since I dropped her off yesterday.

There's not a chance she'll stay now, I think. I remember one Christmas when she was, like, seven years old, we took her to Lapland to visit Santa Claus. We had an appointment to meet the dude in his actual office so she could hand over her list of demands personally. Anyway, we walked in there, with Sorcha carrying the fifteen or sixteen foolscap pages of shit that Honor wanted. All of a sudden, I looked around because I wanted to see the joy and wonder on our daughter's face. Except there was no sign of her. We found her outside in the corridor, staring at her phone, going, 'One bor? Are you focking shitting me? Take me back to the airport!'

Which we did.

The door of the gaff opens and big gaggle of girls comes spilling out into the gorden. I spot Honor right in the centre of them. And it's, like, *the* weirdest thing, because she's telling them some, I don't know, random story and – get this – they all suddenly burst out laughing.

'Oh, Honor,' one of them goes, ''tis fierce funny you are altogether!'

Fierce funny, I'm thinking, what the fock? I'm the only one who finds her hilarious – and that's only when she's being a complete wagon to someone other than me.

They walk over the cattle grid – it's terrifying to watch – and they take a right turn out of the gate. Honor doesn't even see the cor and I end up having to beep the horn twice to get her attention. She turns around, spots the A8 and this look of, like, shock slash disappointment comes over her face. She tells the other girls to go on ahead without her, then she walks up to the cor.

I'm like, 'What story were you telling them? Was it the one where I took you to Deansgrange Library and you tore the last page out of all the Agatha Christie novels?'

'Dad,' she goes, obviously in no mood for nostalgia, 'what the fock are you doing here?'

And I'm there, 'I'm here to end your ordeal.'

'My *ordeal*?'

'Yeah, no, you knew I was going to stick around just in case you wanted to go home.'

'And I told you I wasn't *going* home?'

'What, even though there's no mobile signal?'

'I don't focking *need* a mobile signal.'

'That's not what you said to Thorsten the Elf when you were seven. The exact opposite, in fact.'

'Oh my God, you've no idea how *actually* liberating it is not to have to keep checking my phone.'

'That'll get old pretty quickly. So what did you actually do last night if you weren't buying shit online or trolling celebrities?'

'I talked. To the girls.'

'What, *those* girls?'

'Yes, those girls.'

'That's a bit weird. The focking state of them, by the way. Where are they even from?'

'From all over. Limerick. Tipperary. Cork.'

'Why do country girls always dress like they're wearing their brothers' hand-me-downs?'

'Dad, don't be mean.'

'I'm just trying to get a riff going here.'

'I made this friend called Clíodhna. She's in the bunk above me –'

'You're sleeping in a bunk? Honor, go and get your stuff.'

'– and she's from Louth.'

'Louth?'

'I know!'

'Is she from Louth in the same way that the Kearneys are from Louth? Because with them, the good thing is you'd never actually *know*?'

'She's really nice.'

'I'll have to take your word for it.'

'Dad, they're *all* really nice.'

'The focking state of them – I'm standing by that statement.'

I can hear the – I'm admitting it – *jealousy* in my voice? It's pretty obvious that Honor doesn't need me here.

'So I should just go back to Dublin,' I go. 'That seems to be what you're saying.'

She's like, 'That's *exactly* what I'm saying,' and she goes to walk away. She suddenly stops, turns around and goes, 'Oh, by the way, do you remember that woman you knocked off her bike yesterday?'

I'm there, 'I'm not sure that's how I remember the incident, Honor. She hit me every bit as much as I hit her.'

'Well, her name is Marianne – and she's my teacher.'

'She's pretty foxy for a teacher. And that's no disrespect to your mother.'

'Anyway,' she goes, changing the subject, 'I'm going to go and catch up with the girls. Drive safely, Dad – and give the boys a hug from me.'

She turns then and she hares off down the road after – yeah, no – her new mates. I end up just sitting there for a good, like, ten minutes, feeling the way I used to feel as a kid when Christian's old pair would bring him away to France for, like, the entire summer, like I'm missing not only port of myself, but the *best* port?

I should be, like, happy for her. Yeah, no, she looks like she's already a hit with the other girls, even though country people would get excited about pretty much anything. You only have to watch Nathan Corter singing 'Wagon Wheel' on *The Late Late Show* to know that.

I stort the cor and I drive to the end of the boreen and out onto the actual road. Twenty minutes later, I'm driving back over the bridge into Dingle when my *phone* all of a sudden rings?

It ends up being Sorcha.

She goes, 'Ross, where are you?' and she sounds upset.

I'm there, 'I told you I was staying over just in case Honor wanted to come home. She doesn't, by the way. She's fallen in with a bad lot.'

'Focking formers!' she goes.

'Well, the children of formers is what I'm guessing.'

'I'm not talking about Honor, Ross. I'm talking about *actual* focking formers!'

'Okay, what have they done now?'

'They've flooded the Vico Road – with cows!'

'As in, like, *actual* cows?'

'Yes, as in, like, *actual* cows. There's, like, two or three thousand of them. And there's, like, more arriving every minute. Cors can't get up and down the road because it's, like, totally blocked. Joy Felton has had to cancel her annual summer borbecue.'

'There'll be a meeting of the Residents' Association about this – you see if there isn't.'

'We're all, like, trapped in our homes, Ross.'

'On the upside, they *are* nice homes, in all fairness.'

'Ginny Morton's eldest daughter had one of her anxiety attacks,' she goes. 'She's never seen a cow in real life before. No one around here has. And it's the fear of the unknown that these formers are playing on.'

I'm there, 'Don't worry, Sorcha, I'm on the way.'

'There's no point in you coming home, Ross. You won't get anywhere near the house.'

'Er, what am I supposed to do, then?'

'You might as well stay down there until the road is cleared. Which could take days.'

'Right.'

'You know, I *was* actually prepared to be *reasonable*? I was talking to the Minister for Agriculture about possibly compensating formers for the loss of their herds and helping them to transition to non-ruminant animals, such as pigs and chickens.'

'I'm tempted to say fair focks.'

'Sea-mon said I was mad, of course. She said formers don't know how to compromise – that's how they've brought the world to the verge of destruction.'

'Dicks – I'm agreeing with you.'

'Well, that's it, Ross. I will not rest now until every sheep- and dairy-former in this country is put out of business – focking permanently!'

*

It's, like, *the* strangest feeling to be young, free and single again – well, not so much young, free and single as thirty-eight and married, but with full permission from my wife to be away from home.

Like Honor, I've decided to look on it as – yeah, no – a little holiday away from my life. And, after three days of pretty much solid boozing in the pubs of Dingle, I'm storting to secretly hope that they *never* clear the cows from the Vico Road?

I obviously miss my friends. And I suppose I also miss Brian, Johnny and Leo – in the same way that you might miss a cor alorm that's been going off for hours and hours and then it suddenly stops and you can actually hear yourself think again.

It's, like, two o'clock on a Sunday afternoon and I'm taking a drive around Slea Head, which actually isn't that *unlike* the Vico Road, except without the whiff of dirty money and the private security firm tasering day-trippers who outstay their welcome.

It's – honestly? – some of *the* most stunning scenery I've ever seen and I'm on the record as saying that the only thing worth looking at south of the Loughlinstown roundabout is Una Healy. But I'm prepared to admit that I was wrong.

Even the smell is something that you don't *notice* after a few days? It reminds me of the time I was in UCD and I had, like, a *thing* with a girl called Clodagh from Kinnegad, who was studying, like, Agricultural Science. The girl was a Guinness drinker – she could actually match me pint for pint – and I got so used to the whiff of her forts that I almost didn't need to cover my nose and mouth when I was making love to her.

See, this is the kind of shit that goes through my head – we're talking deep, deep shit – when I've got nothing to worry about. It's like when you delete a load of shit off your iPhone and it frees up all this memory.

Like Honor, I'm storting to think that I could possibly reinvent myself down here. I'm already experimenting with a new hairstyle, although the truth is that I'm all out of pomade and the big Super-Valu in the middle of the town doesn't stock American Crew. So the famous quiff has been replaced by a fringe, which has gone a bit curly in the rain, although the women seem to love it, judging by the amount of giggling and nudging that was going on in Foxy John's last night.

I drive through Ballyferriter and then across to Ballydavid and I stort to think about Ronan and – yeah, no, I'm admitting it – the utter balls we made of trying to steal the evidence against him. I actually blame Nudger and Buckets of Blood for bringing Gull along, knowing all about his history of PTSD, but Nudger says there's no way he's going to risk trying to do it again.

My phone pings. Carmencita Blake – as in, Sally Blake's old dear – says she's in Quinta do Lago and is it true what she's hearing about the Vico Road being full of cows? Rebecca Leahy – as in, like Diva Leahy's old dear – says oh my God, she's in QDL too and they'll have to meet up! Joanne McAuley – as in, Ruth McAuley's old dear – says oh my God, she's in QDL too and they'll have to meet up! Collette Cranny – as in, like, Imogen Cranny's old dear – says oh my God, she's in QDL too and they'll have to meet up! Alva Crowe – as in, like, Ginny Crowe's old dear – says yes, it's true about the Vico Road, but she'll tell her all about it on the Orchestra Moms group.

All of a sudden, I hear a loud bump. Something has hit the windscreen. I'm thinking, oh, fock, please don't tell me I've hit another cyclist.

I slam on the brakes and I get out of the cor with my hort in my literally mouth. But I'm relieved to see that it wasn't an actual person that I hit this time. It was a thing.

And this time *it* really *did* hit *me*?

It turns out it was a ball – but not an ordinary-shaped one. This one is, like, round, with the word 'O'Neills' written on it. I bend down and I pick it up. And that's when I hear two old dudes giving out yords to each other on the other side of the road.

One of them is like, 'God of mercies! Is it not straight you can kick the thing at all – you useless sluggard?'

He's, like, a big chunky dude in possibly his mid-fifties, with jet-black hair that looks definitely dyed and jet-black eyebrows to match.

'The devil mend you!' the other dude goes – he's, like, short and bald and around the same age. 'Is it not hoarse you are yet from all your blathering?'

'Blathering, is it? I own to God and the world, Peatsaí, it's worse you're getting – and 'tis not lies I'm telling!'

'God fire your ribs, Man! Heaven will be your rest tonight if you don't give up your talk without sense this minute!'

The little baldy dude, who – yeah, no – seems to be called Peatsaí, sees me standing there with the ball in my hand.

He's like, '*Dia dhuit!*'

'Ross,' I go. '*Tá mé* Ross.'

They end up just staring at each other with their mouths open – like two culchies on *Winning Streak* who've just seen Morty Whelan in the flesh for the first time.

'Have you the use of two languages?' the dude with the black hair goes.

I'm like, 'Jesus, no! I'm still struggling with one. I presume this is your ball, though?'

''Tis,' the same dude goes. 'And you may throw it to us now so that we might have it!'

Instead of, like, throwing it, just for the sheer hell of it, I put my foot *through* the thing? And to my surprise, even more than theirs, it ends up travelling a good, like, seventy metres – we're talking over their heads and right into the middle of the pitch behind them.

The dude with the black hair goes, 'Put it upon my soul, that was a kick! What name have they on you, did you say?'

I'm like, 'Er, Ross?'

'Is it a Yank you are?'

'I'm not a Yank, no.'

'You have the way of the Yank about you!'

'Yeah, no, where I come from we all talk like this.'

'Have you time to pass? Would you like to play football with us?'

'Er . . .'

'There's no hurry home on you, is there?'

'Not really. I'd say the *opposite* in fact?'

'So will you play?'

Again, I'm thinking about the whole, like, changing it up thing that Honor was talking about. I've got the new hairstyle. I tasted broccoli for the very first time last night and, even though I spat it onto the floor straight away, I love that I'm suddenly open to new experiences.

'Yeah, no, why not?' I hear myself go, then I cross over the road to them.

'I'm Canice,' the dude with the black hair and eyebrows goes. 'Let me knock a hundred shakes out of that hand!'

I shake hands with the dude, and then with Peatsaí, who definitely seems *less* keen on me? Then I follow them onto the pitch, where I notice there's, like, fifteen or twenty other dudes standing around, all of them, like, fifty-plus, and they're all wearing the same white jerseys with a red, diagonal stripe across it, which reminds me of the sash that Sorcha's sister wore the night she was named the 1999 Dalkey Lobster Festival Queen and she tried to take my mickey out of my chinos in the doorway of Select Stores when Sorcha and her old pair were walking, like, ten metres ahead.

Oh, except there's also, like, a sealion on the front with something foreign written underneath – we're talking, *Iasc Uí Mhathúna Teo*, which obviously means something.

I'm there, 'So are you goys, like, an actual team?'

Some dude with literally silver hair walks up to me and goes, 'A life of ease on you and all belonging to you! We're the An Ghaeltacht veterans football team.'

I'm there, 'Fair focks!' and – believe it or not – I genuinely mean it.

'I'm Muiris,' he goes, shaking my hand. He has about seven teeth in his head. ''Tis the captain I am.'

Canice is there, 'I own to God and the world that he has a kick on him that is the equal of that of the great Bryan Sheehan himself!'

'Is it so?' Muiris goes, looking me up and down.

Canice is like, 'Yerra, 'tis!'

'Are you a football man?' Muiris goes – talking to me.

I'm there, 'Rugby would be more my sport. But when in Rome – blah, blah, blah.'

'You may get him a jersey,' Muiris goes to no one in particular, 'and a shorts and a stockings. And boots, if anyone has a pair they haven't the use for.'

They manage to get me all the clobber and I throw it on me while standing on the side of the pitch. Then Muiris hands each of us either a yellow or an orange bib to divide us into actual teams. And five minutes later, I am quite literally playing Gaelic football with this bunch of, like, total randomers.

The goys are all, like, super-, super-fit, especially for men in their, like, fifties. But I quickly get into the pace of the game, despite not having a focking clue what I'm doing. Muiris, who's on my team, ends up having to pull me to one side after, like, sixty seconds. He goes, ''Tis not *throwing* it you should be. You pass it this way, look it,' and he sort of, like, demonstrates hitting the ball from underneath with the top of his fist.

I'm there, 'Would it not be easier to, like, throw it?'

'It might or it might not,' he goes. 'But 'tis not rugby you're playing – do you get me? 'Tis football – and that's how we pass the thing around.'

'Yeah, no, I'll give it a go.'

'And don't be a bit shy of throwing it forward. 'Tis not only backwards it can travel.'

'Okay, that's going to take a bit of getting used to.'

But I end up surprising myself. The next time I get my hands on the ball, I do exactly what Muiris showed me, hitting it with my fist and sending it looping over Peatsaí's head and straight into the hands of Canice.

'*Maith an fear!*' Muiris shouts, clapping his hands together. ''Tis how it's done, Rossa!' which is what everyone is suddenly calling me, by the way.

I end up really settling into the game then. I sort of, like, gravitate towards the centre of the pitch and I spend most of the match there, spraying long passes around – all those Sunday afternoons of unsupervised access that I spent with Ronan, booting the ball backwards and forwards to each other on Dollymount Strand, definitely paying off.

I end up doing – I think? – okay. Then, when the kickaround is sort of, like, coming to an end, I leap about – I swear to fock – four feet in the air to claim a high ball. With my confidence up, I set off in the direction of the goal. I ride one tackle, then another, and suddenly a huge space has opened up in front of me. I put my foot through the ball and I send it sailing over the bor and between the posts for a point, which seems to be *their* equivalent of a drop goal, except obviously easier to score.

Or so I think. But when I turn around, expecting fair focks from my teammates, there ends up being none. Everyone is sort of, like, looking awkwardly away.

Canice goes, 'You were travelling, Rossa.'

And I'm there, 'Yeah, no, thanks,' thinking it's a compliment about my turn of pace from a standing stort.

'No,' he goes, ''tis against the rules what you did. You're not allowed to travel more than four steps without either bouncing the ball or dropping it onto your foot and kicking it back into your hands. Did you see us doing that?'

I'm like, 'Yeah, no, I thought you were just showboating.'

'No, 'tis one of the rules.'

'Random. But fair enough.'

When it's over, it ends up being handshakes all round. I'm saying to each and every one of them, 'Thanks for the game!' and I'm not even being sorcastic.

I genuinely, genuinely enjoyed myself, even if I made a bit of a tit of myself with the point that wasn't actually a point.

I can nearly hear Ronan going, 'You bleaten tulip, Rosser!'

I watch Muiris exchange a look with Canice, then he goes, 'Have you plans for Thursday night, Rossa?'

I'm there, 'Thursday night? Er, I'll probably just be getting shit-faced in Dingle – same as the last few nights.'

He's like, 'Would you come out here and train with us again?'

And again – not even being a dick about it – I go, 'Yeah, no, I'd absolutely love that.'

So I'm in the big SuperValu in the middle of, like, Dingle – Gorvey's, as they call it around here – and I'm buying toothpaste, because after a week of not brushing my teeth, they feel like they're wearing little mohair jumpers.

I'm heading for the second checkout, where there's, like, no queue at all, but when I get there, I notice that someone – almost certainly a woman – has abandoned her shopping trolley and the dude on the till is just sitting there, waiting for her to come back.

'There was a couple of things she forgot,' he goes, and we end up exchanging what would have to be described as a *knowing* look?

My old man has written letters to the *Irish Times* about the problem.

That's when, all of a sudden, my phone rings. It ends up being Sorcha and, for a split-second, I actually consider not answering it. More than a split-second, to be fair. I let it ring out five times – it's a sort of life-hack that I invented to test whether a call is important or not. But – yeah, no – she keeps on ringing, which means it must be, so I end up answering.

She's like, 'Oh my God, were you screening me again?'

I'm there, 'I was trying to figure out if it was important. It's a system I developed.'

'I'm your wife, Ross. It's *always* important.'

'Definitely one way of looking at it. So what's up? Have the cows gone home?'

'No, they haven't gone home.'

'Jesus, are they not, like, storving at this stage? There's not exactly a lot of grass there for them to eat.'

'They're bringing in new cows all the time. There are, like, cattle trucks arriving on Coliemore Road constantly. They unload thirty or forty new cows and they join the slow parade all the way to Victoria Road.'

'Cattle trucks? Jesus, I'd say you're the talk of the Dalkey Open Forum.'

'They reach Victoria Road, then they're driven off, by which time another truck will have arrived and added thirty or forty more to replace them.'

'I'm pretty sure they're ripping the back off you on the Mount Anville Orchestra Moms group as well – not to rub your nose in it. In other news, I'm trying out a new hairstyle.'

'Excuse me?'

'Yeah, no, it's gone a bit curly in the rain. But it's a good look for me – I think you'd definitely approve.'

'Anyway,' she goes, changing the subject back to her, 'your dad is sending the Government helicopter for me and the boys this afternoon. He's evacuating us to the Áras. We're going to live there until this is all over.'

'Yeah, no, cool.'

'So you can come home now.'

I'm like, 'Riiiiiight,' and she immediately picks up on the hesitation in my voice.

'What's that supposed to mean?' she goes.

'The thing is, Sorcha, I'm playing football tomorrow night with these sort of, like, *old* dudes I met? And before you ask the obvious question, yes, I'm talking about Gaelic football.'

'Ross, you are *not* staying down there. I want you home – tonight.'

'Bear in mind, the mobile reception isn't great here, Sorcha. I might end up losing you any second.'

'Ross, don't you *dare* hang up on me!'

All of a sudden, I hear a voice behind me go, 'I'm sorry to keep you waiting,' and it's obviously the – not being sexist – but *woman* back with whatever she forgot to throw in her trolley the first time around.

I turn around and I'm about to tell her that I haven't got time to waste just because her head isn't in the focking game when I suddenly realize that I know her. It's Honor's teacher – yeah, no, the woman who hit my cor with her bike.

I hang up on Sorcha and I go, 'Hey.'

The woman's like, 'Hi,' as surprised to see me as I am to see her.

I'm there, 'I'm trying to remember did I catch your name?'

'Marianne,' she goes.

I'm like, 'Right.'

'Yes.'

'I'm Ross.'

'I remember you.'

'So how *are* you?'

'Grand.'

'Good to hear.'

'And you?'

'Cracking form.'

'I'm sorry I –'

'It's cool.'

'– just forgot something.'

'It happens.'

'The man had already started putting my messages through –'

'Hey, it's not my first time in a supermorket.'

'And I remembered I didn't get –'

'Toilet roll.'

'Yes.'

'So I see.'

'Grand.'

She hands it to the dude. Ultra-quilted, I notice. Three-ply. You wouldn't focking blame her. She's actually hotter than I remember her. I think I mentioned Marisa Tomei. There's, like, silence between us for a good ten seconds, before I'm the one who ends up filling it.

I'm there, 'A little birdie tell me you're an Irish teacher.'

'I am,' she goes.

'I have to admit –'

'What?'

'– I was surprised to hear it.'

'Why?'

'I don't know.'

'There must be a reason.'

'What do you mean?'

'A reason for saying it.'

'It's just –'

'What?'

'You don't *look* like an Irish teacher?'

'Don't I?'

'Not really.'

'Right.'

'Not at all, in fact.'

'So what do Irish teachers look like?'

'Horrendous usually.'

'Excuse me?'

'It's a compliment, Marianne.'

'Is it?'

'Meant every word.'

'Okay.'

'Call as I see.'

'Fine.'

'Always have.'

'Right.'

She hands the dude her plastic to pay for her messages.

I'm there, 'Hey, I'm sorry again – about what happened.'

She's like, 'Happened?'

'Yeah, no, you crashing into my cor with your bike.'

'That's not how I remember it.'

'Are you saying you banged your head?'

'I'm saying you just pulled out –'

'Not sure I did.'

'– without checking your blind spot.'

'Agree to differ.'

'We'll have to.'

I watch her pick up her two bags of – yeah, no – messages and I'm like, 'Whoa, horsey! You're not cycling back to Muiríoch with those, are you?'

She goes, 'I am.'

'You can barely lift them.'

'I'll hang them from the handlebars.'

'I've the cor outside.'

'I'll be grand.'

'I'll give you a lift.'

'I couldn't ask you to.'

'I honestly don't mind.'

'Well, if you're sure.'

'I'm totally sure.'

'Thank you.'

'Not a problem. Jesus, you're already a danger to other road users *without* shopping bags.'

I pay for my toothpaste. Then, a few minutes later, I'm lifting Marianne's big, heavy bike into the boot of the A8. I point out the scratches on the paintwork to her – although hopefully not in an *accusing* way? – before I throw her two bags of messages on the back seat. Then I stort the cor and I point it in the direction of Muiríoch.

'By the way,' I go, 'the reason I know you're a teacher is because my daughter is in your class.'

She's like, 'Your daughter?'

'Yeah, no, that's why I'm down here.'

'Who is she?'

'Honor?'

'Honor?'

'Yeah.'

'Oh, you must mean Onóir!'

'Do I?'

'Onóir Ní Cheallaigh?'

'Could be.'

'Are you saying that Onóir is your daughter?'

'Okay, tell me first what she's being accused of.'

'She's a beautiful girl.'

'She's what?'

'So kind.'

'Riiiiiight . . .'

'And polite.'

'I'm not sure we're talking about the same girl here.'

'All the other students adore her.'

'Although she did say she was going to make the effort.'

'And her boyfriend is a lovely young man.'

'Although I didn't think she'd keep it up for this long.'

'They make such a cute couple.'

'Wait a minute.'

'What is it?'

'Did you just say boyfriend?'

'I did.'

'Who is he?'

'Reese.'

'Reese?'

'That's right.'

'He sounds like a tool.'

'He's in the class above her.'

'A real piece of work.'

I can feel my hands tightening on the wheel.

'I'm here,' she goes.

I'm like, 'What?'

'This is where I'm staying.'

'Right.'

'Here on the left.'

I pull up outside this, like, thatched cottage with whitewashed walls. We get out and she takes her bags of shopping off the back seat while I lift her bike out of the boot of the cor.

'Have you any faith?' she totally out of the blue goes.

I'm there, 'Faith? As in?'

'Do you go to Mass?'

I'm there, 'Oh, I do,' lying through my back teeth.

She's like, 'Regularly?'

'You could say that.'

'That's good.'

'Mostly for weddings.'

'I see.'

'Or when someone dies.'

'Right. Father Reddin does a lovely Mass.'

'Who?'

'He's, em, sort of a relative of mine.'

'Right.'

'Here in Muiríoch.'

'Fair focks.'

'Eleven o'clock. On Sundays.'

'Right.'

'This Sunday is the Nativity of the Birth of John the Baptist.'

'God, it comes around quickly, doesn't it?'

'If you were interested.'

'What?'

'In going.'

'Going?'

'Only if you wanted.'

'What, to Mass?'

'To Mass.'

'With you?'

'There's no pressure.'

'Er . . .'

'Like I said –'

'Yeah, no, I will.'

'Will you?'

'Yeah, why not?'

'Right.'

'Right.'

'So I'll see you there so.'

'You will.'

'Goodbye.'

'Bye.'

I watch her lean her bike against the wall of the cottage, then disappear inside. And I'm thinking, Did I just agree to go on a date with Honor's teacher – to, like, Mass?

This is going to sound possibly creepy, but – yeah, no – it's half nine at night and I'm hiding behind a fuchsia bush outside Bean Uí Chuill's gaff, waiting for Honor to come home from the *céilí*.

I haven't been able to stop thinking about it all day. Honor has a boyfriend. And I know literally nothing about him, except that his name is Reese and he's about to get his focking jaw punched loose.

Actually, no, I have no intention of hitting the dude. All I'm looking for is information as to who he is and obviously what school he goes to. It's not like I'm standing here with a tyre iron in my hand – although I did take it out of the boot and put it on the front passenger seat just in case it's Terenure College.

Bored waiting, I whip out my phone and check Twitter. I notice my old man has tweeted for the first time since he became, like, Taoiseach. It's like:

Charles O'Carroll-Kelly √ @realCO'CK – 4h

Was forced to send out Government helicopter today to rescue a young mother and her children who were trapped in their home by farmers for SEVEN DAYS! It's irrelevant that the woman in question also happens to be the Minister for Climate Action and my daughter-in-law! She and her children have been bullied out of their home by thugs!

Reply 2,007 Retweet 6,566 Like 22,772

And then an hour later, he was like:

Charles O'Carroll-Kelly √ @realCO'CK – 3h

For too long, farmers have had it all their own way with their EU grants and their FFG friends bending over backwards to please them! Time to smash the Political-Agricultural Complex, I say!

Reply 3,116 Retweet 8,207 Like 29,555

I feel – yeah, no – a little bit guilty for not being there. But then I tell myself, 'Fock it!' and I feel a little bit better.

Then, suddenly, in the fading light I see two figures approaching, a boy and a girl, holding hands. I duck in behind the bush again and I listen out for their voices.

Eventually, I hear *her* go, 'I just feel like my Irish is improving – oh my God – *so* much!'

Believe or not, it *is* actually Honor.

She's like, 'Marianne is, like, *so* an amazing teacher.'

'What's the story with her?' the dude – this, presumably, Reese – goes. 'She doesn't look like an Irish teacher.'

Honor's there, 'What do Irish teachers look like?'

'Horrendous usually. What's her deal? Is she, like, married and shit?'

'The story I heard was that she's, like, *separated*?'

Interesting to know, I think. Interesting to know.

'Anyway,' Honor goes, 'the point I'm making is that I'm actually *glad* my mom left it until the very last minute to book? I'd much prefer to be here than in, like, Lurgan – or even, like, *Spleodar*?'

And he's there, 'I'm glad I got focked out of Lurgan last year for bullying and this was the only place that would take me. Because otherwise I would never have met you.'

He's got the gift of the gab – there's no doubt about that. One player recognizes another. I poke my head out again and I see that him and Honor are, like, facing each other. She has her back up against this – I can barely bring myself to say it – wooden form gate and *he* suddenly throws the lips on her.

It's every father's worst nightmare and I'm standing here watching it, this worthless piece of shit getting off with my daughter, her running her hands through his hair and him with his two hands on her – hord for me to say this – but *orse*?

Which goes some way to explaining what ends up happening next.

I morch straight over to them, going, 'Okay, that's enough! Get your hands off her! I said get your focking hands off her!'

He looks at me over his shoulder. He's, like, a tall dude with blond hair and – I can't help but notice – big guns.

He goes, 'Who the fock are you?'

And I'm like, 'Who the fock am *I*? Who the fock are *you*?'

Honor – who's totally lost in the moment – suddenly opens her eyes and goes, 'Dad?'

The dude's like, 'Dad?' looking me up and down and laughing. 'I thought you said your dad played rugby?'

Which hurts. Which hurts a lot.

I'm there, 'I happened to play the game in an era when the emphasis was on skill and mobility rather than bulk,' shooting him a look of absolute disgust, 'certainly in terms of backline play.'

'Oh! My God!' Honor goes.

I'm there, 'How about I hit the deck there, Player, and show you what fifty push-ups look like?'

'Dad,' Honor goes, 'you're focking embarrassing me!'

'Oh, am I? Aren't you going to introduce me to whoever this focker happens to be?'

'I'm Reese,' the dude has the actual balls to go.

He seems to be from South Dublin – that's some consolation at least.

I'm there, 'And what are you – my daughter's boyfriend?'

He's like, 'Er, we're not really, like, *defining* it at the moment? It's sort of, like, *casual*?'

I go, 'Casual, is it? How about I knock that focking smirk off your face right now?'

Honor comes at me then, shoving me in the chest.

She's like, 'Oh my God, Dad, are you focking following me? Do you know how – oh my God – *creepy* that is?'

'I don't like this dude,' I go. 'He's a ladies' man, Honor. I can see it because I was one myself. I like to think I still am.'

'What the fock are you even *doing* here?' she goes.

'I've been staying in Dingle for the last week.'

'What? Why?'

'The Vico Road is full of cows, so I decided to stay put. I've got involved with this crowd of old dudes playing – believe it or not – Gaelic football.'

Reese laughs. He reminds me so much of myself that I feel like nearly finding out if I ever rode his mother.

I'm like, 'Something funny, Player?'

He's like, 'Gaelic football is funny.'

'Is it?'

'I think so.'

'And I suppose you play rugby, do you?'

'I do, yeah.'

'And what have you actually achieved in the game – if anything?'

I swear to fock, he goes, 'I captained St Michael's to victory in the Leinster Junior Cup this year.'

Which leaves me literally speechless – as in, my mouth is just, like, slung open, like the focking Aillwee Cave.

He goes, 'No comeback, huh?'

And I end up doing something stupid then. It's, like, a pure spur of the *moment* thing? I hit the deck and I stort doing push-ups, counting them off as I go: 'Three . . . Four . . . Fiiive . . . You want to join me down here, Player?'

Honor goes, 'Oh my God, I am *so* embarrassed!' and bursts into tears. 'Reese, I'm so sorry!' She storms off, into Bean Uí Chuill's gaff, slamming the door behind her.

I'm left there, mid-push-up, staring up at Reese, with his good looks and his blond hair and his big guns and – I'm presuming – his Leinster Junior Cup winner's medal in the pocket of his beige chinos.

It's the one thing I've feared more than anything else in the world – aport from obviously Kielys of Donnybrook closing down, or Ian Madigan signing for one of the other Irish provinces. My daughter has fallen for a teenage version of me. And the worst thing is, she seems to have no idea how hopelessly out of her league he is.

'Maith an fear, Rossa! Maith an fear!'

I'm on fire tonight and it's not only Muiris saying it.

Look, I'm not suggesting I'm the next, I don't know – I'm trying to think of the name of a Gaelic footballer. Jesus Christ, I don't know the name of a single Gaelic footballer.

My point is, I'm not the best player on the pitch by any stretch of the imagination. But I'm drawing on the strengths I had as a rugby player to more than hold my *own* here? There's, like, my physicality – yeah, no, I'm knocking over some of these old dudes like they're focking bowling pins. And then there's my ability, as a former out-half, to make the ball do anything I want it to do.

We're, like, twenty minutes into the kickaround and I launch it, like, fifty yords, straight into the hands of Seán Bán, the team's first-choice centre-forward, who buries it in the back of the net.

'That kick of his,' I hear him say to Muiris, 'I never saw its equal for length and accuracy! By my palms, it would take a great deal of believing that that big Dublin bucko has never played the game before – and God's blessing on all who hear it!'

It's a nice thing for me to hear, even though most of what he said goes straight over my focking head.

Not everyone is, like, happy for me, though. Peatsaí is, like, constantly sledging me, trying to fock with my mind, going, 'There's no hard work in them hands of yours!' and 'Yerra, 'tis only a home-bred lamb you are!' even though it's supposed to be a friendly kickabout between two teams of ten and he's on my actual side.

The reason for this becomes clear at the stort of the second half when we win a free near the sideline and Peatsaí goes to take it.

But Muiris is like, 'Peatsaí, will you give the half-Yank one or two kicks to take?'

Peatsaí goes, 'I'll not – and he only a scrap of turf from the rick!' and it's suddenly obvious that – a bit like ROG when Sexton storted getting rave notices for his performances at provincial level – he feels possibly threatened by my ability with the boot.

Peatsaí ends up taking the kick and putting it wide of the posts. But the next time we win a free, we're talking forty yords from goal, Muiris makes a point of putting the ball in my hands and going, ''Tis yours to take, Rossa!'

Peatsaí tries to take it off me, but I hold on tightly to it, and we end up, like, pushing and shoving each other for a few seconds.

'Oh, don't be a bit shy!' he goes, daring me to throw the first punch, which I don't want to do because obviously he's a good bit older than me. 'One blow and I'll settle you – you Dublin gobaloon!'

Canice ends up having to drag him away, going, 'Do yourself a benefit, Peatsaí, and let's just see what the half-Yank does with it.'

I put the ball down and I take a deep breath. Whether it's Donny-brook Stadium, the old Lansdowne Road, or a field in the middle of – yeah, no – Kerry, the approach is the exact same. Oval ball, round ball, square ball – it doesn't matter a fock. I rub my hand through my hair, take four steps backwards, then three to the side. I look from the ball to the posts, then back to the ball, then back to the posts again. I run my hand through my hair, then I take a run at the thing and I send it, straight as an arrow, between the chopsticks.

Canice is there, 'He kicks the ball in a way that would put you in mind of the great Maurice Fitzgerald!'

'Stay talking forever and I'll stay listening to you!' Colman, one of the team's goalkeepers, goes.

Anyway, eventually, the match is over and I'm standing next to my cor, changing back into my usual chinos, Dubes and Leinster rugby jersey. I whip out my phone and I notice that I've got a shitload of WhatsApp messages. Alva Crowe – as in, like, Ginny Crowe's old dear – says she's just arrived in QDL and where is everyone tonight? Rebecca Leahy – as in, like, Diva Leahy's old dear – says she's in Gigi's! Rachel Lynch – as in, Eponine Lynch's old dear – says she's in Gigi's! Roz Matthews – as in, Sincerity Matthews's old dear – says she's in Gigi's! Carmencita Blake – as in, like, Sally Blake's old dear – says she's in Gigi's and so is Joanne McAuley and Cho Hye-ji. Alva Crowe says she'll see everyone in Gigi's so.

I look up again and that's when I pick up on, like, an *air* of something? It's like all the goys are – yeah, no – whispering among themselves.

I'm there, 'What's the story?'

It's Muiris who ends up going, 'Will you give us your ears so that we might talk to you?'

I'm like, 'Er, yeah, no, what about?'

Canice is there, 'You have the full story in your gob, Muiris. Begin at the start of it and tell it to him properly.'

Jesus, they don't believe in short conversations around here.

'A match is to be played,' Muiris goes, 'between An Ghaeltacht and Sneem.'

I'm like, 'Sneem? Is that a genuine place?'

'Oh, 'tis. And isn't it my blood that shivers whenever I think of that cursed town! You see, there is great spite between our two peoples. 'Tis a bitterness as old as Brandon itself!'

'Sounds like us and Terenure,' I go. 'A school for dicks.'

He's there, 'Last year, we met them, as we do every year, and 'twas for the ninth time in a row they beat us. All of us here have given the love of our breasts and our souls to this club over a great many years, ever since it's gasúns we were. If we were to lose ten in a row to the team that has been our heart's torment for many's the year, well, the sorrowful weeping would be heard across the water in Springfield, Massachusetts, as equally as it would in Ceann Trá.'

'I'm, er, still trying to figure out how I fit into the picture,' I go.

And he's like, 'Faith and begod, we think you might be the very man to scatter the gloom!'

'As in?'

'We'd like you to play.'

'But how can I? I'm not from round here. And I'm definitely not in the same age bracket as you goys – no offence.'

'The rules has it that, every year, each team is allowed one wild-card pick.'

'What, and you see *me* as that wild cord?'

'Yerra, I do!'

Again, Peatsaí isn't happy, though.

He goes, 'There isn't a patch of ground in all of Kerry that would beat this one for talk in the air at this moment in time!'

'All that comes between me and my sleep,' Canice goes, 'is to win this match and stop Sneem winning ten in a row. Have done with your whining, Peatsaí – for the bloom has gone off your game and 'tis well you know it.'

'There's a power of nonsense in your head,' Peatsaí goes, 'and 'tis no heed any man here should give it.'

Muiris is like, ''Tis far from nonsense! We need a man can kick! Then along comes this young half-Yank – and he knocking tally ho out of the ball all night!'

'But we don't know him from a crow!' Peatsaí goes, talking about me like I'm not even *there*?

Canice is like, 'Musha, even fine meat couldn't please the like of you, Peatsaí!'

Peatsaí is there, 'He may show his heels to the road – and with a long stride to give him the appearance of a man!'

'Have sense for yourself,' Muiris goes. 'Look at us, fighting among ourselves like hens – and the match only a fortnight away!'

He turns to me then.

He's like, 'Well? Is your tongue withered? Will you play?'

And what else am I going to say, except, 'No better focking *buachaill*!'

*

'Honor,' I go, 'please don't hang up!'

She's like, 'I *am* hanging up!'

I'm there, 'I need to talk to you.'

I'm using – believe it or not – a pay phone in a pub to ring her on Bean Uí Chuill's landline, having pulled the number out of – believe it or not – a telephone directory.

Seriously, it's like the millennium was only a focking rumour down here.

'Make it quick,' she goes. 'We're getting ready for the *céilí* tonight and I promised Clíodhna that I'd let her borrow some of my clothes.'

'As in, like, Clíodhna from Louth?'

'Yeah – so?'

'It's just you sometimes hear of kids going to Irish college and becoming radicalized.'

'What?'

'It happened to a kid from Knock-Na-Cree Road. He came back knowing all the words of the national anthem. And I'm not talking about "Ireland's Call".'

'Dad, what do you want?'

'Yeah, no, I just wanted to apologize to you. I acted like a dick.'

'Yes, you did.'

'It's just, well, it's hord for me to see you with someone – as in, like, *with* with?'

'Then why were you spying on me from behind a bush?'

'I don't know the answer to that question.'

'Because you're a focking weirdo.'

'You'll understand one day when you have a daughter of your own.'

'You embarrassed me in front of Reese.'

'I'd hordly say I embarrassed you.'

'What is it with you and push-ups?'

'I'm admitting that I might need to talk to someone about the push-ups.'

'A focking psychiatrist.'

'It's possible.'

'You threatened him with violence.'

'I'd hordly say I threatened him with violence.'

'You said you'd knock the smirk off his face.'

'Sorcha's old man used to say shit like that to me all the time. He still does. Look, it's entirely natural for a man to hate the dude his daughter is dating and want to kill him.'

'Reese is a really nice goy, Dad.'

'St Michael's College? I'm reserving judgement on that one. Why did you tell people your name is Onóir Ní Cheallaigh?'

'Because I don't want people to know who I am, Dad. I told you, I wanted to stort here with a clean slate.'

'Denying your own name, though?'

'Dad, I'm doing what Erika told me and I'm being nice to people. And I have – oh my God – *so* many friends!'

'I don't know how important that is in the scheme of things.'

'The teachers all love me.'

'Again –'

'And Reese is, like, *the* hottest goy on the whole course. Oh my God, every girl wants to be with him – but, like, *I'm* the one he wants to *be* with?'

I'm there, 'I'm just worried that you're not being true to yourself, though.'

'Hold on,' she goes, 'how did you know I'm calling myself Onóir Ní Cheallaigh?'

Fock – obviously, I can't tell her that I've been sort of, like, sniffing around her teacher, so I just go, 'Er, Bean Uí focking Chuill told me.'

She's like, 'Did she? When?'

'Er, just now when I rang. I was like, "Can I speak to Honor?" and she went, "Do you mean Onóir? Onóir Ní Cheallaigh?" '

'Oh, right.'

I'm actually patting myself on the back for how quickly I came up with it.

I'm there, 'Anyway, I have to go. I think I mentioned the other night that I'm playing Gaelic football down here.'

'Were you actually serious?' she goes. 'Oh my God, wait until Ronan hears about this!'

'I know! He'll be genuinely worried! Anyway, I'm actually in the famous Páidí Ó Sé's pub with a few of my teammates now, having a few scoops.'

Honor laughs. She's like, 'You must be having a mid-life crisis or something.'

'It might be that alright,' I go. 'Anyway, look, I'll talk to you soon.'

I hang up, then I tip back over to the goys. They're sitting at the bor, drinking pints of Guinness, chased down by shots of – yeah, no – whiskey, even though it's not even six o'clock yet.

There's me, Canice, Muiris, Seán Bán and our right corner-forward, who's called – I *think*? – Éamonn Óg? Canice hands me a pint of Guinness. I definitely told him Heineken, but he's obviously made up his mind that it's some weird quirk in my personality that he should just ignore.

'And there's a small fella on the bar for you there,' he goes, pointing to a glass with at least three fingers of Powers in it, 'so it's not lonesome the big lad will be on his journey down!'

I'm going to be on my focking ear in about an hour.

'So,' I go, 'how long have you goys been playing together?'

'Yerra musha,' Muiris goes, 'let me show you,' and he leads me across the floor of the pub to where there's loads of, like, framed black-and-white photographs of football teams on the wall.

''Tis us there,' Muiris goes, pointing at a picture of a group of kids with a humungous trophy.

I'm there, 'You're shitting me.'

''Tis not shitting you I am,' he goes. 'Nineteen hundred and seventy. It was the Kerry under-eights football championship that we won – and God save the hearer!'

I look at it closely. I can actually pick them all out. I recognize Muiris straight away. He's the one holding the trophy, although he obviously had a full set of teeth in those days. I spot Canice, whose hair is, like, fair, not dyed jet black, and he's got a big smile on his face. There's Colman, the goalkeeper, and Seán Bán, the centre-forward, as their seven-year-old selves. And there, standing on the edge of the group, is Peatsaí. He has a full head of hair and he looks the happiest of them all.

I'm like, 'Look at Peatsaí.'

'Yerra,' Muiris goes, 'a finer full-back I never saw in my fifty-five years in this world and a better free-taker was not to be found anywhere from Listowel to Portmagee. A wonder it was that he never played senior football for Kerry.'

I'm like, 'He's no fan of mine,' bringing the conversation back to me.

''Tis true for you,' he goes. 'But it's no heed you should pay him. 'Tis frustrated he is, for God has stripped him of the power of his limbs – and he suffering like the Lord Himself with the arthritis.'

'Which is why you need a kicker?'

'Now you have it!'

I stare at the photograph again. They remind me so much of me and the goys when *we* were younger? And it's incredible that they're all still playing together nearly fifty years after this picture was taken.

''Twas Sneem we beat that day,' he goes. 'And 'twas the start of the spite that lies between us still.'

I'm there, 'What, you've basically been replaying this match ever since?'

'Put it upon my soul, we have.'

Then he suddenly shushes me because the Angelus is on, on the TV behind the bor. We make our way back over to the rest of the goys. They all bless themselves, so – yeah, no – I end up doing the same and we sit there listening to the bongs and watching the people on the screen stop what they're doing and stare wistfully into the distance.

The *Six One News* comes on then and I'm just about to ask the goys what they do for an actual living when Canice all of a sudden goes, 'Ah, will you look at her there in her posture! I'd call her a bitch except I'd be in fear of committing a slander against the animal kingdom!'

And it's only when I look that I realize he's talking about my wife.

Yeah, no, Sorcha is on the TV, with the famous Simone behind her, going, 'These protests are unlawful, as well as being a gross invasion of my privacy, my freedom of movement and my civil liberties. And my message to the formers is . . . you will not win!'

'Ah, the back teeth must be worn out of her head,' Colman goes, 'with all her hugger mugger and her flim flam and her brilla bralla!

And she totally ignorant about rural Ireland! 'Tis doubtful I am that she's ever spent a day outside the city of Dublin! And she voicing her opinions at the height of her head!'

Oh, fock.

I'm there, 'So are you goys, like, formers?'

'Yerra, we are,' Muiris goes.

'As in, like, sheep and cows?'

'In the here and the now anyway,' Colman goes. 'But it'll not be for much longer if this *liúdramán* of a Dublin Minister has her way.'

I'm staring at the TV again. There's, like, an aerial shot of the Vico Road, with cows literally everywhere. Then – holy shit – there's a shot of, like, North Frederick Street, where her supposed office is, and it's absolutely swamped with sheep. Then there's a shot of, like, the Dáil and it's a similar scene of, like, pandemonium, except it's sheep *and* cows?

And Sorcha's back on the screen again, going, 'As Minister for Climate Action – and, I'm proud to say, a woman – I am determined to tackle our shameful emissions record in a way that is meaningful. What I want to say to Ireland's sheep- and cattle-formers is that I will not be intimidated by you. You have driven me from my home. You have driven me from my place of work. But you will not – I repeat, *not* – drive me from my course.'

Seán Bán is there, 'Oh, isn't it for her the life is hard!'

'Ah, 'tis small blame on *her*,' Canice goes, 'and she only a marbles-in-her-mouth *asalín* of a girl. The blame is on him that appointed her. Charles O'Carroll-Kelly – and hasn't he declared war on all farmers!'

Jesus Christ. I don't even know where to look, so I just stare at the screen and nod along, like I do when I'm watching a Christopher Nolan movie.

'And how is it that a woman like that is in the job in the first place?' Éamonn Óg goes. 'My soul to the devil, sure isn't she riding his son?'

Muiris is like, 'No, 'tis betrothed unto him she is!'

I possibly should say something here – declare my interest – except I'm really storting to like these dudes and I don't want to let them down.

But then Muiris suddenly remembers something.

'I forgot to ask you,' he goes, 'what family name is on you, Ross?'

I'm like, 'Family name? *On* me?' playing for time. 'You're asking what family name is *on* me? *On* me. *On* me. *On* me.'

'Your second name,' he goes. ''Tis for the team sheet I need it.'

I'm suddenly thinking about Honor calling herself Onóir Ní Cheallaigh. I'm like, 'It's Ross, em . . .' at the same time staring at my whiskey chaser.

'Spit it out, Man,' Canice goes, 'so that we might hear it!'

'Powers,' I suddenly hear myself go. 'Ross Powers.'

'Ross Powers,' Muiris goes, pulling a bookie's pen from behind his ear and writing it onto a beer mat. 'Rossa de Paor.'

The news report ends.

'The curse of Naomh Eithne on Sorcha Lalor!' Canice goes, raising his glass. 'And the same to Charles O'Carroll-Kelly! And he wanting to drive us from our land like a modern-day Custer! Curses on both their heads! May they both die roaring!'

And I have no choice but to go, 'Yeah, no, I'll drink to that!'

Getting the hang of Gaelic football is one thing – but Mass is a different *scéal* altogether. I'm always sitting when I should be standing, or standing when I should be kneeling, or kneeling when I should be sitting.

What's making it even more confusing for me is that it's being said in presumably Irish, which means I wouldn't have a clue what was going on even if I did have the attention span to follow it.

At the same time, I don't want Marianne to think I'm a total heathen, because she seems to be genuinely into it, so I make sure to keep going, 'Amen to that!' and 'Oh, Amen! Amen! Amen!' whenever Father Reddin makes some important-sounding point.

He's not a fan of mine, by the way. I can tell from the way he keeps staring at me, obviously wondering who's this handsome hero sitting in the front row with this – what did Marianne say? – *relative* of his?

Anyway, after a whole load of blahdy blah, the entire – I suppose – congregation stands up and storts shuffling out of their pews. I head for the door, but Marianne ends up following me, then tugging at my sleeve.

'It's not over,' she goes. 'We're just going up for Communion.'

Of course, I end up having to turn around then – dying for myself – and I join the line of people slow-walking their way towards Father Reddin, who's standing in front of the altar, dishing out the holy bread.

When I reach him, I stick out my tongue for him to drop the thing onto it, except he doesn't. He pauses and just, like, glowers at me for a good ten seconds, making it pretty obvious that he doesn't like me.

'Take your hands out of your pockets,' he goes, through gritted teeth.

Anyway, happily, the whole thing does eventually end and we all spill outside into the cor pork.

'Did you enjoy it?' Marianne goes.

I'm there, 'Er, yeah, no, I suppose.'

'You suppose?'

'As in, I *think* I did?'

'You certainly sounded like you did.'

'Did I?'

'You did.'

'As in?'

'You were saying Amen a lot.'

'Was I?'

'A lot.'

'I don't even notice myself doing it.'

'And you were crying.'

'Don't remind me.'

'During St Paul's Letter to the Ephesians.'

'He wrote a good letter.'

'And during the Consecration.'

'I love a good Mass. I'm on the record.'

Then, totally randomly, she goes, 'Will we go for a cycle?'

I'm there, 'A cycle?' because I'm thinking – yeah, no – if this is a date, it's the weirdest date I've ever been on.

'To the beach,' she goes.

I'm like, 'Which beach?'

'Ballydavid.'

'Er . . .'

'You don't have to.'

'Yeah, no, I'd *love* to?'

'But?'

'For storters, I don't have an actual bike.'

'I've a spare bike.'

'Right.'

'You can use it.'

'Okay.'

'Only if you want to.'

'I do.'

'Do you?'

'I suppose I do.'

'I'm just going to say hello to Father Reddin.'

'Oh.'

'Do you want me to introduce you?'

'Er, no.'

'No?'

'I have to, em –'

'What?'

'I have to pop into Londis.'

'Right.'

'Do you want a Wibbly Wobbly Wonder?'

'A what?'

'A Wibbly Wobbly Wonder.'

'I don't know.'

'They're very nice.'

'I don't –'

'We're talking strawberry and banana ice cream –'

'I like ice cream.'

'Do you?'

'I suppose I do.'

'– then the top is just, like, frozen lemon jelly –'

'Frozen lemon jelly?'

'– coated in, like, *chocolate*?'

'It sounds –'

'What?'

'It sounds grand.'

'Grand?'

'Yeah.'

'In a good way?'

'I suppose.'

'So will I get you one?'

'Maybe.'

'Maybe?'

'I don't know.'

'Right.'

'Yes. Do.'

So she focks off to talk to Father Reddin, while I pop into the shop for the ice creams.

Anyway, fifteen minutes later, I'm around the back of the cottage with Marianne and I'm throwing my leg over this, like, ancient bone shaker. I'm talking about this spare bike of hers, just to be clear.

Then five minutes after that, the two of us are on the road – it's, like, a baking-hot day – and we're eating our ice creams and basically just shooting the shit.

I'm there, 'So where are you from – as in, like, originally?'

'Skerries,' she goes.

'Jesus.'

'Do you know it?'

'Yeah, no, I played rugby there.'

'Right.'

'Once or twice, in fact.'

'Right.'

'I meant what I said, by the way – the day I met you in, like, Gorvey's?'

'What do you mean?'

'You're nothing like the Irish teachers who used to chase me out of the grounds of Coláiste Íosagáin when I was at school.'

'Right.'

'It's a compliment, Marianne.'

'Okay.'

'I'm saying you don't seem angry like a lot of people who are into the Irish language.'

'No.'

'You seem cool.'

'Well, you seem *cool* too!'

'I don't think Father Reddin is a fan.'

'A fan of what?'

'A fan of mine.'

'Oh.'

'The looks he was giving me.'

'Was he?'

'Er, during *Mass*?'

'I didn't notice.'

'When I went up for Communion.'

'What happened?'

'You didn't see?'

'I suppose I didn't.'

'He was a dick to me.'

'I'm sorry.'

'It's not your fault.'

'Don't take it personally.'

'It'd be hord *not* to?'

'I think he's just –'

'What?'

'Concerned.'

'Concerned?'

'I suppose.'

'About what?'

'About me.'

'Why would he be concerned about you?'

'It's a long story.'

'Right.'

'He's wondering is there –'

'Is there what?'

'– is there something going on.'

'In terms of?'

'In terms of . . .'

'Like, sex?'

'I suppose.'

'Right.'

'He asked me who you were.'

'And what did you tell him?'

'I told him your daughter was in my class.'

'Which is true.'

'I told him that we were friends.'

'Friends?'

'That's right, isn't it?'

'Er, I suppose.'

'And that nothing is going to happen between us.'

Jesus, you could have told me that before I bought you a Wibbly Wobbly Wonder, I nearly feel like saying – *and* let you drag me to focking Mass. I don't say it, though. I just sulk for a bit and we ride our bikes in silence.

'Onóir is getting on great,' she goes, changing the subject.

I'm there, 'Good for her,' pretending to care. 'That makes focking one of us.'

Yeah, no, I say the last bit under my breath.

She's like, 'Her Irish is as good as you'd hear from a native speaker.'

'I'm delighted,' I go.

'Everyone adores her.'

And the fair focks keep on coming!

I'm like, 'Yeah, no, that's great.'

We eventually arrive at the beach. We lean our bikes up against the wall of the pier, then we take off our shoes and socks and our bicycle clips and we step onto the sand and walk down to the edge of the water.

The sea is calm this morning – like a sheet of actual glass.

I'm thinking, this is one of *the* most random mornings of my life.

She hoicks up her trousers and she steps into the water. I follow her in, pulling a face to, like, brace myself against the cold. The water is focking freezing and pains shoot up my actual legs.

'So, like, are you married?' I go, just trying to find out what the actual *craic* is here?

She's like, 'Separated.'

'Same,' I go – force of habit.

She's there, 'But we're working on things.'

I'm like, 'You and –?'

'Donnacha.'

'Donnacha, right. And, er, how's that going?'

She stares into my eyes. Then out of nowhere, with literally no pre-warning, she makes a lunge for me – as in, she full-on throws the lips on me. So obviously I stort kissing her back and suddenly the two of us are standing there, up to our knees in water, our lips cold and tasting of strawberry and banana, her going at me with her tongue like she's licking the melted ice cream off the inside wrapper of her Wibbly Wobbly Wonder.

After maybe thirty seconds of swapping spits, she suddenly pulls away – her face all red with embarrassment – and she goes, 'I'm so sorry. I'm so sorry,' and she turns around and runs back up the beach towards her bike.

And I'm left standing there, thinking, what the fock? What the *actual* fock?

7.

The King of Corca Dhuibhne

There's a story on the front page of the *Irish Independent*. It's, like, the headline that catches my eye and I ask the dude at the next table if he's finished with his paper. He says no – 'Can you not see I'm still reading the thing?' – and I tell him there's no need to be a focking dick about it.

But the headline – which I *can* read? – is like, 'Where is New-grange?' and then underneath it's like, 'Prehistoric Passage Tomb and World Heritage Site Mysteriously Vanishes', and I can see the photograph of a humungous hole in the ground like an, I don't know, asteroid landed in the middle of the countryside.

Nuala puts my full Irish breakfast down on the table in front of me and follows my line of vision.

'Disappeared overnight,' she goes. 'And the story that's being told on *Morning Ireland* is that it's to the Russians he's given it for a gift!'

I'm there, 'It definitely seems random alright.'

'Yerra,' she goes, 'a polished Jackeen trickster that Charles O'Carroll-Kelly is. And hasn't he declared war on those that earn their living from the land –' and then she suddenly stops, because it's like she's suddenly *copped* something? 'Is he a blood relative of yours at all?'

I'm there, 'Excuse me?'

''Tis only now I see it – 'tis the same surname ye have.'

Fock it.

I'm there, 'I honestly don't follow you, Nuala.'

'Charles O'Carroll-Kelly is *his* name . . .' she goes.

I'm there, 'Okay, it'll be interesting to see where this is going.'

'. . . and Ross O'Carroll-Kelly is *your* name.'

'Who said Ross O'Carroll-Kelly was my name?'

''Twas you – when you filled in your registration card.'

'What are you, Mrs focking Morple all of a sudden?'

'And 'tis also the name on your credit card.'

By now, the dude reading the paper is, like, glued to the conversation and so is his wife – not great in terms of looks – and the few stragglers who are still finishing off their breakfasts.

'Yeah, no,' I go, 'my point is that it's probably just a coincidence. Whatever happened to client confidentiality, by the way?'

My *phone* all of a sudden rings? I check the screen and it ends up being Honor and I'm thinking, okay, how does she have mobile reception all of a sudden?

I answer, going, 'Honor, where the fock are you? You haven't gone back to civilization without telling me, have you?'

But she's like, 'No, I'm in Dingle! They've brought us in to go shopping for the day.'

Nuala focks off back to the kitchen.

'Shopping?' I go, knowing the girl is in for a serious culture shock. 'You do know there's no BTs down here, don't you?'

She's like, 'I know that.'

The dude with the paper mutters something about some sign that says mobile phones aren't allowed in the breakfast lounge, so with my free hand I snatch his newspaper from him and I fock it across the room and go, 'You're on about signs? How do you like that for a focking sign?'

Honor's like, 'Are you talking to me?'

'No, I was just, er, dealing with a situation that's been building up here.'

'I was wondering did you want to meet up?'

'Meet up? With you? Oh my God, definitely!'

'I know you two got off on the wrong foot, but – oh my God – I'd love you to meet Reese again.'

'Reese? He's still on the scene, then, is he?'

'Yes, Dad, he's still on the scene!'

'I only asked.'

'I'd also like you to meet Marianne.'

I go suddenly quiet.

She's like, 'It wouldn't be awkward between you, would it? After what happened?'

I'm there, 'Nothing happened, Honor. I don't know who's been talking. Someone with a big mouth obviously.'

'Er, you knocked her off her *bike*?'

'Oh, that! Er, I didn't, by the way. But I see what you mean now.'

'I'd love you to get to know her, Dad. She's *so* an amazing person.'

'Er, yeah, no, cool.'

'She says I speak Irish like a native speaker,' she goes. 'She also says I'm a pleasure to teach and that I'm a real leader.'

'Sounds like she's full of compliments.'

'So I'll meet you outside the Tourist Office in, like, fifteen minutes.'

I stand up and I grab the last sausage from my plate. The dude at the next table – obviously some kind of last-word freak – goes, 'Are you going to pick up that paper?'

And I'm like, 'Er, no – I'm going to do this instead,' and I dip my sausage in his wife's egg yolk, then I take a bite of it, then out the door I saunter, grinning like a superhero, into the sunshine of a beautiful, sunny day.

Honor is waiting for me outside the – like she said – Tourist Office. She literally squeals when she sees me and she comes running towards me, all smiles, with her orms outstretched. She gives me a hug, then she pulls away from me and she's like, 'Oh my God, your hair!'

I'm there, 'Yeah, no, it's gone all curly – there's no product in it.'

I wait for the nasty put-down, but there isn't one. She goes, 'It really suits you!' and I'm thinking, who the fock are you and what have you done with my daughter?

I spot Reese then, standing a few feet away.

She goes, 'Dad, you remember my boyfriend, don't you?'

I'm there, 'Boyfriend? I thought you weren't actually defining it.'

'Yeah, no,' Reese tries to go, 'we're actually going out now – as in, like, going-out going out?' and I just stare him down.

Honor's there, 'Dad, we were going to go out on a boat trip to see Fungie the Dolphin! Will you come?'

Seriously, it's like talking to a focking changeling.

I'm like, 'Yeah, no, that'd be great.'

And she goes, 'Marianne is meeting us here in, like, five minutes! I'll go and get the tickets!' and she rushes off – I swear to God – without even asking me for my credit cord.

I'm left standing there with Reese. I'm looking at him the same way that Sorcha's old man looks at me – like I'm trying to decide how I'd dismember his body if the situation ever arose.

'Onóir tells me you played number ten,' he goes when the silence becomes too much for him.

I'm there, 'If you knew anything about the history of the game, you wouldn't focking need so-called Onóir to tell you that. But since you brought it up, yeah, no, I won a Leinster Schools Senior Cup medal as the captain of Castlerock College, but then I also coached Pres Bray this year to their first Senior Cup win since 1932.'

'Fair focks.'

'I don't need a fair focks from you.'

It *is* nice to hear it, though.

'Dude,' he suddenly goes, 'I totally get that you're, like, super-, super-protective of Onóir, which is kind of cute. But I really, really like the girl.'

I'm there, 'Don't give me that. You're way out of her league in terms of looks and you know it.'

'That's, er, a pretty strange thing to say about your own daughter.'

'You're a player. I don't want to see her hurt.'

'I've no intention of hurting her.'

'I'm calling bullshit on that one.'

'Seriously, Onóir is the most amazing girl I've ever met.'

All of a sudden, Honor arrives back with the Lemony Snickets and the famous Marianne with her. I literally haven't set eyes on the woman since that scene on the beach in Ballydavid a week ago and it's as awks for me as it is for obviously *her*?

Honor's there, '*Tá Marianne anseo! An cuimhin leat Ross, Marianne?*'

'*Is ea, is cuimhin,*' Marianne goes, barely able to meet my eye. 'Er, *conas atá tú, Ross?*'

And I'm like, '*Bhí,*' because the odd word is definitely coming back to me – just from being immersed in it down here. '*Go raibh mé.*'

Honor goes, '*Níl aon Gaeilge aige,*' whatever the fock that means. '*Caithfidh tu labhairt as Bearla.*'

Marianne smiles at me awkwardly.

She's like, 'Hi.'

I'm there, 'Yeah, hi. How are you?'

'Grand. I suppose.'

'Right.'

'How are you?'

'Cracking form.'

'That's good.'

'Yeah.'

'Right so.'

'Right.'

Honor doesn't seem to pick up on the weirdness between us.

'Come on, Dad,' she just goes, 'the boat's about to leave.'

We pull on our life vests, then we end up having to sprint down the metal gangway so we don't miss the actual boat. We make it with, like, seconds to spare.

Out into the middle of the bay we go. Honor and Reese head for the front of the boat because Honor wants to get a selfie of them doing a 'Jack and Rose' – exact quote – even though she laughed at me, threw Quality Street wrappers at my head and called me pathetic for crying at the end of the movie three Christmas Eves ago.

God, I miss that girl.

I watch her standing at the front of the boat with her orms stretched out by her sides. And Reese is standing behind her with one orm wrapped around her waist and the other one taking their picture, then he storts kissing her ear and the back of her neck, and I somehow manage to resist the temptation to smash him over the head with something, then hold his head under the water and drown him like a focking –

'They make a lovely couple,' Marianne goes.

I'm there, 'Do you think so?'

'He's mad about her.'

'Yeah, no, he seems to be.'

'He does.'

'I suppose.'

'How have you been?'

'Great. Like I said. And you?'

'Yeah. Grand.'

'That's good.'

'It is.'

'I'm happy for you.'

'Look, I just wanted to say –'

'You don't have to say it.'

'I *want* to say it.'

'It's not a major deal.'

'It is to me.'

'Go on, say it so.'

'I will –'

'Fine.'

'– if you'll give me a chance.'

'I will.'

'I wanted to say sorry.'

'For?'

'For kissing you. The way I did.'

'I've been kissed worse.'

'For kissing you at all, Ross.'

'Oh. Right.'

'It wasn't fair.'

'I wasn't exactly fighting you off, Marianne.'

'We're both married.'

'I thought we agreed we were both –'

'What?'

'Er, *separated*?'

'I am separated.'

'So what's the biggie?'

'Father Reddin –'

'What about him?'

'He's an uncle of Donnacha's.'

'Okay. Explains why he was a dick to me.'

'He wants us to try to fix our marriage.'

'And you?'

'It's difficult.'

'As in?'

'Donnacha had –'

'Had what?'

'An affair.'

'Whoa.'

'With a colleague.'

'There's no excuses.'

I have literally *no* shame?

She's there, 'He's a teacher as well.'

I'm like, 'What a dick.'

'So I threw him out.'

'Wouldn't blame you.'

'He's renting in Swords.'

'Good enough for him.'

'Father Reddin wants me to forgive him.'

'What, even though he did the dirt?'

'We made vows to each other.'

'Vows, *shmows*.'

'My faith is very important to me, Ross.'

'Is it?'

'Of course. Just as yours is to you.'

'What?'

'I was listening to you. In the church that morning.'

'Oh, yeah, that.'

'How *moved* you were by the Mass.'

'It *was* a good one, in fairness to it.'

Honor all of a sudden shouts, 'Oh my God, I just saw Fungie! Dad, did you see him?'

I'm there, 'I did, Honor, yeah,' even though I didn't.

Dolphins have never really impressed me. But then I'm not as easily won over as *other* people?

'That's why I'm here,' Marianne goes.

I'm like, 'Where?'

'In Kerry.'

'Right.'

'Father Reddin thought it might do me good –'

'What?'

'To come here for the summer.'

'Got you.'

'To teach Irish.'

'Right.'

'And to think things over.'

'Hmmm.'

'And after five weeks, I really felt I was beginning to –'

'What?'

'Feel less confused. I suppose.'

'Right.'

'I was getting to a place where I thought I could forgive Donnacha.'

'Okay.'

'And maybe take him back.'

'Right.'

'And then you knocked me off my bike.'

'Yeah, that's not what happened.'

'When I looked at you that day –'

'I still say *you* hit *me*?'

'– I was attracted to you.'

'Right.'

'Instantly.'

'Can I be honest?'

'Please do.'

'I picked up on it.'

'Did you?'

'Your face was all flushed and you kept licking your teeth.'

'Did I?'

'No one looks at me like that – except obviously Glenda.'

'I was a bit overwhelmed.'

'And Mary Kennedy once, after I clipped her wing mirror in the RTÉ cor pork.'

'It was a very intense, physical attraction.'

'I think Mary would say something similar. She didn't even ask me for my insurance details.'

'I've never felt anything like it before.'

'Not even with, em –?'

'My husband.'

'Sorry, I've forgotten his name.'

'Donnacha.'

'I didn't do that on purpose, just in case you think –'

She's suddenly staring into my eyes – the same way she did on the beach in Ballydavid. It's like she's totally forgotten herself. For a second I'm convinced that she's going to throw the lips on me again.

But in that moment, Honor suddenly shouts, 'Oh my God, Dad! Fungie just jumped fully out of the water!'

And I look over my shoulder. 'That attention-seeking focker!' I mutter between gritted teeth. 'I wish he'd just, like, fock off!'

When I turn back around, the moment has passed. Marianne has obviously remembered that she's my daughter's teacher and she's moved to the other side of the boat.

I'm there, 'Marianne!'

But she goes, 'I can't, Ross. I want to. But I just . . . can't.'

'Come on, goys, you've got more to give!' I hear myself shout. 'Seán Bán, I heard you got a new hip last year!'

He's like, ''Tis true as the Lord's word, Rossa! The High King of Creation be praised and thanked!'

'Well,' I go, 'you're not playing like a man with a new hip! Come on, you can move faster than that!'

It's, like, my third training session with the goys and I'm proving what Father Fehily always said about me, that you could throw me into literally any situation – as long as it wasn't a matter of life and death and didn't involve handling money – and I would always, always, *always* emerge as the leader of the group.

That's just the alpha in me.

'Canice,' I go, 'let your opponent know you're there.'

He's there, ''Tis sticking to him I am – like a new-born lamb to its mother.'

I'm there, 'You're not. He's scored four points off you in the last six minutes. You can't afford to let that happen against Sleen.'

'Sneem,' he goes.

'Sneem, then.'

Seriously, ten days ago I didn't know how to play this game – I honestly thought they were making the rules up as they went along – and now I'm not only playing it, I'm talking to my team-mates like I'm the one who's going to be leading them into battle.

Even Muiris – the *actual* captain – ends up going, 'God of fortunes! 'Tis like a weaver's shuttle your mind is – and it moving non-stop!'

Although ten minutes later, he shouts, 'That's it, fellas! We'll call it a night, Rossa.'

I'm like, 'Call it a night? It's only, like, nine o'clock. Do you think the Sreen lads will be calling it a night? Shmeem. Sleem. Sneem.'

'Ah, 'tis an hour ago they'll have finished,' he goes. ''Tis pissed in the pub they'll be now.'

I have to keep reminding myself that this isn't rugby.

I'm like, 'Fair enough.'

''Tis well we've trained,' Muiris goes. 'And there's a question I need to ask you, Rossa?'

'Er, yeah, whatever.'

'Will you play centre half-back for us against Sneem?'

'Dude, I'll play anywhere.'

''Twill mean you'll be marking the great Séamuisín Joyce.'

'Er, right.'

'He's their centre half-forward – their danger man.'

'Not a problem.'

'He has All Ireland medals won. Putting a stop to his gallop will be vital, Rossa.'

'If that's what I have to do,' I go, 'then that's what I will do.'

I stand next to the cor and I change back into my civvies. Then I tell the goys I'll see them on, like, Thursday night – our last training session before the actual match.

'*Oíche mhaith!*' they all go, which I take as a compliment.

I'm like, 'Yeah, no, thanks.'

It's as I'm opening the door of the cor that I notice two figures step out of the dorkness about, like, twenty feet away from me.

It's Peatsaí, who didn't even train with us tonight. And with him – oh, shit the focking bed – is Father Reddin.

Peatsaí goes, 'There you are, you Dublin devil! Haven't I been listening to you all night? And isn't it a great power of noise you've been making with your rulla-bulla and your wim-wam and your blither-blather?' and then he turns to the priest. 'Well, is it him, Father? Is it the lump of a Jackeen lad that was seen on the beach with your niece-in-law – and he all over her like a harvest midge?'

''Tis him,' Father Reddin goes, 'for 'tis well I remember him! And I sitting in my car outside Tigh TP, looking at him kissing her!'

I'm there, 'Er, *she* actually kissed *me* – if you want to get your facts right?'

'A wanton woman!' Peatsaí goes. 'And she going about the place on a pushbike! Doesn't the Book of Revelation have it that a sign of the world ending would be a woman riding around on a wheel?'

Father Reddin walks up to me. For a second, I actually think he's going to deck me. Instead, he goes, 'I'd like to ask you, in regards to Marianne, what are your intentions?'

I'm like, 'My intentions? Jesus, you sound like my father-in-law!'

'I'll not lie to you – it's not one bit I liked or trusted you from the first time I saw you in the church!'

'I'm not everyone's cup of tea.'

'You have a horrible sneering face on you! You and Old Nick are lick-alike – prosperity to all who hear it!'

'Well, if you must know, me and Marianne are friends.'

'Friends, is it?'

'Yeah, no, men and women *can* be friends.'

I'm saying shit that I don't even believe now.

He goes, 'And you kiss all of your friends that way, do you?'

I'm there, 'Like I said, she was the one who lobbed the gob.'

Peatsaí decides to get involved again then.

'Yerra,' he goes, ''tis a flimsy tale that would take a great deal of believing!'

I'm there, 'It's true.'

Father Reddin goes, 'Listen to me now so that I might educate you. There'll be no more of your kissing.'

I'm like, 'I can't make that promise.'

God, I really am a prick sometimes.

He goes, 'She's a married woman.'

I'm there, 'Separated is the story I heard.'

'Oh, you're a class of plucky, aren't you? Well, I'll make *you* a promise – in the here and the now. If you ruin that woman – and you know what I mean by ruin –'

I'm there, 'Presumably *ride*?'

'After your final breath is drawn,' he goes, 'it will be to the fires of Hell you'll go.'

'You're what?' Ronan goes.

I laugh.

I'm there, 'Yeah, no, it's true.'

'Gaedic?'

'Absolutely.'

'Footbalt?'

'That's right – and I'm pretty good at it as well.'

'You used to say it wadn't a proper spowurt, Rosser.'

'I know what I said.'

'You used to say thee were making the rules up as thee weddent along.'

'We're playing this local team – it's, like, a *grudge* match?'

'Jaysus, I'd lubben to be theer to see that. Addyway, the reason Ine rigging, Rosser, is to say thanks.'

'For?'

'Ine oatenly arthur hearton about you and Buckets and Nudger and Gull breaking into the Geerda Headquarthors in the Pheodix Peerk to steal the ebidence.'

'Yeah, no, we focked it up, though. I got bitten by a rat and Gull's PTSD storted playing up. But don't worry, Dude, I'm going to come up with another plan.'

'There's no neeyut, Rosser. I doataunt waddant to go away addy mower.'

'To the States? Why not?'

'I hab a job with Heddessy, Rosser. It pays weddle. And Cheerlie's arthur gibbon me and Shadden the house in Foxrock.'

I'm like, 'Yeah, no, so I heard.'

He goes, 'Be a roof oaber Shadden and Ri's heads when I go to jayult. Plus –' and then he lets it just hang there.

I'm there, 'Please don't say it.'

'I've anutter birra news.'

'I know this is going to be bad.'

'Shadden's pregnant.'

I'm there, 'For fock's sake, Ro,' sounding less enthusiastic than I maybe should at the thought of a second grandchild.

He goes, 'It was a total surproyuz, Rosser.'

I'm there, 'Yeah, you had unprotected sex with a woman during the few days of the month in which she was ovulating and then, as if by magic –'

I feel bad that I can't be happy for him. It's just, I still had a hope of getting him away from my old man and Hennessy and now that hope has gone.

'In addyhow,' he goes, 'I'd bethor go. Ine going through Paschal Duddahue's rubbish hee-or and I've Eamon Ryan's to do arthur.'

He hangs up and I hit the floor – I'm in my room in the B&B, by the way – to do my nightly sit-ups. With match day only, like, five days away now, I want to make sure I take the field in absolute peak physical condition. That's what a pro I am. I burn through fifty of the things, only having to stop twice to catch my breath, then I decide to do fifty more, especially because I'm planning to have another few scoops in Foxy John's tonight.

I'm just storting my second set when my phone all of a sudden rings again. This time, it's, like, a local number, so I end up answering.

'Hello?' a woman's voice goes.

It's *her*.

I'm like, 'Oh, hey.'

'It's Marianne,' she goes.

'Yeah, no, I gathered. How are you?'

'Grand. I suppose. And you?'

'Cracking form.'

'That's good.'

'I was just doing some sit-ups.'

'Right.'

'That's why I'm out of breath.'

'Right.'

'Just in case you thought I was –'

'I didn't.'

'Good.'

'Grand.'

'I, er, had a visit from your mate last night?'

'Who?'

'Father Reddin.'

'He saw us on the beach, Ross.'

'So he said.'

'He followed us. After Mass.'

'Well, just to let you know, he threatened me.'

'Threatened you?'

'He told me I'd go to Hell if anything happened between us.'

'I shouldn't have invited you to Mass that day.'

'Why did you?'

'It was a way of spending time with you –'

'Right.'

'– in a way that looked innocent.'

'I didn't mind.'

'The other reason –'

'Go on.'

'It doesn't reflect very well on me.'

'Say it anyway.'

'I thought if Father Reddin saw us together –'

'What?'

'– it'd get back to Donnacha.'

'Right.'

'I'm sorry.'

'What for?'

'I used you.'

'You're attracted to me.'

'Ross, please don't.'

'And I'm attracted to you.'

'Nothing is going to happen between us, Ross.'

'Then why are you ringing me?'

'I'm ringing about Onóir.'

'Who?'

'Your daughter.'

'Oh, her. What about her?'

'She's not well.'

I'm like, 'Not well?' quickly jumping – well, slowly climbing – to my feet. 'What kind of not well are we talking here?'

'It's nothing serious,' she goes.

'I'll be the judge of that.'

'It's just she said she felt a bit off –'

'Off?'

'– when she came off the camogie field this afternoon.'

'Camogie?'

'Yes.'

'Jesus.'

'And she said didn't feel up to going to the *céilí* tonight.'

'So, er, why are you telling *me* all this?'

'Well, she's staying home tonight –'

'Right?'

'– and she wondered would you call out to her –'

'Absolutely, I would.'

'– just to keep her company.'

'Like I said, I'm on my way.'

So – yeah, no – I drive out to Muiríoch, not even caring about the pints that I'm being denied. Half an hour later, I'm knocking on Bean Uí Chuill's door and I'm going, 'Hi, is Honor here? Slash, Onóir?'

She invites me in, then leads me along a hallway to the last room on the left, knocks on the door and goes, '*Onóir, tá d'athair anseo.*'

Then I hear Honor go, *'Tar isteach!'* which obviously means something because the woman opens the door for me and in I go.

I'm like, *'Go maith mé,'* just to say thanks, then off the woman focks.

There's, like, two sets of bunk beds in the room. Honor is sitting up in the bottom bunk of one of them, reading – I shit you not – a book.

I'm like, 'Is everything okay?'

'I'm not feeling great,' she goes.

I'm there, 'Obviously. Is this something to do with Reese?' hoping and praying that the answer is yes, 'because I will deck him, Honor, for the slightest thing.'

'No,' she goes, 'I'm just feeling a bit, like, *crampy* tonight?'

I'm there, 'Crampy?'

'Yeah – as in, you know, I've got my *thing?*'

'What thing?' I – like an idiot – go.

She's there, 'Er, my *period*, Dad?'

'Jesus Christ!'

'What?'

'Yeah, no, forget it. I'm sorry I asked.'

She smiles at me.

'Thanks for coming,' she goes.

I'm there, 'Hey, it's not a big deal. I was just going to have a few pints in Foxy's. Although that's obviously gone out the focking window now. But I honestly don't mind.'

'It's just that, I don't know, I've kind of *missed* you?'

'Hey, I've kind of missed you too!'

'Yeah, I miss us just, like, hanging out together and having, like, a *laugh?*'

'Same!'

'Even though I do love it here. Sit down.'

So – yeah, no – I plonk myself down on the edge of her bed.

I'm there, 'I was hoping that it was something to do with Reese – just so I could smash his head through a wall.'

She's like, 'Oh my God, Dad, you have to stop! He's *such* a lovely goy!'

'I still say it's an act.'

'I still can't believe that someone like him would want to be with someone like me!'

'Don't talk rubbish.'

She's not talking rubbish. I can't believe it either. It's focking mind-boggling.

'I mean, he's, like, *so* good-looking,' she goes. '*And* he's a year older than me. *And* he goes to Michael's. *And* he plays rugby.'

I'm there, 'He definitely seems to be the complete package alright.'

'Dad, he told me he has feelings for me.'

'Again, it could be just a line – reel you in.'

'He said he's never felt about any girl the way he feels about me.'

'All I'm saying, Honor, is don't put all your eggs in one basket.'

'What are you talking about?'

'I'm talking about you keeping your options open. I'm sure there's other goys on the course who are into you, is there?'

'I'm not interested in anyone else.'

'What about that kid with the big ears?'

'What kid with the big ears?'

'He was on the boat when we went out to see Fungie. He had a massive underbite as well. He was staring at you the entire time.'

'He's not on the course, Dad. I think he was the captain's son.'

Okay, that explains why he was wearing the sailor's cap and kept telling me to put my life vest back on.

I'm there, 'He was still into you. And if *he* was into you, then others will be as well.'

She goes, 'He bought me jewellery!'

'Who, the half-wit with the ears?'

'No, Reese!'

'Oh, did he now?'

'Yeah, no, Cliodhna – as in, like, my *friend* Clíodhna? – saw him in the Celtic Jewellery Store and he was buying a necklace with, like, a *dolphin* on the end of it?'

Oh, he's good. He's better than good. It's like he's taken my correspondence course.

I'm there, 'All I'm saying, Honor, is that there's such a thing as a holiday romance. You've watched *Grease*, haven't you?'

She goes, 'That's not what this is, Dad. As a matter of fact, we've already decided that we're going to carry on being boyfriend-girlfriend after next week. He lives on Shrewsbury Road.'

Shrewsbury focking Road! She has literally no idea how out of her depth she is here.

I'm like, 'Hmmm,' just letting her know that I'm still dubious.

She goes, 'Dad, I'm also going to stop being a bitch when I go home.'

I'm there, 'Don't do that. I definitely don't want you to do that.'

'Dad, look at what happened when I storted being nice to people. I'm the most popular girl on the course – and I've got this amazing, amazing boyfriend who, oh my God, *every* girl wants to *be* with?'

'I just don't want you to become boring.'

'I'm not going to become boring.'

You're focking boring now, I nearly feel like telling her.

'Erika's right,' she goes. 'It's, like, exhausting being horrible all the time.'

I'm there, 'You can be very funny when you're horrible. I'm throwing that in there, just in the interests of balance.'

'But I don't *want* to be horrible any more.'

'You might change your mind. You might arrive home and feel like being a bitch again. Leave your options open is all I'm saying.'

I end up staying with her for a couple of hours.

'It's nearly ten o'clock,' she eventually goes. 'The girls will be home from the *céilí* soon.'

I'm like, 'Yeah, no, I'm going to hit the road. Might still get one or two pints in – and that's not a dig at you.'

I don't bother telling her that her brother is going to be a dad again. I haven't, like, properly processed it myself.

'Hey, will you come to the show?' she goes.

I'm there, 'What show?'

'There's, like, a show. On our second last night. Every house has to, like, *do* something? As in, like, a song or play?'

'And what are you doing?'

'I've translated *Get Lucky* into Irish.'

'Fair focks.'

'Well, I just cut and pasted it into Google Translate.'

'I'm still saying it.'

'I'm going to really miss Marianne when I go home. She's so amazing.'

'She is amazing. No doubt about it.'

So – yeah, no – we say our goodbyes and I bid farewell to Bean Uí Chuill with a cheeky wink and a '*Céad míle fáilte!*' on my way out the door.

I get into the cor and I stort driving back down the boreen, slowly because – like Honor said – the kids are all returning home from the *céilí* in little huddles.

I'm passing this, like, bornyord, and I just happen to look to my right, when I spot something that causes me to slam on the brakes. I can't believe what I'm actually seeing – and yet, at the same time, I *can*?

There's, like, a tall, blond dude and he's standing there with this much shorter, red-headed girl. He's wearing the absolute face off her and I know – without even having to get out of the cor – that it's Reese.

I get out of the cor anyway and I morch straight up to him. The dude is obviously a good kisser because the girl looks like she's in her element, just like Honor did.

I go, 'Typical focking Michael's,' because I really want to hurt him.

He's like, 'Er, Dude –'

Except I cut him off.

I'm there, 'Don't call me Dude!' and I end up roaring it at him. 'You don't *get* to call me Dude!'

'Who's this?' the girl goes, with her half-Nordy voice.

And Reese is there, 'It's Onóir's old man.'

The focking state of her, by the way. I think I mentioned the red hair. Your confidence would never recover if a dude picked her over you. You'd end up with a focking complex.

I'm there, 'So you have feelings for my daughter, huh?'

And that's when I spot the little box in *her* hand. I snatch it from her and she's like, 'Hey!'

Her face looks like something her neck puked up.

I open the box and I look inside. And – yeah, no – just as I suspected, it's a little dolphin on the end of a chain.

I'm there, 'I'll take this,' snapping the box shut and slipping it into my pocket.

The girl goes, 'That's mine!'

And I'm there, 'Not any more it's not.'

Reese is like, 'Dude –'

And I end up exploding. I'm there, 'I already told you – *you* do not *get* to call *me* Dude!'

He goes, 'Whatever.'

I'm like, 'So here's what's going to happen. I'm not going to mention this incident to Honor slash Onóir and neither are you. You're going to carry on going out with her for the last week of the course and you're not going to do the dirt on her with anyone, including this yoke. After that, you can do whatever the fock you like – but you will *not* break my daughter's hort while she's here.'

The dude just nods. He's terrified of me. That'd be Michael's all over, I'm tempted to say.

I turn around to the girl then and I notice that she's wearing Honor's pink RIXO top.

I'm there, 'I'm presuming you're Clíodhna, are you?'

And she's like, 'Er, yeah – how did you know?' a look of, like, shock on her face.

And I'm there, 'Let's just say I understand human nature better than my *daughter* obviously does?'

'So how many actual cows do you have?'

Talk about lines you never thought you'd hear yourself say.

'Four hundred, my dear man,' Canice goes. 'And two hundred sheep. But, my sharp woe, they will soon be gone the way of Mór's wealth if that stump of a fool from the land of the enemy is to have her way. May hardship and distress follow her wherever she goes and may she be separated from the good people of the world on the Day of Judgement and her father-in-law with her!'

Jesus.

I'm there, 'So, er, what will you do instead?'

'I haven't a notion in this wide world what I'll do instead,' he goes. 'For cows and sheep is all I know, Rossa. Same as my father and seven generations of us that's under the clay. 'Tis far from a life of ease, but I never knew hunger – and now I'm as vexed as a tethered calf.'

'Could you maybe, like, switch to something else? As in, like, chickens, wind, blah, blah, blah?'

He laughs, then slaps me on the back.

He's there, 'Have sense for yourself, Man! 'Tis too late I am in the run of this life to be learning about turbines – and I a man with fifty-five summers lived! Will you have a drink? For you have it well earned!'

Yeah, no, we're all back in Páidí Ó Sé's, by the way, having one or two after our final training session.

'I'll have a Rock Shandy,' I go, because I've decided to go off the booze until after the match.

'A pint of Guinness it is,' Canice goes, 'and a small one that'll be a comfort for it.'

All of a sudden, the door of the pub opens – and in walks the famous Peatsaí.

'The cross of God between all here and harm!' he goes.

There's no such thing as a simple hello in these ports.

'You saying it,' everyone shouts in response, 'and me saying it after you!'

'So how was the training tonight?' Peatsaí goes – he seems a bit jorred.

Muiris looks up from his pint. 'There was no sign of you at it,' he goes. 'Again.'

Peatsaí's like, 'There wasn't – neither tonight nor the last night! For hadn't I more important matters requiring my attention?'

'Is that the truth?'

''Tis God's own.'

Something's going on. He seems, I don't know, more cocksure of himself than usual, like he's got something *on* me?

'Rossa, my old butty!' he goes. 'How's every little thing?'

I'm like, 'Er, good.'

Seán Bán goes, 'Peatsaí, take yourself home now – for your five wits are scattered from the drink you have taken.'

'Oh, 'tis not drunk I am,' Peatsaí goes. ''Tis happy. For I have news to tell!'

'News?'

'News such as would put a crease of consternation on the royal foreheads of the mountains of Kerry!'

'Well, spit it out, Man,' Muiris goes, 'and be done making a production out of it!'

'It turns out young Rossa here is a rogue – and he's put his treachery across on us.'

'The fock are you talking about?' I make sure to go.

''This afternoon, I was inside in Dingle – and didn't I chance upon a cousin of my wife's who runs one of the finest bed-and-breakfast establishments in that fine, fine town. You've met Nuala, haven't you, Rossa?'

Oh, fock.

'I'm, er, just trying to place the girl,' I go.

But Peatsaí's there, 'Ah, 'tis well you know her! And haven't you been the top and bottom of her heart's torment ever since the day you landed in on her? Well, Nuala had the full *scéal* in her gob, boys – and it's not sorry I'll be to see him meeting his comeuppance on this floor tonight.'

Canice goes, 'Peatsaí, will you tell your story – for we've all had our share of your chatter!'

'I will so,' he goes. 'Young Rossa has taken ye all for a band of fools. For haven't I discovered his secret, that his name is not Rossa de Paor at all. His name is Ross O'Carroll-Kelly.'

There's, like, silence in Páidí Ó Sé's. They all just look at each other.

Canice goes, 'You mean –?'

'He is the husband of the woman who wants the sheep and the cow to go the same road as the buffalo. And the son of the man with his heart set on doing to the people of rural Ireland what the

Americans did to the poor, cursed Indians – and may all be safe and well wherever the tale is told!'

Muiris looks at me, but I can't meet his eye.

'Has his story truth?' he goes.

There's no point in lying to him. But I decide to give it a go anyway.

I'm there, 'I honestly haven't a clue what he's talking about, Muiris.'

'Every word I'm telling you,' Peatsaí goes, 'could have come from the mouth of the Pope inside in his palace in Rome! Didn't I see the guestbook and wasn't his signature in it – in his own hand? Ross O'Carroll-Kelly! The eldest son of that gangster up above in Dublin who gave a passage tomb to the Russians for a gift! Oh, the prophet wasn't far wrong when he said that every child follows his rearing!'

I'm there, 'Goys, you've got to listen to me –'

'You may hold your whisht! For we've all had our share of your chatter!'

'Yeah, no, okay, Chorles O'Carroll-Kelly *is* my old man. And Sorcha Lalor *is* my wife. But that's where the relationship ends. I don't believe the shit that they believe.'

''Tis small thought you have for the people of An Ghaeltacht!'

'Maybe that was true before. But now I can put my hand on my hort and honestly say I'd consider you friends.'

'Oh, doesn't the vein of poetry pulse in him, fellas!'

'Look, I totally get why you'd hate my old man and my wife. *He's* a dick and *she* can be a bit much at times. But I've never been anything but nice to you. And – yeah, no – I think it was actually fate that brought me to you. If you just give me a chance to prove to you what I'm all about, I promise you we can beat Sleen. Sreem. Sneem.'

'The devil take the match!' Peatsaí roars. 'And let him fire your ribs while he's about it!'

I look around the pub. I haven't convinced anyone. None of them can bring themselves to even *look* at me? Muiris is just, like, staring into space with, like, tears in his eyes. I've hurt him – a man who liked and genuinely trusted me. I've hurt them all.

'You may cut the wind,' he goes.

I'm there, 'Does that mean fock off?'

And he's like, 'You're a smart one.'

So I'm guessing that it does.

I'm standing on my tiptoes on a rock, near the edge of a cliff, staring out at the Three Sisters. The good news, though, is that I've got one bor of signal. I dial the number. Sorcha answers on the third ring.

She's like, 'Where the fock are you?'

I'm there, 'Er, I'm still in, like, Kerry?'

'I told you to come home.'

'And I told you I was going to stay down here. I have this Gaelic football match – well, *had* this Gaelic football match. And that's kind of the reason I'm ringing.'

'Ross, I'm too busy for this.'

'Sorcha, you know the way you're talking about possibly banning sheep and cows from, like, Ireland?'

'I'm not talking about it. I'm preparing the Bill to put it before the House in the autumn.'

'Right – well, could you maybe, like, *not*?'

'Excuse me?'

'As in, like, *not* ban sheep and cows? I'll tell you what it is, Sorcha, I've kind of fallen in love with rural Ireland.'

'Have you been drinking?'

'Not today, but – yeah, no – I have had a fair bit over the past few weeks. But I've also developed an understanding of these people, Sorcha. I'm actually friends with some formers and they're – believe it or not – good people.'

'Good people?' she goes, her voice travelling up through the scale. 'Formers are the reason my family has been driven from its home! Formers are the reason I can't work from my office! Formers are the reason the Dáil is having to sit in the National Convention Centre!'

'Maybe there's some kind of compromise, like, I don't know, get rid of the sheep but let them hang onto their cows. I'm just thinking out loud here.'

'You drive our daughter to Irish college,' she goes, 'and then you disappear for three weeks while everything here is falling aport! Then you ring me up out of the blue and you ask me to feel sorry for formers and – oh, yeah – maybe hold off on that legislation you're preparing that's going to drastically reduce Ireland's green-house gas emissions! You've got a –'

She all of a sudden stops.

I'm like, 'Sorcha, are you okay?'

'Oh! My God!' she goes.

I'm there, 'What is it? What's wrong?'

'I'm just watching CNN here! They're rebuilding the Newgrange passage tomb in Gorky Pork!'

'Where?'

'Gorky Pork! Ross, I have to go.'

She hangs up.

I jump down off the rock and I walk back across the field. I climb over the stone wall and cross the road to the little school hall where the show is happening tonight. I walk in. The place is rammers and full of excited chatter. All these kids from different ports of the country who've become friends over the past few weeks will be say-ing their tearful goodbyes to each other two days from now.

I spot Reese in the middle of the hall, chatting to two girls and giving it – it has to be said – *loads*? He reminds me so much of myself that I know I could never warm to him. He cops me staring at him and he obviously gets the message I'm sending him, because he wanders over to Honor and he puts his orm around her shoulder and she looks up at him and they kiss.

'Ross?' a voice behind me goes.

I turn around and it ends up being Marianne. She looks well.

I'm there, 'Hey.'

She goes, 'Hi.'

'How are you?'

'Grand.'

'Right.'

'And you?'

'Yeah, no, great.'

'That's good.'

269

'Yeah. No. Good.'

'Are you here for the –'

'For the show. Is that okay?'

'Of course.'

'Right.'

'It's nice to see you.'

'Yeah, no, it's nice to see you, too.'

'I just, em –'

'What?'

'I've decided to take him back.'

'Who?'

'Donnacha.'

'Right. Whatever.'

'Don't be like that.'

'Like what?'

'You sound –'

'How do I sound?'

'– disappointed.'

'Why would I be disappointed?'

'For what it's worth, Ross –'

'What?'

'– I think us meeting was an act of God.'

'In terms of?'

'I think He sent you to me.'

'Sorry, I'm getting mixed messages here.'

'To tempt me. To test my faith.'

'Is that what you genuinely think?'

She suddenly can't bring herself to look at me.

I'm there, 'Well? Is that what you think?'

She goes, 'It's what Father Reddin thinks.'

'I thought so.'

'I suppose this is the last time we'll ever see each other.'

'What do you mean?'

'Onóir will be going home in two days.'

'I suppose.'

'And she tells me you have a match tomorrow.'

'I don't.'

'Oh?'

'Long story.'

'Call into the house to see me. Before you go.'

'I might.'

'I don't want you to go without saying goodbye.'

All of a sudden, I hear music. I look up at the stage and there's, like, twenty-five boys and girls up there. Honor is at the front and she's singing:

Tá sí ina dúiseacht ar feadh na h'oíche go n-éirí an ghrian
Táim i mo dhúiseacht ar feadh na h'oíche chun roinnt a fháil,
Tá sí ina dúiseacht ar feadh na h'oíche chun spraoi a bheith aici,
Táim i mo dhúiseacht ar feadh na h'oíche chun go mbeadh an t-ádh liom.

It doesn't really fit the tune, to be honest. But you'd still have to say fair focks to her.

Then the rest of them are like:

Táimid in ár ndúiseacht ar feadh na h'oíche go n-éirí an ghrian,
Táimid in ár ndúiseacht ar feadh na h'oíche chun roinnt a fháil,
Táimid in ár ndúiseacht ar feadh na h'oíche chun spraoi a bheith againn,
Táimid in ár ndúiseacht ar feadh na h'oíche chun go mbeadh an t-ádh linn.

The song eventually ends. I give Honor the guns and she gives me a big wave and a smile, then all the other girls stort hugging her, including Clíodhna, the two-faced bitch.

I step outside again – and I'm not prepared for the sight that ends up greeting me.

There's, like, ten or eleven of them standing in the cor pork. We're talking Muiris. We're talking Canice. We're talking Colman. We're talking Seán Bán. We're talking Éamonn Óg.

At first I think they're here to drive me to the border. But they're not.

'The sins of the father,' Muiris goes, 'are not the sins of the son. The same as the sins of the wife are not the sins of the husband. Will you play for us against Sneem?'

And what else am I going to say?

I'm there, 'You better focking believe I will.'

I'm nervous. More nervous than I've ever been before a big match and I'm including the 1999 Leinster Schools Senior Cup final in that.

Even though it's taking place in just, like, a field in the middle of Kerry. Even though there's only, like, fifty people here to watch it. Even though the result literally doesn't matter a fock to anyone outside of here. The point is that it matters to these people – and I don't want to let them down.

I watch the Sneem players get off their bus and make their way to the dressing room. There ends up being quite a bit of pointing and shouting between *our* players and *their* players?

It's all, 'This field will see blood and tears spilled today, the like of which has not been seen since Dark Rosaleen was in slavery!' and ''Tis true, but 'tis *your* tears and blood will be spilled – and you only a bunch of fooken caubogues with a fine gift for the gabbing!'

It's like listening to the Seoiges with drink on them.

I'm about to walk into the dressing room when I hear a familiar voice say my name.

'Rosser – you bleaten flute!'

I spin around and he's standing right there – we're talking Ronan.

I'm like, 'What the fock are you doing here?'

'Ross O'Cattle-Keddy playing Gaedic footbalt?' he goes. 'I woultn't miss it for the wurdled! I hab to go straight back, but – Heddessy dudn't know Ine godden.'

He looks down at my general crotch area then.

'Hee-or,' he goes, 'them showurts you're wearton doatunt leave much to the imagidation, do thee, Rosser?'

I'm like, 'Yeah, no, they're definitely *tighter* than rugby shorts?'

'And is that a chayun arowunt your neck?'

I end up just laughing.

'Yeah, I only threw it on to see what it looked like,' I go, 'but I thought it kind of suited my new look.'

He's there, 'Is that a dollaphint on the eddend of it?'

'Yeah, no, I think it's supposedly Fungie.'

'Rosser with a chayun – moy Jaysus.'

'Ro,' I go, 'I'm sorry, I should have said – yeah, no – congratulations. On the baby.'

He's there, 'Ah, you're alreet. I know you're woodied about me.'

'I worry constantly about you.'

'It's all godda woork out. We're arthur moobin into the gaff in Foxrock. Moy Jaysus, there's some amount of muddy on that roawut, idn't there, Rosser?'

'Yeah, no, there is.'

'Addyhow, you bethor go and get chayunged. Good luck, Rosser.'

Into the dressing room I go. All the goys are already in there – we're talking Muiris, we're talking Canice, we're talking Seán Bán – and it's, like, a world away from the rugby dressing rooms I've been in in the past. I'm looking around at men bandaging their knees and their ankles, and putting corn plasters on their feet, and pulling on – Jesus! – thermal under-layers, even though it's, like, July.

I haven't seen a more unimpressive-looking group of athletes since Sorcha's granny and her mates walked a kilometre of the Dublin Mini Marathon course for osteoarthritis. But I know they've got horts like, I don't know, *lions*?

I walk over to the bench and I sit down. Canice hands me my jersey and I spread it across my lap, which is something I used to do when I played for Castlerock, and later for, like, Seapoint, just to think about who I'm representing today.

I look at the crest, which has, like, an island on it – the island where Peig Sayers lived, according to Seán Bán, even though I thought she was a made-up person – and a triangular hut made out of stones, which I've passed once or twice on the road, then the writing underneath that says, *Sprid Croí Caid Teanga*, which is probably something like 'kick orse' in Irish.

And something happens to me in that moment. I stort to feel actual pride in that jersey, even though it's made of micro polyester and the letters GAA are spelled out over the right tit. I pull it on, standing up at the exact same time and I suddenly slip into leadership mode.

I turn to Muiris and I go, 'Would you mind if I said a few words here?'

And he's like, 'Yerra, any man may exercise his windpipe – so long as it's wise words coming through it!'

I'm there, 'I don't have a lot to say. I suppose the main thing would be, like, thank you – for letting me play for this incredible team, even though I'm the son of a man who – like you said – wants to lay waste to rural Ireland and married to a woman who wants to slaughter your animals. Yet you were prepared to put that aside in the name of sport. And I want you to know that I will not let you down today.'

It's pretty heady stuff.

The players whoop and holler and shout about how there'll be bonfires burning on specifically named beaches and mountains in the region tonight. The referee bangs on the door and tells us that it's time, then out we walk.

Even though there isn't much of a crowd, there's still, like, serious, serious *tension* in the air? The two sets of players trade insults out of the sides of their mouths. They go, 'I'll send you off home with your bus fare, you dirty fooken gobaloon!' and they go, 'By me palms, 'tis you who'll have the sorrowful faces before long!' and they go, 'A drove of asses is all you are and it's much we'll enjoy putting the bridles on you! Yahoo!!!'

Like I said, it's like Síle and Gráinne being refused a late drink in Renords back in the day.

I walk out onto the pitch and take my position at the hort of the defence. The dude I'm morking – the famous Seamuisín Joyce – is, like, a big fat dude in his fifties. He introduces himself to me by giving me a hord shoulder nudge and going, 'You'll have the fill of trouble on your hands today!'

And I'm there, 'Is that right?' because he doesn't look like much of a player.

'Oh, 'tis,' he goes, shoving me in the chest then. 'And you with only a soft shell on you!'

I haven't been verbally abused by a bogger like this since I tried to blag my way into the VIP cor pork at the 2002 Witnness Festival.

I clap my hands together and shout, 'Come on! Let's drive through these fockers for a shortcut!' which, coincidentally, is what I said to

Sorcha when they tried to tell us we didn't have a valid pass and *she* was stressing about missing the Dandy Warhols.

The referee throws the ball up in the air and the game is suddenly underway. The first few minutes end up being total chaos. Anyone who has ever watched Gaelic football will know. It's just, like, pulling and dragging and biting and kicking until everyone remembers that the actual point of the exercise is to try to get your hands on the ball.

But after, like, five minutes, the game settles down and a sort of, like, *pattern* storts to emerge? That pattern is that Sneem take chorge and stort to build up a score. They've got this dude in the middle of the pitch called Podge – he's, like, *their* wild-cord player? – and he's, like, spraying balls everywhere, with pretty much pinpoint accuracy as well.

Twice, it embarrasses me to say, he pops balls over my head and right into the hands of Seamuisín and the dude puts the ball over the bor.

Canice is really struggling with Podge, which is no surprise given that he's old enough to be his father. After, like, twenty-five minutes, we're 0–10 to 0–3 behind and I pull him to one side and go, 'Dude, do you want me to, like, switch with you?'

Canice is like, 'Switch with me? Switch with me, is it?' like he can't believe that I'd even, like, *suggest* such a thing?

I'm there, 'Dude, he's controlling the match,' because – yeah, no – he's pulling the strings like ROG in his prime. 'At least I'm closer in age to him.'

''Tis the divil-a-bit you should worry,' Canice goes. 'Sure, haven't I a plan made for the famous Podge!'

That plan turns out to be a punch in face the next time the referee's back is turned. The ball goes out of play and Canice walks straight up to him and literally chins him. The poor dude's knees buckle and he flops down onto his side like a limp penis. All *hell* breaks loose then? The players from both teams suddenly steam in and we're all pulling the front of each other's shirts, or shoving our palms into each other's faces, or grabbing each other in a headlock.

Everyone has, like, totally lost it. Like a mob, we're caught up in the madness of the moment and it reminds me of the time Paul Costelloe made an in-store appearance in Dunnes Stores in the Beacon Court – except my old dear isn't standing on a table this time, drunkenly threatening to stove some total stranger's head in with one of the dude's trademork opulent, golden-toned toilet brushes.

Some randomer who isn't even playing calls me a Dublin yahoo and that's when I realize that there's been, like, a pitch invasion and the two sets of supporters are getting involved, grabbing each other by the throat and calling each other gannets and *dúramáns*, whatever the fock that's all about.

Suddenly, I hear Ronan behind me, going, 'You're a bleaten embadassment, Rosser.'

I turn around and I'm like, 'What?'

'The fedda you're meerking is nearly twedenty years older than you and he's arthur scording fowur points off you.'

'Yeah, Gaelic football isn't my sport, Ro.'

'He's got wooden leg, Rosser.'

'Well, he doesn't move like it's wooden.'

'I doatunt mean wooden, as in wooden. I mean wooden, as in wooden, two, tree, fowur . . .'

'Oh, *one* leg? You're trying to say he's got *one* leg?'

Seriously, sometimes it's like trying to communicate with Skippy the kangaroo.

'That's reet,' he goes. 'Ine arthur been watching him for the whole match, Rosser – and durding the wardem-up. He caddent kick with he's left foot. So all's you hab to do is force him odden to that soyud – do you wontherstand me?'

I'm there, 'Every second or third word – but I think I'm getting the general gist.'

'Force him odden to he's left soyud.'

'His *left* side – got it.'

The fight is eventually broken up, the pitch is cleared of members of the local community and Podge is helped to his feet. He looks pale and shaken and very definitely *not* on solid legs – again, like Paul Costelloe when they covered his head with a luxury, faux-fur throw and carried him back to his bulletproof SUV.

The match restorts and you can tell instantly that there's been a shift in the balance of power. I end up doing exactly what Ronan told me to do. Every time Seamuisín gets the ball, I force him onto his left foot – and Ro is completely right. Suddenly, the dude couldn't hit a hippo's orse with a badminton racquet. Even though he still beats me to pretty much every ball, he ends up kicking five wides in a row and he knows I have the measure of him because he goes, ''Tis vexed you have me!'

Podge is barely involved now and suddenly *we're* the ones who are playing with energy? Muiris is everywhere. And, despite his age, I can see why he won, apparently, county medals – whatever the fock they're worth – in his younger days. It's not long before we stort chipping away at their lead. Seán Bán kicks three points and Muiris adds one, then a minute before half-time we're awarded a free-kick, right on the sideline near the halfway line.

I grab the ball and I place it on the ground. I can hear one or two of the Sneem players sniggering behind their hands, going, 'He'll not get it from there! And he only a gasún from the city of Dublin!'

I just, like, blank it out, though. I take four steps backwards, run my hand through my hair, then take three steps to the side. I look down at the ball, then up at the posts, then down at the ball, then up at the posts. The Sneem players are booing and whistling. They don't respect the kicker. But I've got more than enough love for myself. I run my hand through my hair again, then I run at the ball and I strike it absolutely perfectly. And I know from the very second it leaves my boot that it's going over the bor.

People are going, 'Faith and begad, 'tis never I've seen the likes of that!' and 'By my baptism, 'tis unbelievable!'

It's, like, half-time and we're suddenly only 0–10 to 0–8 behind.

Back in the dressing room, the goys are suddenly allowing themselves to believe that we can win this match. Maidhc, our left corner-forward, goes, ''Tis a miracle unfolding before our eyes this day,' while Seán Bán goes, 'They'll not get the ten-in-a-row – and I couldn't be happier if I was with the Lord Himself above in Heaven!'

I'm the one who's warning them against getting carried away, though.

I'm like, 'Goys, let's not stort patting ourselves on the back – we're on top but we're still behind on the scoreboard.'

And it's a good warning. Because Sneem come out stronger in the second half. Podge's head has obviously cleared because he doesn't look as dizzy as he did after Canice decked him and he goes back to popping perfect passes around the place. I manage to keep Seamuisín to just one point in the second half, but I'm absolutely out on my feet from the effort, as are the rest of our goys.

The second half absolutely whizzes by, though. And with, like, a minute to go, we're trailing by 0–14 to 0–12 and I decide to take chorge of the situation. We're, like, attacking the Sneem end and I leave my station and make my way forward.

Canice has the ball, except he can't get in a clean kick at goal because he's surrounded by Sneem players. I call for it and he plays a handpass, which I run onto and solo my way towards the goal. I wrong-foot one player, then another.

And that's when *the* weirdest thing happens.

Instead of, like, blasting the ball past the keeper, I go around him. He tries – and fails – to bring me down. Instinct takes over in that moment. And, instead of kicking the ball into the open goal, I end up carrying the ball over goal-line to the right of the post . . . and putting it down for a try.

All of my teammates are looking at me like I've just slapped a widow's orse at her husband's wake. There's just, like, silence – except for the sound of my son going, 'It's not rubby, you bleaten spanner.'

I'm thinking, Oh, fock! Oh, fock! Oh, fockety, fockety fock-fock! I can't believe I actually did that!

'By my sorrow,' Maidhc goes, thinking our chance has passed, ''twas a good shot we gave it!'

I can see the Sneem players laughing. One of them turns to me and goes, 'You haven't the brains you were born into the world with!' and the rest of them all laugh. 'You big Dublin ass!'

My teammates have their heads down. They can't even bring themselves to look at me. I've let them down – and I've let them down in a major, major way.

But it's not over yet. That's what I end up telling myself.

Yeah, no, there's, like, thirty seconds remaining as the Sneem goalkeeper prepares to kick the ball out and that's good enough for the Rossmeister General.

I never, ever stop believing in myself. That just happens to be my superpower.

The goalkeeper kicks the ball high into the middle of the field. I've actually stayed where I am rather than return to the defence. I'm standing next to the famous Podge and we're both looking up, watching the ball come falling out of the sky towards us.

I spring into the air – it's an unbelievable leap from, like, a standing stort – catching Podge totally unawares, and I grab the ball in my two hands. I hit the ground and I set off in the direction of the goal, zigzagging one way, then the other, channelling the great Dricster Himself when He scored that try for the Lions against Australia, feinting one way, then going the other, leaving players grasping at air, or sitting on their orses, or panting in my slipstream, until I'm bearing down on the goal again and my teammates are shouting, 'He's in!' and 'The proverb didn't leave much out when it held that youth was a precious thing!' and the goalkeeper is rushing towards me, performing a stor jump to try to make the torget smaller.

And, though it seems utterly focking ridiculous to me that you get three points in this game for kicking the ball *under* the bor, I strike it hord and low and to the keeper's right. And suddenly I'm watching the net ripple and I'm hearing the roars of my teammates, then I disappear under an avalanche of jubilant An Ghaeltacht players. And it's from underneath this pile of bodies that I hear the referee blow the final whistle.

My teammates all climb off me and they pull me to my feet. Then ten pairs of hands seize me and I'm lifted up on to Muiris's and Canice's shoulders, then we set off on a lap of honour.

The Sneem players look seriously, seriously pissed off.

'Oh, you're not too happy for your bargain now,' Seán Bán shouts at them, 'and you denied the pleasure of the ten-in-a-row! Praise the Lord for delivering him unto us – a blow-in from the land of the enemy! And now 'tis ye who have the heavy hearts!'

I hear Ronan calling from the sideline. He's going, 'Rosser!

Rosser!' and when I look at him, I notice that he has, like, tears in his eyes. He never got to see me play rugby in my prime and I'm glad he was here to witness this. He goes, 'Ine proud of you, Rosser!'

And I shout back, 'Yeah, no, thanks!'

The goys do a full circuit of the pitch with me, then they put me down on the ground again and it ends up being back-slaps and hugs, and I can't say that there aren't a few yeehaws and yaroos as well.

I'm thinking about the trophy presentation until I remember that there's no actual trophy. It's pretty much literally a non-event. But then I end up getting something that's even better.

All the goys go quiet for some reason, then suddenly they port and I notice Peatsaí – the famous Peatsaí – standing ten feet in front of me.

Muiris goes, 'You may do yourself a benefit now, Peatsaí, and show your heels to the road. For this is a day of a celebration – and may it be remembered by the people of Kerry for as long as Mother Carey's chickens have a home in the Kingdom!'

But Peatsaí isn't here to make trouble. He looks me dead in the eye, then he sticks out his hand. Again, instinctively, I grab it and shake it.

''Tis sorry I am,' he goes, 'for I had you misjudged. Ross O'Carroll-Kelly, husband of the black-hearted woman who would take away our animals and our livelihoods, son of that ass of a man who would rob us of our land – you are an honorary Kerryman!'

She opens the door and I can tell from her face that she's surprised to see me standing there – although delighted might be *more* the word?

I'm there, 'Hey.'

And she's like, 'Hi.'

'I thought I'd swing in –'

She smiles at me.

She's like, 'I'm glad you did.'

I'm there, 'Just to say goodbye.'

'Come in,' she goes, opening the door for me.

I step inside.

'I only have a few minutes,' she goes.

'Right.'

'The final *céilí* is tonight.'

'So are you not going to say congratulations?'

'What for?'

'Er, we won our *match*?'

'Oh.'

'An Ghaeltacht against Sleem. Sbeen. Sneem.'

'That's great.'

'I actually scored the winning *goal*?'

'*Go h'iontach!*'

'Hero of the hour.'

'*Maith an fear!*'

'Thanks.'

'It's me who should be saying that.'

'Saying what?'

'Thank you.'

'For?'

'For helping me see the light.'

'Hey, all I did was buy you a Wibbly Wobbly Wonder.'

'That's not true.'

'And then I sort of, like, went with it when you storted getting off with me on the beach.'

'You helped me get everything straight in my mind.'

'Right.'

'I really do believe we met for a reason.'

'Yeah, no, definitely.'

'I do.'

'Definitely, definitely.'

My God, she suddenly looks beautiful to me. I need to get out of here.

'I'll let you get ready for the, er –'

'For the *céilí*.'

'That's right.'

'Well, it was lovely to have met you –'

'Yeah, no, you too.'

'– and your beautiful daughter.'

We, like, move in for a hug, but it doesn't feel like a *goodbye* hug? It feels like one of those hugs where something is being, I don't know, communicated – as in, like, our feelings for each other. It's one of those hugs where you both lose track of time. It's me who ends up pulling away in the end.

I've got a focking horn on me like a cruise liner.

I'm there, 'You better get ready.'

But then the most un-focking-believable thing happens. She kisses me again – even more passionately than she did on the beach. And suddenly, without a thought for Donnacha, or her marriage vows, or Father Reddin, or even God, our hands are all over each other and Marianne is slow-walking me backwards into the living room, tearing at my belt and my chino buttons like a woman hoping for a Death Row pordon who's just received a letter from the Governor.

And it's there, as usual, that I'm going to ask the director to fade to black, out of respect for Marianne's reputation as a married woman and someone who teaches children for a living. All I will say – and it's just to flesh out the story a bit – is that it ends up being wild, furious, sweary sex, and I'm saying that from *her* POV?

I'm not going to use the phrase *revenge* sex? All I will say is that Marianne ends up working out more anger in the minutes that follow than she has in all the weeks she's been teaching Irish to kids on the Dingle Peninsula. Poor Donnacha's name gets mentioned more than a few times during the exchanges and not in, like, a *complimentary* way?

'Gráinne fucking Thorpe,' the woman goes, bending me like a balloon animal, trying to find the position that works for her best. 'A fucking religion teacher. Just your fucking kind, Donnacha. A fucking hypocrite.'

She eventually finds her sweet spot, sitting astride me like she's, I don't know, sitting on a focking milking stool, then she storts bouncing up and down on me, going, 'How do you like this, Donnacha? Are you watching? How do you fucking like this, huh?'

Once or twice, I'm going to be honest, she sounds so pissed off that I have to remind her that her husband isn't actually *in* the room?

But she goes, 'Thank you, Ross. Thank you, Ross. This is really helping. This is really, really helping.'

Seven, possibly eight, minutes later the entire transaction comes to a shuddering end, with my face buried in Marianne's blorps and her shouting, 'You bastard! You bastard!' while bouncing up and down on me like Daenerys Targaryen riding Drogon into battle.

When the show's over, she stays seated, with her sweaty forehead resting on my shoulder, then when she manages to get her breath back, she kisses the side of my face and whispers in my ear, 'That was very nice,' a rare five-stor review.

I'm like, 'What about, I don't know, God?'

'I'm sure He has it in Him to forgive me,' she goes.

'He sort of, like, has to, doesn't He?'

'I suppose.'

'It's kind of, like, His *thing*?'

'Yes.'

'What about –'

'What?'

'– what's-his-face?'

'Who?'

'Focking Donnacha.'

'Like I said, my faith is very important to me.'

Which presumably means she's taking the dude back.

We kiss again, then she climbs off me.

She's like, 'I have to go.'

I get my shit together. I find my boxer shorts in the coal scuttle, where she focked them.

'This thing that happened,' she goes as I'm walking out the door.

I'm there, 'Yeah?'

'It has to –'

'What?'

'– has to stay between us.'

'Hey, I'm cool with that.'

Then she goes, 'Goodbye.'

And I'm like, 'So long, Marianne.'

'Thank the Maker who sent you our way!' Maidhc goes. 'I couldn't be happier this day if I had a currach full of mackerel!'

Yeah, no, the goys have driven into Dingle to say goodbye to me and it's a nice touch.

I'm there, 'It should be me thanking you. The thrill I got from scoring that winning goal.'

'Rossa Ó Cearbhall-Ceallaigh,' Muiris goes. 'It's not quickly you'll be forgotten in Corca Dhuibhne.'

Peatsaí's like, 'God save the hearer! May your creel always be filled with turf! And may every man who speaks your name give it the full love of his tongue – in spite of who your people are!'

I'm like, 'Thanks, Dude. And, by the way, I'm going to have a proper talk with Sorcha – and my old man – and ask them to maybe *not* go ahead with the whole banning cows and sheep thing?'

I shake each and every one of them by the hand.

'Oh, man of my soul,' Canice goes, 'our hearts are soaring this day like the great black Guillemot in flight! 'Tis a king's welcome that will be rolled out for you, Rossa, whenever 'tis this part of the world you visit!'

And with that, we say our goodbyes.

I hop into the cor and I point it in the direction of Muiríoch. Somewhere along the road, my phone storts pinging. It ends up being a bunch of pictures from Rebecca Leahy – as in, like, Diva Leahy's old dear – of the whole crew drinking cocktails in Gigi's. She's like, 'Final night out with The Girlies in QDL! All CLEARLY looking forward to seeing our children tomorrow!' and then my phone pings again. Alva Crowe – as in, Ginny Crowe's old dear – goes, 'Did anyone hear which Gaeltacht HORROR O'Carroll-Kelly ended up in?' and then a few seconds later, she's like, 'Sorry! Blonde moment! Orchestra group!'

I just think, fock *their* shit. I swipe left, then I hit 'Exit Group' and I throw my phone on the seat beside me. Then I continue driving the long and winding road into Muiríoch.

The cor pork in front of the school hall is full of kids, most of them in tears at the thought of saying goodbye to each other. There's, like, a bus there that's going to the train station in Tralee – for the kids who aren't middle class enough to have their parents here to drive them home.

I spot Honor standing with her back to the school building – yeah, no – getting off with the famous Reese. I get out of the cor and I make my way over to them. I tell her that it's time to say good-bye to Reese and make tracks. She's clinging to the dude like shit to a shovel and I end up having to clear my throat to get her actual attention.

She opens her eyes and goes, 'Oh, hi, Dad!'

I'm there, 'Yeah, no, let's, er, hit the road,' not able to even look at him, holding my daughter in his orms.

'I don't want to say goodbye,' she tells him.

And he's like, 'Er, yeah, no, me neither,' laying it on thick like Panda chocolate spread.

She goes, 'I just want to quickly say goodbye to Clíodhna and I'll be back!' and she runs across the cor pork to say a tearful farewell to the not-even-good-looking girl, from Louth of all places, who bor-rowed her clothes and got off with her boyfriend behind her back.

Reese doesn't know what to say to me.

He's there, 'So, like, er –' except there's fock-all going on in his head. He's so like me it's terrifying.

I'm there, 'I suppose you'll be getting off with Clíodhna on the train back to Dublin, will you?'

He just goes, 'Dude –' and he gives me a shrug that seems to say, hey, you played rugby yourself – you know the deal. And I do. I know it only too well.

I reach into my pocket and I whip out the box with the Fungie chain in it. I'm there, 'Here,' and I hand it to him.

And he's like, 'Oh, er, thanks.'

'Don't thank me,' I go. 'You're going to give it to Honor.'

One quick look at me tells him that I'm not focking around here and I don't expect to *be* focked around either.

He's like, 'Er, yeah, no, cool.'

I look up. Across the cor pork, I spot Marianne. She's hugging Honor and they're both in, like, tears saying goodbye to each other. I catch Marianne's eye and we both sort of, like, smile at each other. We don't need to say anything. Let's be honest, we only ever spoke in short sentences anyway. But there are times when, like, no words are needed.

I walk back to the cor and I get in. Twenty minutes later, Honor finally opens the door and slips into the front passenger seat, wiping tears from her face with her open palm.

'Look what Reese bought me,' she goes, showing me the chain.

I'm there, 'Wow!' cracking on that it's the first time I've seen the thing. 'Is that, like, Fungie?'

She goes, 'Oh my God, he's *so* romantic!' as she puts it on.

I'm there, 'It was hord saying goodbye to him, I'd say, huh?'

'Well, it's not *actually* goodbye?' she goes.

Yeah, you keep telling yourself that, I think.

'We're going to carry on seeing each other when we get back home,' she goes.

I'm there, 'He definitely said that, did he?'

'We both said it.'

Honor is suddenly staring at her phone.

She goes, 'I can't wait to get a signal. I want to send Reese a picture of me wearing the chain.'

I'm like, 'Or just leave it.'

'Oh my God, that's so weird.'

'What's weird?'

'Er, I asked him to put his number in my phone – but it's, like, one digit *short*?'

And, even though I hate the dude, there's a little bit of me that wants to go back and high-five him.

I'm there, 'Buckle up, Honor – we're going home.'

8.

Reese is the Word

The old man ends up nearly choking on his Cucumber Jalapeño Morgarita when he hears the news.

'Gaelic football?' he goes.

And I'm like, 'Gaelic football.'

'Gaelic?'

'That's right.'

'Football?'

Ronan's there, 'He was veddy good, Cheerlie – eeben though he was playing wirra buddench of bleaten auld feddas.'

I'm like, 'Yeah, no, thanks for that, Ro,' at the same time picking Mellicent up off the ground and sitting her on my knee. 'I scored the winning goal. Thought I'd just throw that into the conversation and see how it plays.'

We're having a family borbecue in the gorden of the Áras, where we're still living, by the way, as the Vico Road protest enters its fourth week. It's, like, a scorcher of a day and the boat has been well and truly pushed out. There's, like, tables and tables of food and an actual deer, roasting on a spit. Brian, Johnny and Leo are standing over the fire, pushing sticks into it.

The old dear is, like, holding little Hugo. She turns around to Honor and she goes, 'And what about you, Moxy? Did you have a good time?'

And Honor just stares back at her with this, like, confused look on her face. She goes, 'Er, Moxy is the name of Rihanna-Brogan's *pony*?'

The old dear's like, 'What?'

'You called me Moxy,' Honor goes.

The old dear's there, 'Did I?'

Then the old man suddenly pipes up. He's like, 'No, you definitely said Honor, Dorling. That's what I heard anyway – clear as a

289

bell,' and I'm suddenly staring at him, thinking, I thought you said you were going to change her meds, or at least stop her boozing when she's on them?

'Well, anyway,' Honor goes, 'I had an amazing time. And I learned – oh my God – *so* much Irish!'

'And what about boys?' the old dear goes. 'Were there any boys?'

Honor's like, 'There was one boy,' and her face reddens a little bit.

I steal a sneaky look at Sorcha, except there's no reaction from her. She storts taking a sudden interest in her phone. The old man can't help himself, though – has to ask the question that's on everyone's lips.

He's like, 'Do we know what school he goes to?'

'Michael's,' I go.

And he's there, 'Oh,' unable to hide his disappointment. 'Oh, well. Does he have a name, this chap of yours?'

Honor's like, 'His name is, like, Reese. And he bought me this chain. It has, like, a *dolphin* on the end?'

Ronan looks at me. He's about to say something, but I give him a tight shake of my head.

Shadden goes, 'And are yiz godda caddy it on now yisser howum or was it just a subber romaddence?'

Honor's there, 'No, we're going to carry on seeing each other,' and she's, like, staring at Sorcha as she says it, looking for her reaction, except there's none.

'I'd say yiz are texting the whole toyum,' Ronan goes, 'are yous?'

And Honor's like, 'No, because when he put his number into my phone, he accidentally left *out* a digit?'

That *does* get a reaction from Sorcha? She has a sly look at me – recognizing it as a classic Ross move.

'Has *he* not texted *you*, but?' Ronan goes, obviously concerned about the girl.

Honor's there, 'Oh my God, give him a chance, Ro! We're only home, like, two days!'

The old dear takes a sip of her Tom Collins and goes, 'Well, he sounds absolutely divine!'

The old man changes the subject. He's there, 'How's our friend coming along, Kennet?'

Yeah, no, I forgot to mention, Kennet is turning the deer on the spit. He's there, 'She's n . . . n . . . n . . . neerdy ready, T . . . T . . . T . . . T . . . T . . . T . . . Teashocked.'

'Wonderful!' the old man goes, then he turns to Rihanna-Brogan, who's holding Cassiopeia. 'Have you ever eaten venison, little one?'

She obviously goes, 'No,' because Shadden never fed her anything that didn't come out of the freezer or the Hole in the Wall. Even her focking breast milk came with a shovel of chips.

'Well, you have your grandfather to thank for it!' the old man goes. 'He ran over the thing near the Papal Cross while fumbling for his vape pen!'

'That's reet,' he goes, giving the girl a wink. 'Least she ditn't d . . . d . . . d . . . d . . . d . . . d . . . die in vayun, wha'? Did you hear that, Teashocked? Said at least she ditn't d . . . d . . . d . . . d . . . d . . . d . . . die in vayun!'

Sorcha goes, 'How are you feeling, Shadden?'

And Shadden's like, 'Ine feeding alreet – no morden sickness like I had with Ri.'

'And how are you goys settling in to Foxrock?'

'It's veddy diffordent to Finglas.'

Thanks be to focking Jesus, I think.

Sorcha's there, 'But you do like it, do you?'

'It's alreet,' she goes. 'I like the house, but the neighbours are a bit snoppy. The bleaten faces on them when they saw Moxy.'

'What,' I go, 'you're keeping the pony in the focking gorden? Okay, *that's* hilarious.'

Hennessy reaches into his suit jacket and whips out three humungous Cohibas. He hands one to the old man and one to Ronan.

'Fucking *Irish Times* is still going on about Newgrange,' he goes. 'Frank McDonald is calling it Ireland's Elgin Marbles.'

The old man actually laughs at that. He's like, 'It's the silly season, of course! By the way, I was watching the Russian news this morning! You know they've had a hell of a job reconstructing the thing! It seems they can't get the alignment for the solstice right! They've built it, then knocked it down, then rebuilt it again!'

Sorcha shifts uncomfortably in her seat. She's there, 'Taoiseach, I'm being asked to comment on it pretty much *every* time I talk to the press? Apparently, they dropped the entrance stone and it cracked in two. Fine Gael are calling it an act of historic vandalism. Like, what's the Government's line on this?'

'The Government's line,' the old man goes, 'is that we have far more important issues to concern us than a bunch of useless rocks!'

Leo pulls his stick out of the fire and tries to push the red-hot end into Johnny's face. But Johnny ducks out of the way, then punches him in the side of the head. He storts bawling and Honor goes over to them to try to restore order.

She's like, 'Come on, boys! We're having a lovely day! Don't spoil it for everyone!' and I can see Ronan and Hennessy and one or two others looking at the girl, wondering what the fock has gotten into her.

I watch Ronan puff away on his cigor, holding it like a dort, the exact same way as Hennessy.

'It suits you, Ro-Ro,' Shadden goes, smiling at him.

He's like, 'Dud it, Shadden?'

And she's there, 'You're like a Midi-Me version of Heddessy theer!' like that's somehow a *good* thing?

'Anyway,' the old man goes, 'the so-called paper of record will soon have something far juicier to write about! I've decided that the referendum on whether Ireland should leave the European Union will take place on Saturday, the eighth of September!'

'Oh my God,' Sorcha goes, 'that's only, like, six weeks away.'

'Well, the presidential election is scheduled for the end of October and I don't want it detracting attention from the most important question that Irish voters will have to answer in their lifetime! Oh, speaking of which, did you hear that our friends are finally moving out? I'm talking about the famous Michael D. and his good lady wife!'

I'm there, 'Where are they moving?' because I actually *like* them?

'Oh, they've found a couple of rooms for them in the Mansion House!' the old man goes. 'I think the Lord Mayor is a fan!'

Sorcha's like, 'Well, I'm still hoping to change your mind about Europe, Taoiseach. Yes, I'm having a hord time trying to persuade them that a total ban on ruminant animals will be good for the planet, but I still believe we're stronger *in* Europe than, like, *out* of it?'

'Taking back control of our country was the promise on which I was elected!' the old man goes. 'I said I would repeal the Third Amendment to the Constitution and I fully intend to deliver on it!'

Hennessy's there, 'I'll tell you who *wants* us to stay in Europe – those formers who've chased you from your home.'

'Well, let's see how clever they are,' the old man goes, 'when they no longer have Brussels paying them to do nothing from one end of the year to the other!'

I'm there, 'When are we moving back to Killiney, by the way? Is there any sign of that protest ending?'

'It's running out of steam,' Hennessy goes. 'My spies tell me it won't last more than a few more days. Although it might take a week to clean up all the shit.'

Sorcha's there, 'It's been lovely staying with you, Taoiseach, and you too, Fionnuala, but it will be – oh my God – *such* a relief to get back home to Honalee.'

Fionn steps out into the gorden then, holding little Hillary.

I'm like, 'Hey, Fionn, how the hell are you?'

He's just, like, staring at Kennet and Ronan as they lift the deer off the spit.

'Is that what I think it is?' he goes.

I'm there, 'Yeah, no, Kennet ran over it near the Papal Cross.'

Kennet goes, 'I had to ch . . . ch . . . ch . . . ch.. chase it across two fields foorst!' and I know that he's not even joking.

Fionn just stares at the blackened corcass of the thing.

Sorcha's there, 'How did you get on?'

Yeah, no, the dude spent the morning in, like, Trailfinders on Dawson Street.

'All booked,' he goes. 'We set off on the first of September,' and he sounds genuinely excited.

I'm like, 'Where are you going? Go on, make me sick,' even though I probably won't have heard of any of the places.

'Buenos Aires,' he goes. 'Rio de Janeiro. Montevideo. Santiago. Lima. Machu Picchu. Quito. Galapagos.'

Told you.

I'm there, 'Those are all actual places, are they? You checked?'

'Yeah, I checked,' he goes – and he's not even a dick about it. 'Then we're going to do New Zealand and Australia – might even see Erika while we're there. Then Kuala Lumpar. Hanoi. Ho Chi Minh City. Phnom Penh. Mandalay. Ulaanbaatar –'

'Such random names,' I go. 'You couldn't blame me for asking are they actual. I suppose they'd know in Trailfinders, wouldn't they?'

'And then back through Europe via Moscow.'

'Moscow?' Hennessy, quick as a flash, goes. 'You could visit fucking Newgrange while you're there!'

The old man and the old dear crack their holes laughing, as do Kennet, Shadden and Rihanna-Brogan.

Fionn looks at them like he thinks they're animals. And, let's be honest, he wouldn't be far wrong.

'I, er, ran into President Higgins and Mrs Higgins in the hallway,' he goes. 'I see they're moving out.'

'Into the famous Mansion House!' the old man goes. 'Ross, get young Fionn there a drink of something!'

I'm there, 'Ro, would you do the honours? I just have to pop into the gaff to, er, change Mellicent. Yeah, no, she's shat herself again.'

She actually *hasn't* shat herself? It's actually just an excuse for me to go into the gaff to say goodbye to – like he said – President Higgins and Mrs Higgins.

They're actually getting into the back of the presidential limo as I'm walking through the house. I wave at them just as they're about to be driven away. *He* winds down the window.

'We're moving out,' he goes.

I'm there, 'Yeah, no, so I heard. I'm going to miss having you around.'

'Well, I can't fight a presidential election campaign from the attic of the Áras. Thank you for your kindness, Ross.'

'Yeah, don't mention it. I'm, er, sorry about *him*? As in, like, my old man. He used to be alright. He was a bit of a knob, but he turned into a complete dick the second he put that wig on his head.'

'Ross, he's planning something.'

'Planning something? In terms of?'

'I don't know what it is, but I overheard him this morning, talking to that odious solicitor person.'

'Hennessy? Good description. Sums him up.'

'They have a plan, for before the referendum, if the opinion polls are in any way close. Something spectacular.'

'But you don't know what it is?'

'Your father kept referring to them hitting the doomsday button.'

'Jesus.'

'Can you find out what it is, Ross?'

With my brains? I seriously doubt it. But then I'm suddenly wondering does Ronan know anything about it? And – even worse – is he possibly mixed up in it?

I'm there, 'Leave it with me, Mister President,' and I really love the way the words sound coming out of my mouth. It's very *West Wing*.

As the limo pulls away, the dude looks at me through the window with, like, sadness in his eyes and goes, 'Ross, the future of our democracy could be in your hands.'

'You had sex with your daughter's Irish teacher?' JP goes.

And he doesn't say it in a good way either – certainly not a way that suggests a high-five is in the post.

I'm like, 'Why are you saying it like that?'

He's there, 'What way did I say it?'

'You said it in, like, a *judgy* way?'

'I'm trying to process it, that's all.'

'What's there to process? It's, like, an anecdote – in, like, a *Sex in the City* sort of way.'

This is us in, like, Kielys, by the way, having our usual Friday night scoops and waiting for the rest of the goys to arrive.

He goes, 'It's just, I don't know, a weird thing to be bragging about.'

He's changed since he got together with Delma. She's even

dressing him now, judging by the Pringle sweater he's wearing, which I've gone out of my way not to mention, even though it's killing me to stay quiet about it.

Oisinn and Magnus decide to show their faces then and they've got some, like, random dude with them.

'Ross, JP,' Oisinn goes, 'this is Kevin. And, Kevin, these are our friends. That's Ross – and the one in the Pringle sweater there used to be JP!'

I laugh.

'I'm glad someone brought it up,' I go. 'Delma must be focking dressing you now, is she . . . Jay Dorling?'

JP just shrugs like it's not a major deal. He's like, 'It was a present from Delma, yeah.'

I'm there, 'The focking state of you, I'm tempted to say. It'll be a pipe and slippers for you next. I'm just saying, Oisinn, it'll be a pipe and slippers for him next!'

While I'm saying this, I'm also sizing up this – like he said – Kevin dude. I'd say he's in his, like, early thirties, with a neck beard and black, hipster glasses. He's wearing a black hoodie, three-quarter-length boardshorts and black-and-white checkered Vans. He's got, like, a swipe cord in his hand and a distant look in his eye.

'It ish okay, Kevin,' Magnus goes, 'you will not need your shwipe card tonight. You are in a pub in Donnybrook.'

I turn around to Oisinn and I'm like, 'Who the fock *is* this total randomer?'

'We sprang him from Google three days ago,' Oisinn goes. 'He's our seventh extraction in the last month and he's by far the severest case we've seen. He can't do anything for himself. Doesn't know how to cook. Doesn't know how to operate a washing machine. Doesn't know how to make his bed.'

'Jesus,' I go, even though – hand on hort? – I can't do any of those things either and it's never really been an issue. 'The poor, poor focker.'

'It was his sister who contacted us after seeing the TED Talk. He literally hadn't set foot outside the Velasco Building for, like, four weeks.'

'So how did you, like, capture him?'

'Google were playing softball against Yelp,' he goes, 'and Kevin was fielding. Me and Magnus just walked onto the field and literally dragged him to his sister's cor.'

'Fair focks. I'm saying it.'

'Now we're trying to, like, de-programme him. He can't even approach a door without whipping out that swipe cord and every so often he'll blurt out something about his deportment's coding output being up seven percent in the second quarter. Slowly but surely, though, we're reacquainting him with the real world. Where are Fionn and Christian, by the way?'

I'm there, 'Fionn can't make it. He's got shit to do before he heads off with, like, Hillary on their travels.'

'And Christian texted me to say he's just porking across the road,' JP goes. 'He's bringing his girlfriend, by the way.'

I'm there, 'Girlfriend?' because he's supposedly my best friend and this is literally the first I'm *hearing* about it? 'What girlfriend?'

Oisinn laughs. He's there, 'Oh, you haven't heard? Happened while you were away in Kerry.'

'Who is it?' I go. 'Here, it's not one of Delma's mates, is it? From the focking Ballsbridge Active Retirement?'

JP has no comeback to that.

Oisinn goes, 'No, think younger. Think way, way, *way* younger!' and I'm suddenly staring at the door, going, 'Who? Who is it?'

And then the door opens and in they walk – we're talking Christian, hand-in-literally-hand with Lychee Greenhalgh.

I'm like, 'Her? What the fock is he doing with *her*?' and unfortunately they happen to be standing two feet in front of me when I say it.

I can't actually help it.

'What's his *problem*?' she goes, obviously referring to me.

Lychee focking Greenhalgh is my problem! She's, like, nineteen and a total focking airhead, which is saying something coming from me – a man who couldn't put a bag of M&Ms in alphabetical order.

Christian's like, 'Drink, Lychee?'

And she goes, 'I'm going to have a Cab Sav, but I'll get it because I want to film myself pouring it!'

That's, like, word for word.

She focks off to the bor and I turn around to Christian and go, 'What happened to you not wanting to get involved with anyone and prioritizing your children's happiness?'

He tries to change the subject, though. He turns around to Magnus and he's there, 'So, how's business?'

'The bishnesh ish flying,' Magnus goes. 'We have done sheven exshtractionsh shinsh the shtart of the shummer. But – shad to shay – we could and should be doing a lot more.'

Christian's there, 'So it's obviously a massive problem?'

'Mashive ish the word. We are hearing from two or perhapsh three new people every day. Hushbandsh worried about their wivesh, or wivesh worried about their hushbandsh, or parentsh worried about their shons and daughtersh, or, in shome cashesh, very young children worried about their mumsh and dadsh becaush they cannot talk about anything outshide the world of the multinational tech company.'

Christian's like, 'Fock.'

'Ideally,' Oisinn goes, 'what we'd like to do is buy a property that we can turn into a rehabilitation facility. Treatment for this condition involves more than just removing someone from their workplace environment. They need a safe space where they can totally disconnect from all talk of internet-related services and products.'

There's, like, a pause in the conversation then and we can suddenly hear Lychee talking to Kevin up at the bor.

She's going, 'It's, like, a social media platform where you can make, like, short-form videos of, like, a bunch of people doing a dance, or singing, or even something hilarious that you, I don't know, *witness*?'

She shows him her phone and it's like we're all watching it happen in slow motion.

'Look, I'll show you an example,' she goes. 'These are the most popular videos today. Okay, this is one of a family in Copenhagen who've storted this, like, *dance* craze? Look, that's four generations of the same family. Look at the great-grandmother doing the high kicks – *so* cute!'

Kevin's there, 'Do you know does the app use AI technology to offer targeted content based on previous user activity?'

And suddenly Magnus is going, 'SHTOOOOOOPPPPPP!!!!!!' and making a dive for him.

Kevin is going, 'Because in Google –' as Magnus basically rugby-tackles him to the ground, knocking Lychee's phone out of his hand.

'Oh my God!' Lychee goes.

And Oisinn's there, 'Sorry, Lychee, we should have told you, he's in recovery.'

I'm thinking – yeah, no – this is turning out to be one of *the* most random nights I've ever spent in Kielys. But, of course, I don't know the actual half of it yet. I'm knocking back a mouthful of the wonder stuff when I notice that Mary has stepped out from behind the bor. She's smiling at us in a sad way and I'm wondering is she going to remind us that rugby tackles have been banned from the pub since the night in 2004 when I took down Shane Byrne while he was holding a tray of flaming Sambucas and there ended up being a bit of a fire.

'I want to talk to you about something,' she goes. 'Pat and I have some news.'

We're suddenly all ears.

She's like, 'We've decided to retire.'

And we're all there, 'Whoa! Fair focks!' because we're obviously *delighted* for them?

'So what's going to happen?' I go. 'Are you going to get someone in to, like, run the place for you?'

She's like, 'No, we're closing it, Ross. From the first week in September, I'm sad to tell you that Kielys will be no more.'

I suddenly feel weak, like my legs are about to go from beneath me. And then they literally do. My knees buckle and I can suddenly feel myself falling backwards towards the floor. The only thing that stops my head hitting the deck is JP and Christian, who've seen it happening and they've caught me, like, mid-faint.

And in my groggy state, I can see Lychee pointing her phone at me and I hear her go, 'Oh my God, I got it on camera!'

I'm sitting with Ronan in, like, the Dáil bor and he's saying all the right things to me.

He's there, 'You're pudding me woyer, Rosser.'

And I'm like, 'I'm not pulling your wire, Ro. It's an actual fact.'

'Kiedys of Doddybruke?' he goes. 'Godden?'

'Yeah, gone – well, *going*. I literally can't get my head around it.'

'What'll you do, Rosser?'

'I don't know. Jamie Heaslip's obviously been on. Said he'd love to see us in The Bridge.'

'He's a heerdo of yooers.'

'And vice-versa. I was very nearly a groomsman at his wedding, except Dave Kearney accused me of jamming a supermorket trolley token in the Johnny machine the previous Paddy's Day and Jamie said it would have been awkward to have us both at the top table.'

'Which is feerd enough.'

'But Kielys was like a second home to me. Literally. How many times did Pat and Mary let me sleep upstairs when I'd pissed my chinos and no taxi would take me home. I don't think it would be an exaggeration to say that Kielys closing is our generation's Diana moment.'

Ronan raises his eyes to the borman.

He goes, 'Sayum again,' and we watch the dude pull two pints, we're talking Heineken for me and – yeah, no – focking Bulmers for Ro.

'Hee-or,' Ronan goes, 'what's the stordy with Hodor and that fedda she's seeing?' because he's very protective of his sister.

I'm there, 'There's no story, Ro.'

'Is he messing her arowunt? Will I hab a woord wirrum?'

'Have you seen him, Ro?'

'Yeah, she showut me pitchers of him on her phowun.'

'So you know that he's way out of her focking league.'

'Is he a player, Rosser?'

'What do you think? He gave her a number that was one digit short.'

'I've dudden that to boords.'

'And you got it from me. But Honor hasn't a clue. She thinks it was a genuine mistake.'

'She's veddy iddocent when it comes to feddas.'

'She spent the entire day today adding digits to the end of the number – from 0 to 9. Then she storted working back through the number, doing the same thing.'

'The pooer geerdle.'

'I tried to tell her when we were in Kerry to possibly lower her sights. There was a dude from, like, Tipperary who wore Wrangler focking jeans. He would have been more in her league.'

'She wouldn't listodden, but?'

'No – and this Reese dude was getting off with at least one of her mates behind her back.'

'Are you shewer?'

'Saw it with my own eyes, Ro.'

'Did you ted her?'

'I couldn't. It would have broken her hort.'

'Pooer Hodor.'

'Poor Honor is right.'

The phone behind the bor rings. The dude answers it, then – randomly – tells me that it's for me. I ask him who it is and he just, like, puts on this posh voice and goes, *'Is there a Ross O'Carroll-Kelly drinking in the bor?'*

I take the phone from him. I'm like, 'Hey, Sorcha.'

She goes, 'I've been ringing your phone for the last focking hour.'

I'm there, 'Yeah, no, I thought if it was important, you'd maybe leave a message.'

She sounds upset, way more than she'd usually be at me for ignoring – I check my phone – nineteen calls.

I'm there, 'Are the kids okay?'

She's like, 'The kids are fine.'

'Thank God.'

'Did you see the *Six One News* tonight?'

'I, er, recorded it on the Sky Box. Yeah, no, I was going to watch it later.'

'So you didn't hear what Lenka Lippmann said?'

'Who the fock is Lenka Lippmann?'

'She's the German agriculture minister, Ross. She said today that my Ruminant Animals Bill was a salutary lesson on the dangers of nepotism.'

'What's that in English?'

'She's basically implying that I'm only in Government because my father-in-law happens to be the Taoiseach.'

'Hmmm.'

'I just don't understand how a woman can say something like that about another woman.'

'Sucks alright.'

'I need you to come back to the Áras – right now.'

'Yeah, no, you're breaking up there, Sorcha.'

'We're both on *landlines*, Ross?'

'Fair enough.'

'Sea-mon is coming over and she's going to help me formulate my response. I want to put out a statement this evening, so I need you to look after the kids. Kennet is on the way to collect you.'

She hangs up on me and I hand the phone back to the borman.

Ronan goes, 'Evoddy thing alreet, Rosser?'

And I'm there, 'Yeah, no, she needs me back at the ranch. How are things with you, by the way?'

'Ine moostard, Rosser. Shadden's lubben redecordating the new gaff. And Ri's arthur widding anutter jiddum kada. I think she has real tadent, Rosser.'

'I'm not asking about them, Ro. I'm asking about you.'

'Ah, Ine alreet. Still woodied about me case is all.'

I smile at him in, like, a sad way.

'I remember when you were a kid,' I go, 'you used to say you weren't scared of jail. You used to say you'd love twelve months inside just to clear your mind.'

He smiles at the memory.

He goes, 'Cheerlie used to say that the woorst thing about prison idn't where you are – it's where you're not.'

I'm there, 'I remember he used to say that.'

'I wadn't scared of jayult – but that was cos I didn't hab athin to lose. It's diffordent now.'

'In terms of?'

'What'll happen if I end up doing a ten-stretch, Rosser? Shadden's still a young wooban – she's still veddy attractive.'

'You're being ridiculous.'

'She'll foyunt some wooden else while Ine insoyut. Some utter sham will end up raising me thaughter and the new babby.'

'Ronan, that's not godda happen. I'm going to find some way of getting you out of this. That's a promise.'

There's, like, silence between us then. Eventually, I go, 'Ro, do you know if my old man and Hennessy are planning something?'

He's like, 'Pladden someten?'

'Yeah, no, something big – for the night before the referendum?'

'You're arthur losing me, Rosser.'

'Yeah, no, I was talking to, like, Michael D. *Higgins*? He said he overheard them and they were talking about hitting the doomsday button.'

'The doomsday buttodden?'

'That's what the dude said. I was wondering have they said anything to you about it? Or have you, like, overheard anything?'

'Nutten, Rosser.'

'Because the President seems to be of the view that the future of our democracy is in my hands.'

'Moy Jaysus.'

'What's that supposed to mean?'

'Ine joost wondorden is that not a bit oaber the top?'

'All I know is that he seems to think that something is going to go down the night before the big vote.'

'Ine shewer it's just political tactics thee were thalken, Rosser.'

Behind me, I hear a voice go, 'Howiya, F . . . F . . . F . . . F . . . Feddas?'

It's my lift home.

'How's things, Kennet?' Ronan goes.

Kennet's like, 'Ine g . . . g . . . g . . . gayum balt, so I am, Ro. Ine hee-or to b . . . b . . . b . . . b . . . b . . . b . . . brig your auld fedda howum. So this your new locoddle, is it, Rosser?'

'The fock are you talking about?' I go, standing up and throwing on my jacket.

'The T . . . T . . . T . . . T . . . Teashocked was tedding me that they're c . . . c . . . c . . . closing that b . . . b . . . b . . . b . . . b . . .

boozer you go to in Doddybruke. Says I to himself, the amount of m . . . m . . . m . . . m . . . m . . . m . . . m . . . muddy that young fedda of yooers is arthur spending in theer oaber the yee-ors, he could have bought the bleaten p . . . p . . . p . . . p . . . p . . . p . . . p . . .'

I suddenly smile – because without knowing it, the dude has just given me an incredible idea.

'Ro,' I go, 'I'll talk to you soon,' and I head for the door.

And Kennet's like, '. . . p . . . p . . . p . . . p . . . p . . . p . . . p . . . pub.'

The Vico Road protest is finally over. That's the big news of the week. The formers have focked off home with their cows, the Ormy has cleaned up and disposed of fifteen hundred tonnes of shit and the Dalkey Open Forum has gone back to discussing the real issues that affect the people of the area, like whether bring-and-buy sales – while well-intentioned – lower the general tone and should be broken up by the Gords, using force if necessary.

In the end, Sorcha didn't bother calling out Lenka Lippmann. It was actually Simone who talked her out of it. I could hear Sorcha ranting and raving through the wall, going, 'If our fellow-EU members are so against us taking steps to reverse the damage we've done to the planet, then maybe the Taoiseach is right – God forgive me, but maybe we *are* better off out of it?'

But Simone has come up with a new plan – to invite the agriculture ministers from all the other EU countries to join Sorcha for a video conference, at which she's going to explain to them exactly what she's trying to achieve.

So – yeah, no – she's very excited this morning about that and the fact that the O'Carroll-Kelly family are finally going home. So we're, like, driving back to Killiney. Sorcha, Fionn and little Hillary are up ahead of us in Kennet's cor, while I'm driving the A8 with Brian, Johnny and Leo sitting in the back and Honor in the front passenger seat, staring at her phone, almost willing it to ring, or even just beep.

I'm there, 'Honor, it's been, like, a week.'

And she's like, 'So?'

'I'm just making the point that maybe he's not going to ring you.'

'Oh my God, you sound like Erika.'

'When were you talking to Erika?'

'She FaceTimed me last night. Er, why *wouldn't* he ring me?'

'Because – you know, mad as it might seem – maybe he's not interested in you.'

'That's what Erika said. But I was like, "Why would he buy me a chain if he wasn't, like, interested in me?"'

'Yeah, no, that's a definite mystery, that one. But then – devil's Advocaat – why would he give you a number that was, like, one digit short?'

'I was thinking about that – we were, like, *walking* when he typed it into my phone?'

'But you gave him your number, didn't you?'

'Yeah.'

'So why hasn't *he* phoned *you*?'

'Yeah, no, I was thinking about that as well. Maybe he, like, *lost* his phone and doesn't actually *have* my number any more?'

'You don't think you're just making excuses for him?'

'It could easily happen. He could be out there thinking, 'Oh my God, how am I going to, like, contact her?' That's why I sent him a message on Facebook.'

Oh, fock.

I'm there, 'Is that not a bit –'

'A bit what?' she goes.

'I want to say *desperado*?'

'It's hordly desperado, Dad. I just said, Hey, it's Honor, hope you got home okay, sucks to be back, really miss you, blah, blah, blah, haven't heard from you, was thinking maybe you lost your phone, here's my number again, ring me or text me anytime, day or night.'

I'm like, 'Jesus Christ.'

I can't help it. I'm suddenly thinking about the damage she's doing to the O'Carroll-Kelly brand.

And that's when my *phone* all of sudden rings? I answer it on speaker and it ends up being Christian. I'm like, 'Dude, how the hell are you?'

He goes, 'Yeah, I'm fine. I got a message to say you needed to talk to me urgently.'

'Yeah, no, brace yourself, Christian. I'm thinking of putting together a consortium to buy Kielys.'

Even Honor looks up from her phone when she hears that. She obviously knows I've said fock-all about it to her mother. I don't end up getting the reaction I was expecting from Christian, though.

He's like, 'Er, okay.'

I'm there, 'They reckon the asking price is going to be somewhere in the region of five mills. I can always get money from my old man. You're not exactly short of a few sheks. I'm going to call in to see JP tonight. Oisinn and Magnus might even throw in a few yoyos. So what do you think?'

'In terms of?'

'Jesus Christ, don't make me beg – in terms of you, like, *investing*?'

'Look, I can't speak for JP, but I just don't see myself running a pub.'

'You wouldn't be running it, Dude. We'd hire, like, a manager. The point is we'd be saving actual Kielys.'

'It's just that, well, we're working on this potentially huge deal at the moment – it could be worth, like, hundreds of millions of euros if we get the tender.'

'Yeah, I'm focking delighted for you both.'

'It's just that we don't want anything stealing our focus at the moment.'

Holy focking shit!

I say it out loud as well.

I'm literally like, 'Holy! Focking! Shit!' because something has suddenly stolen *my* focus?

Yeah, no, it just so happens that I'm passing our old school and I'm looking to my right and sort of, like, blessing myself as I *always* do? And that's when I notice that the famous sign outside no longer says 'Castlerock College – Established 1919'.

Instead, it says 'St Ignatius of Loyola Secondary School for Boys – Established 2018'.

Christian goes, 'What's wrong?'

And I'm like, 'They've changed the name of the school!'

'What school?'

'What focking school do you think? Castlerock College.'

'Yeah, did you not read the Past Pupils Union newsletter?'

'Is that a serious question?'

'There was a whole thing about it. McGahy just decided he wanted to break from the past, especially with the centenary coming up.'

I'm like, 'McGahy?' meaning Tom McGahy, the school principal, a man who's never made any secret of how much he hates rugby.

I go, 'We'll focking see about that,' and I suddenly slam on the brakes and perform a U-ey in the middle of the road.

'Oh! My God!' Honor goes.

And Leo is like, 'Where did you get your driving licence – in a focking Lucky Bag?' which is something he's heard me say to other motorists at traffic lights.

Sixty seconds later, I'm pulling into the school cor pork and I'm in an absolute rage – we're talking *literally* fit to kill? I'm wondering is McGahy even here, what with it being the middle of July, but then I remember that he doesn't take holidays, and right enough I spot his shitty little Kia Rio porked in his usual space.

I tell Honor and the boys that I'll only be a minute, then into the school I morch.

I borge into his office, leading with my shoulder and nearly taking the door of its focking hinges. He looks up from his desk in fright, then he cops the Rossmeister standing there and goes, 'What is the meaning of this?' which is a line they must teach them on day one of teacher training college.

I'm there, 'I could easily ask you the same thing. Saint Ignatius of Loyola?'

'Yes,' he goes, with a big, fock-you smile on his face, 'he was the co-founder of the Society of Jesus and its first Superior General.'

I'm there, 'Yeah, I know who Saint Ignatius of focking Loyola is!'

I didn't know. I hadn't a focking clue.

I'm there, 'What was wrong with Castlerock College?'

And he sort of, like, chuckles to himself.

'Many, many things,' he tries to go.

I'm there, 'This is about rugby, isn't it – which you've always hated.'

'I have no idea what you mean. Rugby is not played at this school any more and hasn't been for a number of years.'

'Yeah, no, you saw to that, didn't you?'

'Well, as you know, as a member of the rugby team who brought –'

'Honour to the school – and glory.'

'Really? Because I was going to say shame.'

'Agree to differ.'

'I fail to see that there's any honour involved in being associated with performance-enhancing drugs. Or any glory in having to hand back a trophy and it being splashed across page one of the newspapers and discussed at length in the Dáil.'

'Like I said, that's because you hate rugby.'

'Well, it's not *just* rugby, is it?'

'I don't know. You tell me.'

'Over the last twenty years there have been quite a number of former students of this school who have – allow me to be frank here – disgraced themselves in public life. A number of notable figures in the areas of business and politics who've caused us a great deal of embarrassment with their connections to this institute of learning.'

'You're talking about my old man, aren't you?'

'Let's just say that Castlerock College was too closely associated with a brand of education that turned out men lacking integrity, character and any kind of moral compass. We don't want to be synonymous with those things, especially as we enter a brand-new era . . . as a non-fee-paying school.'

'Excuse me?'

'Don't you read the Past Pupils Union newsletter?'

'Why do people keep asking me that?'

'We're planning to abolish fees. From September of 2020, we're going to be a State school.'

I literally don't know what to say.

I'm there, 'You're out of your focking mind.'

He just smiles at me and goes, 'If you'd followed my thirty-year career as an educator, you would know that I hold very, very dearly the principle of access to education for all. That means regardless of a student's social background.'

I can't believe what I'm hearing. I suddenly feel this urge to hurt him – to come up with a line that will cut the dude right to the focking core. Then I remember that he had a thing that time with, like, Ronan's old dear.

'How's Tina?' I suddenly hear myself go.

He's there, 'Tina? What does she have to do with this?'

'She dumped your orse in the end, didn't she?'

'My private life is none of your concern.'

'How private *is* your private life, though? That'd be my question.'

'What the hell are you talking about?'

'Yeah, no, Tina's jaw gets a bit loose with a few drinks on her. I was in her gaff the night of Ronan's daughter's sixth birthday and she had all her mates around. Oh, she'd had, like, five or six White Russians and she was full of the chats. Especially about you.'

'Get out.'

'She said you'd a mickey on you like a fun-size packet of Rolos and you cried your eyes out whenever you two did the deed.'

I'm not making that up, by the way. Voddy is like truth serum to Tina.

McGahy's face turns suddenly red and he storts shaking with rage to the point where I actually think he's going to throw a punch at me. He points at me, his finger trembling in the air between us, and he goes, 'Get out!' and then he says it again, except he just, like, roars the words this time at the top of his voice.

'GET OOOUUUTTT!!!'

JP says he's sorry and I tell him that he has nothing to apologize for – even though he does. He was a dick to me that night in Kielys. He knows it and I know it.

He's there, 'I was possibly out of line.'

'No possibly about it,' I go. 'All I was trying to do was tell you a funny story about me having a thing with Honor's teacher – I didn't expect to have it thrown back in my face.'

'Come in,' he goes, stepping to one side.

So I walk into his aportment and straight away I can see the changes that have come over the place. It looks like something from a magazine and it's no coincidence that Delma happens to own an interiors shop in Ranelagh.

You can see the woman's influence everywhere.

'Nice soft furnishings,' I go, making sure to get the dig in. 'That screen wasn't here the last time. What do you call that design again?'

'Chinoiserie,' he tries to go. 'It's, like, a European spin on Far Eastern ort.'

'Is that a fact? Delma's changed you.'

'For the better, I hope.'

I don't comment either way.

He tells me to sit down, which is what I end up doing.

'The thing is,' he goes, 'Delma has made me want to be a better man.'

I'm there, 'I'm going to throw up all over this . . . okay, what the fock even is it?'

'It's a Helen Moore faux-fur throw.'

'I'm going to throw up all over this Helen Moore faux-fur throw in a minute.'

'Just hear me out, Ross. Look, it's different with Delma – different to the way it was with other girls.'

'That's because she's not a girl – she's, like, sixty-focking-five.'

'Yeah, no, maybe it *is* that? But what we have is, like, a proper, mature relationship.'

'I should have heard the alorm bells ringing when you told me to get rid of your bag of screwvenirs.'

'The thing is, the goy who kept those, Ross – I don't want to *be* him any more? Do you understand that?'

'Not really, but I'm going to say I do.'

'See, Delma's husband was a complete orsehole, by all accounts.'

'Yeah, no, he used to drink in The Wellington. He was a dick then – I can vouch for him – and I can't imagine he's changed much since.'

'Delma's only been with one goy since they broke up.'

'Okay – and, er, what was he like?'

'The same.'

'She said that, did she? She went into actual specifics?'

'Well, no, she didn't tell me who he was.'

'Right.'

'But, yeah, she said he was a dickhead.'

'Okay.'

'And didn't care about her needs from a sexual point of view.'

'Yeah, I get the point, Dude.'

'She was storting to worry that she maybe had a type. And I just decided, okay, I don't want to be that type. Do you want a drink?'

'Yeah, no, stick of Heinemite if you have one.'

He goes to the famous smort fridge, whips out two and hands one to me.

He's there, 'So, er, what did you want to talk to me about?'

'In a word,' I go, 'business.'

'You and Sorcha looking to buy a vertical bed, are you? The best discount I can do is twenty per cent.'

'No, it's about Kielys.'

'Kielys? Oh, right.'

'I think it's fair to say we all got a major shock when Mary broke the news that night. Sorcha took one look at my face when I walked through the door and she thought Johnny Sexton had gone back to Racing.'

'It's not surprising. Kielys was a huge port of our lives.'

'Jamie Heaslip rang me – touting for our business.'

'Dave Kearney's obviously forgiven you for jamming that super-morket trolley token in the condom machine.'

'There was no proof that it was me.'

'Even though it *was* you and he stood there watching you do it.'

'Anyway, I was thinking, even though I'm a massive, massive fan of The Bridge, Friday nights wouldn't be Friday nights without a feed of pints in Kielys of Donnybrook.'

'But you heard what Mary said. It's closing.'

And I go, 'It wouldn't have to close,' like I'm revealing a winning poker hand, 'if *we* bought it!'

He's like, 'We?'

'Dude, I'm putting a consortium together. So what do you think? Are you in?'

He puffs out his cheeks. 'I'd, er, obviously have to think about it,' he goes.

I'm there, 'Another one who needs time to think about it.'

'It's just that, well, me and Christian have this tender in at the moment.'

'Yeah, no, he told me earlier.'

'We can't say anything about it, but it would be worth a hell of a lot of money if we got it.'

'Blah, blah, blah. I still don't understand how that's stopping you from buying Kielys.'

He's un-focking-believable. He goes, 'Leave it with me, will you?'

I'm like, 'Leave it *with* you?'

'Yeah, no, I'm going to have a think about it.'

I put my beer down on the table and I stand up.

'Yeah, well,' I go, 'you enjoy your focking *think*, JP.'

He obviously hasn't picked up on my anger because he's there, 'And I'll obviously have to talk to Delma as well.'

I'm like, 'Delma? What focking business is it of hers?'

'She's my portner, Ross.'

'Your portner? She's a mate of my old dear's from the Move Funderland to the Northside campaign – and, what, she's calling the shots now, is she?'

'Ross, I love her.'

'You've only known her a wet week.'

'I've known her since I was a teenager.'

'Yeah, wanking yourself cross-eyed with her Hermès scorf balled up in your gob. Have you told her about that?'

'No.'

'No, didn't think you had.'

'Ross –'

'Don't touch me, Dude.'

'Ross –'

'It's Kielys!'

'I know it's Kielys.'

'*Kielys!*'

'Dude, I'm as upset as you are.'

'Yeah, I seriously doubt it. I'll see you round.'

I pick up my beer and I storm out, accidentally on purpose kicking over his Chino-whatever-the-fock screen on my way out the door.

I grab the lift and I head downstairs to the cor pork. I'm still seething as I throw open my passenger door. And that's when my phone all of a sudden rings.

I answer it by going, 'Yeah, you look down your nose at me for riding Honor's Irish teacher, yet having sex with an old-age pensioner is perfectly normal behaviour.'

There's, like, silence on the end of the line. Then a voice goes, 'Ross, it's Fionn.'

I'm like, 'Hey, Fionn, sorry, I thought you were someone else. How did it go?' because he was supposedly going to the Tropical Medical Bureau this afternoon to get his shots for the big trip.

'Ross,' he goes – and I can tell straight away that something has happened. 'You haven't heard the news, have you?'

I'm there, 'News? What news?'

'I'm talking about Tom McGahy.'

'McGahy? That prick with ears? Yeah, no, what about him?'

'He's dead.'

'Dead?'

'It looks like a hort attack.'

'No way.'

He goes, 'This morning apparently. He was found on the floor of his office.'

I'm like, 'Jesus Christ!' because I'm obviously thinking, was I, like, the last person to ever speak to him? Did he keel over the second I walked out the door? Did I, like, cause this?

Fionn goes, 'At least he died doing the work he loved.'

And I just gulp and I'm like, 'Er – yeah, no – bummer.'

Honor steps into the kitchen, dressed for a red corpet event and reeking of *Ariana Grande Sweet Like Candy* eau de parfum.

She goes, 'Dad, can you drive me to Riverview?'

I'm like, 'Riverview? You're not exactly dressed for the gym, Honor.'

'I know.'

'A full face of make-up as well.'

'I'm not going to the gym – as in, I'm not, like, *using* the gym?'

'So why do you want to go there?'

'Because Reese is going to be there this morning?'

I end up nearly spitting coffee all over the island.

I'm there, 'Reese? Honor, do you not think you should possibly move on?'

'I just need to find out once and for all if it's, like, definitely, definitely over.'

'It is, Honor. Trust me. I know.'

'Well, I want to hear it from him.'

'How do you know he's going to even be there today?'

'I saw it on his Facebook page. He was arranging to meet his friends. Today is Legs Day.'

Legs Day. God, that brings back a few happy memories.

I'm there, 'Honor, are you sure this is a good idea – as in, confronting him on his home patch?'

'Dad,' she goes, 'I'm going whether you drive me there or not. I'll use public transport if I have to.'

I'm there, 'I don't want you to do that, Honor.'

So I decide to just drive her there. It's probably best that she hears the truth straight from the horse's mouth. Then she can move on. Plus, I'll be on hand to deck him depending on how upset she ends up being.

I put my phone away and I try to prepare Honor for the massive land she's about to get.

I'm there, 'The thing is, Honor, you should play the field while you're young – in other words, try to be with as many people as you possibly can.'

Honor says nothing. She's, like, tense for the entire journey. But we eventually reach Riverview and I pull into the cor pork.

'Oh my God,' Honor goes, excitement in her voice, 'there he is!'

I turn my head and I see him – the handsome bastard – walking up the driveway with four other rugby jock dudes.

I'm there, 'Okay, so how are you going to handle this?' but she doesn't stick around to listen to my advice. She throws open her door and gets out without even closing it, then walks across the cor pork towards the five dudes.

They're all big goys as well.

Reese stops walking when he sees Honor – well, *she* sort of, like, bors his way. His four mates are all looking at each other, as if to say, Who the fock is this total randomer?

I watch her talk to him in, like, a really – I think it's a word – *animated* way? And he's just standing opposite her, kitbag slung over his shoulder, shrugging in a way that I recognize all too well. I've been in his position a thousand times – maybe more.

I actually feel a bit sorry for the dude. But it also kills me to imagine what he might be saying to her, even though it's obviously something she needs to hear. Cruel to be kind and blah, blah, blah.

It's only when I notice the four mates cracking their holes laughing that I decide it's time for me to intervene. I throw open my door, get out of the cor and morch over to where they're standing. I notice that Honor is, like, bawling her eyes out.

I'm like, 'Alright, that's enough – she's got the message.'

One of the mates looks me up and down and goes, 'Who the fock is this dude?'

I'm there, 'Yeah, you'd want to learn your rugby history. Come on, Honor, let's go.'

But Honor hasn't finished. She's a total last-word freak. Like her old dear, I'm *tempted* to say?

'But I don't understand,' she goes, clutching the little Fungie hanging around her neck. 'Why did you buy me this chain if you didn't like me – as in, like, *like* like me?'

And Reese is there, 'I didn't buy it for you, Onóir. It was your old man who made me give it to you.'

'Excuse me?' she goes.

I'm like, 'Honor, let's get out of here. Let's not give them the satisfaction.'

'I bought it for Clíodhna,' he goes.

'Clíodhna? As in, like, Clíodhna from Louth?'

'Yes, Clíodhna from Louth. I was sort of, like, seeing her behind your back.'

Honor turns and looks at me. She's there, 'Did you know about this?'

And I'm like, 'Hand on hort, Honor, this is the first I'm hearing of it.'

'He did,' Reese goes, seizing on the opportunity to suddenly land *me* in it? 'He saw me getting off with her – the night you were sick and couldn't go to the *céilí*. And he threatened me. He told me if I didn't keep going out with you, he'd deck me.'

I'm there, 'I'm not sure if those were the *exact* words I used?'

'Then he took the chain off Clíodhna. And before you left – that day in the cor pork – he gave it back to me and told me to give it to you.'

Honor just stares at me. It's the angriest I've seen her since the Christmas when she was five years old and Sorcha tried to pass off a pair of Dunnes Stores knock-off Uggs as the real thing.

I'm there, 'Let's not forget who the real villain is here, Honor.'

But the dude is good. He's like, 'I didn't mean to hurt you, Onóir. It's, like, Irish college. I thought you understood that.'

Honor looks at me, rivers of – Jesus Christ – mascora flowing down her face, and storms off.

I tell Reese he's a bastard – and not in an admiring way – then I chase after my daughter, going, 'Honor, how are you going to get home?'

It's a mork of how upset she is that she goes, 'Stay the fock away from me. I'm getting the Dort.'

I'm there, 'I can't let you do that, Honor,' but she suddenly breaks into a sprint.

I get back into the cor, then I follow Honor along Beaver Row in the direction of Donnybrook, slow-crawling alongside her, trying to apologize to her through the front passenger window.

I'm there, 'Honor, I honestly didn't see him getting off with Clíodhna. He's a focking liar.'

'You're the one who's a focking liar!' she goes.

'And even if I did see him getting off with her, the only reason I didn't tell you was because I was trying to stop you getting hurt.'

'Yeah, the reason you didn't tell me was because one rugby wanker recognizes another.'

'That hurts, Honor.'

'You're just like him – *that's* why you focking protected him.'

I'm like, 'Come on, please, just get in the cor.'

She's there, 'No!'

'Come on – get in the cor!'

Some old biddy walking past decides to stick her beak in then. She's like, 'Is everything alright?'

And Honor – I swear to fock – in a little, tiny voice goes, 'I don't know who this man is. He keeps asking me to get into his cor.'

'He what?' the old biddy goes.

'He says he has sweets in the glovebox.'

It's not the first time, or even the fifth time, that Honor has pulled that stunt and I've spent enough afternoons in the security office of Dundrum Town Centre, trying to prove that I am her actual father, to stick around and wait for the Feds to arrive. I put my foot down and I'm out of there in a screech of rubber.

So I'm sitting in the church, staring at the coffin, with the framed photograph of the dude on top. They couldn't even find one of him with a focking smile on his face. On the other side of me, Tina is blubbering into her hand. Christian hands me a tissue and I pass it on to her.

'Thanks,' she goes. 'Ine soddy.'

I'm like, 'Yeah, no, don't be sorry. You two had a thing together – even though it still feels random.'

'I lubbed him, Rosser.'

'Again, weird.'

'We bumped into each utter.'

'Did you?'

'A few munts ago. On Heddenry Street.'

'Jesus, what was he doing on Henry Street?'

'We went for a thrink, just to say, you know, no heerd feedings oaber it not woorking out.'

'Henry Street. I can't get my head around it.'

'Ine joost glad he didn't die hating me.'

'Yeah, no, that's, er, a definite plus alright. A definite, definite plus.'

Fionn steps out of the pew behind us to go up and say his few words. He hands little Hillary to me, then he heads for the – I want to say – *pulpit*?

'Good morning,' he goes. 'It's great to see so many of you here today to celebrate the life of Tom McGahy.'

The church is pretty much empty, by the way.

He's like, 'My name is Fionn de Barra. I was fortunate enough to be a student of Tom's and then later a colleague on the teaching staff. Tom was a brilliant teacher who dedicated his life to importing knowledge to others. It was his passion and his reason for being.'

I'm looking at the front of the church. There's no grieving wife or even girlfriend. No kids, no mother or father, no even brothers or sisters. No one close at all. It makes me feel, I don't know, sad for the dude, even though he had no love for me and no love for the sport of rugby.

'He did have other interests,' Fionn goes. 'He enjoyed a glass of port and a good book, especially the works of Thomas Hardy and Gustave Flaubert. I know *Tess of the d'Urbervilles* and *Madame Bovary* were two particular favourites of his and I remember he told me once that he'd read both of them many, many times.'

Jesus Christ, he's doing best up there, but there's not a lot to work with.

'He never took holidays,' Fionn goes, 'even when school finished for the summer. But he *was* a keen gardener. In his later years, I know, he was especially proud of the award-winning, organic vege-table gorden that he helped the students create at the school.'

I'm thinking, yeah, on the hallowed ground of our former rugby pitch. Fionn says fock-all about us destroying it by doing wheelspins on it in our cors. Probably not the right audience.

He goes, 'Tom was, in essence, a selfless man whose only real ambition in life was to see his students succeed in school and in their lives beyond it. There are a great many of us who owe him a debt of gratitude that can never be repaid. May he rest in peace.'

He gets a round of applause, then he steps down from the – again – pulpit. I hand Hillary back to him.

'Well dudden, Fionn,' Tina goes.

And I'm like, 'Yeah, no, you did your best.'

The priest says a few more words, then it's the closing hymn – we're talking 'I am the Bread of Life' – and then four dudes who work for the funeral home carry the coffin down the aisle and outside for the drive to Deansgrange Cemetery.

I spot JP and Delma standing outside and I tip over to them.

I'm just like, 'Hey,' deciding to be the bigger man. If there's a lesson from today, it's that I don't want to die having literally no mates.

'Hey,' he goes.

I'm like 'How *are* you, Delma?'

And she's like, 'I'm fine.'

'That's good to hear.'

'Look –' JP goes.

And I'm like, 'Dude, there's no need to apologize.'

'Yeah, I wasn't going to apologize, Ross.'

'Okay, wrong end of the stick.'

'I was just going to say, I've decided – after talking it over *with* Delma – that I want to buy a stake in Kielys.'

'Are you serious?'

'Yeah, I'm serious.'

I punch the air and I literally go, 'WHAAA-HOOOOOO!!!!!!'

Admittedly, my timing couldn't be worse, as they just so happen to be loading the coffin into the back of the hearse at that very moment and I get more than a few filthy looks from the other – I suppose you'd have to call us – *mourners*?

'This is fan-FOCKING-tastic news!' I go. 'GET IN!'

Christian and Fionn tip over to us then. Oisinn and Magnus are with him and they've got the famous Kevin in tow, still looking for somewhere to swipe that cord that's permanently in his hand.

I'm there, 'JP said yes, Christian. The pressure's on you now.'

'What's this?' Oisinn goes.

I'm there, 'We're putting together a consortium to hopefully buy Kielys – for a cool five million yoyos.'

Oisinn's like, 'Whoa!'

Christian goes, 'I've had time to think about it as well, Ross – and I'm in too.'

'The thing is,' Oisinn goes, 'me and Magnus were talking about this the other night and Magnus said, "Why don't you all get together and buy it?"'

'That'sh right,' Magnus goes. 'It jusht sheemsh like the perfect sholution to me.'

Oisinn's there, 'So – yeah, no – count us in as well.'

Fionn doesn't say shit. He's obviously keeping his money for his big round-the-world trip.

'Hey, Fionn,' Oisinn goes, 'good job in there.'

And Fionn's like, 'Thanks,' giving Hillary a kiss on the top of his head. 'I wonder what's going to happen now.'

I'm there, 'In terms of?'

'Is the school going to go back to being called Castlerock College?' he goes. 'I know there were a lot of members of the Board of Governors who weren't happy with the name change.'

Kevin suddenly pipes up then. He's like, 'Collaboration and innovation are central to what we do here,' and we all crack our holes laughing, which draws even more disapproving looks.

'Yesh, you don't work for Google any more,' Magnus ends up having to remind him.

It's funny.

JP's there, 'Is anyone going to the graveyord?'

I'm about to say, you must be focking joking, except Christian goes, 'I suppose we probably should – just to fill out the numbers.'

I'm there, 'Er, yeah, no, that's what I was going to say. Why don't you, Oisinn and JP come in my cor? That way we can talk turkey on the way.'

So that's what ends up happening. Oisinn jumps into the front passenger seat and Christian and JP hop into the back. But then, of course, Delma insists on coming along as well. She's got JP by the nuts so tight I'm surprised the dude doesn't talk in falsetto.

I'm driving out of the church grounds when my *phone* all of a sudden rings? I can see from the screen that it's, like, Sorcha. Still buzzing from the goys agreeing to buy Kielys, I make the mistake of answering it on, like, speakerphone.

'Sorcha,' I go, 'how's it all going?' because – yeah, no – she's supposedly prepping for her video conference with the agriculture ministers from the other however-many EU countries this afternoon.

Her opening line is, 'What the fock, Ross?'

And I'm there, 'Er, bear in mind, Sorcha, that I've got you on speakerphone and there's people in the –'

'What the fock is *this*?' she goes.

And I'm there, 'Er, you're probably in a better position to judge than me, Sorcha.'

'It's a bag of women's underwear,' she goes. 'I found it in the bottom of your focking wardrobe.'

Everyone in the cor is suddenly silent.

I'm like, 'Er . . .' trying to come up with an excuse quickly. At the same time, I'm looking in my rearview mirror at JP, who doesn't know yet that it's *his* collection. 'Yeah, no, I just remembered – they accidentally gave us someone else's laundry in the cleaners.'

She's there, 'These haven't been cleaned, Ross. And they've all got, like, names and dates stapled to them,' and that's when I see the blood suddenly drain from JP's face.

I'm like, 'Sorcha, I can explain everything – if you just give me a few hours to think.'

'You don't have to explain,' she goes. 'This is a bag of souvenirs from your focking sexual adventures. Grainne Curley – 18/8/2006. Oh my God, isn't she your second cousin? Sally O'Rourke – you had sex with her on our focking wedding anniversary!'

I can hear Delma tutting in the back.

I'm there, 'Sorcha, they're not mine.'

'Oh my God,' she goes, 'why have you got Delma's scorf in here? Ross, this is an actual *Hermès*.'

I watch Delma turn suddenly pale.

I'm there, 'Again, Sorcha, I'm looking after them for someone else.'

'Oh, I'm *sure* you are,' she goes. 'Fock you, Ross,' and then she just, like, hangs up on me.

There's, like, total silence in the cor. No one knows what to say next. Typical me, I decide to just style it out.

'Anyway,' I go, 'five million yoyos divided by four is what? It's a pity we don't have Fionn in the cor with that big brain of his.'

'Sorcha,' I try to go, 'it was all a big misunderstanding.'

She's like, 'Ross, I don't have time to talk about this right now.'

'Do you honestly think I'd be stupid enough to keep a bag of women's knickers at the bottom of my wardrobe?'

Of course I wouldn't. Mine are in Christian's.

She goes, 'I have a conference call in, like, ten minutes with the agriculture ministers from the other twenty-seven EU member states.'

I'm like, 'Sorcha, they're JP's.'

A little robot voice goes, 'Calling JP.'

Sorcha goes, 'No! Silas, cancel call.'

I'm like, 'That thing is so focking annoying.'

Silas goes, 'Call cancelled.'

I'm there, 'JP asked me to mind them for him because things are getting serious between him and Delma.'

She changes the subject then. She's like, 'I heard Honor crying in her room tonight.'

I'm there, 'Crying? What about?'

'I don't know. I told you months ago that I have zero interest in the girl and what she gets up to.'

'I must go and check on her.'

'I presume it's something to do with that boy she met in Irish college.'

'Yeah, no, he gave her a bullshit number, then she turned up at Riverview to confront him. It was Legs Day.'

'Is he a rugby wanker, Ross?'

'Excuse me?'

'The boy who broke your daughter's hort? I'm asking is he a rugby wanker?'

'He goes to Michael's – draw your own conclusions.'

'It's interesting, isn't it?'

'In terms of?'

'That she would fall for someone exactly like you?'

'I'm nothing like him.'

'Yeah, you keep telling yourself that.'

The front doorbell rings.

'That'll be Sea-mon,' Sorcha goes. 'Ross, let her in, will you?'

I'm like, 'Why is this conference call happening at, like, eleven o'clock at night?'

'Because Alejandro Posades is being a total dick about it.'

'Who's Alejandro Posades?'

'He's the Spanish agriculture minister. He said he's too busy running his deportment, that he doesn't have time during the working day to indulge the insane whims of other countries.'

'Is that an actual quote?'

'That's an actual quote.'

'You do know he's going to have an advantage over you, don't you?'

'Excuse me?'

'I'm talking in terms of shorpness. If he's Spanish, he'll have been in bed for the afternoon.'

'Oh my God, I can't believe you just said that.'

'What, is it racist?'

'If you have to ask, Ross, the answer is always yes.'

The doorbell rings again.

'Let Sea-mon in,' she goes. 'And tell her I'm in the study.'

So I open the door and – yeah, no – the girl is standing there. The focking state of her, by the way. She's wearing, like, a green, woolly jumper that looks like it came from the Blorney Woollen Mills and itches like fock, white combat shorts and – again – navy Toms. I notice she's holding her folded-up bike in her right hand.

I'm like, 'Hey, See-mon.'

She goes, 'It's Sea-mon.'

I'm there, 'Did you have far to cycle tonight?' at least making the effort with her.

'From Cabinteely,' she goes, giving me very little back. 'Can you let me in, please?'

I step to one side and she steps past me into the gaff, leaning her bike up against the hallway wall.

I'm there, 'Do you want to maybe take a shower?' because Cabinteely to Killiney is a long way, especially in a sweater like that.

She obviously thinks it's a dig about her general lack of hygiene – which it sort of *is*? – because she totally blanks me and I'm just like, 'She's in the study,' and off she focks in that direction.

So I'm standing there in the hallway, thinking about Honor, crying alone in her room. And I think to myself, it's been, like, three days – hopefully, she'll have forgiven me by now.

I decide to go and check on her, even though I know it'll probably mean a mouthful of abuse. I tip up the stairs and I gently tap on her door.

'The fock do *you* want?' she goes.

Yeah, no, she definitely doesn't *sound* as angry as she was?

I push the door and I stick my head around it.

'Yeah, no,' I go, 'I just wanted to see how you were.'

She looks shit – like she's been crying for three days solid. Which, of course, she pretty much *has*?

She goes, 'I made a focking fool of myself, Dad.'

I step into the room. I'm there, 'You didn't make a fool of yourself, Honor.'

She did. I was there.

She's like, 'This is what being a nice person gets you.'

I'm there, 'I don't know what the fock Erika was thinking, giving you that advice.'

'People end up treating you as a doormat.'

'They take the piss, Honor – that's what they do.'

'From now on, I'm going to go back to being an absolute bitch to everyone.'

'I love hearing you talk like this.'

'Fock Reese. Fock Mom. And fock you, by the way.'

'This is all great stuff. Look, Honor the reason I didn't say anything to you about him doing the dirt was because, well, I couldn't bear the thought of you being hurt.'

She goes quiet for about twenty seconds. Then, totally out of left field, she goes, 'If I ask you a question, will you give me an honest answer?'

I'm there, 'Of course I will.'

'Was there something going on between you and Marianne?'

'Marianne?'

'As in, like, my *Irish* teacher?'

'Irish teacher. I'm trying to place the woman.'

'Er, you knocked her off her bike, Dad.'

'Yeah, I *didn't*, by the way? But why do you think something was going on?'

'Because I rang Clíodhna, just to tell her that she's a two-faced ginger bitch and I hope she focking dies in a cor accident –'

'I love hearing you talk like this.'

'– and she said one of the girls saw you out cycling with her after Mass one Sunday morning.'

'Mass?'

'She said you were both eating Wibbly Wobbly Wonders.'

'Does that not sound like bullshit to you?'

'And then she said Pádraig from Cloughjordan said he saw you going into her cottage on the last night.'

'Cloughjordan? Don't insult me, Honor.'

'So you're saying nothing happened?'

'We already know this Clíodhna is a cheat. It turns out she's a liar as well.'

'I'm going to make her life hell, Dad.'

'It's great to have the old Honor back.'

'I'm going to bully the focking shit out of her on social media.'

I give her a little smile and I go, 'You do you, Honor. You do you.'

I say goodnight to her, then I tip downstairs.

The famous video conference has already storted. I can hear

Sorcha in the study going, 'Good evening. *Bonsoir. Guten Abend. Buona-sera. Dobry wieczór. Buenas noches . . .'*

And then a woman's voice – I'm guessing it's the famous Lenka Lippmann – goes, 'Minister Lalor, we all speak English perfectly well. It is sufficient, I think, to say good evening – you are not read-ing out the Eurovision Song Contest votes from the Republic of Ireland jury.'

It's a real slap-down for Sorcha, because that's how she used to stort *all* of her debates in school? The message seems to be, you're not in Mount Anville any more.

A man's voice – he sounds sort of, like, French – goes, 'I think what Minister Lippmann means is that it is very late and perhaps it would be best if you got to the point.'

Sorcha's there, 'On a point of order, Minister Brizard, I just want to point out that the meeting was set for this time to facilitate Min-ister Posades, who's obviously very busy during the day. But thank you, I will proceed.'

I push the door. Sorcha is sitting at the desk with the laptop open in front of her. On the screen, there's twenty or thirty boxes with, like, faces in them. The famous Simone is standing on the opposite side of the desk, giving her the thumbs-up and other signs of encouragement.

Sorcha takes a deep breath and goes, 'Ever since I was a little girl, I have been proud to describe myself as a European. As a matter of fact, whenever I'm in, like, the States or wherever, and I'm asked where I come from, I always say Europe.'

She does. It's focking embarrassing. I always say, 'Killiney – Dublin's Bel Air.'

'It's Europe first,' she goes, 'and Ireland second. And the thing that makes me most proud to describe myself as a European is the European Union. The European Union – formerly the European Economic Community – grew out of the rubble of the Second World War, when the citizens of this continent decided to set aside their differences and work together in the interests of peace and obviously mutual prosperity.'

I can hear tutting and more than a few sighs. She's losing them.

'As Europeans, the EU has taught us to celebrate our great cultural diversity, which is obviously a good thing. But, equally important in terms of achievements, the EU has helped bring peace to our continent after, like, centuries of conflict. This was recognized in 2012 when the EU was awarded the Nobel Peace Prize, a proud day for the citizens of all twenty-eight member nations, I think we'd all agree.'

Simone is drawing circles in the air with her finger, telling her to get on with it.

'Now, we,' Sorcha goes, 'as the political leaders of this great, great continent, have an opportunity to do something even more important – to save this planet for future generations.'

The French dude has heard enough. He just, like, cuts her off and goes, 'Are you suggesting, Minister Lalor, that we also ban the sheep and the cows?' and he's cracking his hole laughing as he says it.

Sorcha's there, 'I prefer to use the term ruminant animals – it's, like, less *emotive*?'

This Lenka Lippmann one goes, 'The German beef industry is worth an annual €27 billion to my country's economy, Minister Lalor. How do you suggest we fill this hole?'

I watch Simone scribble something on a sheet of paper. She holds it up for Sorcha to read.

Sorcha goes, 'I promise you, Minister Lippmann, it will be a lot easier than filling the hole in the ozone layer,' and Simone gives her another thumbs-up, even though I didn't think it was that good a line. 'It's a matter of weighing up the short-term cost to the German economy against the long-term cost to the planet.'

I hear someone go, '*Ciao*,' and someone else go, '*Vaarwell*,' and I notice a few heads stort disappearing from the screen.

The French dude – again – goes, 'So we all follow this madness that you are proposing –'

Sorcha's like, 'With respect, it's not madness, Minister.'

'We stop the breeding of the cows and the sheep in France and Germany and elsewhere and we all live on vegetables –'

'Not *just* vegetables,' Sorcha goes – basically just repeating the words that Simone is mouthing to her. 'There are meat substitutes, made from tofu, or even tempeh, that have almost the same texture, flavour and appearance as actual meat. And they're getting better all the time.'

'So we take this step, and perhaps we stop people from driving their cars, and we stop people from flying in airplanes, and we close down all of the factories that cause pollution. As a matter of fact, we turn off all the lights in Europe and we live in darkness in our cold homes, eating our vegetables. It will not lower the temperature of the planet by even one-quarter of one degree Celsius.'

The Spanish dude – Alejandro whatever-he's-called – goes, 'What this woman is suggesting is that we destroy the European economy just to reduce our carbon emissions, while China and the United States and India continue to do whatever they want.'

I can tell from Sorcha's face that she didn't love being called 'this woman'. But she lets it go and reads out whatever message Simone is holding up for her.

She goes, 'We can't control what other countries do. All I'm saying is that, if we do our bit, we can set an example for the likes of – you mentioned – China, India and the States. It's like the whole *peace* thing? They will hopefully see in time how it benefits us all.'

'*Godnat!*' I suddenly hear, and then, '*Kali-nichta!*' as more faces disappear from the screen.

'You're not listening,' Sorcha goes. 'Okay, I'm going to read you out the main points from my Ruminant Animals Bill and hopefully –'

'No,' the famous Lenka Lippmann goes, 'it is you who is not listening. You are not a sixteen-year-old girl any more, impressing your teacher with your clever science project. You need to act like a grown-up.'

'*Excuse* me?' Sorcha goes – like she always does when she's about to lose her shit.

'You are a stupid girl,' the Spanish dude goes. 'You are a dreamer.'

And Sorcha's like, 'Yeah, this coming from the man who probably spent the best port of the afternoon in bed.'

'*Hasta luego!*' the dude goes and then Lenka Lippmann is like, '*Gute Nacht!*' and, ten seconds later, Sorcha is staring at a blank screen, going, 'Oh my God! Oh *my* God? Did you hear the way they spoke to me, Sea-mon?'

Simone's like, 'They're idiots. They just don't get it, Sorcha.'

And Sorcha goes, 'That's it. That's the last straw. If the European Union refuses to act to safegord the future of the planet, then maybe we *are* better off out of it.'

9.

While EU were Sleeping

There's, like, a definite buzz in Government Buildings this afternoon. The word is obviously out. I hear Richard Chambers off TV3 say it to someone on the phone.

'What we're *hearing* is that Sorcha Lalor has changed her mind,' he goes. 'Yeah, she's now supporting the Government's campaign for a Yes vote.'

The room is, like, totally rammers. I'm here to try to hopefully get back into Sorcha's good books by showing her some – I *think* it's a word? – *solidarity*?

I take a seat in the back row, next to Simone. She's wearing the same puke-green jumper as the other night, except this time with black, Adidas tracksuit bottoms and – I shit you not – brown Birkenstock sandals. Seriously, she's always dressed like it's focking laundry day. I somehow resist the temptation to go, 'Would it focking kill you to throw on a trouser suit and a nice blouse?'

Instead, I go, 'Hey,' because I'm trying not to be the wanker that I can sometimes be.

'Hi,' she pretty much grunts at me.

'So, Sorcha's changed her mind, huh – about the whole, like, Irexit thing?'

'The Minister has come to the realization that the kind of radical reforms that are required to save our planet are not achievable as long as Ireland remains part of a bureaucratic machine obsessed with petty rule-keeping and beholden to special interest groups.'

'Hey, I'm on the fair focks side of the fence.'

Suddenly, a door opens and the room comes alive. In walks my old man, followed by Sorcha, followed by Gordon Greenhalgh, followed by Hennessy. They all sit down at the top table, with big, shit-eating grins on their faces and camera flashes going off everywhere.

After a few minutes, the old man calls the room to order.

He's like, 'Thank you very much, ladies and gentlemen of the – inverted commas – mainstream press! Thank you for coming here today for the launch of the campaign to repeal the Third Amendment of the Constitution of Ireland, which was passed in the year of Our Lord, nineteen hundred and seventy-two, which permitted the State to join the European Economic Community, later to become the European Union, and provided that European law would take precedence over our own!

'As you all know, New Republic, the porty of which I am President – for my sins! – won an overall majority in the last General Election on the strength of my promise to follow our good friends in the United Kingdom out of the European Union! Well, today, with the launch of the Leave campaign, we are taking the very first step towards that end! Now, does anyone have any questions?'

Pretty much every hand in the room shoots up.

'Questions about Ireland leaving the European Union,' Hennessy snaps. 'The Taoiseach won't be talking about Newgrange, or trees, or the Book of Kells, or the President's living arrangements.'

A load of hands go down.

'You say that you won an overall majority,' this, again, Richard Chambers dude goes, 'on the strength of your promise to deliver on what's being called Irexit. How do you square that with the results of two recent opinion polls that suggest a majority of Irish people want to remain within the European Union? One of the polls had it as seventy per cent to thirty.'

'If opinion polls mattered a jot,' the old man goes, 'Leo Varadkar would still be the leader of this country – which, you may have noticed, young man, he isn't! Chorles O'Carroll-Kelly is, despite the fact that the opinion polls had us trailing FFG throughout the last election! Opinion polls can be made to say anything, especially when they're commissioned by a biased media that has a vested interest in maintaining the status quo! Quote, unquote!'

Some dude from, I think, RTÉ goes, 'Taoiseach, would you agree with the comments of Fine Gael's Richard Bruton –'

I laugh – we have his focking coffee machine in our kitchen.

'– that membership of the European Union has been the single most important factor in Ireland's emergence as a modern nation with a competitive economy?'

'Europe has been good for Ireland!' the old man goes. 'I'm on the record as saying it many, many times! But the relationship altered in 2008 and there's no use pretending that it didn't! We saw – all of us in this country – just how valued we were within this marital union! When we got into trouble, we felt *not* the warm embrace of a loving and understanding portner, but the cold shoulder of a hord and unfeeling spouse, who let us know, in no uncertain terms, that we could go and sleep on the lumpy mattress in the spare room for all they cared!

'I think we all know that it's been a loveless marriage since then, notwithstanding the efforts of our political and media elite to pretend that it's still a relationship with meaning! But the people understand that it's over – the people who were forced to pay for the irresponsible lending practices of the German banks, who had years and years of austerity foisted upon them to cover losses that had nothing to do with them whatsoever, who paid for the folly of the so-called European project with their jobs, their homes, their pensions, their life savings!'

The RTÉ dude tries to interrupt him. He's like, 'What do you say to people who accuse you of singing from the same populist hymn sheet as Donald Trump and Boris Johnson?'

The old man's there, 'I say, how bloody well dare you? How bloody well DARE you suggest that this is all just some wheeze to me? I have eight children – as well as God knows how many grandchildren!'

I'm thinking, that sounds like a focking dig at me.

'It's *their* future I'm thinking about!' he goes. 'Especially the six innocent little babies that my wife, Fionnuala, and I were recently blessed with! I don't want them growing up in a country that will still be paying the price for the 2008 bailout, which Ireland was forced to accept, at gunpoint, by the European Union and their pals in the European Central Bank and the International Monetary Fund!'

'If you really believe that's an issue for people,' some random woman reporter goes, 'why was there no clamour for Ireland to leave the EU at that time? Why has it taken ten years?'

'Because nobody walks away from the marriage the first day it starts to go wrong! You hang on in there, remembering the good times, hoping that it gets better, not wishing to face up to the fact that it was all a waste of time! And people were frightened! They're still frightened! They have no idea what the future outside of the European Union looks like! That is why, over the course of the next six weeks, I, along with my colleagues, will be travelling the length and breadth of this country, telling people about the bright and exciting future that awaits us once we throw off the yoke of our European oppressors and our so-called debt obligations to them!'

Another hand goes up. It's another woman. Not that I've a problem with that.

'Speaking of your colleagues,' she goes, 'Minister Lalor, I think a lot of people will be surprised to see you here today, advocating a Yes vote, given that you have been vocal in your opposition to Irexit.'

I watch Sorcha suddenly stiffen in her seat and I feel this instant urge to, like, protect her.

'As a matter of fact,' the woman goes, 'when you stood unsuccessfully for election to the Dáil, you said that leaving the European Union would be – and I quote – "Oh my God, *the* biggest mistake that Ireland could make."'

Sorcha goes to answer her, except the woman is, like, on a *roll* now?

She goes, 'Also, during your first term in the Seanad, you said, in relation to Brexit, that you hoped Boris Johnson would one day have to face the young people of Britain and explain why there was going to be no Erasmus programme for them.'

Sorcha stares hord at the woman – like she does to me sometimes when she catches me sniffing my socks to see if I'd get another day out of them.

She goes, 'Sorry, are you just making a statement? Because I didn't actually *hear* a question there?'

'I suppose what I'm asking,' the woman goes, 'is why are you flip-flopping on this issue?'

Sorcha's there, 'I'm glad you asked me that question,' like she's being interviewed for a summer job in the focking Build-A-Bear Workshop in Dundrum. 'And I'm happy to answer it, even though I strenuously object to you describing me as a flip-flopper. My position has not changed, in the sense that I still believe that the European Union is an amazing, amazing institution that has helped bring peace and economic prosperity to the continent after – oh my God – *so* much war!

'But as Ireland's first dedicated Minister for Climate Action – and obviously a woman – I have come to the realization that the kind of radical reforms required to save our planet are not achievable as long as Ireland remains port of a bureaucratic machine that's obsessed with petty rule-keeping and beholden to special interest groups.'

I turn around to Simone and I'm like, 'That's, word for word, what *you* said! Er, Jedi minds or what!'

Sorcha goes, 'It saddens me deeply that the Governments of the other EU member nations aren't prepared to support Ireland in our response to the climate emergency. What I'm proposing in the Ruminant Animals Bill 2018 might seem radical – but it's actually *necessary*? If the European Union can't see that, then it's a club I no longer wish to be a member of.'

All of a sudden, I hear clapping coming from the back of the room. I look over my shoulder and it ends up being Sorcha's old pair. They're both wearing – I shit you not – t-shirts with '#Irexit – Towards a New Republic!' on them. *He's* the one doing the actual clapping while her old dear is going, 'Well said, Dorling! We're very, very proud of you!'

I'm watching *Home and Away* and enjoying a couple of cheeky lunchtime cans when my *phone* all of a sudden rings? I can see from the screen that it's, like, Tina and my first thought is not to bother my hole answering it.

In the end I do. Just in case it's about Ro.

I'm there, 'Tina, what's going on?'

She goes, 'Ine rigging about your sudden.'

'What about him?'

'He's tweddenty-foorst is cubbing up.'

'I'm well aware of that, Tina.'

'Ine wontherding are you cubbing to the peerty or not?'

'Of course I'm focking coming!'

'It's joost Shadden said you habn't RSVP-ed yet.'

'Hey, as I said at Devin Toner's wedding, my face is my RSVP!'

Mind you, I got turned away from the Cliff at Lyons that day – as did Jordi Murphy, who used the exact same line. The two of us ended up toasting the happy couple sitting on the wall of the Texaco on the Celbridge Road, splitting a chicken fillet roll and a can of Monster Pipeline Punch. I think that was the day me and Jordi properly bonded, going from distant admirers to genuine friends.

I'm there, 'Refresh my memory – where is it happening again?' pretending I even looked at Shadden's email.

'They're habbon it in the new house,' she goes. 'Doing what suits *her* – just because she's supposedly pregnant again. Fox bleaten Rock. Miles away from addything.'

'It's miles away from focking Finglas, yeah.'

'There's no eeben buses go theer.'

'Well, you've my old dear to thank for that. She battled against a public transport service for Foxrock for years. She even got the Luas diverted through Leopardstown, in fairness to her. Anyway, you can tell Shadden I'll definitely be there.'

'Hee-or, wait a midute – doatunt hag up.'

'What's wrong?'

'There was sometin else I was wanton to thalk to you about. It was about Tom.'

'Tom?'

'My Tom.'

'As in, like, Tom McGahy?'

'Yeah.'

'Oh, he's *your* Tom now, is he?'

'Ine arthur been thalken to he's secretoddy.'

'Right.'

'The last thig he did befower he died was to steert writing me an e-mayult.'

Oh, fock it, I think. Fock it, fock it, fock it!

'Er, what was it about?' I go.

She's there, 'I've no idea. He oately madaged to write wooden loyun befower he keeled oaber.'

'And, er, what was the line? Do I want to know?'

'Here's what he writ: *Dear Tina, I've just had the dubious pleasure of a visit from that insufferdobble imbecile . . .*'

'Okay?'

'That's all he writ.'

'So it doesn't say who it actually was? As in, there's, like, no proof?'

'It wadn't you, wad it, Rosser?'

'Excuse me?'

'I was wontherden wad it you?'

'Why would you read a line like that and automatically assume it was me?'

'Because that's what he used to altways calt you – that insufferdobble imbecile.'

'Hey, that's nice for me to know.'

'So me foorst thought was that you must have godden to see him.'

'I didn't go to see him.'

'You might have been the last peerson to ebber see him aloyuv.'

'I just told you, it wasn't me, okay?'

'Well, he was obviously woorked up about something befower he had he's heert attack.'

'Yeah, no, it certainly sounds like it.'

'And no wooden could get under he's skidden like you, Rosser.'

'Yeah, no, there was a definite clash of personalities.'

'He used to be thalken to you in he's sleep, so he did.'

'What?'

'He'd be shouting, "Ross O'Cattle-Keddy – you insufferdobble imbecile!" Shouting it, Rosser!'

'A lot of that was based on rugby.'

'But you definitely didn't go and see him?'

'I didn't.'

'Do you swayor?'

'Absolutely.'

'It's a musterdoddy, then.'

'What is?'

'Why was he writing to me, Rosser? What was he pladding to say in he's emayult before he's heert weddent on him?'

'Yeah, no, it's a real head-scratcher, that one – genuine.'

I suddenly hear a loud bang upstairs. Something has hit the floor above me and nearly come through the focking ceiling. I'd usually just think, hey, it's probably Brian, Johnny and Leo killing each other in their room – focking leave them to it. Except they're in, like, *crèche* at the moment?

I'm like, 'Tina, I have to go,' and I hang up on her.

I tip out to the hallway and shout from the bottom of the stairs. I'm like, 'Honor?' because it's only the two of us in the gaff. 'Honor, are you okay?'

But there's, like, no response from her.

I'm there, 'HONOR?' except louder this time. 'HONOR, ARE YOU OKAY?'

Again, nothing.

So I take the stairs – we're talking two at a time – then I rush along the landing and throw open the door of her bedroom.

I'm not ready for the sight that ends up greeting me. Yeah, no, Honor is lying face-down on the floor and she's not moving. I rush over to her, going, 'HONOR! HONOR!' and I turn her over.

Her eyes are closed.

I'm, like, roaring into her face, going, 'HONOR? HONOR, WHAT THE FOCK? WHAT THE ACTUAL FOCK?' except there still ends up being no response from her.

And that's when I smell it – the sickly sweet smell of something alcoholic. I spot the empty Peach Schnapps bottle on the floor a few feet away from us and I think, Oh, fock!

I've found my old dear in a similar state often enough to know that the girl is focking mashed.

Holy! Focking! Shit!

337

I'm there, 'HONOR, WAKE UP!' lightly slapping her face. 'WHAT THE FOCKING FOCK? HONOR, WAKE UP!'

She sort of, like, half opens her eyes and her expression changes to one of annoyance – her normal face, in other words.

She's like, 'Whaaat yooouuu waaan?' slurring her words.

I'm there, 'HOW MUCH DID YOU DRINK? HONOR, CAN YOU HEAR ME? HONOR, IT'S YOUR DAD! HOW MUCH DID YOU DRINK?'

'Aaalll of it,' she goes. 'Whole focken b . . . b . . . bockle.'

I'm there, 'HONOR, YOU'RE GOING TO NEED TO GET SICK, OKAY?' and I grab her under the orms and drag her into her *en suite*.

'Fffock offfffffff,' she goes, 'you fffffocking rugby fffffocking waaanker fffffocking priiiiiick!'

I sort of, like, set her up in a kneeling position over the bowl – and not a moment too soon either.

'Fffffoooooock,' she goes, at the same time gripping both sides of the bowl like it's the steering wheel of a cor she's about to drive over a cliff.

Then it storts.

'BBBWWWWWWEEEUUUGGGHHH!!!!!!' she goes, throwing up her lunch – and I mean liquid lunch.

'BBBWWWEEEEEEUUUGGGHHH!!!!!!'

I hold back her hair for her – feeling like a proper father – while she spews up everything in her stomach.

At the same time, I'm going, 'Honor, what the fock were you thinking? Jesus Christ, I knew this day would probably come, but I thought you'd wait until you were, like, fifteen, the same as other girls.'

But she's like, 'BBBWWWWWWEEEUUUGGGHHH!!!!!! BBBWWWWWWEEEUUUGGGHHH!!!!!!' until eventually there's nothing left inside her and she's just, like, dry-retching.

Then she flops down onto the floor with her flushed face pressed against the cold bathroom tiles.

She's there, 'I fffffoooooockinggggggg hate yooouuu!!!'

And I'm like, 'You don't hate me, Honor.'

'Why doesn't fffooocckiiinggg Reeeeeese like me, Dad?'

'I don't know what to tell you, Honor. There's obviously no attraction from his point of view.'

'Hhhow can I mmmake him liiiiike me, Dad?'

'It doesn't work like that, I'm afraid, Honor. If it did, I'd be married to Emily Blunt.'

'I ffffeeeeeel so sick.'

'I can imagine, Honor. You drank the whole focking bottle – presumably without a mixer. Just promise me there'll be no repeat of this.'

But she doesn't say shit.

Fionn's in the kitchen, getting Hillary his breakfast while listening to the radio, except it's not actual *music* he's listening to? Typical of him, it's – yeah, no – talking.

I pick Hillary out of his high-chair and I go, 'Hey, Hill! How are you doing this morning?' and he smiles at me and goes, 'Unkon Yoss!'

It still hasn't got old.

I'm there, 'Hey, turn that focking radio off, would you, Fionn? Whoever that is, she's doing my focking head in.'

He goes, 'Er, that would be your wife, Ross.'

I actually laugh.

I'm like, 'Is that really Sorcha?' because she always sounds a few postcodes posher when she's being interviewed.

'She's on *Morning Ireland*,' Fionn goes, at the same time mashing up a bowl of sweet potato for the little lad, 'talking about her reasons for changing her mind on Europe.'

I'm there, 'And you definitely want to listen to it, do you?' taking the bowl from him.

'Yes, I do, because she's always been a big believer in the European project.'

'Do you remember the euro coin collector? She actually filled that thing in the end.'

'Sorcha always described herself as European first and Irish second.'

'Yeah, no, I remember that as well.'

'I'm just interested in understanding her thought processes.'

'Yeah, no, so am I – definitely.'

I sit down at the table with Hillary on my lap and I stort feeding him, making airplane noises as I move the spoon towards his mouth, which he loves. And, at the same time, Sorcha is going, 'I would like if we could stop talking in terms of flip-flops and u-turns and about-faces and focus instead on the issues at hand. But what I will say is that I believe people would have far more faith in our democracy if all politicians had the courage to say, "Yes, I used to think that yesterday, but today I think the complete opposite."'

Whoever's interviewing her tries to get a word in edgeways – 'But, Minister . . . but, Minister' – but it's, like, impossible when Sorcha is on a roll. I know that more than most.

She's like, 'Please let me finish, Áine – you asked me a question and I fully intend to answer it. Yes, I *was* a supporter of the European Union. And I like to think I *still* am? But I've always felt that their torgets in relation to cutting greenhouse gas emissions weren't nearly ambitious enough and I'm on the record as saying –'

'So this *isn't* just a fit of pique,' this apparently Áine person goes, 'in response to, well, we've had various EU officials, including our own commissioner Phil Hogan, rubbishing your plan to place a ban on the farming of cows and sheep. We've had various other member countries – Germany, France, Poland, the Netherlands, to name just a few – who've criticized what you're proposing and said that it's completely against the interests of the European Union.'

'This upcoming referendum,' Sorcha goes, 'is about our continuing membership of an economic and political union that is – let me be frank here, Áine – actively attempting to stymie our efforts to do something, yes, radical but also necessary to achieve a climate neutral world.'

'You mean destroying the farming sector?'

I'm there, 'Here comes another, Hillary – *mwwweeerrr*!!! Open up! Good boy!'

'I'm not destroying the forming sector,' Sorcha goes. 'What I'm proposing we do – and I'm planning to bring this bill before the Dáil in the autumn – is to phase out our overreliance on the breeding of ruminant animals and to incentivize formers to explore other forms of forming.'

'Other forms of farming?'

'Other forms of forming, yes.'

'And what will happen to this bill of yours if the electorate decides that it wishes to remain within the European Union?'

'I don't believe that will happen.'

'Well, the early opinion polls suggest that almost sixty per cent of voters say they are against Irexit.'

'Well, the campaign has only just storted, Áine, and I'm confident our orguments will be heard. The choice here is very simple. Do we, as a people, want to do our bit to save this planet – or are we happy to remain a member of a club whose obligations to the environment are secondary to keeping agriculture, industry and other vested interests happy? That's why – please let me finish, Áine! – it's important that people vote Yes on the eighth of September.'

I'm there, 'Last one, Hillary! Open up! *Mwwweeerrr*!!! Who's the best boy? Who's the best boy?'

'And what happens,' this, again, Áine goes, 'if this referendum is passed and we trigger Article 50? Micheál Martin has said that Ireland will be consigned to the economic wilderness.'

'As the Taoiseach said yesterday,' Sorcha goes, 'we can continue to have a trading relationship with the European Union, just as we can have a trading relationship with our good friends in the United Kingdom.'

'And Russia?'

'The world is changing, Áine – and I'm talking, like, *geopolitically*? There's nothing wrong with making new friends and allies.'

'Even if that means giving them our national treasures?'

'If you're referring to Newgrange, I think the Taoiseach has dealt comprehensively with that issue.'

'I'm looking at a photograph of it in this morning's *Irish Times*, sitting in the middle of Gorky Park. How does it make you feel, Minister, when you see this great World Heritage Site stolen –'

'Just to correct the record, Áine, it wasn't actually *stolen*? A decision was made to offer it to President Putin as a gesture of friendship from the Irish people. Let's be clear, Ireland has had this thing –'

'It's a Stone Age passage tomb, by the way.'

'That's exactly my point – Ireland has had it since the Stone Age. I saw that photograph in the paper this morning and I thought how – oh my God – amazing it is that Russian kids are going to get to enjoy it now, just as generations of Irish kids got to enjoy it as well.'

'Minister Lalor, we're out of time – thank you for joining us this morning.'

I'm there, 'Well, I'm proud to say I didn't understand a single focking word of that.'

Fionn goes, 'Aren't you worried about her, Ross?'

'Er, no – like I said, straight over my head.'

So much for Michael D. saying the future of our democracy depends on me. God focking help us all if that's true.

'It's just that it doesn't sound like her,' he goes. 'It's like *her* voice – but it's like someone else is talking.'

I'm there, 'I'm guessing it's See-mon.'

'You mean Sea-mon?'

'Okay, I'm going to have to record myself saying her name, because I'm pretty sure there's no difference between what I said and what you said.'

'Yeah, she does seem very influenced by her,' Fionn goes.

I'm there, 'She's, like, her Special Adviser.'

'But the whole banning sheep and cows idea. That wasn't Sorcha.'

'Yeah, no, it was focking See-mon's idea.'

'Sorcha was always a great critical thinker, even going back to her All Ireland debating days. But this Sea-mon seems to have taken over her mind – which isn't a positive thing, because the woman is obviously a fanatic.'

'Not when it comes to washing herself.'

'I was checking out her social media presence from before she went to work for Sorcha. She was port of the whole Extinction Rebellion thing – there's photographs of her taking port in a sit-in in Penneys against fast fashion.'

'She's against all fashion. I'm no Brendan Courtney, but some of her outfits are a focking disgrace.'

'She moved away from them because she didn't feel they were extreme enough. Her profile on Instagram describes her as an eco-terrorist.'

'Jesus.'

'She's been arrested at loads of demonstrations.'

'Fock.'

Listen to me sounding shocked – a man whose old pair have both done jail time and whose son could be about to go down.

'I'm just saying,' he goes, 'what if all Sea-mon wants to do is create chaos? And you know Sorcha when it comes to guru figures – if she's impressed by someone, she can be very suggestible.'

'She paid fifty-eight snots to learn how to yawn like Gwyneth Paltrow.'

'I just think we need to watch her, Ross.'

I'm there, 'And watch her, we will. So what are you up to today?'

He goes, 'I, em, have a meeting this morning,' acting all shady on me.

I'm like, 'A meeting? Is it something in relation to your round-the-world trip?'

He's there, 'Er, kind of, yeah,' and then he quickly changes the subject. 'I was going to make some breakfast – is Honor getting up today?'

I sort of, like, chuckle to myself.

I'm there, 'Yeah, no, I'd leave her for now. I'd say she has some head on her this morning.'

He's like, 'What do you mean?'

'I mean she'll be hungover to fock.'

He looks at me in, like, total shock. It's straight out of left field, in fairness to it.

'Yeah, no,' I go, 'she drank a bottle of Peach Schnapps yesterday.'

He's there, 'What?' like a thirteen-year-old drinking a bottle of spirits is the most shocking thing he's ever heard.

You'd never know he even played rugby.

I'm like, 'Yeah, chill out, Fionn. You were drinking alcohol at her age.'

He's there, 'My parents let me have half a glass of wine with dinner when we were on holidays. And I never finished it.'

'Sounds like you alright.'

'Why did she drink a bottle of Peach Schnapps? Is this because of that boy she liked?'

'Yeah, no, it looks like he's a definite player.'

Fionn – again with the open-mouthed stare – goes, 'Have you checked on her?'

And I'm there, 'Yeah, no, I got up twice in the night and rolled her onto her side. Sorcha knows fock-all about it, by the way, and I'd prefer to *keep* it that way?'

'Do you not think you should go and talk to her – as in, like, have a conversation about what she did?'

I'm like, 'Yeah, I was actually just *about* to do that?' and I stand up and hand Hillary to him.

So – yeah, no – I focking troop up the stairs to Honor's room. I knock on the door and I'm like, 'Honor?' in as quiet and gentle a voice as I can manage.

'Fffffock off,' she goes – yeah, no, we've all been that soldier.

I'm like, 'How's the head?'

She's there, 'I'm dyyying,' and I decide it's safe to push the door and enter. 'Don't turn that fffffocking light on.'

'I wasn't going to turn the light on.'

'It feels like my fffffocking . . . brain is bleeding.'

I sit down on the side of her bed.

I'm there, 'I'm not surprised. You'd usually drink Peach Schnapps with a mixer – orange juice maybe, or even white lemonade. I'm saying that for future reference.'

'I'm never drinking again,' she goes.

'Now you sound like your grandmother.'

'I've got the fffffocking . . . shhhakes.'

'I'll get you a glass of water in a minute. I wouldn't mind a quick word *first*, though?'

'Fffffock off. I'm too fffffocking sick to talk.'

'Hey, I've been there – many, many times. It's just, I wouldn't be any kind of father if I didn't ask you, well, why you felt the need to drink a bottle of Peach Schnapps – with or without a mixer?'

'I just fffffelt . . . sad, that's all.'

'In terms of?'

'The fffffocker told me he loved me.'

'It was a line, Honor. To goys like Reese, it's just something you say – a figure of speech.'

'Goys like you . . . you mmmmmmean. Fffffocking orseholes.'

'It sounds like you're feeling definitely better. You're saying there's definitely going to be no repeat of this, right?'

'Never ffffffocking drrrrrrinking again.'

'Consider this a – what do they call it? – a learning moment?'

'Get the ffffffock . . . out of my rrroooooom.'

'Good talk, Honor.'

I decide to just leave her to it. I step out of the room and my phone all of a sudden beeps. It's, like, a text message from JP.

It's like: 'Me and Christian have the money. Oisinn and Magnus have got loan approval from the bank. What's the Jack with you?'

Fock, I think. Kielys. With everything else going on, I nearly forgot.

I text him back, going: 'I'll go and see my financial adviser today.'

The old man is standing outside the GPO on, like, O'Connell Street with his famous megaphone held to his lips, even though he doesn't need it, even though this crowd of, I don't know, however-many-thousand people could hear him perfectly fine if he just used his regular indoor voice – the voice he uses to heckle politicians when they come on the TV in Doheny & Nesbitt, or to compliment a waitress in Shanahan's on her overall attractiveness.

'The EU,' he goes, 'is an affront to democracy!' which goes down well with the crowd, judging by the cheers. 'A group of self-regarding, unelected bureaucrats telling us how to run our affairs – and doing so in the interests of a German- and French-dominated *über staat* that cares NOTHING for this country! NOTHING!'

Again, there's a roar from the crowd. I spot Ronan standing on the platform, next to Hennessy, in front of a backdrop that says '#IREXIT – Towards a New Republic!' like the focking t-shirts that Sorcha's old pair were wearing that day.

'Of course,' the old man goes, 'in the last day or two, since our campaign began to gather momentum, we've had a steady stream of Jean-Claudes and Gerhardts coming out and assuring the Irish people how valued we are within the European family! But then I'm sure none of us has forgotten how they referred to us during the economic crisis of a decade ago! Portugal! Ireland! Italy! Greece! Spain! The countries who were forced to wear the hair-shirt of austerity! They called us PIIGS, ladies and gentlemen! PIIGS!'

Everyone storts booing.

He's there, 'They had contempt for us! And they didn't even bother to disguise it!'

He's good value, in fairness to him, even though I wouldn't be that into, like, world affairs and I'm only really here to shake the focker down for the money to buy Kielys. It's rare that I'd find myself deliberately on O'Connell Street. Shows you what I think of that pub.

'And now they love us!' he goes. 'Because they've known, from the very moment that our good friends in the United Kingdom voted to leave, that the European project – quote-unquote – is doomed! Mork my words, the EU is in its death throes and will be gone within a decade! By which time *we* will have formed new trading alliances with new portners and new friends! But only if we're brave enough to make the right choice on the eighth of September!'

Again, more cheers. I stort making my way to the front of the crowd.

He's like, 'You're going to hear lots of talk in the coming weeks from our friends in the fake news media, speculating as to what's behind this? What's in it for Chorles O'Carroll-Kelly? Well, I'll show you! Bring them out, Fionnuala!'

All of a sudden, the old dear steps up onto the platform, holding one of the babies – I can't make out which one it is from here – followed by five members of the old man's presumably staff, carrying the *others*? The audience goes absolutely bananas.

'I want to introduce you to the newest additions to the O'Carroll-Kelly family!' he goes. 'Hugo! Cassiopeia! Diana! Mellicent! Louisa May! And Emily!'

The crowd cheers each and every name – even though there wouldn't be many Cassiopeias or Mellicents over this side of the world, never mind Dianas, Emilys and Louisa Mays. There'd be quite a few Hugos, although they'd be mostly kids in Belvedere College whose parents wanted them to be mistaken for Protestants.

'These children are the reason I'm doing what I'm doing!' the old man goes. 'I want them to grow up in a country free from the enterprise-crushing, creativity-suffocating influence of the European Union! I want them to grow up in a country where they don't have to spend their entire working lives struggling to pay back tens of billions of euros in bailout money that has nothing whatsoever to do with them! That's why I'm doing this! Are you with me, O'Connell Street?'

Everyone's like, 'YEAH!!!'

He's there, 'I said, are you with me, O'Connell Street?'

And, even louder this time, they go, 'YEEEAAAHHH!!!'

He steps away from the mic and I squeeze my way through the throng of people at the front and step up onto the platform.

'Kicker!' he goes when he sees me coming. 'Did you hear the speech?'

I'm like, 'Yeah, no, I did. Jesus Christ, I was going to give you a fair focks if you'd just give me a focking chance.'

He goes, 'Very nice of you to say, Ross! Very nice of you to say!'

I don't bother beating around the bush. I'm there, 'I need one point something million euros.'

The focking face he pulls. He goes, 'Do you mind my asking what it's for?'

I'm there, 'I don't see what business that is of yours.'

'It's just that, well, it's not like you've asked me for fifty-thousand euros, Ross! One point . . . how much was it again?'

'One point something million euros.'

'Yes, one point something million euros is a lot of money!'

'If you must know, me and the goys are putting a bid in for Kielys of Donnybrook.'

'How wonderful! You should have said!'

'I shouldn't have had to say.'

'The answer is yes, Ross, I'd be happy to underwrite your investment in the business!'

'Does that mean you'll give me one point something million yoyos?'

'Yes, it does! By the way, Sorcha is playing an absolute blinder! I thought she wiped the floor with your friend and mine – the bould Áine!'

'I'm worried about her, and so is Fionn.'

'Why on Earth are you worried about her?'

'We think possibly See-mon is using her for her *own* ends?'

'What, that adviser of hers?'

'Yeah, no, the whole banning sheep and cows thing was, like, *her* idea?'

'Nonsense, Ross! The Sorcha Lalor I know is a strong-willed woman who's not afraid to speak her mind! Speaking of which, she's on the campaign trail in Kilkenny today!'

'Yeah, no, she set off early.'

'I thought we'd stort her off in Phil Hogan's home-town! That'll wipe that self-satisfied grin off his face!'

Suddenly, people stort coming up to my old man and telling him that he has their vote and it's about time someone said the things that he's saying. I hear a woman go, 'We had a French student once and she never wore deodorant!' and she just lets it hang there for us to make of it what we will.

I decide to just leave him to his fan club. I tip over to where Ronan is standing. He's wearing an '#Irexit – Towards a New Republic' t-shirt too.

I'm there, 'Alright, Ro, what's the Jack?'

He's there, 'Er, howiya, Rosser?' except he seems a bit, I don't know, *preoccupied*, if that's a word?

I'm there, 'I'm looking forward to your birthday porty – you can tell Shadden that I'm definitely coming, by the way.'

He goes, 'Could you mebbe seddend her an RSVP, Rosser?'

'As I told your old dear, I don't do RSVPs. My *face* is my RSVP?'

He just nods. He seems – like I said – a bit *sad* about something and definitely not excited about turning twenty-one in a couple of weeks.'

I'm there, 'What's wrong, Ro? You don't seem your usual chirpy self.'

He goes, 'It's alt steerting to get on top of me, Rosser.'

I'm like, 'As in?'

And that's when he all of a sudden bursts into tears. He goes, 'I doatunt waddant to go to jayult, Rosser.'

I'm there, 'You won't go to jail, Ro.'

'You caddent probiss me that, Rosser. I'd a nightmeer last neet that I got ten yee-or and some udder sham was brigging Ri to her jiddum kadas.'

'Ah, Ro.'

'Ine godda plead giddlety, Rosser.'

'What?'

'When me case cubs up.'

'But you're not guilty.'

'I am giddlety. I took the gudden from the choorch and I thrun it in the lake.'

'Maybe if I found out who this witness was, I could pay them off. That's how we do things in our world, Ro.'

'No, I've me mind med up, Rosser. If it goes to throyal, Ine godda plead giddlety. Be bethor to do two or three yee-ors than tedden.'

The old dear says she's going to miss these mornings as she hands me a Bloody Mary that looks big enough to transfuse a focking rhino.

I'm there, 'Jesus Christ! I'll be on my ear!'

'Oh, it's Friday morning!' she goes. 'Practically the weekend!' and I'm thinking – yeah, no – there's no prizes for guessing where Honor got it from.

Brian, Johnny and Leo are singing – I shit you not – a German lullaby to the babies. Yeah, no, they're going:

> *Guten Abend, gut' Nacht!*
> *Mit Rosen bedacht,*

Mit Näglein besteckt
Schlupf unter die Deck.

And the babies are genuinely loving it.

Astrid goes, '*Sehr gut,* Johnny! Brian, *du hast eine schöne Stimme!*'

Brian's like, '*Dankeschön!*'

She's like, '*Singe ihr!*'

The old dear grabs her swizzle stick and gives her breakfast a good stir. She goes, 'They're such beautiful boys, Ross.'

I'm there, 'They're nothing like that at home – I can assure you of that.'

'Well, it's been an absolute pleasure having them.'

Yeah, no, it's their last day coming here. They're storting in St Kilian's first thing on Monday morning and they'll be someone else's problem to deal with then.

Morgen früh, wenn Gott will,
Wirst du wieder geweckt,
Morgen früh, wenn Gott will,
Wirst du wieder geweckt.

'Of course,' the old dear goes, 'it's the end of this as well, isn't it?'

I'm like, 'What are you talking about?'

'Well, when the boys stort in their new school, you'll have no excuse to come here, will you?'

'I shouldn't need an excuse to visit my old dear, should I?'

'So you'll still come?'

'I probably will.'

I probably won't.

'Obviously not every day,' she goes.

And I'm like, 'Yeah, no, my liver couldn't take it – and I'm not even joking.'

I watch her nose suddenly twitch.

'Oh,' she goes, 'someone's done their dirty business! Was it you, Diana?' and she says it without even having to check her swatches. 'I think it was! Come on! Let's get you changed, Dorling!'

She hands me her drink, then she bends down to pick Diana up and she carries her over to the changing table. She lays her down on her back, then she whips off the old nappy, wipes her bits and pieces clean and puts on the new nappy with the speed and skill with which I've seen her mix a Mojito, or a Mai Tai, or a Cosmopolitan. Or a Mint Julep, or a Morgarita, or a Piña Colada. Or a Caipirinha, or a Whiskey Sour, or a Brandy Alexander.

You get the idea.

Or a White Russian, or a Tequila Sunrise, or an Old Fashioned. Or a Long Island Iced Tea.

I'm there, 'You've gotten good at that. Your fingers don't even shake like they used to.'

'Thanks to you,' she goes.

She picks Diana up and she rubs her nose off hers.

I'm there, 'It's not thanks to me at all. You're good with them. I'm saying that as a compliment to you.'

She smiles at me – and, for once, I don't even mind looking at her.

She goes, 'I really do wish I'd been a better mother to you, Ross.'

I'm like, 'Hey, it's cool – the damage is done now.'

She puts Diana back down on the giant playmat with the others.

'I wish I'd known then what I know now,' she goes, 'about the sheer joy that comes from being a parent.'

I'm there, 'It definitely has its moments alright.'

'How's Honor, by the way? I phoned her once or twice. I gather all is not well between her and this boy of hers.'

'Yeah, no, he turned out to be a bit of a player.'

'Is she *terribly* upset?'

'You could say that. She drank a whole bottle of Peach Schnapps last week.'

'Did she mix it with something?'

'Er, no, she drank it straight.'

'Tell her that orange juice is very nice. Or white lemonade.'

'Yeah, no,' I go, 'I was more concerned with the idea that she would drink a bottle of spirits at the age of, like, thirteen.'

She goes, 'There's a lot of nonsense spoken about young people drinking. My father allowed me to have wine with dinner from the age of seven!' and I wait for her tell me what she thinks the moral of this story might be, except she doesn't.

I hand her back her drink and I'm like, 'Right.'

Then we go back to listening to Brian, Johnny and Leo sing their little horts out.

> *Guten Abend, gut' Nacht!*
> *Von Englein bewacht,*
> *Die zeigen im Traum*
> *Dir Christkindleins Baum.*
> *Schlaf nun selig und süß,*
> *Schau im Traum's Paradies.*
> *Schlaf nun selig und süß,*
> *Schau im Traum's Paradies.*

Suddenly, out of literally nowhere, the old dear goes, 'I've been forgetting things, Ross.'

And I go, 'I know. It's your various meds – you shouldn't be drinking with them.'

'It has nothing to do with my meds.'

I end up just, like, staring hord at her.

I'm there, 'Are you being serious?'

She goes, 'It's my mind, Ross. Most days I'm fine. But some days, I just can't remember people's names or things that happened. You know, I have no memory of the day of the christening.'

'That's saying something – given that a gun was fired in the church.'

'I can't remember a single moment of it.'

Okay, that would also explain why she's forgotten about Delma telling her I rode her.

I'm there, 'Have you mentioned any of this to the old man?'

She goes, 'Oh, Chorles doesn't want to hear it, Ross.'

'As in?'

'I've told him several times what I told you. I'm forgetting things. He just said, "Oh, we're old, Fionnuala! None of our memories are what they once were!" He's not listening to me.'

'Focking typical of him.'

'He's the most powerful man in the country, Ross. He's just brought six children into the world and he has a wonderful vision for the country in which they're going to grow up. He doesn't want to hear that he has a wife at home who's losing her mind.'

'You're hordly losing your mind.'

She sort of, like, smiles sadly at me.

She goes, 'This *thing* – I don't even want to say its name – it's in our family, Ross. My grandmother had it. And *her* mother. And, well, you met *my* mother, of course.'

I don't know what to say. I just stand there, staring dumbly at the woman until she puts her hand on my face and sort of, like, strokes my cheek with her thumb.

She goes, 'I love you, Ross.'

And I can't say that it's the first time she's ever said that to me – but it's the first time I've heard her say it and felt like she definitely meant it.

And there's fock-all I can say back to her in that moment except, 'Yeah, no, I love you too, Mom.'

I'm like, 'No! Focking! Way!'

And Christian's like, 'Come on, Ross, it'll be a laugh.'

'For who?'

'For everyone!'

Yeah, no, his girlfriend – we're talking the lovely Lychee – wants me and the goys to do a dance to a song called 'Chicken Noodle Soup'.

I'm like, 'What the fock is she going to even do with it?'

And he's there, 'She's going to put it up on TikTok.'

'What,' Oisinn goes, 'for the whole world to see?'

'Yeah,' Christian goes, 'she's trying to grow her account and she needs as much content as she can get.'

I'm there, 'That's all we are to these kids. Focking content. I see it with my own daughter – focking millennials.'

This is in, like, Kielys of Donnybrook, by the way – soon to be ours hopefully, provided there are no rival bids. All the goys are here – we're talking me, we're talking Christian, we're talking JP, we're talking Oisinn, we're talking Magnus, we're talking Fionn – and, yeah, no, we're supposed to be discussing our plans for the place, except Christian is clearly in the first flush of love and can't even focus.

He's like, 'Come on, goys, it'll take, like, sixty seconds,' and he walks into the middle of the floor and storts, like, demonstrating it for us. 'You walk like this, then you do this and this, then you stick your elbows out like that, like they're wings, then you do this, then you turn around this way, then you turn around that way, then you do this with your neck three times, then you shout, *Chicken noodle soup!*'

We're all just, like, staring at him. I don't know who I'm more worried about – him dating a girl who's, like, eight years older than his son, or JP dating a woman who's, like, a year older than his mother.

See, this is what happens when you let the likes of Lillie's, Renords and even the Club of Love close down. It's hord to meet women of the same age with similar interests. That's why we have to make sure this place survives.

I'm like, 'Dude, we're not doing the stupid focking dance, okay?'

Christian looks back at me, all hurt.

I'm there, 'Okay, are we ready?'

And Fionn goes, 'Maybe I should I absent myself – you know, not being port of the consortium and everything.'

I'm like, 'Stay where you are, Fionn. You might not be an actual investor, but you're port of the circle of trust – and we still value your input.'

I love the way my voice sounds when I say shit like that.

JP goes, 'So, before we stort talking plans, can everyone get their hands on the one-point-two-five mills?'

Me, Christian and Oisinn are all like, 'Yeah, no, got it.'

'And can anyone go any higher – in case there's other interest and we get into a bidding war?'

Oisinn goes, 'We can probably pull together – what do you think, Magnus? – one-point-five?'

Magnus is there, 'That shoundsh about right, yesh.'

I'm like, 'Yeah, no, I'm getting the money from my old man, so it shouldn't be any problem for me.'

'So we'll put in an offer of five mills,' JP goes, 'but we *can* go as high as six – is that what we're saying?'

We're all like, 'Yeah, no, sounds good.'

'So what are we going to do,' Oisinn goes, 'in terms of bringing more people in?'

Fionn's there, 'What about Wednesday night table quizzes?'

He literally, literally says that.

I'm there, 'Okay, I've changed my mind. Fock off, Dude – you're out of the circle of trust.'

Fionn laughs, in fairness to him, and goes, 'I'll go and help Kevin with the pints.'

I forgot to mention – yeah, no – Kevin, the famous Google escapee, is *also* here?

Christian's there, 'Presumably, we're talking about ripping everything out and doing a complete refurb?'

'The fock are you talking about?' I go. 'Then it wouldn't be Kielys.'

JP's like, 'We have to put our own mork on it, though, Ross.'

'Not by turning it into a totally different pub.'

'No – by turning it into a better pub.'

'There's no such thing,' I go. 'You can't improve on perfection.'

Magnus goes, 'We can figure all of that out. Let ush not shtart with the – how to shay – counting of the chickensh jusht yet.'

JP's there, 'Yeah, no, Magnus is right. Anything can happen.'

'No way,' I go. 'We're going to be the next owners of this place. I can feel it in my bones.'

Fionn and Kevin arrive back from the bor with the round.

'So,' Fionn goes, 'I, em, have a bit news, by the way.'

We're all like, 'Go on,' because he's treating it like it's a major, major announcement. Which is what it ends up being.

He goes, 'I've been offered Tom's old job,' and he just lets it hang there for, like, ten seconds.

I'm there, 'Are we talking Principal of Castlerock College?'

'St Ignatius of Loyola College,' JP goes, putting me right.

But Fionn's like, 'No, the Board of Management want to change the name back. And they asked me to be the new Principal – starting from when the school reopens next week.'

I'm there, 'But hang on, you can't. You're about to –'

'Yeah, no, I told them that the timing was unfortunate,' he goes, 'that I was about to go on a round-the-world trip with my son and I was going to be away for a year – so, regrettably, I would have to say no.'

I'm there, 'Fock,' unable to hide my disappointment. 'It's making sense now. That's what your meeting was about.'

'And that's how I left it,' he goes. 'I walked out of the office and out of the school.'

I'm like, 'Why couldn't he have waited a year to die? He did that to focking spite us. That's how much he hated rugby.'

'But then –'

JP's like, 'What?'

Fionn takes a deep breath.

'Then,' he goes, 'I looked at the statue of Father Fehily outside – and, well, he seemed to speak to me.'

'And what did he say?' I go – and I can actually feel the butterflies in my stomach.

'He said I was being offered the opportunity of a lifetime,' Fionn goes. 'I could nearly hear him saying, "A round-the-world trip? Are you out of your mind?" So I said to Hillary, "What if we put it off until you're a little bit older? All of these places will still be there in five years' time." Well, some of them won't if the seas keep rising the way they are.'

I'm there, 'So what happened next? Don't leave us on, I don't know, tender hooks.'

'I stort first thing Monday morning, Ross.'

I punch the focking air.

I'm like, 'Yes! And will you be bringing rugby back?'

He's there, 'There'll be trials after school on – oh, I don't know – Tuesday?'

I throw my orms around him – we *all* do? – and we take it in turns to hug the shit out of the dude.

I'm like, 'Bottle of champagne, Mary!' because the moment definitely, definitely calls for it.

Kevin pipes up then.

He's there, 'I'm, er, going to go now.'

Magnus is like, 'Okay, sho I will shee you tomorrow, yesh?'

'No,' the dude goes, 'I mean I'm going to . . . *go*?'

Magnus and Oisinn smile at him and then at each other.

'You are ready?' Magnus goes.

And the dude just nods.

He's like, 'Thanks – for everything. If it wasn't for you, I don't know where I'd be right now.'

'Sitting at your focking desk would be my bet,' I go – and everyone laughs – even Kevin, in fairness to him.

Oisinn's there, 'What are you going to do?'

The dude just shrugs. He's there, 'I was thinking of maybe going on a holiday. I haven't had one in years. I had, like, six months' worth of leave built up when I left . . . I don't even want to say the name of the place.'

Fionn goes, 'I hear Buenos Aires is very nice at this time of year,' and he reaches into his inside pocket and – I swear to fock – pulls out his famous Lemonys. 'And Rio de Janerio. Montevideo. Santiago. Lima. Machu Picchu. Quito. Galapagos.'

Kevin is like, 'You can't do that.'

'I can,' Fionn goes – by a focking mile, the kindest, most generous dude I've ever focking met, even though I'd never let him know that. 'I'll ring Trailfinders tomorrow and transfer everything into your name.'

It's shaping up to be one of *the* greatest nights ever in Kielys of Donnybrook Town – even better than the night Johnny Ronan exited NAMA and put ten Ks behind the bor.

And that's when my *phone* all of a sudden rings?

It's a number I don't instantly recognize, but I answer it anyway, thinking literally nothing could actually ruin my mood tonight. But, of course, I have no idea yet how wrong I could be.

I'm there, 'Hey, you've got Ross,' which is how I used to always answer the phone and I was thinking of maybe going back to doing it.

'Ross O'Carroll-Kelly?' a voice goes.

And I'm like, 'The one! The only!' because – fock it – I'm bringing that one back as well.

The voice goes, 'Er, this is Reese,' and my entire mood changes instantly.

I'm there, 'Reese? What the fock do *you* want?' and I can see the goys all looking at me, wondering what the fock's upset the Ross-meister General? What's yucking his yum?

The dude goes, 'I'm in Vincent's Hospital,' and I know what's coming next before he even *has* to say it? 'Dude, it's Onóir.'

'What happened?' I go. Then I shout, 'What the fock did you do to her?'

'I didn't do anything to her. She turned up at a porty in my gaff tonight and she was, like, wasted.'

'My daughter wasn't at a porty tonight. She was going to her friend Sincerity's house and they were going to cover their school-books . . . okay, that sounds like total focking horseshit now that I'm saying it out loud.'

'She turned up uninvited. She was, like, all over me like a –'

'Hey, you're speaking to her old man, remember.'

'She drank a naggin of vodka before she even got here. Then when I told her I didn't want to be with her – as in, like, *with* with? – she turned totally schizo. She drank all my old dear's tequila.'

'I am going to deck you when I see you. Then I'm going to wait until you pick yourself up off the ground and I'm going to deck you again. And every time you get up again, you're going to be the subject of another decking. We're talking decking after decking after decking after decking.'

'Dude, I was the one who called the ambulance.'

'You're getting decked.'

'I was the one who went with her to the hospital.'

'There will be deckings.'

'Fock's sake.'

'Is she okay?'

'I don't know. They're pumping her stomach out.'

Jesus Christ. It's every parent's worst nightmare.

I'm there, 'At least tell me she's in the private hospital.'

'Er, no,' he goes, 'they brought her into A&E.'

I focking take it back.

'I'm on my way,' I go. 'And you better not focking be there when I arrive. Or the first of those deckings will be administered straight away.'

I hang up and Christian's like, 'What the fock is going on?'

I'm there, 'Honor's in Vincent's Hospital. She's having her focking stomach pumped out.'

Fionn's like, 'What?' because he gets on very well with her, in fairness to him.

I'm there, 'Goys, I'm going to go and grab a taxi.'

'Jesus Christ,' Fionn goes, 'she's thirteen years old, Ross.'

I'm like, 'Yeah, you're going to make a focking great Principal, Fionn. I'll text you as soon as I know something.'

I step outside onto the road. I go to hail a taxi, except it drives straight past me, even though its *lights* are on?

I end up screaming, 'TURN YOUR FOCKING LIGHTS OFF!' at no one at all, because that's how *worried* I suddenly am?

And that's when I notice a woman standing outside Bren's Borbers. She's so beautiful that it actually hurts my eyes to look at her. She's wearing – yeah, no – a short skirt that shows off her suntanned, perfectly shaped legs. She's got eyes so brown and so deep that you could basically drown in them and lips that you just can't help wanting to kiss.

'Hello, Ross,' she goes. 'Do you have a hug for your sister?'

'Fock's sake,' Erika goes, 'can you stop staring at my legs for, like, five seconds?'

The answer is clearly no. Even with my daughter in A&E, having her stomach pumped out, I can't take my eyes off those – oh my God – smooth, suntanned thighs.

'Do you want to touch them?' she goes as we're driving past RTÉ. 'Is that it?'

I'm there, 'No – well, no, but at the same time, *yes*, if that makes sense?'

She's like, 'Ross, I'm your focking sister.'

'Half-sister,' I go. 'Plus, you've been away for a few years. Plus, I've always had a thing for denim cut-offs. My mind is bound to be confused.'

'Oh my God, you've *literally* got drool on your chin.'

'Can we possibly change the subject, Erika?'

'Happily,' she goes, taking the left turn onto Nutley Lane. 'You need to see someone, Ross. As in, like, a psychiatrist?'

'Thanks,' I go. 'What are you doing home anyway?' at the same time sneaking what I promise myself will be one last look at those gorgeous, caramel-coloured getaway sticks.

'We're home for good,' she goes. 'Mom, me and Amelie.'

I'm there, 'I can't wait to see them.'

'She wants a divorce, Ross.'

'Helen?'

'She wants to serve *him* with the papers herself.'

'I'd love to be there – see the look on the focker's face.'

'Please keep that to yourself.'

'Yeah, no, I will. You should have told me you were coming.'

'I wanted it to be a surprise. Instead, *I* was the one who ended up getting the surprise?'

'In terms of?'

'In *terms* of? I get in a taxi at the airport and Sorcha's on the radio talking about how the European Union is, like, an anti-democratic institution and it's, like, complicit in the destruction of our *planet*?'

'Yeah, no, this girl called See-mon got inside her head.'

'Then I get in my cor to go to see my brother and it turns out that my thirteen-year-old niece is in an accident and emergency ward having her stomach pumped out.'

She turns right into Vincent's.

'Yeah, no,' I go, 'I'm holding you responsible for that one, by the way.'

She's like, 'Me?'

'I heard you talking to her on FaceTime, telling her she should try to be a nicer person. What kind of bullshit advice was that?'

'I said she'd have more friends if she wasn't so openly hostile all the time.'

'Exactly.'

'She told me she made loads of friends in Irish college.'

'Yeah, people from the focking country, Erika. Tipperary and God knows where else.'

'What's wrong with people from the country?'

'Oh, you've certainly changed your tune. The old Erika would never have said that. She'd have said the opposite, in fact. The girl who refused to learn the counties of Ireland in primary school because she said she'd never need to know them.'

She throws her Porsche Cayenne into the multi-storey cor pork and we head for the hospital itself.

I'm there, 'My point is that I preferred Honor as a bitch. At least that way she never got hurt.'

'I see you still haven't grown up,' she goes.

Into the hospital we go, and we find the A&E ward. Reese has cleared off – a clever boy, despite the obvious disadvantage of a Michael's education. The waiting room is full of people, some sitting, some standing, and everyone's just, like, staring into space, bored out of their focking tree, like they've been waiting there for, like, hours on end, which they probably *have*? There's a strong smell of disinfectant and a less strong smell of whatever the disinfectant is supposed to be hiding.

We make our way to the desk, where a middle-aged nurse gives us a look, before we've even opened our mouths, that says she's already bored with us.

'I'm here to see my daughter,' I go. 'She's, like, being pumped out?'

I possibly say this in too jaunty a tone, certainly judging by the mutters of disapproval I can hear from quite a few heads in the waiting room.

'What's her name?' the woman goes.

Erika's there, 'Honor O'Carroll-Kelly.'

The woman checks her list. 'No one here by that name,' she goes.

Then I remember that it was, like, Reese, who arrived with her in the ambulance. 'What about Onóir Ní Cheallaigh?' I go.

The woman rolls her eyes, annoyed at having to look again, then goes, 'Yes, she's here.'

Erika's like, 'Is she okay?'

The woman goes, 'What, do you mean *apart* from the alcohol poisoning?' and she says it in a definitely judgy way. 'The doctor is going to want to speak to you. Wait over there.'

Me and Erika end up leaning against the wall for, like, twenty minutes. I try to make conversation by asking her if she's wearing foot socks with her white Converse or if it's just, like, bare feet and she tells me that I need focking therapy, which is possibly true.

Eventually, a doctor appears and I hope it doesn't sound too racist if I mention that he's black.

'Who is here for Onóir Ní –' and – not being from around here – he doesn't even attempt to pronounce the last name. He doesn't need to because we're straight over to him, going, '*We're* here for her.'

'You are her parents?' the dude goes.

I laugh. I'm there, 'God, no – even though there would have been an attraction *before* we found out we were brother and sister?'

This draws more than a few sniggers from the people in the waiting room and I turn around and tell them to keep their focking noses out of other people's business.

'This is Onóir's father,' Erika goes.

I'm there, 'That's what I was trying to say.'

The doctor goes, 'Your daughter should not be drinking alcohol at thirteen years of age,' and – I have to say it – I do not like the tone he takes with me.

I'm there, 'I didn't focking give it to her. She was supposed to be covering her schoolbooks – with a girl called Sincerity Matthews.'

I don't know why I'm trying to shift the blame onto someone else's daughter. It's possibly a South Dublin thing.

'She drank a lot of alcohol,' the dude goes. 'She could have died tonight.'

Oh, that brings me to my senses. I'm suddenly conscious of the smell of booze off my *own* breath?

I'm there, 'I'll have a good talk with her,' trying to sound more sober than I *am* after nine pints?

He hands me a leaflet and goes, 'You should take some time to read this and discuss it with your daughter.'

I look at it. It's like, 'Teens and Alcohol – What Parents Should Know'.

I'm there, 'Oh, I'll definitely be doing that, Doctor – you mork my words.'

'You can go and see Onóir now,' he goes. 'She is through there – the fifth bed on the left.'

We step into this ward, which is full of, like, beds slash trolleys with people on them. I count them off. One, two, three, four –.

Honor's bed has a light-blue curtain drawn around it. I grab it and I pull it to one side. Honor doesn't even stir. She's lying there with a drip in her orm and a clear tube feeding oxygen into her nose. She's staring into space with the same look of utter boredom on her face that she had when she came out of Sorcha's womb.

I'm there, 'Hey, Honor – you have a visitor.'

She slowly turns her head, obviously thinking I'm referring to myself, but then she cops Erika standing next to me at the foot of her bed – looking fantastic, by the way – and her expression of boredom turns to one of shock. I watch her little mouth working, trying to form words, except she can't, because there *are* no words for what she feels, so she just bursts into tears, and Erika bursts into tears as well, and she rushes around the side of the bed, and she takes her in her orms and holds her, and they end up staying like that for, like, a good five minutes, hugging each other and trembling with the emotion of it all.

A nurse is suddenly standing beside me.

'It's a definite moment,' I go.

She's there, 'You dropped your information leaflet on the risks of children drinking alcohol.'

'Yeah, way to focking ruin it,' I go, snatching it out of her hand.

Erika pulls away from Honor and sort of, like, studies her face.

'You didn't tell me you were coming home,' Honor goes.

Erika's there, 'I wanted it to be a surprise. You didn't think I was going to miss Ronan's twenty-first, did you?'

'Is Amelie with you?'

'Yeah, my mom's looking after her back at the house.'

'Are you back for long?'

'No, Honor – we're back for good.'

That sets Honor off again. She bursts into tears of, like, sheer focking happiness and grabs hold of Erika like she has no intention of ever letting go.

Erika kisses the top of her and goes, 'What's been going on, my love? Why are you drinking?'

'Why can't I make him like me?' Honor goes, her face buried in Erika's shoulder. 'Why can't I make him like me?'

Erika's there, 'Oh, Honor,' at the same time stroking her hair.

'And that focking prick knew that he was cheating on me,' Honor goes, pointing at me, 'and he never focking told me because he's a wanker, just like him.'

I'll tell you one thing – the boredom has definitely lifted around the A&E if the sudden chatter is anything to go by.

Honor goes, 'And my stupid bitch of a mother said she wished she'd had a miscarriage with me.'

Erika turns and looks at me. 'Is that true?' she goes. 'She actually said that?'

I'm there, 'Yeah, no, she said it to her old dear. The knob.'

She looks mad enough to kill.

'Ross,' she goes, 'would you mind leaving us alone for a few minutes?'

So I do. I tip back out to the waiting room and I lean against the wall, giving the leaflet the old left to right.

'*Alcohol can affect the normal development of vital organs and functions,*' I read out aloud, '*including the brain, liver, bone and hormones.*'

Jesus, it'd nearly make you think, wouldn't it?

After about fifteen minutes, Erika arrives out.

'They're dischorging her,' she goes. 'She's getting dressed.'

I'm there, 'Cool.'

'By the way, don't tell anyone I'm home.'

'Why not?'

'I want to surprise Ronan at his porty.'

Yeah, no, she loves to make an entrance.

'He'll love that,' I go. 'He's not in a good place right now.'

She's like, 'Why?'

'He's talking about possibly pleading guilty – to possession of a firearm and obstructing the course of justice. Sorry, could you all just continue with your *own* conversations?'

Yeah, no, people are earwigging, left, right and centre.

'Hold on,' Erika goes, 'the last time I spoke to Ronan, Hennessy was going to get the chorges dropped.'

I'm like, 'Yeah, no, he still *hasn't*?'

'Why not? He's the Attorney focking General. Dad is the Taoiseach.'

'Why do think, Erika? They set him up – to stop him going to the States. Now they've got him mixed up in all sorts of shit.'

Erika goes, 'They're bad people, Ross – corrupt, through and through. We have to get Ronan away from them before he goes the same way.'

10.

Oireachtas Has Fallen

Honor laughs.

She's like, 'Oh my God, the focking state of him!'

She's talking about Christian. I'm showing her a video of him doing the 'Chicken Noodle Soup' dance, wearing – I shit you not – an actual chicken costume.

She's like, 'How old is he?'

I'm there, 'That would be my point. I think he's having a mid-life crisis or something.'

She hands me back my phone.

I'm there, 'So are you looking forward to going back to school?'

She shakes her head and she's like, 'Everyone's going to be talking about me making a fool of myself at Reese's porty.'

'I'm sure they won't be, Honor.'

'Dad, there were loads of girls from Mount Anville there.'

'Oh, right – they probably will then.'

'They'll be calling me a desperate bitch.'

'Who *gives* a fock what they think?'

She's quiet then.

I'm there, 'I'm sorry again – for not telling you about Reese.'

She just, like, shrugs. 'Erika said you were trying to protect me,' she goes.

'That's all I was doing, Honor. I didn't want to see you hurt.'

She smiles sadly at me. I wish other people could see this side of her.

'I've storted bullying Clíodhna on social media,' she goes.

I'm there, 'Hey, that's great.'

'I set up an account on Facebook called Clíodhna the Slut from Louth.'

'That's hilarious!'

'I'm using her photograph and everything!'

I smile at her – can't help it.

'Whatever Erika said to you,' I go, 'it definitely seems to have worked.'

'She told me to just be myself,' she goes.

I'm like, 'That's good advice. I genuinely missed you being a bitch.'

All of a sudden, Sorcha is standing in the doorway of Honor's bedroom.

She goes, 'Ross, will you please tell your daughter that it's time to get up for school?' and then she focks off.

'I hate her,' Honor goes.

I'm like, 'Hate's a strong word, Honor, but – yeah, no – she's definitely being a wagon to you.'

I leave Honor to get ready, then I tip downstairs. It's not only *her* first day back at school today, it's also Fionn's first day as the Principal of Castlerock – and Brian, Johnny and Leo's first day at St Kilian's as well.

The kitchen ends up being a scene of pandemonium, except it's, like, *happy* pandemonium? The boys are sitting there in their little uniforms and they're, like, throwing fistfuls of cereal at each other and calling each other every f, b and c word under the sun.

Fionn is standing there in a jacket that has, like, patches on the sleeves and I somehow resist the temptation to go, 'What the fock are you wearing?'

He's feeding little Hillary, who's going, 'Unkon Yoss! Unkon Yoss!' and pointing at me.

Sorcha's there, 'You'll miss him today,' looking up from her phone.

Fionn goes, 'It'll be weird alright, not having him with me.'

I'm there, 'Don't worry, Dude. Astrid will look after him. These three are totally different kids since they storted going there.'

Leo goes, 'You're nothing but a focking wanker, Dad!' and all I can do is laugh.

I'm there, 'Maybe *you're* the focking wanker, Leo. Have you ever considered that?'

He's like, 'Fock you! You focking orsewipe!'

'*Fick dich!*' Johnny shouts at me. '*Fick dich*, you focking fock!'

Sorcha stands up. She's like, 'Let's go. Kennet's outside. I've got a long day ahead of me. I'm campaigning in Wicklow today. You know there's a former down there, just outside Redcross, and six years ago he switched from sheep to alpacas and – oh my God – he hasn't looked back since. I don't know if you know, Fionn, but alpacas are non-ruminant.'

He's like, 'Yeah, I did know.'

I'm there, 'Yeah, I knew as well,' but no one comments.

'You see,' Sorcha goes, 'that's the kind of imaginative, outside-the-box thinking that rural communities are going to have to embrace and that the European Union – oh my God – goes out of its way to actually *discourage*?'

Fionn doesn't say shit. Sorcha knows he's a big fan of the whole Ireland being in Europe thing and she's obviously testing the water with him.

'Come on, boys,' Sorcha goes, 'out to the cor.'

They get up from the table and chorge outside, Brian going, '*Zur Schule! Zur Schule! Zur Schule! Zur Schule! Zur Schule!*'

I'm there, 'They're not going to last a focking day in that place!'

Fionn laughs, in fairness to him.

I'm there, 'Do you want me to –'

And he nods, then picks up Hillary and hands him to me.

I'm like, 'The focking state of you in that jacket, by the way. Sorry, I wasn't going to say anything, but I ended up *having* to?'

He's there, 'It's fine.'

'You're going to be an amazing Principal,' I go. 'I genuinely believe that.'

He's like, 'Thanks, Ross.'

With my free orm, I give him a hug. I don't *give* a shit? I just do. I'm like, 'Good luck, Dude,' and then out to the cor I tip.

Honor's already in the back of the limo, dressed for school. Sorcha is tapping away on her laptop and the two of them are making a big point of totally ignoring each other.

The atmos is horrible.

Kennet goes, 'How's she c . . . c . . . c . . . c . . . c . . . c . . . cutten, Rosser?'

I'm there, 'Whatever.'

'You m . . . m . . . m . . . m . . . must be looken f . . . f . . . f . . . f . . . forward to Ronan's bortdee peerty at the weekend, are you? B . . . b . . . b . . . b . . . be a chaddence for Shadden to show off that n . . . n . . . n . . . n . . . new house of theirs, wha'? It's f . . . f . . . f . . . f . . . far from F . . . F . . . F . . . F . . . F . . . F . . . F . . . F . . . Foxrock she was reared.'

'I'd love to say she hides it well, Kennet, but she focking doesn't.'

I get into the back of the limo and I make sure to close the screen so that he can't hear us.

'That focking stuttering fock,' I go.

Leo – I swear to God – goes, 'K . . . K . . . K . . . K . . . Kennet!' and me and Honor just crack up laughing.

I'm there, 'I can only imagine what the neighbours must make of focking Shadden. The famous Thomas having to look at her shopping in her focking pyjamas. How the fock did Ronan end up with that family of scummers?'

Sorcha looks up from her laptop.

'Speaking of Ronan's birthday,' she goes, 'I thought Erika would have made the effort to come home for it.'

Me and Honor exchange a secret smile.

I'm there, 'She probably doesn't want to see the old man – wouldn't blame her either after the way he treated her old dear.'

But Sorcha goes, 'Their marriage didn't work out, Ross, just like lots of marriages don't work out. I don't know why you always have to take the opposite side to your dad.'

Yeah, no, she's been bought and paid for.

I'm there, 'By the way, did you hear that the theme of Ronan's porty is gangsters and molls?'

'Molls?' she goes. 'I was talking to Shadden on the phone. I thought she said models.'

'No, that's just the way they pronounce molls.'

'Then I'll probably just wear my black pinstriped suit with the wide legs, my high-heel spats and the white fedora that I bought when they were in but then never wore.'

Kennet swings the limo into St Kilian's. The famous Herr

Schwarzenbeck is standing in front of the school, welcoming all the new kids. I open the door and the boys spill out of the back like hazardous focking waste – or at least that's how people react to them.

You can see parents staring at us with shock on their faces. Or they're ushering their kids inside, looking frightened. Like I said, Joe Duffy has done entire programmes on them.

Me, Sorcha and Honor get out.

'*Guten Morgen*,' the dude goes.

Sorcha's like, '*Guten Morgen*. Boys, say, *Guten Morgen* to Herr Schwarzenbeck.'

They're like, '*Guten* focking *Morgen*, Herr focking Schwarzenbeck!'

'They're very excited,' Sorcha goes, by way of explanation. 'They've been up since, like, three o'clock this morning.'

The three of them go chorging into the school, screaming, '*Schuuuuuuuuuuuuule!!!!!!!!!!!*'

We stort backing slowly towards the cor, then we we get back in. Without moving her lips, she goes, 'Kennet, drive!' and then literally ten seconds later we're on the way to Mount Anville with Honor.

I'm there, 'How long do you think they'll last?'

Sorcha goes, 'Have a little faith, Ross. But don't answer your phone if it rings this morning.'

'Hey, it's not our fault if they were stupid enough to take them.'

My phone beeps.

Sorcha goes, 'That's not the school already, is it?'

This from the girl who told me to have a little faith.

I'm there, 'No, it's a WhatsApp message from, like, JP.'

It turns out there's a rival bid in for Kielys and he wants to know if me and the rest of the goys are prepared to go to €5.25 mills.

I text him back and I'm like: 'Focking big time!'

Kennet pulls into Mount Anville and Sorcha doesn't even look up from her laptop as our daughter gets out.

Honor turns to me and goes, 'What are you doing today?'

And I'm there, 'I'm going to drop Hillary off at the Áras. Might have breakfast with my old dear and then maybe meet Christian or

JP if they're around,' and I can tell she's thinking she'd prefer that to being here.

She gives me a kiss on the cheek and goes, 'Bye, Dad!' then she gets out and makes her way across the cor pork.

I notice Sincerity Matthews, standing twenty feet away from her. She waves and goes, 'Hi, Honor! How was your summer?' and Honor gives her the finger and keeps on walking.

And I smile to myself, thinking, well, at least things look like they're getting back to *normal* around here?

I haven't seen the gaff this packed since the porty to celebrate the old dear being cleared of the murder of her second husband. There must be, like, two hundred people in here – all done up like gangsters and molls.

It's amazing how many of Ronan's mates have turned up in their regular clothes and still abided by the dress code.

Sorcha goes, 'Oh my God, Shadden, I love what you've done to the place!' lying straight to the girl's face.

Across the other side of the room, I can hear the old dear going, 'What in the name of God have they done to my house?' which is pretty much the same thing as *I'm* thinking?

Her beautiful wooden floors have been ripped out and replaced with corpet, the furniture is all cheap flatpack and there isn't a wall that doesn't have a flat-screen TV on it.

The old dear goes, 'What's happened to the writing desk that was over there?'

And Rihanna-Brogan is like, 'Me ma thrun it out, Fiddooda. She said it was veddy oawult.'

'Well, of course it was old! It was an antique! It belonged to Maud Gonne!'

'Who's Maud Godden?'

'She was an Irish revolutionary and a feminist. She wrote letters to W. B. Yeats at that desk.'

'Me ma said she wanthed the house to be mower modorden.'

'More what?'

'Modorden.'

'Well, I've absolutely no idea what word you're trying to say,' the old dear goes, then I manage to catch her eye. 'Have you ever heard the like of this, Ross?'

I smile at her. I'm like, 'Good to see you,' raising my stick of Heinemite to her.

She's there, 'Yes, you too. And hello, Sorcha dorling. Oh, I need a drink.'

Ronan walks up to us then. He's wearing a white Man from Del Monte suit with a black shirt underneath it, open to the navel.

He's there, 'Howiya, Rosser?' and he gives me a massive hug. 'Sudeka, looken sheerp! Ine lubben your fedorda.'

Sorcha goes, 'Happy birthday, Ronan!' and she kisses him on both cheeks. 'Yeah, I bought it after seeing Dana Walden wear one in the *Vanity Fair* Power of Women issue.'

'Two hundred snots,' I go, 'and she never took it out of the focking wardrobe. It's one of those things that seems like a good idea when you see a celebrity do it on a magazine cover – but you try to carry it off while you're pushing your trolley around SuperValu in Dalkey. You look like a focking dope.'

As I'm saying it, I spot Erika, looking absolutely stunning in a black cocktail dress and headpiece, the exact same one she wore to the *Great Gatsby* themed porty that Sorcha had for her thirtieth. The only reason I know is because I took about three hundred pictures of her on my phone that night and they're in a file called 'Sexy Sister!'

She walks up behind Ronan and goes, 'Happy birthday, Ronan!' and he spins around and lets out a pretty much squeal of delight.

He's like, 'Edika!' and they throw their orms around each other. 'Ah, Jaysus, Edika – I doatunt belieb it!'

Suddenly, it's as if every conversation in the gaff has stopped and everyone is staring in their direction. Like I said, the girl knows how to make an entrance.

The old man is staring at her like he's seeing a ghost.

Ronan goes, 'You look studden, so you do,' and I end up having to agree. 'I caddent belieb you're hee-or.'

And she's like, 'I wouldn't have missed this night for the world, Ronan!'

Sorcha stares at me while I'm quietly admiring how well the dress still fits the girl, especially around her hips and her orse.

She goes, 'Did you *know* she was home?'

And I'm like, 'Er, yeah, no, she wanted it to be a secret.'

She just fake-smiles Erika, then moves in for a hug, going, 'I didn't know my best friend in the world was going to be here tonight!'

I tip over to Nudger, Gull and Buckets of Blood and I'm like, 'Hey, goys – good to see you.'

Nudger goes, 'Some bleaten house, idn't it, Rosser? Veddy heerd to get to, but.'

I'm there, 'Yeah, that's the focking idea, Nudger!' and he laughs, in fairness to him.

'Hee-or,' Buckets goes, 'soddy again about that day of the cop shop, Rosser.'

I'm there, 'Hey, it's cool. We tried – that's the whole point.'

'Haskins is a boddicks, Rosser.'

'He certainly seems determined to put Ro behind bors.'

'A doorty boddicks is alls he is – and crooked as fook as weddle.'

'Well, if he's crooked as fock, I can't understand why my old man can't just, like, pay him off.'

All of a sudden, Ronan has the microphone from the karaoke machine in his hand.

'Hee-or,' Buckets shouts, 'what sog are you godda sig, Ro? "To Alt the Geerdles I Lubbed Befower"?'

A few people laugh. Shadden just glowers at Buckets, obviously not loving the joke, given that Ro was with these *geerdles* while supposedly still going out with her.

'Ine joost wanthon to say a few woords,' Ronan goes, 'I woatunt keep yous log. I joost wanthed to say thanks to me wife, Shadden, and me thaughter, Rihatta-Barrogan, for arranging the best boort-day peerty I ebber could have threamed of. I lub yous boat. And, Shadden, I hope wooden day, I'll be able for to say that I've been as good a husband to you as you've been a wife to me.'

'Wouldn't be focking hord,' I go, a little bit louder than I'd planned. 'She's way out of her depth – saying it for years.'

Kennet turns around and gives me absolute daggers.

Ro goes, 'I waddant to say thanks to me ma for raising me to know the diffordence between what's right and what's wrong.'

Hennessy shouts, 'You won't need that if you're working for me!' and everyone laughs.

It's a decent heckle, in fairness to it.

'Ma, I lub you,' Ro goes. 'I waddant to say thanks to all me ma's famidy who took a haddend in reardon me. Me nanny Delordes, me grandda Johddy and me uncoddle Anto. I altso waddant to say thanks to me utter nanny Fiddooda and me grandda Cheerdles, who boat mean the wurdled to me. And thanks to Heddessy – he's down theer, the cigeer in he's bleaten mout – for taking me odden and offerton me an appredenticeship. I waddant altso to say thanks to Shadden's family, especiady Kennet –'

'Focking K . . . K . . . K . . . K . . . K . . . K . . . Kennet,' I go, except this time I *want* him to hear me?

'– and Dordeen and then Shadden's brutter and sistor, Dadden and Kadden. Ine looken forwart to hearton Dordeen do the Spoyce Geerdles on the Kadaoke lathor!'

The Tuites all focking cheer.

'I waddant to say thanks,' Ro goes, 'to Sudeka and to me sistor, Hodor, the apple of me bleaten eye – where is she?'

She's right at the front – where else would she be?

He's there, 'I lub you, Hodor!'

And Honor goes, 'I love you, Ro!' and she blows him a kiss. And it's a moment. It's a definite, definite moment.

'I waddant to say thanks,' he goes, 'to me Addenty Edika, who thravelled alt the way from Australia. You're arthur making the night for me, Edika, so you are. And, lastly, I waddant to say –'

Oh, fock, he's welling up.

'– Ine wanthon to say thanks,' he goes, 'to this madden hee-or, the fedda wearton the Leddenstor rubby jersery, eeben though he was toawult the theme was gangsters and moddles. I call him Rosser – but he's me da. He came into me life when I was seben yee-or oawult. I'll nebber forget the day he arrived at the doe-er. He was wearton a Leddenstor jersey that day as weddle. I took one look at him and I says to me ma, "Him? What in the name of Jaysus were you thinking, Ma?"'

Everyone laughs.

'But Rosser proved to me a veddy vital lesson,' he goes. 'Doatunt ebber judge a book by the cubber. I know I throve him mad oaber the yee-ors. How many times did I get us fooked out of Doctor Quirkey's, Rosser, for booting the coin cascades?'

I laugh along with everyone else, but I've got, like, tears rolling down my face.

'When he read me bedtime stordies,' he goes, 'I always insisted it was a Paul Widdiams book – eeder *The Generdoddle* or *Gangladdened* or *Eebil Empoyer*. I'd rig him in the middle of the neet to tell him about me latest scheme to rob the AIB on the Main Street in Finglas and he'd nebber put the phowun dowun on me. He'd listen to me all neet long.'

'Still would,' I go. 'Still would.'

'Rosser,' he goes, 'for a madden with no moddle compass of he's owen, you did yisser best to keep me on the sthraight and naddow. And I waddant to ted you in front of all these people that I lub you veddy much, Rosser. I hope yous all hab a great neet!'

I'm, like, literally bawling. Honor comes over to me and throws her orms around my waist and I bend down and kiss her on the top of the head.

She goes, 'That was lovely, wasn't it?'

And I'm there, 'Yeah, no, it was. Have you been drinking again?'

'I had a Peach Schnapps,' she goes. 'Fionnuala said to try it with orange juice?'

'Well, I suppose you've learned enough about drink at this stage to properly respect it. Don't have too many more, though.'

She's like 'I won't,' and off she focks.

The next thing I hear is the old man's voice. He has the mic in his hand and he's going, 'Ladies and gentlemen, if I may just say something!' because he can't *not* be the centre of attention? 'If I may say something before the delectable Dordeen wows us all with that wonderful singing voice of hers. Hennessy Coghlan-O'Hara and I have a gift for the – quote-unquote – birthday boy!'

'You altreddy geb us this house, Grandda!' Ro shouts.

'Hennessy, do you want to join me up here and we can tell him together?'

Hennessy slithers over next to him. He whips a piece of paper out his pocket and the old man takes it from him.

'This morning,' the old man goes, waving it around, 'Hennessy received a letter from the Office of the Director of Public Prosecutions, informing him that the case against Ronan for illegal possession of a firearm and obstructing the course of justice will not be proceeding. All chorges against you, Ronan, have been dropped!'

There's a humungous cheer, especially from the Tuite family and Nudger, Buckets and Gull. I notice Ro hugging Shadden, and Kadden hugging Dadden, and Kennet hugging Dordeen. And I feel suddenly giddy, like a massive, massive weight has been lifted.

Dordeen grabs the mic, shouts, 'Fook the Geerds – every fooken wodden of them!' and then launches into her song.

> *If you wadda be moy lubber,*
> *You godda get wi moy freddens,*
> *Make it last forebber,*
> *Ferrenship nebber eddens.*

Erika is suddenly standing behind me. She turns around to me and goes, 'That's very suspicious, isn't it?'

I shrug. I'm there, 'Well, at least it's over now.'

'I know a girl whose sister works for the DPP. I'm going to ask her to find out what's going on.'

I shush her then because I notice the old man tipping over to us. He looks majorly sheepish.

He goes, 'Hello, Erika!'

She's like, 'Hi,' giving him very little back.

'You look well,' he goes.

I'm there, 'I already told her. Several times in fact.'

He's like, 'How's Helen?'

'Look,' Erika goes, 'I came here tonight for Ronan. I don't want to have a scene with you and ruin his night, so I'm just going to walk away from you, okay?'

Which is what she then *does*?

The old man sighs and goes, 'It'll take time, Ross, but I'm sure she'll come around eventually! Good news about Ronan, eh?'

I'm there, 'What happened? Did you pay off that Haskins dude?'

'Let's just say that a certain piece of evidence that was vital to the State's case – namely, the gun in question – mysteriously disappeared! And now Ronan is free to get on with the rest of his life!'

I go, 'Well, you let him focking sweat on it for long enough, didn't you?' and then I tip over to the goys – we're talking Christian, JP, Fionn, Oisinn and Magnus. JP says he has it on very good authority that the other crowd who are interested in buying Kielys aren't going to match our offer. Which means that by, like, five o'clock on Monday, it's going to be ours.

Yeah, no, it's nothing *but* good news tonight?

I head for the kitchen to grab another stick of Heinemite. Kennet is there, smoking a joint and drinking a can of some cheap, Belgian piss.

He's like, 'G . . . G . . . G . . . G . . . Great news, Rosser – about R . . . R . . . R . . . R . . . Ronan, wha'?'

I don't even look at him. I just stare out the window at Rihanna-Brogan, who's riding around the gorden on Moxy. I can only imagine what they've done to house values on this road. Another few weeks and I'd say the people around here will be nostalgic for the 2008 economic crash.

I'm there, 'I'd still be interested to know why you had the gun in the church in the first place – and how it ended up in the hands of a child.'

Kennet goes, 'It d . . . d . . . d . . . d . . . dudn't mathor now, dud it? W . . . W . . . W . . . Woorked out weddle for evody wooden. The cheerges is thropped. Ronan has a g . . . g . . . g . . . g . . . great job and Shadden has a lubbly howum, albeit on the wrong s . . . s . . . s . . . s . . . s . . . s . . . soyud of the city.'

Something suddenly occurs to me, standing there in the kitchen, talking to Ronan's fockwit father-in-law. The case being dropped means he's going to be getting his passport back, which means he can go to the States after all.

I don't even bother grabbing myself a beer. I go off to search for Ronan.

On my way out of the kitchen, Kennet goes, 'By the w . . . w . . . w . . . way, you know when you're in the back of the k . . . k . . . k . . . keer, I can hear evoddy woord you do be s . . . s . . . s . . . s . . . saying in the back.'

I actually laugh.

I'm there, 'Couldn't give two focks, Kennet. Could not give. Two focks.'

I wander into the hallway, then into the living room, then into the drawing room, looking for Ro, except there's no sign of him. I tip upstairs and that's when I end up hearing – yeah, no – raised voices coming from my old bedroom.

It's, like, Sorcha and Erika and they are going at it in a way that I would probably find hot if one of them wasn't – I have to keep remembering – a blood relative of mine. And I still find it hot anyway.

'How *dare* you?' Sorcha is going.

And Erika's like, 'Seriously, take a focking look at yourself!'

'*Excuse* me?'

'You've totally bought into my dad's bullshit. Since when are you in favour of Ireland leaving the European Union?'

'Er, since they tried to block my efforts to bring down Ireland's greenhouse gas *emissions* rate?'

I'm actually seriously turned on, even though politics would usually do very little for me.

'By banning cows and sheep?' Erika goes.

Sorcha's like, 'I've nothing personal against them, Erika.'

'Oh, focking wake up,' Erika goes, 'you're being used.'

'I'm not being used.'

'Yes, you are. By my dad on one side and whoever that focking adviser of yours is in every second photo I see of you online. Focking See-mon.'

'Don't give me that. Her name *happens* to be Sea-mon.'

'And what about your family?'

'My family are fine.'

'Are they? Were you aware that your daughter had to have her stomach pumped out in St Vincent's Hospital last weekend?'

I can feel myself suddenly losing my erection.

'That's a lie,' Sorcha goes.

Erika's like, 'I was there, Sorcha.'

'How?' she goes. 'Oh my God, did Ross know about this?'

'It's not Ross's fault. Stop always blaming Ross.'

'So he *did* know?'

'It's *your* focking fault that your daughter is drinking, Sorcha.'

'Excuse me?'

'You know she heard what you said to your mother – about wishing you'd had a miscarriage? What the fock is wrong with you?'

'I was angry with her over what happened in New York.'

'Tough focking shit, Sorcha. Because you don't get to do that to your children. She didn't ask to be born. You brought her into the world and you raised her. And how she's turned out is down to you and Ross. You don't get to decide to treat her like she's not your daughter any more – you focking norcissist.'

Okay, I'm turned on again.

Erika's like, 'It's typical of you, Sorcha. Trying to save the planet while your own family is falling aport.'

'Rosser!' I hear a voice go.

Jesus Christ, I end up nearly jumping out of my skin. Ronan is standing behind me on the landing.

He's like, 'Were you looken for me?'

I don't know if he can see that I'm turned on.

I'm there, 'I was, yeah. Thanks for, you know, what you said.'

'I meddent evoddy woord, Rosser.'

'And – yeah, no – good news about the chorges being dropped.'

'Heddessy came good in the eddend, ditnt he?'

'Of course, you know what this means, don't you?'

'What?'

'You're going to get your passport back. You can take that internship in the States.'

He just shakes his head. He's like, 'I caddent go now, Rosser – not arthur evoddy thing Heddessy's dudden for me.'

We arrive home from the porty in a taxi. The boys are already asleep. Me, Sorcha and Honor carry them upstairs and we put them to bed. Then Honor heads for her room and that's when Sorcha goes, 'Honor, I'm sorry.'

Honor's there, 'For?'

'For what I said to my mom. It was unforgivable. And it also wasn't true. You were wanted – wasn't she, Ross?'

I'm there, 'Hey, I never said she wasn't. It was you, remember.'

She's like, 'I did very nearly miscarry. And, if I had, Honor – oh my God, I would have been hortbroken. Because I couldn't imagine a world without you in it.'

'Then why did you say it?' Honor goes.

Sorcha's like, 'Because I was angry,' and it all comes out, there on the landing. 'And because I was selfish.'

I'm there, 'I didn't hear your mother rushing to Honor's defence, by the way. The stupid focking cow.'

'Ross,' she goes, 'you're not making this any easier for me. I'm trying to apologize.'

But then Honor – totally out of nowhere – goes, 'I owe *you* an apology, Mom.'

But Sorcha's like, 'No, you don't, Honor. Erika's right. I brought you into this world. You don't owe me a thing. Not a thing.'

'I phoned the Irish Formers' Association and told them you were going to be at *Samantha Power: The Musical.*'

'And that was only because I rang Sister Consuelo and told her not to cast you as Samantha Power.'

'But that's because I said you were full of focking shit in front of the United Nations General Assembly.'

'And that's because I sent you away to Australia because I thought you tried to poison Hillary.'

It's lovely to hear them talk like this – to get it all out in the open. Sorcha storts playing with Honor's curls – the way she used to when

Honor was, like, three or four. It used to send her off to sleep. I watch all the anger in her little face melt.

'You know, the first time I ever got drunk,' Sorcha goes, 'I was sick in the front footwell of my mom's Daihatsu Charade.'

Honor's like, 'Oh! My God!'

'I was seventeen, in fairness – not thirteen. But the point is that my mom was there to hold back my hair for me while I vomited.'

'Dad held back mine – the first time, when I drank a bottle of Peach Schnapps. Then he came to the hospital the night I had my stomach pumped. He was amazing.'

They both smile at me. Hey, I'll take whatever credit is going.

Sorcha goes, 'Well, I'll never forgive myself that it wasn't me. Honor, I have to ask, why did you feel the need to get drunk like that?'

Honor's there, 'I was just sad, that's all.'

'Because of that boy?'

Honor nods her little head, then she suddenly bursts into tears and throws her orms around Sorcha.

Sorcha's there, 'Oh, Honor!' and then *she* storts crying as well.

I have to admit, I'm feeling a little emosh myself.

Honor goes, 'I just don't understand why he doesn't like me.'

Sorcha's there, 'Oh, my poor, poor girl.'

'I tried to be a nice person. I actually stopped being a bitch. But he still didn't like me.'

'You're going into Second Year next year, Honor. The pressure of the Junior Cert is going to really stort kicking in. If it's a consolation, it's probably not the right time to, like, *have* a boyfriend?'

Jesus Christ, I think. Once a swot, always a focking swot.

Honor's there, 'But it hurts so much,' sobbing into Sorcha's chest. 'I love him, Mom.'

'Oh, Honor,' Sorcha goes. 'I know this is probably hord for you to believe right now, but there *will* be other boys.'

'And they won't love me back either – because I'm not pretty.'

Sorcha goes, 'You are *so* pretty, Honor.'

Seriously, politics has totally corrupted the woman.

'I know I'm not pretty,' Honor goes. 'I'm a focking ugly bitch. I don't have anything going for me.'

Sorcha's like, 'What a load of rubbish. This – what's his name? – Reese? He obviously doesn't know a good thing when he sees it. And frankly, Honor, he doesn't sound like he's worthy of you.'

Honor lets go of Sorcha then. And she's there, 'I just wish I could, like, *make* him like me?'

'Oh, Honor,' Sorcha goes, 'I should have been there for you,' and then she sort of, like, smiles to herself. 'This Reese – he sounds very like your father.'

She's there, 'He's a rugby wanker,' but she means it in a good way.

'That was always my ultimate nightmare,' Sorcha goes, 'that my daughter would one day bring home a teenage version of Ross.'

I'm there, 'Yeah, no, thanks a bunch.'

Sorcha stares into Honor's face and goes, 'You *say* you're not pretty, Honor, but I think you are. For instance, you have lovely eyes.'

Honor's there, 'All the girls in school say I have evil eyes.'

'It doesn't matter what anyone in that school thinks.'

Says the woman who still wears the signet ring she got for being voted Head Girl in 1997.

'Honor,' she goes, 'do you think you can forgive me?'

Honor's there, 'You didn't do anything wrong.'

'I did,' Sorcha goes. 'Erika was, like, so, so right about me. What good is it trying to do my bit to help Ireland achieve corbon neutrality when I don't even have a relationship with my own daughter?'

Honor's there, 'We can *have* a relationship – if you want.'

'I do want,' Sorcha goes. 'I so, so do. I know we'll probably never be, like, best, best friends – like me and *my* mom are? But we could make the effort with each other. And in time, who knows?'

'I want that, Mom. I really want that.'

Sorcha throws her orms around Honor. And I think, what the hell – and I throw my orms around them. It's a lovely moment.

And through the door of the boys' room, I hear Leo go, 'Shut the fock up – me trying to sleep.'

*

Fionn is sitting at the table with Hillary and the boys and he's, like, talking German to them.

He's going, '*Hattet ihr Spaß in der Schule?*'

And the boys are like, '*Ja, wir lieben sie!*'

'*Magt ihr Herr Schwarzenbeck?*'

'*Er ist ein dicker Bastard.*'

Fionn smiles. At least they seem to be talking in full sentences, even if I haven't a focking clue what they're saying.

'Is everything okay?' Fionn goes.

I'm like, 'Yeah, me, Sorcha and Honor had the big-time chats last night. Got everything out in the open. Hopefully there'll be no more drinking now. Although I suppose every parent thinks that.'

'Ross,' he goes, 'can I talk to you about something?' suddenly changing the subject.

I'm there, 'It's not Christian, is it?'

'What?'

'He isn't still pestering you to do videos, is he, for that thick-as-shit girlfriend of his?'

'No, he's not.'

'What do you want to talk to me about, then?'

'I was talking to Tina at the porty last night.'

'As in, like, Ronan's old dear?'

'Exactly.'

'She was saying that Tom was writing her an email when he had his heart attack.'

'It's the first I'm hearing about it.'

'She said she spoke to you about it.'

'In that case – yeah, no, she might have said something alright.'

'She said he mentioned that he'd had a visit from *that insufferable imbecile.*'

'I have a feeling I know where this is going.'

'It's just that, well, that's what he used to call you?'

'Okay, look, hands up, I did go to see him that afternoon. I saw that he'd changed the name of the school and I paid him a visit. Yeah, no, we had a pleasant enough conversation. We both made a lot of valid points, I thought. Then, after I left the office, he must have – yeah, no – keeled over and died.'

'Ross, did you say something to upset him?'

'Did I? I'd have to rack my brains.'

'Jesus Christ, you did, didn't you?'

'Dude, every word that came out of my mouth upset him. The focker used to tut at the very sight of me.'

'Ross, what did you say to him?'

'Fine. It was something I overheard Tina say one night with a few drinks on her – about what he was like in the sack.'

'Okay, maybe don't say it in front of the kids.'

'Ah, they won't understand. She said he'd a mickey like a fun-size packet of Rolos and he cried whenever they did the deed.'

Brian goes, 'He'd a mickey like a fun-size packet of Rolos and he cried whenever they did the deed!'

Fionn's there, 'So those were the last words that Tom ever heard?'

'Yeah, no, I presume so,' I go. 'You can see why I don't want to tell Tina the truth,' and then I suddenly remember something. 'Fock, I must throw out that bag of women's knickers today – I keep forgetting.'

'Women's knickers!' Leo goes. 'Women's focking knickers.'

Fionn's like, 'Ross, I don't want to know what you get up to. Sorcha happens to be a friend of mine, okay?'

I'm like, 'Whoa, it's nothing like that, Dude. If you must know, I've been very faithful to her lately – well, aport from a brief fling I had with Honor's Irish teacher when we were in the Gaeltacht.'

'Seriously, Ross, don't tell me things like that.'

'If you must know, they're actually JP's. He asked me to get rid of them.'

'I'm not interested.'

'Yeah, no, they're basically screwvenirs he got from all the birds he ended up with over the years. One or two bras as well. And Delma's Hermès scorf. He stole it from my old dear's gaff back in the day and spent the entire summer in Irish college –'

'Ross, I get the idea.'

'– focking jacking off to it.'

'Focking jacking off to it!' Brian goes.

I'm there, 'Of course what JP doesn't know – and you probably don't want to hear this either – is that me and Delma had a thing. Not that long ago either. Happened in my old dear's side passage.'

'Ross, enough!' he goes.

I laugh. I'm there, 'Sorry, Dude – TMI, huh? Anyway, I better hit the road. I'm supposed to be meeting JP for a coffee slash investors meeting in Ranelagh. If there's no late counter bid, by five o'clock today, we are going to be the new owners of Kielys of Donnybrook Town, the greatest pub in the world! Wish me luck, Dude!'

And so begins what will turn out to be the longest day of my actual life.

I'm in the cor and I end up accidentally hearing the news. An *Irish Times* opinion poll published this morning suggests that the Government is on course to lose the referendum on Orticle Three of the Constitution. Yeah, no, it turns out that fifty-five per cent of those questioned said they intended to vote for Ireland to remain within the European Union when the polls open in two days' time.

The old man isn't happy about it. He's on the radio ranting and raving, going, 'This is a bogus opinion poll and further evidence of what we are fighting against! There is a consensus among every mainstream media organization and every other political party in this country that Ireland should remain within this failed European so-called Union! They have waged a campaign of misinformation to frighten people out of voting to leave and they are continuing to do so!'

The dude sounds totally unhinged. Sometimes I think, if I could just get that focking wig off his head, things might go back to normal. But, then, they probably wouldn't.

He's there, 'We knew that the EU wouldn't let us go easily! You only have to look across the water to see how difficult they're making it for our good friends in the United Kingdom to deliver on the democratically expressed will of its people! These unelected officials in Brussels don't care about our democracy! Our democracy is an irritation to them and they will stop at nothing – NOTHING! – to prevent us from leaving!'

I pull up outside Cinnamon. I kill the engine and his voice along with it. I get out of the cor and I just happen to check my phone. And that's when I notice that I have, like, forty-seven missed calls.

Shit, my phone must have been on, like, Silent.

Forty-seven missed calls, though? Who the fock is ringing me forty-seven times? I scroll down through the names. It's, like, Christian, Tina, Oisinn, Honor, Tina, Tina, Tina, Sorcha, Erika, Sorcha, Erika, Tina, Ryle Nugent, Tina, Sorcha, Delma, Delma, Delma, Delma, Delma, Delma . . .

Delma?

As I'm about to head into Cinnamon, I notice from the screen that Fionn is ringing, so I end up answering it. I'm like, 'Dude, what's going on?'

And that's when he just blurts it out. He goes, 'Ross, Silas recorded our conversation in the kitchen this morning and sent it to every number in your contacts list.'

My entire body freezes.

I'm like, 'What?' at the same time trying to remember what exactly we talked about.

'They all heard it. Sorcha, Honor, Tina, Delma, Christian, JP – every word you said.'

Shit, I think, trying to remember the conversation. I said Lychee was thick as shit. I mentioned – oh my God – riding Marianne and Delma. I mentioned – oh, Jesus Christ – what I said to McGahy, quite possibly killing him in the process. I mentioned – fock-a-doodle-doo – JP's bag of screwvenirs. And everyone in my phone book will have heard every focking word.

All of a sudden, I look up and I see JP standing, like, ten feet in front of me.

I hang up the phone.

I decide to fall back on my tried and trusted tactic of trying to style it out. I go, 'Hey, Dude, today's the big day, huh? By the way, if you get a voice memo from me, delete it without listening to it. I was hammered. Definitely, definitely don't listen to it, though.'

But he doesn't say shit. He just walks up to me and punches me full in the face. And I am instantly decked. I'm, like, literally sitting on my orse on the Main Street in Ranelagh, with my head spinning and my ears ringing, and I'm going, 'Dude, I don't know what you *think* you heard?'

He's like, 'You had sex with Delma.'

'Dude, it was before you two got together.'

'Why didn't you focking tell me?'

'We did it up against the rainwater butt around the side of my old dear's house – she actually managed to dislodge the thing from the overhead gutter with her constant bucking.'

'I don't want the focking details, Ross!'

'Dude, make up your mind.'

'You've ruined everything.'

'I don't see how that's the case. Like I said, we did the deed before you two were even together. She's allowed to have a past.'

'She listened to the message, Ross. She knows it was me who stole her scorf all those years ago.'

'Fock.'

'Now she thinks I'm a focking pervert.'

'Dude, I'll talk to her for you. I'll explain that you were a pervert at the time, but you've grown out of it.'

'You've done enough damage. I'm focking finished with you, Ross.'

It suddenly feels like I've been kicked in the stomach.

I'm there, 'Don't say that, Dude. We're about to buy Kielys together.'

But he's like, 'Fock you, Ross. I'm out. And I know Christian is as well.'

'I think Delma's big romance is over,' the old dear goes.

I'm there, 'Why do you say that?'

This is us in the crèche in the Áras, by the way. I drove out here to hide from the many people who are looking for me.

'She came to see me last night,' she goes. 'She was in a foul humour. Probably for the best. I don't think she was able for all the sex.'

'Yeah, maybe we should put some boundaries around what we do and don't talk about.'

'She came in here one day and I don't know what they'd been

doing to each other, but the poor woman could barely walk. She had to hold on to that table there for balance.'

'Yeah, again – *over-share*?'

I'm sitting on the playmat with the kids and Cassiopeia is trying to put my finger in her mouth.

'She's already teething,' the old dear goes.

I'm there, 'She's so beautiful. They *all* are?'

'What happened to your face?'

'What do you mean?'

'You have a bruise.'

I touch my cheek. Yeah, no, JP left me with some shiner, although I suspect it's nothing compared to what Tina is going to do to me when she catches up with me.

I'm there, 'I was, er, throwing a rugby ball around with a few of the goys this morning,' managing to make myself sound like a hero. 'I took a bang in a ruck. Still got it, even at thirty-eight.'

I look at my phone. It's still on Silent. The missed calls are really storting to rack up. Four hundred and seventeen since, like, this morning. Sorcha. Tina. Sorcha. Tina. Sorcha. Tina. Delma. Sorcha. Delma. Honor. Honor. Honor. Tina. Delma. Delma. Delma. Tina. Tina. Sorcha. Delma.

And then there's the text messages. Tina going: 'YOU FUCKING KILLED TOM!' and 'I AM GOING TO SNAP YOUR FUCK-ING NECK!'

I'm thinking, I'll give JP and Christian until this afternoon to hopefully calm down, then I'll talk them around with my famous people skills. As it happens, I know where JP's going to be at, like, two o'clock this afternoon, because he mentioned before that him and Christian have a meeting with the old man and Fyodor in, like, Government Buildings.

'Hold on,' the old dear suddenly goes, 'is there an extra one?'

I'm like, 'What?'

'One, two, three, four – there's seven, Ross.'

'Yeah, I know.'

'Who is that one there?'

'That's Hillary. It's Sorcha and Fionn's baby.'

'I was thinking he looked bigger than the others.'

'He's coming here now every day.'

'Yes, I knew that.'

'Did you?'

'Yes, I remembered.'

There's, like, silence between us for about thirty seconds, then I go, 'You need to talk to the old man about it.'

'He won't listen, Ross.'

'You're going to have to make him listen – before it's too late.'

'I'm not dying, Ross. It's just dementia.'

'Right.'

'It's not a terminal illness. It's just that, well, bits of me will slowly disappear.'

'That's, I don't know, heavy shit.'

'I need to ask you something, Ross – a favour.'

'Is it more prosecco?'

'No, it's not more prosecco.'

'Shoot.'

'If anything happens to me –'

'You just said–'

'– if I'm in a position where I can't manage any more, will you look after the children?'

'You don't even need to ask me that.'

She smiles at me. She's like, 'Thank you.'

The phone in the crèche rings and Astrid answers it.

'That'll be Delma,' she goes. 'We're supposed to be playing golf this afternoon. It'll be interesting to see what all that sex has done to her stance. Did I tell you that she could barely stand up straight when she was here recently?'

'Again, Mom, can you maybe *not*?'

The old dear storts making her way to the phone, except Astrid goes, 'No, the call is for you, Ross.'

I'm like, 'For me?'

'It's your wife,' Astrid goes.

I'm there, 'Tell her I'm not here.'

'She says she can hear your voice,' and I end up having no choice but to take the phone from her.

I'm there, 'Sorcha, I was anti the idea of getting that device, if you remember? I've heard horror stories about them.'

'DELMA?' she basically roars at me down the phone. 'HONOR'S IRISH TEACHER?'

'Again,' I go, 'it was supposed to be a private conversation, Sorcha.'

'DO YOU HAVE ANY FOCKING IDEA HOW UPSET YOUR DAUGHTER IS AFTER HEARING THAT?'

'I can probably guess.'

'I'VE HAD TO KEEP HER OFF SCHOOL TODAY! I'VE HAD TO PULL OUT OF THE LAST DAY OF CAMPAIGNING! SHE'S BEEN SITTING WITH ME ALL MORNING, CRYING HER EYES OUT!'

'It sounds like you two are finally bonding. I'm trying to think of an upside to this, Sorcha.'

'YOU PROBABLY SHOULD KNOW AS WELL THAT TINA'S HERE!'

'Tell her I got her texts, will you, and I'll hopefully catch up with her soon?'

'SHE'S SAYING YOU KILLED TOM MCGAHY!'

'Bit of a stretch that, Sorcha.'

'WELL, SHE SAID SHE'S NOT LEAVING THIS HOUSE UNTIL YOU COME HOME! I SAID TO HER THE ONLY REASON HE'LL BE COMING HOME IS TO PACK HIS FOCKING STUFF!'

'Sorcha, you've forgiven me for way worse things than this. I'd give you a list except I don't think it'd help my –'

'OUR MARRIAGE,' she goes, 'IS OVER, ROSS!' and she slams the phone down on me.

It's, like, just after lunchtime when Erika texts me and tells me she needs to talk to me urgently. I'm, like, walking past the Shelbourne Hotel at the time, on my way to Government Buildings. I'm going to try to hopefully nab JP and Christian when they finish their meeting with my old man and Fyodor and explain that, I don't know, the Delma thing meant nothing – it was put in front of me and I took it – and that Lychee, while not the brightest, is a definite improvement on Lauren in terms of looks.

I ring her and I'm like, 'Yeah, I know, Erika.'

She's there, 'What do you know?'

'Er, the message that was sent to everyone in my *contacts* list?'

'That's nothing, Ross.'

'Nothing? My marriage is over. My daughter will probably never forgive me. Tina is threatening to snap my neck. I've lost the trust of my friends and we're going to lose out on Kielys unless I can sweet-talk them around by five o'clock this afternoon.'

'Ross,' she goes, 'trust me, this is far more important than any of that. Are you in town?'

I'm like, 'Yeah, no, I'm outside The Shelly.'

'I'll see you in The Merrion in, like, five minutes.'

'Can it not wait, Erika? It's important that I talk to JP and Christian. Like I said –'

'Fock's sake, Ross, if I told you I was wearing my leather trousers, you'd be in here like a focking shot.'

'Are you?' I go.

She doesn't dignify it with a response.

I'm like, 'Fine, I'll swing in.'

Which is what I end *up* doing?

She's sitting in the lounge when I arrive, with a pot of oolong tea in front of her. She's not wearing her leather trousers, it turns out, but I decide not to make an issue out of it.

'There's no case against Ronan,' she goes.

Those are, like, the first words out of her mouth.

I'm there, 'Yeah, no, the chorges were dropped – you heard the old man say it at the porty.'

'You don't understand,' she goes. 'I spoke to my friend whose sister works in the DPP. There's no paperwork. They've no record of this.'

'But I was, like, there in Donnybrook Gorda Station the night he was chorged.'

'Is it possible they just made him *think* he was chorged?'

393

'I wouldn't put anything past the old man and Hennessy. But hang on, I spoke to the Gord. This John Haskins dude. Holy shit. The penny's suddenly dropping.'

'You think he's on the payroll?'

'Yeah, no, Nudger and Buckets said he was crooked as fock.'

'It wouldn't be beyond them to get a room in a Gorda Station, convince Ronan that he was being interviewed in relation to a crime and then tell him he was chorged.'

'But I was there in the court when . . . oh my God, it was a supposably *secret* sitting? Hennessy said he used his contacts to keep the press away.'

'Fake police interview. Fake court appearance.'

'Jesus Christ, all to stop Ronan going away to the States? Hennessy has him doing some seriously, seriously dodgy shit, Erika.'

'You have to get him out of the country.'

'I think the Feds still have his passport.'

'Jesus, keep up, Ross – they never had his focking passport.'

'Yeah, no, I keep forgetting. So, like, where is it?'

'I'm guessing it's across the road.'

I'm there, 'I'll go and get it,' and I stand up.

Erika's like, 'I'll ring Ronan and tell him to meet me here.'

'You know,' I go, 'if I'd thought it through, it's not really the weather for leather trousers, is it?'

'What?'

'Nothing. I said I wouldn't make an issue out of it.'

I walk out of there and I cross the road. Fock. I remember that I have no security pass. I'm trying to think of a way to blag my way past the dude who stopped me last time. But it turns out he's not there. The security hut is empty and the gates are, like, open.

I walk through them and I cross the courtyord, then into the building I go. The place is, like, deserted. I tip along the corridor, looking over my shoulder every few steps. Then I hear voices. Someone is approaching from the direction of my old man's office. I duck into a little room to my left and I hide behind the door and wait for them to pass.

It's the old man himself and he's with JP and Christian. He's going, 'The initial order will be for half a million beds! But that's just the stort of it, chaps!'

In that moment – hord as it is to believe – I'm not even thinking about Kielys of Donnybrook. All I'm thinking about is getting my son away from these evil fockers.

When I'm sure they've gone, I step out of the room and I head straight for the old man's office. I sit at his desk and I pull open his drawers. I find what I'm looking for in the bottom one.

A passport.

I open it and there's Ronan's little hordman face staring back at me as if from a police mug shot. I remember the day he had the photo taken, in the booth in the Ilac Centre – he must have been, like, thirteen or fourteen – trying to look like he was headed for Wheatfield rather than Playa del Inglés with his old dear.

I stick it into my inside pocket, then I close the drawer and head for the door. It's only then that I notice it. On a table in the middle of the floor there's, like, a model of a giant city. I stare at it for a few seconds, no idea what it even is.

'It is beautiful,' a voice behind me goes, 'is it not?'

I turn around – yeah, no, it ends up being Fyodor.

I'm like, 'What even is it?'

'It is new city,' he goes, 'that we build in Donegal. This, my friend, is Malingrad.'

'Malingrad? So this is what the half a million beds are for?'

'There is lot of oil and gas off west of Ireland. To extract, we need workers. And workers must sleep.'

'Presumably standing up?'

'Of course standing up. We can fit more in less space. Your father persuaded President Putin to pay for Malingrad. It will be model for your father's vision of post-agricultural Ireland.'

'What are you even talking about?'

'When your beautiful wife has slaughtered all of the cows and the sheep, rural Ireland will become – how to say – landfill, yes? All of your population will live in cities just like this one. They will drill

395

for oil or for gas, or they will chop down trees, or they will work for big, multinational corporations that pay no taxes, and they will sleep standing up in space-efficient Homedrobes.'

Okay, this conversation has suddenly turned very James Bond. Then I remember that the villain always tries to kill the dude after explaining the plot to him. I'm suddenly shitting myself.

I'm there, 'I think this is the point where I'm supposed to say you're all crazy?'

'You know,' he goes, 'I am sad that I did not kill you. When I look at your stupid face now, I think that perhaps I would like to plunge this through your fucking heart.'

I notice that he's holding a – believe it or not – *letter* opener?

I'm there, 'I thought Hennessy squared that with you. He paid you off in trees, according to him.'

He just, like, laughs at that.

'Trees are not reason,' he goes. 'Reason I don't kill you is President Putin. He says you are not to be touched. He likes you. He says he sees lot of himself in you.'

'I'll take that as a compliment.'

'He goes home to Russia and he tells all people about Irish man who has sex with Russian man's wife, using Russian man's – how to say? – *prezervativ*? And how *prezervativ* flies out of pocket and onto other Russian man's plate at dinner. And how Irish man's wife is in toilet and comes back and does not know. And how Irish man can kiss his wife and act like is nothing.'

'Again, I'll take it as a compliment. All of this – this plan of the old man's – is presumably dependent on him winning the referendum tomorrow? And, from what I'm hearing, that's not going to happen.'

Again, he laughs.

'As Charles O'Carroll-Kelly says,' he goes, 'forty-eight hours is long time for politics.'

Ronan is struggling to get his head around it. And maybe he *never* will?

I'm there, 'You were set up, Ro – just not in the way that I thought.'

'But I was in Doddybruke Geerda Station,' he goes. 'I was in cowurt.'

'You weren't,' Erika, in the back seat, goes. 'You were just supposed to think that.'

He just, like, stares out the window, watching Dorset Street zip by.

'Stall the ball a midute,' he goes. 'It's all happening too fast.'

I'm there, 'You have to get out of the country, Ro. You're mixed up in some bad shit.'

'I've arranged for a cor to meet you at JFK,' Erika goes. 'And I've booked you into a hotel on the Upper East Side. And don't worry about money, it's on my cord.'

'But I caddent joost throp evody thing and go to Amedica,' he tries to go. 'I've got responsibidities hee-or.'

I'm there, 'Shadden can follow you over in a few days. Wait a minute, can she even *fly* in her condition?'

He fidgets with his passport and goes, 'She's not pregnant, Rosser.'

I'm there, 'Yeah, no, I did wonder when I saw her knocking back the Fat Frogs at your birthday porty.'

'She toawult me this morden that it was a false aleerm. But now Ine begidden to wonther –'

He doesn't even finish the thought. The poor kid doesn't know who he can trust any more.

'Was me Grandda id on it?' he goes.

I look in the rearview mirror and me and Erika exchange a look.

I'm like, 'No,' because I know the truth would kill him. 'This was all Hennessy. Your passport was in his drawer the entire time.'

He's quiet for a few minutes, then he goes, 'You're reet, Rosser – there's a lorra bad stuff is about to go dowun. You doatunt know the bleaten half of it.'

I'm there, 'I know about Malingrad.'

'Maddengrad?'

'No, Malingrad.'

Erika's like, 'What's Malingrad?'

'It's a city,' Ronan goes, 'that Grandda's pladden to build in Duddygalt with Bladabeer Pootin's muddy. It's godda be the model for the way evodybody is going to lib in the future arthur we leab the EU. Woorking sixteen hours a day on starvation wages and sleeping standing up in bleaten wardrobes.'

'Jesus,' Erika goes. 'He's insane.'

He's like, 'They're pladden to turden the whole of the Midlands into a wasteland.'

'Would I sound like a total dick,' I go, 'if I said that's what I presumed the Midlands *already* was?'

'The Rushiddens are godda use it to beddy their waste,' he goes, 'arthur Fyodor cuts down evoddy tree in the bleaten counthroddy.'

I'm there, 'It suddenly makes sense why the old man was so keen on Sorcha's plan to wipe out all the sheep and cows.'

'It's not Sudeka's pladden, Rosser. It wad nebber Sudeka's pladden. It was Cheerlie's pladden. He thinks agriculchudder is a reminder of eer peasant past.'

'Yeah, no, I remember him saying that once in a letter to the *Times*.'

'He wants us to lib in a post-agriculcherdoddle society.'

'Hang on, no,' I go, remembering something, 'it was See-mon's plan, wasn't it?'

'You mean Sea-mon?'

'Oh my God,' I go, the truth suddenly dawning on me, 'she's working for my old man.'

'She's a pladdant, Rosser. Her nayum's not eeben Sea-mon. It's bleaten Alice or sometin.'

'She appeared out of nowhere.'

'Heddessy got some wooden to create a whole past for her on soshiddle media. But it's all boddicks, Rosser. The geerl couldn't gib a fook about the future of the pladdet. They're joost using to Sudeka to desthroy the feermers and take their laddend off them.'

'Fock.'

'Will you teddle Sudeka Ine soddy, Rosser?'

'I will.'

'I oatently found out that bit the utter day.'

'Ro, can I ask you a question?'

'What?'

'Do you know what this famous doomsday button is?'

Erika suddenly looks up from whatever she's doing on her phone. She's like, 'Doomsday button?'

I'm there, 'Yeah, no, Michael D. Higgins overheard the old man and Hennessy talking about some big plan they had if it looked like Ireland was going to vote to stay in the EU.'

Ro goes, 'I, er, habn't a clue, Rosser,' but it sounds to me like he knows something and he's too scared to say it.

'Okay,' Erika goes, 'I've just transferred fifty thousand dollars to your bank account, Ro.'

Ronan's like, 'What are you thalken about?'

'You'll need money to live on,' she goes. 'New York is expensive. Me and your dad will top you up whenever you're running low.'

Me and your dad. I sort of, like, chuckle to myself. It makes it sound like we're a couple.

I'm there, 'I'm going to ring that crowd and tell them you're ready to stort your internship.'

He just nods. He's not happy about it, but he's not *unhappy* about it? He just knows that this is how it has to be.

We arrive at the airport and we get out of the cor. I turn to Erika.

'I was thinking,' I go, 'if anyone asks us any awkward questions, we'll just pretend we're married.'

She just, like, glowers at me.

She's there, 'What the fock are you talking about?'

'I don't know,' I go. 'I just thought it might be a bit of fun.'

She just shakes her head sadly, then me and Ro follow her into the terminal building.

His flight is leaving in, like, less than an hour. He has no luggage and his boarding pass is on his phone, so we end up heading straight to the deporture gate and that's where he storts to become emotional.

'I ditn't get to say goodbye to Hodor,' he goes.

I'm there, 'I'll say it for you. Ro, it's only for a year. I'll bring her over at Christmas – you'll come as well, Erika, won't you?'

'Absolutely,' she goes.

He nods his head.

I'm there, 'I'll put Shadden and Rihanna-Brogan on a flight tomorrow, okay?'

'Thanks,' he goes and that's when the tears really stort to come. He throws his orms around me. He's like, 'Ine godda miss you, Rosser.'

I'm there, 'I'm going to miss you too.'

'You're the best thig has ebber happened in my life,' he goes.

And I'm there, 'And you're the best thing that ever happened in *my* life,' and I realize that I'm crying as well.

We stand there just, like, holding each other for about a minute, before Erika goes, 'Ross, you better let go of him. You don't want him to miss his flight.'

So – yeah, no – I let go of him.

He gives Erika a hug and goes, 'I lub you, Edika.'

And she's like, 'I love you, Ro. Text us when you land, okay?'

He takes a long, sad look back at us as he disappears through the gate. Then me and Erika walk away.

We've only gone a few steps when I suddenly hear a roar behind me: 'Rosser!'

It's Ronan. He's, like, come back through the gate.

'I caddent get odden that plane wirrout tedding you,' he goes.

I'm there, 'Telling me what?'

'The doomsday buttoden, Rosser. I know what it is.'

I'm thinking, I focking knew it!

'They're godda burden Doddle Airdint – toneet.'

I'm like, 'They're what?'

'They're godda burden Doddle Airdint.'

'No, I'm definitely not getting it. Erika, have you any idea what he's trying to say?'

Erika goes, 'Ro, can you say it more slowly? Maybe break up your sentences?'

He's like, 'They're godda –'

'Godda,' Erika goes.

'– burden –'

'Burden.'

'– Doddle –'

'Doddle.'

'– Airdint!'

'Airdint!'

Erika turns her head and just, like, stares hord at me.

I'm there, 'Ro, could you maybe, like, text it to us?'

'Ross,' Erika goes, 'I know what he's trying to say. Jesus Christ, they're going to burn Dáil Éireann!'

I put my foot to the floor. I don't even slow down when I'm approaching the Airport Roundabout and the cor goes up on pretty much two wheels.

Erika has her phone clamped to her ear.

I'm there, 'Who are you ringing? The Feds?'

She's like, 'My mom!' and there's, like, panic in her voice when she says it. 'Why isn't she answering?'

I'm there, 'What the fock can she do to stop it? No disrespect to Helen.'

And that's when she says it.

'She was planning to doorstep him in his office tonight,' she goes, 'to present him with the divorce papers.'

I'm there, 'Fock!'

And Erika goes, 'Does this focking cor not go any focking faster?'

We eventually reach the city centre. Something is happening – you can sense it. People are on their phones and they've got, like, shocked expressions on their faces. As we cross the Liffey, you can see smoke in the air and even with the window closed I can already smell it – the smell of, like, something burning.

I look at the time. It's, like, seven o'clock in the evening. It's too late to save Kielys now. But I'm not even thinking about Kielys – except maybe a little bit. I'm just thinking about Helen and whether she managed to get out.

The air is filled with the sound of sirens. There's, like, fire engines and ambulances coming from every direction.

I throw the cor on Merrion Square. Erika barely waits for it to stop. She hares off and – yeah, no – I hare after her, past the National Gallery and then left onto whatever-the-fock-it's-called Street. The further we go, the thicker the smoke becomes and the horder it is to breathe.

We turn left up Kildare Street. There's, like, fire engines and ambulances everywhere. And there's, like, hundreds of people standing around on the street, just shaking their heads in, like, *total* shock?

We reach the Dáil. Through the thick smoke, I can see that the building is in flames. I can actually feel the heat, even from, like, a hundred yords away.

'ERIKA!' a voice suddenly shouts. 'ERIKA!'

And then we spot her. It's Helen! Thank fock, I think! It's Helen! Erika runs to her and they throw their orms around each other.

'*He* did this!' Erika goes, leading her old dear away from the madness. 'I told you, he's lost it! He's insane!'

I walk through the crowds of people, who are all standing around, holding their phones in front of them, videoing the building as it burns, no one saying shit.

I spot – yeah, no – Michael D. Higgins, staring into space as the flames reach the roof. I suddenly remember what he said about the future of our democracy being in my hands and I feel like nearly going over to apologize for letting him down.

But then there's a series of loud explosions. The windows are being blown out, presumably by the heat inside the building. It's like, 'BAM! BAM! BAM!' and people scream and look around them, thinking we're, I don't know, under attack.

There's, like, a real feeling of paranoia in the air.

I suddenly hear my name being called from behind me. It's like, 'ROSS! ROSS! ROSS!'

I spin around and it ends up being Sorcha. Her face is all black and her hair is covered in soot.

I'm like, 'What the fock? I thought you were at home?'

'The Taoiseach called an emergency Cabinet meeting for this evening,' she goes. 'That was when the fire storted,' and she just, like, throws her orms around me and holds me tight. 'Oh my God, Ross, it was so dork! I couldn't breathe! I thought I was going to die!'

Never one to miss an opportunity, I go, 'It certainly puts all that other stuff into perspective, doesn't it?'

Through the crowd, I spot Simone, watching us with a blank expression on her face.

'Can you believe it?' Sorcha goes. 'Can you believe they would do something like this?'

I'm there, 'Hennessy and my old man? Sorcha, you don't know the half of it.'

She pulls away from me and goes, 'Oh my God, Ross, not you as well?'

I'm like, 'Sorcha, you have to listen to me. They used you – even See-mon was in on it.'

'Who's See-mon?'

'Focking See-mon!'

'You mean Sea-mon? Oh my God, Ross, will you *listen* to yourself?'

'Sorcha, it's the truth. It's all port of the old man's plan – just like that building that's burning behind you.'

'You think your dad did this?'

'I focking know he did it.'

'Yeah, you're just like the rest of the sheeple! How can you not see the obvious?'

'Who do you think did it, then?'

'Europe did it!'

I look in her blackened face and – yeah, no – she genuinely believes what she's saying. I'm about to explain to her all the other shit that Ronan told me when I suddenly hear the old man ranting and raving a few feet away. He's standing in front of a lorge group of reporters, with Hennessy beside him, and he's going, 'We knew they would make it difficult for us to leave – just as they did to our friends across the water! But this is a full-frontal attack on Ireland and the independence for which it fought and it is happening in front of the eyes of the world!'

There's suddenly a humungous crashing and the ground beneath our feet actually shakes. The roof of the building has fallen in. There are more screams. I watch the flames as they lick their way up the flagpole on what's left of the roof, then the tricolour catches and I watch it burn, before the pole breaks and comes crashing to the ground.

In that moment, I turn and I happen to catch the President's eyes.

For a second or two, I can tell that he's trying to, like, *place* me? And then I watch as – yeah, no – tears stort spilling down his cheeks.

I can hear the old man going, 'It echoes back through history, ladies and gentlemen, to an event that presaged the last effort to establish a European *über staat* through tyranny! This burning building you see behind me is what they think of our democracy!'

Acknowledgements

These books would not appear every year without the hard work and vision of a whole team of people. So I would like to thank, as always, my editor, Rachel Pierce; my agent, Faith O'Grady; and the artist, Alan Clarke. *Buíochas le Fionnula Ní Dhúgáin.* Thank you to all the team at Penguin Ireland, especially Michael McLoughlin, Patricia Deevy, Cliona Lewis, Brian Walker, Carrie Anderson and Aimée Johnston. And with love and grateful thanks to my family – Dad, Vincent and Richard. And, most of all, thank you to my wonderful wife, Mary.